BOTS, TO THE ROOF! COVER ME!"

Captain Curt Carson didn't expect confirmation from his warbots. They were programmed to do what they were told. If their Artificial Intelligence Systems didn't understand the order, or detected a conflict in their programming, they'd ask for clarification.

Six of the M-22 assault bots swept the roof with fletchette fire, mowing down four Jehorkhim riflemen who'd been standing guard. Six more assault bots headed for the stairway.

"Bots Alpha and Bravo, defend the roof!" Curt shouted. "All other assault bots down the stairs. Search for the hostages. Shoot any person who attacks you. Move!"

Curt knew he had to move fast, too. He didn't know how long it would take the Jehorkhims to realize what was going on and begin slaughtering the hostages. And he also had to worry about getting the hostages and the warbots the hell out of there when the mission was completed!

WARBOTS

G. HARRY STINE

PINNACLE BOOKS
WINDSOR PUBLISHING CORP.

PINNACLE BOOKS

are published by

Windsor Publishing Corp.
475 Park Avenue South
New York, NY 10016

Copyright © 1988 by G. Harry Stine

First printing: May, 1988

Printed in the United States of America

TO:
Lieutenant Colonel Jack Hettinger, USA (Ret.)

We hear very much indeed, in this day and age, of machines and of war waged with machines. We hear so much that we do not, all of us, stop to think that war is not different, in principle, from what it has been since before the dawn of recorded history. . . . We must not fail to realize that machines are as nothing without the men who man them and give them life. War is force—force to the utmost—force to make the enemy yield to our will. . . . War is men against men. . . . Machines are mere masses of inert metal without the men who man them.

—Fleet Admiral Ernest J. King, graduation address, United States Naval Academy, Annapolis, Maryland, USA, 19 June 1942.

CHAPTER ONE

No one noticed them when they boarded Orient Express Flight Seven in San Francisco. They were only six people sprinkled throughout the one hundred seven passengers boarding the hypersonic transport. They'd gone through all the security check points without a hitch. The psychic screeners had "felt" nothing wrong. The detectors had picked up no weapons.

This didn't mean that these six people carried no weapons. They were all armed to the teeth. When all the available information was pieced together later, nobody could figure out how the hijackers had managed to get aboard with what survivors later reported as an "arsenal of weapons."

The tow wagon lined up the bat-shaped arrowlike black hulk with the runway and, precisely at noon, the pilots of Orient Express Flight Seven—international rules of that time forbade the use of robot pilots in passenger craft without human pilots acting as "system managers" and backups for them—saw the final clearance from Space Traffic Control and the San Francisco tower appear on the display screen. The thunder of aeroturboramjets was quickly dissipated by the phase dampers of the runway's noise controls. When the craft attained a speed of ninety meters per second, the pilots noted with satisfaction that the robot pilot signaled for rotation, the nose came up to the precise angle for generating the maximum amount of lift, and the craft was airborne.

Above the shielding effect of the runway noise dissipators, the ripping roar of the engines echoed off the far hills while the shoreline quickly fell behind the climbing black ship.

Another milk run, the pilots told each other. In two hours, they'd be landing in Toyko, at 8:00 A.M. the following morning, having crossed the international date line at an altitude of more than two hundred kilometers.

But the pilots discovered they were wrong when the aft door to the flight deck was blown off its hinges by shaped charges of plasticex. A man stepped through and barked an order. He was armed only with a short dagger with a dark blade. The copilot discovered that the blade was razor-sharp when it nicked his left arm and wet, red blood flowed from the thin cut that had been made almost painlessly. The blade could have been made from flint, obsidian, or any glasslike material that would have an extremely sharp edge upon being flaked or cracked. Such a nonmetallic weapon would pass undetected through any airport security screening device yet developed.

There was only one thing the pilots could do. The flight commander keyed the microphone, using the voice communications channel rather than the computerized digital system. "Pacific Low Orbit Center, this is Oscar Echo Seven. Code seven-five-zero-zero. We are being hijacked. I repeat: We are being hijacked. We haven't been advised of destination at this time. Please track and clear ahead of us. We'll monitor the navsat system for anticollision vectors. Oscar Echo Seven out!"

There didn't seem to be any reason for the hijacking. When aerospaceline managers checked the manifest, they found no one on that flight who was of any particular political or religious sensitivity. The passengers were tourists and business people who could afford the premium fare charged for going halfway around the world in two hours.

And it didn't make any sense to hijack a hypersonic transport. All five of the national space defense systems immediately came to Yellow Alert and began to track the craft. Space mirrors moved "on target" and billion-watt ground-based lasers began to warm up in case the hijacking turned out to be a suicide mission aimed at Toyko, Beijing, or Singapore. No matter where Orient Express Flight Seven went now, it would be tracked by radar, lidar, and infrared systems because it was an unstealthed commercial craft, designed to be seen clearly and plainly by every possible sort of sensor. If it transgressed the international rules of the road in the opinion of some national defense system evaluator, it would be burned out of the sky. More than a hundred lives were at stake, lives that could be extinguished instantly in the inferno of a hydrogen-oxygen explosion.

Within minutes another message came from the endangered craft: "Orient Low Orbit Center, please be advised that Oscar Echo Seven has been ordered to

11

land at a place called Zahedan. Its coordinates aren't even in the autopilot's computer memory. The hijackers have given the coordinates to us. This place must be out in the boondocks somewhere. I hope you can get us back . . ."

Captain Curt Carson's officers had scouts well out on point with flank guards five hundred meters on either side of his advancing company. The enemy was out there somewhere. Lieutenant Morgan's squads Alpha-One and Alpha-Two, from Alpha platoon, were on reconnaissance but had reported no contact yet. Lieutenant Allen, whose Bravo-Three squad was airborne with sensors out, could find nothing. The communications frequencies were quiet. Only the data channels showed any activity as scouts from Alpha-One, Alpha-Two, and Bravo-Three continued their constant monitoring, feeding back the information they gathered into the Head Honcho company battle computer which was being monitored by Master Sergeant Kester. At this point in the engagement, Carson was using his top sergeant as a control point assimilator and evaluator of data.

This was robot warfare as it was supposed to be fought. No human beings were on the field of battle and thus exposed to the hazards of combat.

The technology of robot warfare had been developing for nearly a century. As long ago as World War II, robot weapons such as the primitive German Henschel Hs 298, an unmanned bomb with a television camera in its nose, had allowed a bombardier to see where it was going and to steer it by radio control. A whole series of "remotely piloted vehicles" and target drone aircraft had evolved from the Henschel until the technology of the "human-machine interface" finally reached the point where true robot warfare was possible. The human soldier remained in a relatively safe and secure position while receiving sensations, from the robot, on television cameras, microphones, and position sensors via radio, microwave, infrared, and laser optical channels. In turn, the human soldier sent commands back to the robot via a similar "duplex" link.

This was different from the robot warfare of the past, however, because data flowed into and out of the human soldier's nervous system which was directly linked to the communication channels.

Captain Curt Carson didn't have an electronic connector implanted in his head. Instead, he lay on a couch whose network of small electrode plates made contact with his skin along both sides of his spine and up his neck. Over his shaved head, he wore a close-fitting helmet that put more skin electrodes in contact with his scalp. When he needed to be mobile, he wore a harness which held the electrodes against his back, and neck.

Electroencephalography, EEG, or applying electrode sensors to the scalp, had been used for over a century by medical doctors and research scientists to detect very strong electrical brain activity. By the 1970s, these external sensors had become so sensitive that they could detect the neural activity taking place in the brain during any given activity. Computers were programmed to decipher and recognize command signals or "event related potentials" transmitted by the human nervous system, and to send these translated thought commands to

13

machines. Thus, a human being could "think" a command to a robot, and the machine would carry out that command.

In the 1980s scientists discovered that the human nervous system would respond directly to signals introduced to the surface of the skin by external sensors. Properly encoded by computers, these signals could be made to electrically trigger the sensations of sight, sound, feeling, and smell. This two-way linkage between a human being and a robot allowed soldiers to conduct warfare through robots of various designs and functions.

The soldiers were always in command. The computer programs were designed to ensure this, and would fail-safe in the event of a malfunction.

Press the advance, Carson ordered. The command was merely an electronic version of his thought passing through a computer, but the master battle computer made it seem a verbal message to him and his people. *Keep moving forward until we make contact. Keep looking for them. They're out there somewhere. When we find 'em, we can decide what tactics we use to smear 'em. Kester, don't lose comm with the companies on our flanks. We may need their help, so we don't want to outdistance them and get pinched off.*

Roger, Captain. We're sitting fat. Suggest we come to a forward speed of two kilometers per hour at this point.

We'll do it. Attention, Alpha Leader and Bravo Leader, this is Blue Oscar Leader! Come to and maintain two klicks.

Alpha Leader, roger.

Bravo Leader, roger.

Alpha Leader, this is Blue Oscar Leader, Carson's thought called out. *I'm leaving the Head Honcho vehicle and going out on point.*

That may not be wise, sir. It was Lieutenant Allen's perceived voice-thought.

Thank you for sharing your opinion with me, Carson replied with the catch-all phrase he used when he wanted to let his subordinates know he'd decided to proceed anyway, but since time permitted, he continued with a brief explanation of why. Experience in the field, had taught Curt that a leader should lead people, not drive them. His operational policy had been formed in battle and honed in service under other officers. It had made a taut unit of his company, the Companions, named after the elite Macedonian heavy cavalry squadron that had accompanied Alexander the Great into battle twenty-three centuries before. *I want to get an idea of the terrain. When we make contact, I don't want to be fighting blind. Morgan, which unit do you recommend I join?*

Alpha Leader suggests Alpha-Seven. He's an Alpha Sierra Victor Eighty-eight. An Amphibious Scout Vehicle robot was a good choice.

Thank you. Blue Oscar Leader leaving Head Honcho command, transferring to Alpha Seven.

The transition was swift, as usual.

Captain Curt Carson actually didn't go anywhere. He merely transferred his sensory data inputs from one robot to another.

As a result, the sights, sounds, and feel of the CGV-22 Command Ground Vehicle were immediately replaced in Curt Carson's mind by those of the Amphibious Scout Vehicle Model 88 going under the code name Alpha Seven. The scout vehicle was literally an extension of Carson because the captain sensed what its cameras and microphones and controls sensed. But Carson didn't take control; he let the robot scout—a tanklike, treaded, all-terrain vehicle—proceed with its own artificially intelligent computer in command. It greeted him with a verbal thought message, *Welcome aboard, Captain.*

Glad to be aboard, Alpha Seven. You're Phil Fingers, if I remember.

Named for the digits that play the eighty-eight keys of a piano. Roger, sir. That reply hadn't been generated by the computer's artificial intelligence or AI circuitry but had been programmed by one of the technicians in an attempt to ascribe some human qualities to a machine.

Captain Curt Carson treated artificial intelligence with caution. Even though he worked with AI constantly, he subscribed to the old maxim that there are only three forms of intelligence: human, animal, and military.

Give me a sit-rep, Carson ordered, asking the computer called Phil Fingers to provide him with a situation report.

No enemy detected, sir.

He's out there somewhere. Curt's thought message passed to the machine.

Yes, sir. I know. I have the briefing stored in memory. But he isn't where Ess-Two estimated.

Staff Intelligence, S-2, was usually wrong because

16

they worked with information that was at best several minutes old by the time the regimental computers processed what battlefield reconnaissance robots reported to make it intelligible to humans. That's why Carson always sent his special recon robots out on point for the latest hot skinny.

Because Carson's own nervous system was linked remotely with the scout's sensors, he too felt the slamming impact and heard the incredibly loud clang of the shell hitting the scout's armored glacis plate.

Contact. Incoming, incoming, Phil Fingers reported in the flat and unemotional tone of its computer-voice data channel. *Antivehicle round taken on my glacis plate. Small dent, but I'm functional. I have contact with the enemy. Bearing one-niner-one magnetic, range three-one-one meters.*

Carson disabled the verbal channel, except for the tactical command signals coming from his human officers. He would have been overloaded with information otherwise. Far too much data were suddenly streaming in.

Phil Fingers swiveled Alpha Seven's turret, laid the thirty-millimeter guns on the computer-derived source of the shelling, and fired a burst. The two eighty-eights on point followed suit.

Fire was immediately returned by the enemy.

Carson got out of the point scout. Doctrine directed that the company commander reduce personal risk by transferring to a suitably protected command, control, communications, and intelligence ("C-cubed-I") robot upon contact or when under fire. *Blue Oscar Leader transferring back to Head Honcho,* he snapped into the

17

human voice channel. The computer read his thought command and acted, switching Carson's sensory inputs. Instantly, Carson was back in his command post.

The tactical situation was displayed for him as though he were seeing it with his own eyes. However, the computer sent him an elevated view of the terrain, a composite derived from television, infrared, and radar sensors in the airborne recon robots. The enemy, now tagged as Red Zulu by the computer, was drawn up in a defensive line on the other side of the small valley Carson's company was just beginning to cross. Initial contact had been made, and the fire fight started when the point descended the north bank of the gulch, putting the units in maximum exposure.

Carson called up a bigger picture on his visual input. To the west, the valley tapered into a series of shallow, branched gulleys. Eastward, a small dammed lake with a swampy ground downstream of it extended into the forward battle area of another Blue company, Walker's Warriors, who were yet unengaged.

Head Honcho, request flanking maneuver from Walker.

Request entered, sir, Master Sergeant Kester shot back in verbal. *No joy, Captain. Walker is engaged, too.*

Carson then knew this would be a loner fight. He'd have to win it without help. But he had good data. He knew what was happening. As the tactical situation began to clear, Carson started to issue orders. *Morgan, engage with Alpha platoon in frontal assault. Jerry, take Bravo platoon around the right flank.*

I can comply only with my nine all-terrains, Captain.

18

That ground is too rough for my heavy tracked vehicles, Lieutenant Jerry Allen replied quickly. Carson could tell from the new lieutenant's computer voice that Allen was unsure. The company commander hoped that the young man's West Point education would prove out. It always had in the past, and Carson knew his own commanding officers had probably harbored the same doubts about him years ago.

Alpha engaging, Lieutenant Alexis Morgan reported. Carson didn't have to worry about her at all. She was one of the people he would be glad to have with him in any sort of a fracas.

Kester, assume command of the reserve units. Tag them as Charlie Force. Detach all Alpha Tango Victors to Bravo, withdraw the heavies, assign them to Charlie Force, and put Charlie Force in fire support of Alpha.

Roger. Kester exiting Head Honcho for Charlie One now. Lieutenant Allen, you just got command of Charlie's former Alpha Tango Victors and I'm taking your heavy Charlie Whiskey Bravos.

You've got my heavies, Charlie Leader. Bravo Leader is on the move, heading two-four-zero. Picking up some light fire. We'll suppress it, Lieutenant Allen responded.

Cover, cover. The warning came from the orbiting Bravo-Three recon aircraft. The data suddenly showed Red tactical air support coming in low and fast, fangs out and hair on fire in the strike mode, going for the moving robot vehicles of Bravo platoon.

The air over the right flank was suddenly filled with smart rounds from the quad-forties of Charlie force which Sergeant Kester had prudently moved into place at Bravo's rear for ground fire suppression as well as the contingency of a Red air strike against the exposed Bravo robots. The smart rounds jinked and zanged, found their targets, and a troika of Red saucer-shaped strike fighters became smoking holes in the ground because their own AI units couldn't or didn't react in time to spook the incoming smarts. *Fortunes of war,* Carson thought.

But there could be more where those had come from. Carson contacted Regimental and requested air cover. It wasn't available. He'd have to fight this one out on the ground with what he had available, which was adequate if he deployed it properly.

Lieutenant Morgan's Alpha platoon was moving forward with unexpected ease against what appeared to be light resistance. A disquieting thought entered Carson's mind: If Morgan was encountering such light resistance, her assault target couldn't be Red's main body. Where was Red's main body?

As Allen and Bravo platoon turned the corner of their flanking attack and began to move east after crossing the gullied terrain and breaking out onto the open, relatively flat mesa beyond, Carson acted on a hunch and extended his sensors deep beyond Red Zulu's forward battle area. Head Honcho, the main company battle computer, noticed and remarked, *I didn't know you wanted deep coverage, Captain.*

I'm looking for the main body, Carson muttered curtly.

And he found it.

It was lurking—unmoving, unseen, camouflaged, and

stealthed—in defilade deep in another gulch five hundred meters to the south and rear.

Now it moved.

Bravo, look at what we've found, Carson warned his platoon leader, meanwhile instructing Head Honcho to artificially enhance and point out the images of the newly discovered Red main body. *Break off the wheel-left and engage Red Main's left flank before it can get out of that valley. Charlie force, I want a rolling barrage in front of Alpha force, but keep the beaten zone to the left and away from Bravo's advance. Alexis, break through there. Crunch that Red forward party and prepare to hit Red Zulu main in frontal assault.*

Carson had done the right thing. In sensing deep, he'd made the critical decision in this skirmish. In the next few minutes, the fight intensified, along with the inevitable "haze of battle" that accompanies such concentrated violence. However, modern sensors and detectors cut through most of the countermeasures and continued to give Carson a realistic picture of what was going on. The science boys in Ordnance Corps had done their job, and the AI units were responding effectively to enemy countermeasures, shifting their own battle-management information inputs around Red Zulu's jamming and spoofing.

Lieutenant Allen caught the Red main force on its left flank as it started to move ahead, and even without air support, Lieutenant Morgan was able to move behind Kester's rolling barrage and break through the light frontal defense perimeter. By the time her platoon reached the van of Red main, Allen was moving through the enemy force and cutting it to ribbons.

21

But then it was suddenly all over. Carson's Companions never got the opportunity to exploit the operation by continuing their deep thrust into Red territory and pursuing the enemy force while maintaining contact.

The call came suddenly from Regimental. Curt recognized the "feel" of the computer "voice" of Colonel Belinda Hettrick: *Cancel the battle simulation. Good job, Captain. Also thank your troops; they did an outstanding job managing several robots. Unlink as soon as practical. The critique of today's exercise is canceled. Assemble for a staff meeting and briefing at Regimental Headquarters. Sorry to rush you, but we've just gotten an emergency mission.*

The data flow from the tactical training simulation computer suddenly stopped. The sensor outputs and displays froze like a videotape in freeze-frame mode. Curt found himself in a totally static situation. He and his human companions, the "warbot brainies" who were running the robots, couldn't remain in a nonchanging situation like this for more than a few minutes. It was almost as bad as being killed in action. Since Carson had twice before lost all input from war robot sensors, he didn't want to experiment with zero-input degradation. So he immediately began the process of reincorporation, pulling his mind and senses back into his body as it lay on the command couch, still linked with the Head Honcho master battle computer which in turn was tied in with the battle simulator computer of the training center.

Captain Curt Carson was wondering to himself what the hell was going on? Why the sudden cut-off of the battle-training simulation? It was not only dangerous to pull people out of linkage quickly, but the colonel's procedure was definitely nonregulation. Even with Carson's extensive training, his nervous system would still be attuned to the electrodes of the combat couch for another hour or so. He'd have to work hard to force himself to accept the perception of the actual world coming in through his normal senses. Any warbot brainy, especially an officer with a command, would normally be given a resynchronization period of several hours after coming out of linkage. Whatever the new assignment was, it had to be something requiring an unusually rapid response.

He mentally steeled himself for withdrawal.

Coming out from under direct linkage with computers and robots was like waking from a dream, a transition from one reality to another. It took a lot of training to enable modern soldiers to discriminate between experience and existence. Sometimes, an officer or NCO got confused in spite of all the training and the subliminal commands. When that happened and battle fatigue set in, it might mean six months to forever under psychological reprogramming. A few never made it back. They became human vegetables and were listed as Missing In Action on the roster. But Captain Curtis Christopher Carson never had trouble coming back. He was a fighter and a survivor; the genes of eight generations of military people were very powerful.

As the operations room took form around him, Curt sensed his body reclining on the couch. Sergeant Helen Devlin, a linkage biotechnician, was at hand, checking him as his mind returned. Helen was one of the pleasant things about coming back; a Biotech Sergeant Second, Helen was as expert at therapy as she was with the biological aspects of human-computer interfaces.

"Back from the wars, Captain?" she asked him pleasantly as she sponged him down to get the stink and sweat of battle off him.

Curt snorted. "Just war games!"

"But they're as realistic as a war." Lieutenant Alexis Morgan declared. She lay nearby on her own couch.

"Except you can't get killed in action in a simulator," her company commander reminded her, as he reached up to remove his skull cap.

"Begging your pardon, Captain." It was Lieutenant Jerry Allen, the new officer under Curt's command, who was just coming out of linkage on another couch. "If the robot quits before you can transfer away from it, it's just as bad."

"Don't ever let me find out that you got caught in that situation, Lieutenant," Curt told him flatly. "No competent, trained Academy graduate should ever delay transferring out of a malfunctioning robot. Machines and computers are cheap; humans aren't! Or have they changed the doctrine at West Point lately?" He sat up slowly, separating his neck and spine from the network of sensors and probes attached to the couch. As usual, being shot at, even in a simulator, had had an effect upon his sexual drive, triggering the gallant reflex. "Sergeant, my fatigues, please," he said to Helen Devlin. He then pulled on and fastened the trim, insignia-bedecked coverall which the biotech sergeant handed him.

Other biotechs were assisting his two officers and

24

three NCOs as they detached their minds and nervous systems from the nonintrusive sensors and probes which had linked them to the electronic circuits of the battle simulator. There was much groaning and stretching of cramped and stiffened muscles, but the loudest complaints came, as usual, from Master Sergeant Henry Kester.

"I'm getting too old for this!" the lean but wrinkled man muttered.

"Want out again, Henry?" Curt Carson asked him. That was part of the unofficial ritual.

"Hell, I couldn't live a normal life now. Probably go out and clobber some innocent vending machine in a flashback," the master sergeant replied. "Besides, if we've got a hot operation comin' up, there isn't time for me to train-up either Nick or Edwina."

"Face it, Henry," the powerfully built Sergeant Edwina Sampson observed, "that's just an excuse. If we wouldn't get caught, I'd suggest we go over to the gym later and see who's trained-up." She knew what she was talking about. The standing order in the RI, the Robot Infantry of the United States Army,* prohibited only one form of physical contact between male and female warriors: hand-to-hand simulated combat. No reasons were ever given, but it was widely assumed that the RI didn't want its male officers and NCOs injured when it wasn't absolutely necessary in the line of duty.

The master sergeant started to say something, but Sergeant Nick Gerard put in, "Yeah, we know, Henry:

*See Appendix A, Organization of The Robot Infantry, p. 470.

25

The Army's gone to hell ever since they let women into the service."

"Naw, only since they got tired of being assigned to dangerous posts but not being allowed to defend themselves," Kester pointed out.

"I'm glad *that's* changed," Sergeant Sampson retorted. "Henry, face it, you just like the good Army life."

Captain Curt Carson listened to this banter as Helen Devlin ran her postlinkage physical checks on him. The little tech sergeant finally looked up at him and reported, "Fit for duty, Captain."

"Fit for duty, but tired. And, unfortunately, duty calls," Curt told her quietly.

"How's the postbattle tension?"

"It's there. It's always there."

"If duty doesn't call tonight, will you need some relief? As your chief biotech sergeant, it's in my line of duty, you know ..."

"I could go for some recreational sacktime ... as you damned well know. But I've got to find out what the colonel has in mind since she pulled us out of the simulator so quickly."

"Rain check?"

"Any time." Provided Alexis doesn't beat her to me, Carson told himself. Battle-stimulated erotic tension often affected women warbot brainies more strongly than men. What was it? They weren't actually on a battlefield, but the stink of fear and adrenalin and other powerful pheromones was still there. He didn't know why. Maybe some scientist types would find out.

Even in modern robot war, as the news media incorrectly termed it, it made no difference that people were no longer physically involved in battle. The minds of men and women alike, linked with computers and intelligence amplifiers so they might run warrior robots, were subjected to the same stimuli and stresses they'd undergo on the battlefield. In the early decades of the twenty-first century, the enormous technological strides made allowed machinery to be placed at risk in war rather than human beings. Machines made the human body far less important, even unnecessary, on most battlefields, but the human mind was still the most important factor in warfare.

And the human mind reacted as it always had, because technology made robot or telewar startlingly real.

The computers had to make it seem real. Otherwise, no warrior would take battle seriously. Players of videogames, those early simulators of the twentieth century, perceived war without jeopardy. "Well, I can quit and disengage and go have a beer if I start to lose." That attitude didn't win battles. Effective warbot brainies had to be involved.

Captain Curt Carson took war very seriously. So did his officers and noncoms.

But Carson's Companions was an elite outfit. As a result, it got all the dirty little jobs. Curt wondered which one it would be this time?

His warbot brainies were dressed and ready now. They looked sharp in the light green fatigues. It was easy to tell they weren't rookies—except for Lieutenant Allen, fresh out of the Academy with no chestful of ribbons and citations.

27

Curt took the brick-shaped telecommunicator from its belt loop and keyed it for Colonel Hettrick's office. "Captain Carson speaking. Where does the colonel wish us to assemble?"

On the front of the telecomm, a miniature image of the colonel's aide saluted and replied, "With the colonel's compliments, Captain, there will be a briefing in Room Foxtrot-two-zero-seven at fifteen hundred hours. All of Carson's Companions should be present. That will give you time to hit the open mess. The colonel specifically remarked that she wanted you and your people to have the opportunity to eat after that simulation, sir."

"Please thank her for me. Carson off." Slipping the telecommunicator "brick" back on his belt, he turned to the five people lined up before him. Although this turn of events worried him, he didn't let it show. Instead, he observed, "I don't think I need to ask this outfit whether or not they want to hit the chow line."

"No, sir," Sergeant Nick Gerard replied, but his smile was broad. "We could also have called ourselves Carson's Chow Hounds."

"Except the company commander would have overruled that. Let's go," Carson told him.

"Eat, drink, and be merry because tomorrow—" Sergeant Edwina Sampson began.

"Tomorrow we may become totally digitized," Master Sergeant Henry Kester put in.

Captain Curt Carson didn't add to the lighthearted postbattle banter among his troops. He was worried. The colonel wasn't one to push her troops to the limit

28

unless it was absolutely necessary. Something big must be brewing. The colonel's willingness to delay a briefing so Curt's company could get a hot meal told him that they were going into action and might not have hot food for several days. Field rations meant combat.

CHAPTER TWO

Briefing Room F-207 was six levels down in the Diamond Point Headquarters redoubt of the 17th "Iron Fist" Division,* Robot Infantry, and it was large enough to hold several dozen people. As Captain Curt Carson led his officers and noncoms into the room, it was apparent to him that whatever the mission was, it wouldn't be a small operation. Not only was the full Regimental staff already there, elements from the Division staff were also present. Curt saw the commanders of the other two companies in the combat battalion of the Washington Greys. He said hello to Captain Edith Walker of Walker's Warriors and Captain Manuel Garcia of Manny's Marauders.

Another company present as well. Curt wasn't happy about that.

A huge man stepped into Carson's path. His round face was distorted by a twisted smile, and his eyes were small and mean. "Fer Chrissake, I thought you were

*See Appendix B, Order of Battle, p. 475.

still playing war games, Carson! I didn't figure on having *you* involved with me in this fracas!"

Captain Curt Carson looked back with equal intensity and distaste. "Too bad we can't pick and choose in this Army, Kelly." It was obvious that no camaraderie existed between Captain Curt Carson and Captain Marty Kelly, leader of Kelly's Killers.

"I *knew* I should have worked you over more in your plebe year. God knows I tried to beat that smart-ass mouth out of you, Carson," Kelly growled.

"Well, you failed," Carson responded. "Incidentally, what the hell are you doing with the Washington Greys? Did Division H-Q feel it needed a slaughter force?"

Their mutual animosity went back to West Point where, as an upperclassman, Kelly had given plebe Carson an extremely rough time. Kelly liked to pick on smaller men. But Curt Carson hadn't caved in. Both cadets had made the football team, and that year Army had beaten the hell out of Navy, Air Force, and Space Service. As a running back, Curt was faster than Kelly whose size and vicious nature made him a perfect linebacker. In four years of scrimmages, Kelly smeared Carson on the practice field, but Carson retaliated by maneuvering the big man into situations in which the offense boxed him and hit from two sides at once. You could always find someone willing to bet that one of these two men would be on the injured list for the next game scheduled.

"Naw, the general wanted this outfit to have a real fighting company run by a real fighting officer," Kelly sneered.

Kelly had become an officer, but the part about being a gentleman had passed him by. Curt had the inside skinny that Kelly and his company had been transferred into the Washington Greys from the Old Guard regiment because Kelly's Killers had made more enemies than friends. The Washington Greys' TO had no slot for Kelly's Killers, so the company was a "floater" outfit. Unattached to a battalion, it operated as a Headquarters unit on assignments involving special weapons or tactics. Curt knew why Kelly and his troops had been assigned this wild-card function. So did every other officer in the Greys.

Kelly's Killers were well named. Kelly enjoyed picking fights and killing. So did his troops, who were a bunch of misfits. The RI had an old saying: "There's one in every outfit." Some people wondered where they came from; Marty Kelly apparently was the supplier. The unvoiced motto of his company was, "Kill 'em all; let God sort 'em out!"

"The Greys have done okay without you, Kelly. Don't come barging in and screwing up our contracts," Carson warned. In any outfit, officers develop unique and unwritten "contracts" with subordinates and commanders, basic working agreements covering who does what and when. Kelly's Killers had no such contracts, but they were predictable. They were out to kill, wasting robots in the process, often to the detriment of the other troops around them. The record of Kelly's Killers was studded with reprimands and commendations, but their successes had been costly. Whether the general knew this or not was immaterial; it was apparent that G-1 Personnel was trying to find out where Kelly's outfit would fit instead of taking the Draconian measure of disbanding it. The Army didn't like to bust up battle-tested outfits.

Curt glanced over his shoulder. Lieutenant Jerry Allen was standing behind him. Allen was bigger than Kelly and, in spite of his youth and inexperience, looked tough and hard and mean. "In the meantime, you're standing where I want to walk," Curt said levelly.

"Tough shit. Walk around me." Kelly was impassive. Two lieutenants and three sergeants stood behind him.

Curt couldn't figure out why Kelly was forcing a confrontation in the briefing room just before what promised to be a major mission. This was not the place or time for it. Curt stood his ground.

He didn't see Colonel Belinda Hettrick step up behind him, but he heard her contralto voice in his ear, "Captain Kelly, you're blocking traffic." She couldn't have been there long, and Curt didn't know how much she'd heard. But with a smooth movement, Hettrick stepped around Curt and confronted the huge captain. Looking up at Kelly, she told him something in a voice so low that even Curt couldn't hear more than a few syllables. Those few sounds he caught surprised him; Hettrick wasn't one to use strong language. Even Kelly's face reddened imperceptibly.

But he merely replied in a subdued tone, "Yes, Colonel. Right away." He turned and muttered something to his men, and together they walked over to the chairs and sat down.

Hettrick then turned to Curt. Without referring to what had happened, she remarked, "Sorry to drag the Companions out of the battle simulator, Captain, but this is an emergency."

33

"So I gathered. No problem."

"There could be. I pulled you out of linkage too quickly. If any of you begin to slip back into robot-control mode during this briefing, don't be heroes; punch the chicken switch and get out of the briefing," she ordered, then added without rancor, "I'm giving Captain Kelly the benefit of the doubt; he and his troops also came out of a battle simulator about two hours ago."

Even before direct linkage between a human's nervous system and a robot had been perfected, some people had a natural affinity with machinery, an ability to extend themselves into their machines and to make whatever device they were operating become an extension of themselves. But withdrawing from the artificial link with a machine was difficult for everyone. It took a lot of training to allow "warbot brainies," the real brains behind the actions of the robots, to discriminate between the real world and the robot world, and even this training couldn't overcome the mental confusion that resulted from coming out of linkage too quickly. It took a strong mind to prevent what the warbot soldiers referred to as "flashbacks" or "crossfades," terms borrowed from old-time moviemakers.

"We're not green, Colonel. We'll manage."

"Do more than just 'manage,' " the colonel told him coolly. "Follow orders."

"Yes, Colonel. I presume the chicken-switch remark was an order?"

"Let me put it gracefully, Captain," she said, with a pleasant smile that belied the hardness of command. "I want anyone to punch out of this briefing and return to quarters if he or she begins to slip or even suspects that is happening. Carson's Companions are going to be heavily involved in this mission, and I don't want you to be undermanned because someone felt heroic and went catatonic in the briefing. Understand?"

"Understood. Care to give me a clue about our possible involvement, Colonel?"

"You'll learn all about it in the briefing."

The colonel didn't want to discuss the mission freely, so Curt figured it had to be quite different from anything the Regiment had handled before. And he got the impression that she didn't like it.

Brigadier General Victor Knox was nowhere near as reticent when he approached Curt and the colonel. Inwardly, Curt cringed. In his professional opinion, General Knox should have retired long ago. Knox had been killed in action more than a dozen times, twice on recent operations. Even a one-star general shouldn't allow himself to get into a position where his robots were destroyed, leaving him in linkage with no robot sensory inputs. Knox was getting sloppy, slowing down, and quite probably becoming increasingly inept; and Curt knew that being killed in action a dozen times had probably affected the general's mind.

Curt had been killed in action twice himself; it hadn't been easy on him, but subsequent tests and evaluations had shown him fit for duty after undergoing therapy. An RI trooper was considered "killed in action" when his robots had been shot out from under him before he'd had the chance to withdraw from his link with them. A person had to be mentally strong, well trained, and highly motivated to remain

35

sane while going through the total destruction of sensory inputs and control outputs, to survive the living death in which the mind suddenly finds itself in limbo. Warbot brainies could withstand the "double-lobed Lebanese systolic stroke" only a few times before it scrambled the brain.

It was different from being killed in action, something which rarely occurred these days. But the RI maintained a list of those who'd posthumously received the Congressional Medal of Honor for making the ultimate sacrifice.

At any rate the general's growing military conservatism bothered Curt and some of the other officers in the Washington Greys. Failure of nerve, some called it. No guts was Lieutenant Morgan's blunt evaluation, made privately to her company commander. Curt would never repeat it to anyone, but he agreed with her.

"Well, Captain, looks like an unusual mission is shaping up for you!" General Knox told Curt in a jovial voice that was almost a bellow. "Hostage extraction mission! Haven't had one of those in many, many years. Was on one of the last ones myself. With my experience in that sort of operation, it looks like I'll earn my pay."

"I don't know anything about the mission, General," Curt replied deferentially. He was glad that he was not under Knox's command, although the general often acted as if he were, much to the dismay of Colonel Hettrick. He was also glad that Hettrick had the job of keeping the general off the backs of Carson's Companions. As brigade commander, Knox had less authority than Colonel Hettrick and considerably less than the Division commander. Unfortunately, Knox maintained a high profile and his shortcomings were evident. Curt knew more about robot combat field operations than Knox, yet military courtesy required that Curt maintain a respectful facade.

"Well, from what I've learned, your outfit is certainly the best qualified for this mission."

"Thank you for your confidence in Carson's Companions, General."

"Nonsense! You've earned your reputation. How is your new Academy man working out?"

"Lieutenant Allen is rapidly becoming an effective member of my team," Curt replied. The general was trying to make small talk, but Curt didn't think this was appropriate when an emergency situation was brewing.

"Outstanding! Pleased to hear that. As it should be. He's a West Pointer." Knox always liked to give the impression that he was a graduate of the Military Academy, but Curt knew that the general had gone to VMI. There was nothing wrong with that. Many of the best officers in America's forces had graduated from VMI, Texas A&M, the Citadel, and NMMI. However, General Knox wanted to be treated as a West Pointer rather than a VMI man. Geriatric pomposity had overtaken Knox.

Curt hoped that Hettrick would, as usual, skillfully keep Knox out of the command loop during the upcoming mission.

Hettrick understood the people under her command. With just a slight edge to her voice, she interrupted,

"Please excuse me, General, but don't you think it's time to give everyone the hot sit-rep?"

"Yes, yes! I'd like everyone to sit down and link up now."

Curt nodded deferentially to General Knox. "By your leave, sir," he said and, without waiting for assent, led his company to seats.

Lieutenant Alexis Morgan sat down beside Curt and observed, "An excellent example of polishing the brass."

"No, I was only trying to keep the frigging lead out," Curt replied cryptically, snuggling down into the seat cushions so that the sensors and transducers in them could make linkage with his spinal nerves. "In Kelly's case, it was a matter of confronting green worms and getting him to fight the real enemy."

"He's a real sonofabitch," Morgan remarked.

"Yeah, don't get near him in the Club after he's hoisted a few."

"That goes any time. If the bastard lays Hand One on me, he'll pull back a bloody stump," Alexis Morgan growled.

Curt snorted. Alexis Morgan was capable of carrying out her threat.

At precisely 1500 hours, Brigadier General Victor Knox, commander of the First Brigade, 17th "Iron Fist" Division, Robot Infantry, stepped up to the podium accompanied by his aide, a young lieutenant. The aide immediately called out, "As you were! Carry on!" It was protocol, traditional but functionally unnecessary. In a military world increasingly concerned with technology, tradition had become more and more important. It gave soldiers a sense of continuity with the past.

No one in the audience had risen; they were all in their own linkage couches, able to receive inputs from the Division's master megacomputer, for which most of the Diamond Point redoubt had been built. Someone had once remarked that this supercomputer had "no blood and no guts, so it uses ours." As a result, it became known as "Old Blood and Guts," then the acronym "OBAG," which was replaced by "Georgie," the nickname of the original "Old Blood and Guts," General George Smith Patton.

As General Victor Knox slipped into his linkage couch in the depressed center of the amphitheater, he seemed to disappear and be replaced by his full-color holographic image which rose out of the center of the pit. Georgie, the megacomputer, created the image, sometimes by holographic projection and sometimes by sending signals through the linkage network to the nervous systems and minds of the people occupying the couches. The spectators didn't care how the image was projected. They were in the room to find out what was going on, what they were supposed to do. Since there was no need for the nonverbal computerized communication of linkage, Georgie suppressed that factor. As a result, those present and Georgie used ordinary voice communication.

"Good afternoon, troops," Knox began. "We're about to become involved in an operation of great complexity. This briefing is being recorded and will be available in the data base for later reference."

He got right to the matter at hand. "Here's the situation: Orient Express Lines' Flight Seven departed San Francisco for Tokyo on schedule with no indication that anything was wrong. Twenty minutes out of San Francisco at altitude over the Pacific, the hypersonic transport was hijacked by an estimated half-dozen people. We don't know how it was done, we don't know the reason, and we've received no demands yet. But we *do* know where the aircraft was taken, and that we must move quickly. A hundred and seven names are on the flight manifest. These people are in grave danger. We've received orders from Pentagon to take immediate—I repeat: *immediate*—action.

"General Carlisle, commander of the 17th Division, has assigned command of this mission to the First Brigade. However, since the Washington Greys is the only regiment capable of making such a rapid response, it is being assigned to Operation Squire, directed at rescuing all passengers and crew members of the aircraft and bringing them to Tokyo—alive. Dealing with the hijackers is a secondary objective which must not—repeat, must not—interfere with the primary one. In short, our mission is rescue, not retaliation, and it is to be achieved with the minimum of bloodshed."

This was indeed news to Curt. Aircraft were rarely hijacked these days. It had been at least twenty years, perhaps more, since a successful in-flight hijacking had taken place. Departure security screening had become very effective, and it had become more difficult for hijackers to get their demands satisfied. Governments had resorted to "stonewall" negotiations and protracted delays.

But most hostage situations had involved less than a

40

dozen people, and had occurred in large cities where media coverage could be quickly and easily obtained.

As war robots had been integrated into military organizations, swift and deadly counterterrorist assault units and weapons were developed. Then, like intercontinental ballistic missiles, they were never used because they were so effective.

And international law had a lot to do with the decline in hijackings. By the end of the twentieth century international jurists and diplomats had worked out antiterrorist procedures that most nations could follow. "The wheels of God grind slowly, but they grind exceedingly fine." The result was the Treaty of Karachi in which all major nations of the world agreed to refrain from utilizing terrorism for national purposes and to deal militarily with terrorists within their borders. The treaty also specified that any nation whose citizens were victims of terrorist acts was free to enter the sovereign territory of another nation: upon notification, in order to rescue its citizens, but the action taken must be within the bounds allowed by the treaty.

Curt found an aircraft hijacking after a *twenty-year* hiatus very odd. Why, robot warfare was only in its primitive stages when the last one had occurred! No one in the United States Army had ever had to utilize the RI for an antihijacking rescue operation. And anyone who'd participated in the last antihijack operation had either retired or, like General Knox, was getting ready to retire. Even Colonel Hettrick would have been a raw lieutenant twenty years ago.

Who was insane or stupid enough to believe that

such a terrorist operation could produce the desired results nowadays?

Or were the motives of the hijackers new ones?

Curt asked himself another question: If the Washington Greys were responsible for the Operation Squire, why was General Knox, the brigade commander, assuming command of Colonel Hettrick's outfit? No wonder the colonel seemed a bit testy!

"This is going to be a difficult mission because of the location of the hostages, provided they're being held in the same place as the aircraft. Our possible courses of action are affected by the location. Here's the situation," Knox went on. A three-dimensional holographic color relief map built up in the pit. It showed a part of the world with which Curt Carson wasn't familiar. Few people were. Knox addressed the Iron Fist Division's megacomputer, "Georgie, give me information about the operational action area, information that is of value to the Zahedan hostage strike and rescue mission."

The supercomputer answered with its synthetic voice, and Curt could almost see an experienced general staff officer talking: "According to in-flight tracking by Low Orbit Orient Traffic Control Center and the latest high resolution satellite imagery, Orient Express Flight Seven is now on the aerodrome at Zahedan in extreme eastern Iran."

As Georgie spoke about places on the map, a very solid-looking arrow-pointer indicated them or the map was highlighted by a spot of light.

"The region is a high semiarid desert with marginal agriculture and some herding, mostly goat and cattle grazing. It hasn't changed in thousands of years except

42

it's become drier. Nomadic herding has stripped the vegetation, allowing erosion to ruin the soil. The hills and ridges are covered with camel's thorn and tamarisk, although there are dwarf and date palms in the oases and along the riverbeds. The highest terrain is the volcanic peak, Kuh-e-Taftan, about four thousand meters high and fifty kilometers southeast of the town.

"Zahedan is a town of about twenty thousand people. It's the regional capital of the Iranian province of Baluchistan. The Iranians control the area politically, which doesn't simplify the operation because they never signed the Treaty of Karachi.

"However, Iranian control of the region is probably minimal because of its isolation. Zahedan is connected to the rest of Iran only by two very poor roads. On the other hand, a railway connects Zahedan to the Indus Valley of Pakistan. The Zahedan aerodrome was probably built during the Second World War. However, our information on the technical status of air transport and defenses in that part of the world is very poor.

"Away from Zahedan, the population is very thin—only about seven people per square kilometer. The local language is Baluchi, a mix of Aryan and Farsi, and most people follow old local folk religions which are mainly animistic. *Jinn*, demons, and angels are part of their Islamic beliefs.

"This is one of the most remote places remaining on Earth in the twenty-first century. Few people have been there, and the region has virtually nothing worth exporting. Conditions are primitive, at best. This is all the information I have been able to locate. Very little additional information is available in the worldwide data base. I even checked the data base in the Explorers Club.''

The place is a thousand kilometers or more from anywhere! was Curt Carson's immediate thought. And Georgie hadn't obtained anywhere near enough information about the area, especially if the Washington Greys were going to conduct a military rescue mission in it. More information was essential. Getting it would be difficult and time consuming.

Was there any time?

He could understand the urgency; what he'd been taught about antiterrorist military operations had stressed the need for rapid deployment in case diplomatic negotiations failed.

General Knox resumed his briefing, ''I'm informed that the Secretary of Defense believes that rapid deployment of a rescue mission is mandatory. The President supports this. The reason is quite simple, but it's classified Sensitive D, T, and O.''

There was an audible stir in the briefing room. Any matter that carried a classification of being security sensitive in the diplomatic, technical, and operational areas was extremely rare.

Knox revealed why. ''Two of the hostages are high-ranking Army officers who are involved in classified research and development on robot warfare at McCarthy Proving Grounds. Orient Express Lines doesn't know they're military personnel because our high-level sensitive people travel as civilians. Ever since the United States military forces pulled out of Japan, there's been no way to maintain the requisite level of secrecy by traveling in military aircraft.

"One is Dr. Robert Armstrong. The other is Colonel Willa Lovell, who was traveling under her civilian title of medical doctor. You don't need to know what their work at McCarthy involved—it's highly classified—and the Pentagon will not divulge the nature of their trip.

"Because the two of them were working on very advanced and highly classified robot warfare technology, we believe their presence on the aircraft motivated the hijacking," General Knox declared. "We'll work on that premise until another is known."

The tension in the briefing room was electric. The RI took care of their own. Although they were Army with old traditions behind them, robot infantry soldiers —men and women—thought of themselves as being something new and different, a cut above the old-time doughboy, GI, grunt, and sand pounder. No one in the briefing room had the slightest doubt that they'd go in and get Armstrong and Lovell. Their fervor would have been intense if only civilian hostages were involved, but the involvement of two Army people working on RI research increased it.

"So we're going in as quickly as we can," Knox stated, and began to outline the mission. "Here is the basic plan. My staff will be fleshing it out while the First Battalion of the Regiment is being airlifted into the Zahedan area. The robot command and control base will be established at some suitable nearby site. Carson's Companions will locate the hostages, penetrate to wherever in Zahedan the hostages are being held, release them, and transport them. Aerodrome security will be provided by Walker's Warriors. Manny's Marauders will create a diversion on the outskirts of the city, and

Kelly's Killers will be held in reserve at the command post."

Curt Carson signaled that he had a comment. Knox recognized him.

"Excuse me, General," Carson began carefully, "unless there's additional intelligence data that hasn't been revealed to us, there's a very good chance we're charging right into a trap."

Knox paused before he responded. "What sort of a trap, Captain?"

"I'm not sure," Curt admitted. "But we're not really sure of anything right now except that a hypersonic transport has been hijacked, one hundred and some people were aboard, two of the passengers were sensitive robot researchers, and the aircraft landed in eastern Iran. We've got at least two divisions of motorized infantry on the PetroPeace Force in the Persian Gulf, and we know the Iranians don't like that. They're going to like it a hell of a lot less if we put the Washington Greys into Iran proper. Furthermore, the Pakistanis want that region, and it's a possible route to the Arabian Sea for the Russkies who still lust for those warm-water seaports. Shouldn't we get more intelligence data and make a threat analysis before we move?"

"We've been given orders, Captain," Knox reminded him.

"And I'll follow them," Curt promised. "But before we go in there and get our asses shot off, we ought to have a better estimate of the total situation and some hard intelligence. The hostages may be in Teheran, or even Kabul or Moscow by now."

Knox was momentarily flustered. Then he cleared his

throat and replied, "We have all the available data, and it will take at least thirty-six hours to position the Regiment. We'll have more information by then. In the meantime, I want to get the operation moving."

Curt Carson didn't like that at all. The Regiment was blundering into action without adequate intelligence. But he was a soldier. He'd follow orders. That's what he'd been trained for and was paid to do. Still, the idea of being ambushed in the wilds of eastern Iran and of having to shoot his way out didn't appeal to him.

He felt that Operation Squire could be a suicide mission with an inept general in command.

He remembered what had happened at the Little Big Horn.

CHAPTER THREE

"General, you'd better hold off further discussion," Georgie suddenly announced. "Defense Intelligence Agency has just transmitted a videotape to me."

"Videotape? Where did it come from?" General Victor Knox wanted to know.

Georgie explained that the tape cassette had quietly appeared on the doorstep of the Rome bureau of Reuters only about an hour ago. Reuters had intended to use it as an exclusive, but a mole in Reuters had notified the Defense Intelligence Agency of the transmission time, satellite, transponder, and scramble parameters in time for DIA snoops to make a clandestine intercept of the data when it was transmitted from Rome to New York.

"Is there any information on the videotape that identifies the responsible party?" Knox asked.

"Yes. I'm currently downloading information from a data base in Baghdad. The responsible party is a relatively new Muslim sect that calls itself the Jehorkhim. Do you want the videotape or my new threat analysis first?"

"The videotape, please, Georgie," Knox requested. In this case, the threat analysis would mean little without having seen the raw data.

"I don't think this will be a very pleasant thing for humans to watch," Georgie warned.

It wasn't.

The image that built up on the flat video screen in the briefing room was that of a short and ascetic man of indeterminate age, wearing a white kaftan and turban. Threads of white ran through his scraggly black beard. His appearance was unforgettable because of his dark, piercing eyes, though he was handsome and virile and obviously attractive to women.

Behind him, on the otherwise blank wall, was a solid green flag, a yellow crescent emblazoned across its field.

The videotape was a terribly amateur effort. Georgie attempted to correct for the color imbalance and fuzzy edge effects caused by a dirty videotape and hand operation of a cheap videocamera whose framing pulses were erratic.

The image spoke in excellent academic English, with a British accent.

"I am Abdul Madjid Rahman, Imam of the Jehorkhim Muslims. Under my command and at my direction, the Jehorkhim are responsible for the taking of the aircraft, Orient Express Flight Seven, and all of its passengers and crew members. The artificial eyes and ears that you have placed in Allah's heavens have certainly told you that the aircraft is at the aerodrome of our holy city of Zahedan. We have taken as prisoners one hundred and five of your people. We hold them at our mercy in Zahedan. Each day at sunrise, we will begin to torture one of these individuals. At sundown that person will be permitted to die. We will use a videocamera to record each torture and each death. The following day, a videotape will be delivered, always to a different location in the western world. The description and commentary on the tapes will be provided by the United States Army scientists who were aboard the flight. Finally, on the one hundred and fourth and one hundred and fifth sundowns, these two will be allowed to experience merciful deaths.

"But we Jehorkhim are not sadistic fiends. We can be convinced to return these people to their homes and families. You want these people released and returned. You cherish them, and we have little that we can trade for the things we need. We have something of value to you; you have the money to obtain the things we require. Let us therefore exchange things of value.

"What is the price of a human life? I have established it at ten million dollars in gold bullion. When I receive word via Voice of America radio, the BBC overseas service, or Radio Tokyo that the head of state of the United States or of Japan will guarantee that this amount in gold will be delivered to us in exchange for each person, I will specify the time and place for the exchange of these valued items.

"To demonstrate that I mean what I say, I am now willing to sacrifice ten million dollars in gold bullion. Many of you may not want to watch what follows. We will use old methods of torture; but time has shown them to be extremely effective."

The videocamera zoomed back jerkily to reveal a man and a woman tightly restrained against a limestone-block wall by shackles. The pair looked dazed but defiant.

"You may know these two people. The woman is Colonel Willa Lovell of the United States Army's Fort McCarthy Proving Ground. The man is Dr. Robert Armstrong of the same organization," the Imam's voice explained. "I shall now require that Dr. Armstrong continue the narration by describing what is being done to one of the prisoners we have taken."

The videocamera swung wildly to a young man hanging from chains attached to the ceiling and to the shackles around his wrists. He was spread-eagled by additional restraints and was stark naked. He stared ahead, dazed but obviously terrified and in pain. He was bleeding from several wounds.

"You may hold us prisoner, Imam," came the voice of Dr. Armstrong, "but I won't participate in your cruelties."

"I anticipated that," the Imam replied. "Therefore, I will change the planned sequence of torture. I require your cooperation, Colonel Lovell. Therefore, a little persuasion is in order."

"Bob!" It was the woman who screamed.

"Willa, they're going to kill us all anyway! Imam, let her alone! Kill me first! Let's get this over with!"

The Imam shook his turbaned head slowly. "No, we intend to make use of you. I have many means of persuasion, but this one suits my present purposes."

The videocamera panned back to Willa Lovell, an attractive dark-haired woman clad in torn and tattered clothing. As torturer approached her, she let out a high shriek of terror which changed to a gasp and then a cry of pain. For a moment, she was hidden from the camera's view by the torturer. Her scream rose, became a ululation. The Imam spoke roughly in a strange language to the torturer, who then stepped back from her. Wet red blood covered her breasts.

"Shut it off!" It was Colonel Hettrick who cried out. While men are extremely sensitive to testicular pain, women suffer the same trauma with respect to their breasts. Few sane people can stand to watch such forms of torture.

"Yes, Colonel," Georgie replied as the video screen went black.

The violent emotions stirred by that crude videotape had shattered the linkage between Georgie and those in the room. Everyone was now, abruptly, in the real world, looking at the others in shock and anger or staring at the amphitheater pit where General Knox was sitting on his linkage couch.

There was absolute silence in the briefing room. War was one thing. Robot war involved destroying machines with other machines, and only occasionally did a human being get hurt. But sadistic torture was inhumane insofar as modern soldiers were concerned. Worse, it was barbaric. Utterly repugnant.

Suddenly the briefing room erupted into a babble of sound.

Curt's throat was dry and he was having trouble controlling his anger. But Lieutenant Allen was shaking with rage, and Lieutenant Morgan had her face buried in her hands.

"Alexis, are you all right?" Curt asked.

"No . . . no, I'm not. I may be sick to my stomach.

. . . On the other hand, I don't want to be. Every minute we waste gives those bastards a minute more to work the hostages over."

Lieutenant Allen swallowed. "My history prof told me they still practice mutilation in that part of the world. I didn't really believe him at the time."

"I hope you don't want to watch the rest of that tape, Lieutenant," Sergeant Sampson said quietly. "I sure as hell didn't join the Army for that! It's *sick!*"

Master Sergeant Kester and Sergeant Gerard looked grim. Kester was shaking his head sadly. "Goddam world hasn't changed a bit," he muttered.

Curt took a deep breath and let it out explosively. "I was hoping to get a good night's sacktime. So much for that . . . I won't be able to sleep worth a damn now."

"All right! Hold it down! As you were!" General Knox shouted, trying to quiet the bedlam. It didn't work. Everyone was highly charged.

It was Henry Kester, the oldest soldier in the room, who barked in a voice loud and piercing enough to command a regiment on parade: " *'Ten-HUT!'*"

The command almost echoed, even though the briefing room was acoustically proofed.

The room fell quiet as if by magic.

Knox seemed a bit dazed, but he quickly recovered his composure. "Thank you, Sergeant," he told Kester. "Georgie, is there anything on that tape other than torture?"

"Yes, the killing and death throes of the young man, one of the pilots, is shown quite explicitly. But by the time they finished with him, there wasn't very much of him left to die."

"Colonel Hettrick, are you fit to continue?" General Knox asked solicitously.

"Yes . . . uh, I'm all right, sir," she replied. And she was. Hettrick knew a commander had to think coolly and logically. The ability of women soldiers and officers in the RI to turn off their emotions was legendary; it was the source of the rumor that women warbot brainies were frigid and dispassionate. The rumor was wrong. Those submerged and controlled feelings burst forth with great intensity under other circumstances.

"General!" Captain Marty Kelly bellowed. He was going directly over his colonel's head, making an end run around the chain of command. Typical Kelly maneuvering. Nobody missed it, and no one liked it. "I don't share Carson's reluctance to go in there and hit hard and fast. We've got to do that now! Give me the point command! I'll get in there and kill those bastards! All of them!"

"Captain Kelly, I appreciate your willingness to act," General Knox replied quickly, an edge on his voice now. "But your request is denied. Our orders are to rescue the hostages with a minimum of killing. We may be madder than hell right now because that Imam showed us scenes that would infuriate us. Why? That was unusual behavior. Terrorists like to keep hostages hidden and give very little information about them."

Captain Edith Walker spoke up. "General, exactly who are we fighting? I've never heard of the Jehorkhims."

"Georgie, brief us on this Jehorkhim sect," Knox

snapped to the megacomputer. "Who and what are we going up against?"

Georgie paused. It was a perceptible pause, which meant that the megacomputer was manipulating an enormous amount of data. Georgie was capable of carrying out trillions of operations per second, and his memory was so large that the contents of the books in all of the great libraries of the world would take up less than one percent of it. In Georgie's memory banks reposed all extant military books and reports, from Sun Tzu and Caesar to the latest dispatches from Tunis and Java. So a pause was significant when it was long enough to be perceptible to human beings who processed information much more slowly and had far less available memory.

"The Jehorkhim sect is a religious splinter group of the Shiite Muslims," Georgie reported. "They're believed to be extreme traditionalists. They split with their Teheran colleagues about fifty years ago and went off in an even more doctrinaire Muslim direction. One of the major rifts between the Jehorkhim and the rest of the Shiite Muslims is the Jehorkhims' almost fanatical opposition to the development of machines as extensions of human muscle power in manipulating the universe. The reasons for this aren't known in light of the Koran and other Muslim teachings and writings."

"They sure as hell use torture machines!" Marty Kelly's voice rang out.

General Knox's voice was disproving. "Captain, I think if you review the tape carefully, you will see that the torturer used nothing but his bare hands. We weren't allowed to see how he did what he did. Consider their motives in showing us this torture. The Jehorkhims and their holy man want us to be upset and outraged. They want to cloud our thinking. Now, I don't know why the Jehorkhims did this. It doesn't make any sense to me, and I don't understand their religion. But that's beside the point. The Iron Fist RI has its orders. So do the Washington Greys. Our job: Go in and get 'em! Without killing if possible. Without being killed, for sure. We don't have to answer all those other questions. So, Captain Kelly, my orders regarding the organization of Operation Squire stand."

That remark told Curt that Knox really didn't know what to do with Kelly or Kelly's Killers. Although the outfit had a long list of reprimands, when everything had gone to worms, Kelly's Killers would fight just for the sheer joy of it. They could be useful, but they were like a loose cannon, loaded and rolling wildly with the ship.

Knox went on, "Operation Squire will proceed as previously presented. I'll see to it that the proper announcements are made by the book through channels, but I must presume that the Iranians won't cooperate and we'll have to blast our way into Zahedan through Iranian air defenses. I'll also assume the Pakistanis will cooperate, but I don't want their help in Iranian territory. Any questions?"

Curt spoke up. "Yes, General. We still don't have enough information. Let me take the Companions in ahead of time on a reconnaissance snoop."

"We can't delay the mission," Knox told him flatly.

"I won't delay it," Curt fired back. He didn't want to go into Zahedan without knowing more about the place. His butt was in a sling if something went wrong. "It's going to take time to get everything in place. While you're doing that, I'll be scouting Zahedan. I can move faster with two or three people than you can move the Regiment halfway around the world."

Knox knew the Washington Greys were short on good intelligence data. He believed there wasn't enough time to mount a recon mission, but if Curt Carson had worked out something, he was willing to listen. "What do you want to do?"

"Get out of Diamond Point within an hour or so with Master Sergeant Kester and Platoon Sergeant Gerard. We can move fast if we can get robots and aircraft."

"What do you need?"

"The fastest possible airlift to international waters in the Gulf of Oman. Georgie, project that map of the Zahedan region," Curt said to the megacomputer. The map sprang into three-dimensional reality in the holo tank.

Curt studied it for a moment. "Georgie, can you increase the scale? I need better resolution."

"I can go down to three meters resolution with the data I've got. If you want better, I'll have to program a high-resolution recon satellite to pass over the area, and that will take about twenty-three hours."

"Best you can do?"

"Best I can do."

"Then do it. I've got to get a good picture of where we'll be." He thought he had his recon mission pretty well worked out except for confirmation of the details and of the technical equipment he needed. Indicating the geographical location as he spoke, Curt went on,

"I'd like to rendezvous in the Gulf of Oman with any ship that can bring the equipment we can't take along on the airlift."

"That means Air Force and Navy support. That will complicate the situation," Knox complained. "Well, I'll have to call in some favors. Navy's got a task force there. The flyboys are always happy to log more time."

"I'll want to use two aerodynes going in from the Gulf," Curt went on, referring to the Army's new saucer-shaped jet-powered aircraft that could take off and land anywhere. Because of its shape, it was difficult to spot on radar. A helicopter made noise, was a mechanical monstrosity. It showed up on even the most primitive radar sets because of the thrashing rotor blades. An aerodyne had only one moving part: the sheet of high-velocity air blown by a fanjet engine out through slots near the center of the dish and over its curved upper surface. Similar to big non rotating frisbees in appearance, aerodynes were quiet as a whisper, and had given the Army's vertical envelopment doctrine a whole new lease on life.

"One of those aerodynes will be cover and contingency; it should be armed, maneuverable, and capable of carrying us out of Zahedan if the mission goes to slime. We'll operate our recon robots from a mobile robot command and control center in the other aerodyne, which will be heavy and not as maneuverable because it will be carrying two of us plus the recon bots' equipment. I'll need as many of the latest recon robots as I can get, preferably birdbots in the shape and coloring of local falcons and other large birds." Carson was referring to flying robots that carried on-board television cameras.

"Those are hard to get, Captain," Knox pointed out. "They're just completing development tests on them at McCarthy Proving Ground. No operational unit has them yet."

"I can get birdbots for you, Captain," Colonel Hettrick stated. "I'll call in a few of my own favors. No sweat. Want some of the new ratbots, too?"

Curt hadn't worked with those. The superminiaturized robots that looked like large rats, squirrels, cats, or dogs were still under development. "Sure! We haven't used them yet, but command and control can't be too difficult. Easier than operating a birdbot," he observed.

"I'll see how many of the preproduction units I can weasel out of Ordnance Corps. And I think you'll find that the additional artificial intelligence circuitry in the new birdbots will relieve you of some of the flying duties," Hettrick added.

"Okay." Curt felt he was on a roll, and he feared to let up lest he lose momentum. He was selling this recon mission, even though it meant a lot of additional work on the part of the staff. Perhaps Knox was too overwhelmed to object. "Here's my mission plan: Lean, mean, and simple; myself and two of my sergeants, that's all. We'll depart a blue-water ship of some sort—whatever can be made available—and go in from the Gulf of Oman to the Zahedan region, trimming the tops of the palm trees as we go. Not over ten meters altitude. We'll go in at night, stealthed and flying by passive I-R nightscopes. Before dawn, we'll have the command

59

post established on the slopes of Kuh-e-Taftan, that four-thousand meter volcanic peak about fifty klicks south of Zahedan. I don't want to get too close to Zahedan; this is a recon mission that shouldn't be detected. Locating on that mountain should give us line of sight to Zahedan so we can set up and maintain our microwave and laser command and our data channels with the bots.

"I'll use the big birdbots to lift the ratbots into Zahedan from the command post, and we'll use both types of bots for recon in Zahedan," Curt finished. "Does that sound feasible and workable, Colonel?" He deliberately directed his question to his regimental commander rather than General Knox. At least Colonel Hettrick was "can do" and didn't throw up bureaucratic roadblocks.

"I like it, Captain, except for one thing," Hettrick told him. "The power packs on the birdbots will be badly depleted if you use them to air-carry. I'll have Supply lay on some additional birdbots to be used strictly for recon and give you additional birdbot power packs as well. Speaking of Supply, how long do you intend to stay there?"

"Uh, we'd better configure the supply of the bot command post with food, water, and power for, oh, say a maximum of fifteen man-days with a six man-day contingency factor. I don't think I'll be there that long, but I've got to have some flexibility and I don't want to be caught short of rations or power. This mission is based on speed and stealth. We're gonna get in, get the data, and get out," Having reminded them of the tactical doctrine under which he intended to work, Curt made further requests. "Finally, I need carbines, grenades, a sixty-millimeter mortar, and air defense capability in the form of smart flak rockets and shells. I want to be able to carry out personal recon if it becomes necessary because we may not be able to get in there a second time. And we must be able to fight our way out if necessary."

Colonel Hettrick quickly turned to him. "I don't want you and your people to abandon the bots and try to get out of there on your own. Too dangerous."

"Colonel, I want to be prepared to do it if we have to," Carson responded, adding, "I don't like the idea of exposing my pink bod to physical combat unnecessarily, and I don't relish crawling on my belly in the sand, either. But if going physical means saving our butts, we will. That's a godforsaken part of the world, but I want to be able to walk out of it if I have to."

"You won't have to," Hettrick promised him. "The full Regiment will be in there with Operation Squire if you don't get out. I won't dump you out there in the desert and forget you."

Curt smiled, for the first time in hours. "Thanks. That's nice to know." He turned to his company, "Lieutenant Morgan will be in command during my absence."

"Yessir! But just be careful. I don't relish the idea of having to go in there to snatch the three of you . . . sir." Alexis Morgan's remark was a tad sarcastic, Curt noted, but perhaps that was because he'd excluded her from the recon mission.

Curt looked at her noncommittally. "Lieutenant, please see me privately afterward."

"Yes, sir."

"That's it, Colonel . . . General," Curt declared. "Will you buy it?"

"Georgie, please recap the mission plan and point out any holes in it." Hettrick was the one who had presence of mind to use the megacomputer's capabilities.

Georgie pulled back on the map scale to reveal the Gulf of Oman at the bottom and Zahedan at the top. Three dimensional symbols appeared and moved on the holo as the megacomputer spoke. Georgie integrated the inputs that Division and Regiment staffs had made with Curt's mission outline. "A supersonic aerodyne will be on the pad at Diamond Point ready for departure at oh-seven-hundred local time tomorrow morning."

"We need to get moving sooner than that!" Curt objected.

"Captain, you said you wanted to go in from the Gulf of Oman to Kuh-e-Taftan under cover of darkness," the megacomputer pointed out in unemotional tones. "If that is still your intention, an oh-seven-hundred local takeoff time will put you at your rendezvous point in the Gulf of Oman at twenty-one-hundred local time there, well after sunset, following a four-point-eight-hour flight."

"Can't you get us there any sooner?"

"Captain, this planet is round and Zahedan is approximately one-hundred-seventy-two degrees longitude away from here. Dawn is breaking over Zahedan at this time while we have yet to experience sunset here. It's possible to get you to the gulf in less than five hours, but you'll land on the water for pickup by the Navy before sunset. You'd be a very attractive potential target . . . in case this whole affair is indeed a trap as you suspected earlier."

"Shit!" Curt muttered in frustration. Another hostage was going to die simply because the Earth happened to be spherical. "That blows the recon mission, Colonel! I can't get in there and get out before the Greys get into position if I have to wait overnight."

"Maybe not, Captain. Continue, Georgie."

"At oh-six-hundred local time tomorrow morning, the three humans involved in the mission should report for suiting-up and checkout of their ambulatory linkage harnesses. The Navy has no support vehicle available in the Gulf of Oman, but one of the carrier submarines supporting the Cottonbalers in the Persian Gulf can be diverted. The air transport vehicle *Foulois* will rendezvous with the carrier submarine *McCain* at twenty-four degrees thirty-five minutes North, sixty degrees thirty-five minutes East no later than seventeen hundred Zulu time or twenty-one hundred local time. The *McCain* will be transporting a Victory Class heavy-lift aerodyne with a recon bot command center plugged in, along with sufficient power cells for a seven-day operation. Also aboard the *McCain* will be an escort aerodyne, type PF-51D. The ratbots and birdbots will be aboard the *Foulois*. Captain Carson and Sergeant Kester will man the heavy-lift aerodyne, call sign Beauregard. Sergeant Gerard will man the escort aerodyne, call sign Pickett.

63

Departing the *McCain* no later than seventeen hundred Zulu time, the two aerodynes will reach Kuh-e-Taftan, three hundred seventy-three kilometers away, no later than twenty hundred Zulu which is oh-three-hundred local time, one hour before first light. Support troops consisting of the rest of Carson's Companions and the other companies of the Washington Greys will be air-lifted out tonight to make rendezvous with the *Raborn* off Abu Musa Island. The *Raborn* will rendezvous with the *McCain* in the Gulf of Oman by sunrise day after tomorrow, and will be ready to launch the hostage extraction mission the following sunset."

Georgie's words came out slowly and distinctly as the symbols moved across the map. It was the usual dry, straightforward presentation of an initial mission plan. Georgie completed it by asking, "Comments? Critique? Questions?"

"No way to get the Washington Greys in position sooner than that?" Hettrick asked.

"No. We don't have the airlift capability and the necessary naval support to do it any sooner. I'm discounting the need for air support, which would take even longer."

"Damn! General, if we take on any more of these quick response hostage extraction missions, we'd better be able to shag our tails a whole hell of a lot faster than *this*!" Hettrick snapped. "Forty-eight hours to get into position for launching the mission is too god-damned long . . . sir!"

"Army hasn't done one of these in more than fifteen years, Colonel. We're going to have to relearn some things," Knox told her.

"Other than the fact that it's taking too long to get in gear, I have no heartburn over the recon mission, but I'll be working to speed up mobilization tonight," Hettrick muttered. "Well, it's the best we can do under the circumstances, I guess. I'll buy off the recon mission."

"Comment." It was General Knox. "Captain, I think you should be more economical. One aerodyne is far harder to spot than two. The reliability of our equipment is top-notch, so you shouldn't worry about an aircraft malfunction. With only one aerodyne, you might be able to get in during daylight hours."

Curt merely looked at his buffer, Colonel Hettrick, who said, "General, Carson and his people need to be able to defend themselves and to have viable alternatives open to them if something should go wrong. But let's look at the success ratio. Georgie, calculate probabilities of success if the recon force strength is halved to eliminate active defenses and the contingency air cover of the second aerodyne."

"Probability of successful mission as presently structured is five in one with a ninety-percent confidence level. Probability of successful mission if force is realigned as General Knox suggests is diametrically the opposite: one in five."

"Very well!" General Knox conceded. "Proceed as planned."

"Sign-off time. I buy it with reservations; I'll smooth the details tonight," Colonel Hettrick said wearily.

"Very well. Recon mission approved," General Knox said. "But you must be made aware, Captain Carson, that we may not have time to properly analyze and evaluate all the data from your recon mission."

"General, I just want to make sure I know where I'm going when we put ourselves into Zahedan," Curt told him bluntly.

"Very well. Briefing completed. Dismissed! Move out!"

As the room was vacated, Hettrick came up out of the pit, sought out Curt, pulled him to one side, and quietly remarked, "Remember that videotape. These are mean bastards in Zahedan. Don't drag your ass."

"We're going to lose two more hostages before we can even get emplaced," Curt reminded her, bitterness in his voice. Then he added, almost as an afterthought, "Uh, Colonel, excuse me, but why the hell did General Carlisle turn Operation Squire over to Knox?"

Belinda Hettrick sighed. "General Carlisle has the rest of the Iron Fist Division to run, and we're in the middle of a troop rotation in Iraq as well as the annual budget battle. I understand that General Knox got command of Operation Squire because of his previous experience on a hostage strike about seventeen years ago."

"Jesus, that's a long time! Everything's changed since then!" Curt gritted his teeth. "Why the hell did Carlisle do that? You're regimental commander. You're in charge of the Greys, and we're the only outfit involved."

Hettrick shrugged. "That I am, but Carlisle is 'Old Army,' " she said quietly. "I'm the first female regimental commander Carlisle's had. He isn't chauvinistic;

66

but he may be uncomfortable with me in command of what's turned out to be a major mission. And it's none of your business anyway, Captain! Carry out your orders just like I'm doing."

"Sorry. Does Knox know where the bodies are buried or something?"

"Just between you and me, I detect the subtle fickle finger of the Old Comrades Network in this," she told him. "I've caught the vibe that Knox convinced Carlisle to let him have this operation because Knox desperately needs a combat command to maintain his rated staff position code. Without it, Knox could be dropped into a noncombat position and find himself running a support command."

"Shit! Will you buffer me as usual?"

"Best I can. I know where a few bodies are buried myself." She looked closely at him. "You've got a tough mission coming up. You were in combat sim for two hours today, plus this briefing. Get some sleep before you shove off."

"I'd rather work the sims tonight and sleep on the flight over."

"Captain Carson, this is a direct order: Go to bed."

"Yes, Colonel."

"And I mean get some sleep . . . in spite of consequences of linkage, you hot-blooded young war-horse." Hettrick obviously wanted to say something else, but Carson's Companions were standing nearby. She turned and walked out the door.

Curt looked around at Carson's Companions. "Sergeant Kester, Sergeant Gerard, be in the suit-up room tomorrow at dawn patrol time. The rest of you will be moving out in a few hours, so I'll see you on the ocean somewhere. Let's get cracking."

Lieutenant Jerry Allen snapped a sharp salute. Surprisingly, his action was followed by the other four. Curt returned the respectful gesture, and then all filed out except Lieutenant Alexis Morgan. She was now alone with Curt in the briefing room.

He looked at her. "Lieutenant?" he asked.

"You wanted to see me privately, Captain," she reminded him.

"That was before the planning indicated you'd be standing by on the *McCain*."

"I'm standing by any time you want, Captain."

"If you're pissed off because you're not going on the recon mission, forget it. I need you in command while I'm gone."

She was noncommittal and unargumentative. "Yes, sir. I'll do the best job I can, along with the rest of the company, sir."

"I know you will. That's why you're my second in command. You're dismissed, Lieutenant," he told her, signifying that their official relationship was temporarily terminated. "Uh, Alexis, this is the first time since you were posted to Carson's Companions that we've gone into action separately, isn't it?"

"Yes, Curt. And this is a lot more dangerous than a standard skirmish. You could damned well get killed for real."

"Not if I can help it."

"I won't be leaving for four hours. I'll be in my quarters. The door is open. . . ."

68

"We're officially off duty, Alexis. Rule Ten isn't in effect right now."

She didn't say anything. Instead, she reached up, put her arms around his neck, and kissed him fervently. For a soldier, she was soft and round in all the right places, even in her fatigue uniform. "Now!" she whispered. "We don't have much time!"

CHAPTER FOUR

"I ain't gonna like wearing this damned thing for six days!" Sergeant Nick Gerard complained as he wriggled under the pickups of the ambulatory linkage harness the biotech was adjusting over his head and down his back. The harness was a mobile version of the sensor and electrode network in a standard linkage couch. It was used on missions when soldiers had to move around, when there was no room for a linkage couch in a vehicle or command post, or when soldiers might have to quickly plug into or unplug from a command center's circuitry.

"Aw, golly gee!" Master Sergeant Henry Kester said sarcastically. "Such a hardship, Nick! Why don't you transfer to the paratroops where you can jump out of perfectly good airplanes, or to a swat team where you can eat dirt?"

"We may damned well be eating some dirt before this is over," Gerard observed.

"Not unless you go into idiot mode and blow your neural fuses," the old soldier told him.

"Recon mission," Gerard grumbled. "That means we don't shoot first."

"Would you be happier in Kelly's Killers, Sergeant?" Captain Curt Carson asked unnecessarily.

"No, sir!"

"How does that feel, Captain?" Helen Devlin stepped back and made a small readjustment on Curt's harness.

"Like cold, icy fingers up and down my spine," he told her.

"The electrodes will warm up shortly."

"I know. But never fast enough. Well, it's about as comfortable as a harness can ever be. Thanks. You got it adjusted pretty good." Carson rotated his bare shoulders and flexed his back.

"Anything else?" the little biotech sergeant asked coyly.

Curt shook his head.

"There you go, disturbing the sensors again," she admonished him. Leaned close to his ear as if to readjust an electrode pickup on the back of his neck, she whispered, "Drat! You officers always stick together, don't you?"

Curt turned his eyes to her without moving his head. He simply said, "RHIP, Sergeant."

"You should have called me. I'm a well-qualified biotech. I'm trained to handle all sorts of premission problems as well as postlinkage trauma."

"And I'm certified as an officer and a gentleman, so I must politely let your remark and its implications pass. We're on duty." The time for playfulness was past insofar as Curt was concerned. He was about to go into action, and this particular mission was far more dan-

71

gerous than he liked. He didn't mind battle risk; that was part of the job of being an RI officer. But this was not the usual sort of mission. Its consequences could be dire indeed. There could be no thought of capture. Curt had the images of the videotape in mind. Had it not been for Alexis Morgan, he would have had trouble getting what little sleep he'd managed last night. Premission sleep was always difficult. It had been even worse last night.

Now it was morning. Although he could see no daylight in the windowless bastion of Diamond Point, he somehow felt the chill and anticipation of the dawn that was breaking outside.

Tech Sergeant Helen Devlin helped him don the skintight body stocking of composite filament yarns. Developed on the same principle as the tightly-woven silk armor of Genghis Khan's Mongol cavalrymen, it wouldn't stop a 4.45-millimeter high-velocity bullet, but any projectile traveling less than two hundred meters per second would, at worst, simply drive into his skin. He could remove the projectile by pulling the fabric out of the wound. Nearly impossible to cut, the silken armor also protected its wearer against shrapnel or bayonets. RI troopers weren't supposed to be placed in physical danger, but they wore body armor when they might be.

Curt, who'd been on remote missions before, didn't put on the cooling garment with fluid-filled tubes which carried body heat into a heat exchanger. And he didn't like, nor did he want, the additional weight and complexity of the backpack and its power cell, which might go flat and leave him encased in what would quickly become the world's most efficient sweatsuit. If he'd been planning to wear a powered combat suit, the pack would have been mandatory. But the combat suits were bulky and heavy, and they became deep freezes or ovens if the power packs and life-support units quit.

Instead, Curt and his sergeants chose to wear coveralls with a loose, open weave to the cloth and light, desert camouflage coloring. He zipped on thigh-high tan leather battle boots, and strapped the protective helmet over the skull cap of the linkage harness.

For the recon mission, Curt had chosen his favorite close-quarter weapon: the Winchester CG-17 bullpup autoload carbine. It took 4.45-millimeter high-velocity caseless cartridges, and it sported an all-vision variscope sight along its top rib. It wasn't much good beyond a hundred meters, but he'd never had to fire a personal weapon at an enemy at a greater range. The firearm-type weapons utilized by war robots, far more powerful and accurate, were deadly up to one thousand meters because they didn't have to be designed to suit the limitations of human soldiers; specialized weapons robots were made to bear their weight and their recoil.

Curt had been educated and trained by old-line soldiers who'd been in combat before war robots had become part of the U.S. Army. He knew, understood, and appreciated personal firearms, and felt naked and vulnerable when unarmed, even if the enemy were only shooting at his warbots. The Winchester carbine was strictly for last-ditch personal protection, but he liked the heft of the 2.4-kilogram weapon as he picked it up and slung it from his shoulder. He then attached the bandolier of six fifty-round clips to both sides of his chest, gently slipped a composite-plastic general-purpose knife into his boot top. The final fillip was the pair of all-vision binoculars that hung against his chest from an elastic neck strap.

Master Sergeant Kester preferred something more substantial in the way of a personal weapon: an old rebuilt Ingram MAC10 that fired .45-caliber ACP rounds. The MAC10 was an antique; it belonged in a museum. But Kester, an amateur gunsmith, had rebuilt it. He once told his captain, "If somebody gets close enough to me that I've gotta use a hand gun on him, I want to be damned sure I stop the bastard cold. Those subcaliber BB guns you carry, Captain, they'll wound but they won't lift a hundred-kilo man off his feet and toss him back three meters." Every time Curt looked at the gaping muzzle of Kester's little hand cannon, the bore appeared to be larger. But he'd never seen Kester kill a man with the MAC10 because he'd never been with Kester in a situation where they, not the bots, were taking and returning fire. He'd once watched Kester fire a burst of three rounds into a watermelon. There wasn't enough of it left to eat.

The choice of Sergeant Nick Gerard was the RI's standard-issue personal sidearm, a 7.62-millimeter Hornet machine pistol, which he slipped into his service belt's holster. Curt felt the Hornet didn't have enough range or accuracy, and, Kester maintained that the Hornet was a "social purpose weapon," useful only for giving an assailant a bad scare. Gerard paid no attention to this jibe, however, every year he continued to qualify at Expert level with the Hornet, repeatedly putting a five-shot rapid-fire burst into a ten-centimeter circle at one hundred meters. Curt didn't like the gun, but he respected it in Nick Gerard's hands.

"Captain Carson, report now with your detail to Departure Ramp Foxtrot." The announcement came over the suit-up room's intercom.

"Move out," Curt told his men. On impulse, he gave Helen Devlin a quick pat on the fanny as he left, and told her quietly, "See you when I get back."

"Promise?"

"Promise."

"Don't get shot up. Or down, either."

"Neither. You'll find me up as usual when I get back . . ."

"A woman can hope . . ."

The sun was just over the Mogollon Rim and a cold wind was blowing across the departure ramp as the three men emerged from the lift and hurried to the open, belly cargo hatch of the transport. The *Foulois* was a new supersonic aerodyne that had the usual curved upper surfaces, but there was a hint of swept-back stubby wings at the rear. It was big—fifty meters across—because it carried enough fuel for long-range operations. In contrast to an ordinary aircraft, which had to move through the air in order for the wings to generate lift, the *Foulois* aerodyne got its lift from the air blown over its upper surface. Several fanjet engines drove the moving sheet of air from their exhausts. The bottom of the sprawling black hull looked vaguely like the bottom of a boat. This design allowed the *Foulois* to land on the water or on inflatable landing bags on a ramp such as the one at Diamond Point.

Curt took a quick look around. He was sorry he

hadn't spent more time outside in the last several weeks. He might live through many days and much action before he saw this place again. He promised himself that when—not if—he returned, he'd take some accumulated leave and go up into the high, isolated back country of the White Mountains, just to get the hell away from it all. It had been a long time—a year?—since he'd had leave.

But, in the meantime, there was a job to do.

Once the *Foulois* had lifted from the Diamond Point ramp and made its transition into forward flight, it climbed into the high stratosphere and began accelerating to supersonic speed. The aerodyne shape of the *Foulois* made it easier for designers to reduce the intensity of the ship's shock wave, thereby cutting the sonic boom to something akin to distant thunder to listeners on the ground ten kilometers below. The fast, quiet ship drove eastward through the skies to a destination half a world away.

The *Foulois* was a military cargo aircraft designed for hauling freight and not for human comfort. There wasn't much room to move around in it. Packaged equipment and supplies for Operation Squire took up most of the space in the cargo bay.

Kester found a reasonably comfortable place on top of a covered pallet and went to sleep. Gerard squirmed into a position near a window, where he could sit and read; he had managed to stuff a sex novel into his kit, and he quickly became engrossed in it.

The cargo bay was far too noisy for a decent conversation, so Curt climbed over equipment and pallets to the control compartment. The pilot waved to him, indicated a place where he could sit, and went back to watching video. After an initial few minutes of small talk, Curt and the man fell silent; they had little in common to talk about. From time to time, the pilot looked up to see how well the autopilot was doing its job. He was an Air Force noncombat transport driver, a "trash hauler." He could have been delivering a load of blankets to Bahia for all he cared. He was along for the ride, a pilot in name only, in the cockpit just to make sure the computer that flew the plane did what it was supposed to do.

Curt decided that kind of work would bore the hell out of him.

The displays told Curt where the *Foulois* was at any given time. The flight distance was just shy of sixteen thousand kilometers, and would have been shorter if the *Foulois* had been able to overfly Russia. As it was, the cleared course took the ship over Gibraltar and Suez. When they were over Saudi Arabia, the sun set behind them.

It was pitch black outside when the *Foulois* dropped to subsonic speed and began to descend under automatic robot pilot control commanded via satellite by the Air Force master traffic control computer complex at Colorado Springs. The pilot monitored the displays with greater interest as the ship settled down through the blackness, finally splashing gently into the dark waters of the Gulf of Oman.

The situation display on the pilot's panel showed:

Time: 2054:04 Z
Position: 24° 35′ 07″ N 60° 35′ 02″ E

Altitude: 0 meters above sea level
Speed: 0 km/hr
Course heading: NONE

It was now deadly quiet in the aircraft, which rocked and bobbed slightly in the long swells.

"Where's the *McCain*?" Curt wanted to know.

"We had some tail winds. Jet stream. We're ahead of schedule. Got six minutes yet. Don't get your water hot . . . sir." The flyboy was not only no conversationalist, he had the flippant attitude of most Air Force personnel. To Curt, flyboys were airliner drivers who couldn't cut it in the competitive commercial world. They even looked the part right down to their sky-blue uniforms. Theirs was a world of hot coffee, pocketfuls of plastic spoons, and latrine parts to be hauled to Singapore . . .

Curt turned on his all-vision binoculars and scanned the ocean's surface. There was very little wind outside because, even on this moonless night, he could see no waves other than the one-meter swells that rocked the aerodyne. No ship. Nothing out there.

Suddenly, the *Foulois* stopped rocking, and Curt felt a sudden surge of upward motion.

"Right on time," the pilot remarked. "And right on target."

The *McCain* had surfaced beneath the aircraft, positioning it neatly on the forward flight deck. Outside, Curt saw the hulking black shape of the submarine carrier's conning tower, water running out of its scuppers. Beneath the *Foulois* was a level black deck.

Curt had not seen or been inside any of the new two

hundred-meter submarine carriers laid down by the Navy only a few years before. They were among the biggest submersibles afloat, even larger than the fabled old Soviet "Typhoon" class. Displacing forty thousand tonnes submerged, the *McCain*, on whose forward flight deck the *Foulois* now rested, was the best transportation device for clandestinely by moving soldiers and warbots around the world.

A dark hatch opened on the forward deck of the *Foulois*. Time to get moving, Curt told himself.

He thought he'd have to awaken Kester, but found the Master Sergeant was up and had his equipment on. Gerard was also ready. They had to wait for Curt while he strapped on his gear and sidearm.

"This way, Captain," the voice of a deck seabot told him as he stepped out of the bottom hatch of the *Foulois* onto the *McCain's* deck. The sea robot, designed for deck operations, looked like a fifty-gallon oil drum with outriggers to keep it from rolling over on pitching decks. It was covered with a rubbery substance that shed water, and had several specialized arms and appendages. It extended one of these to Curt. There were no lights visible; the seabot was getting its direction by infrared viewing. "Let me show you the way, sir."

Curt permitted this. Although the *McCain* was rolling only slightly in the long swells and although the seabot was under the control of an AI computer, he knew that somewhere in the ship a human was overseeing the activity and was ready to step in if something went wrong. Besides, Curt was used to solid land under his feet, so he was perfectly happy to let the seabot steady him on the short walk across the stubble-plated deck to the open hatch.

Carefully shaded deep red lights illuminated the companionway inside the hatch, but Curt used the handrail as he descended. At the bottom waited the officer of the deck, clad in navy whites. As the other two members of Carson's Companions joined him, following ancient custom, Curt saluted in the direction of the ensign on the fantail, then the OOD. He intoned, "Request permission to come aboard, sir!"

The OOD returned the salute. "Permission granted, Major," he replied, automatically bucking Curt up one rank because by tradition there's only one Captain aboard any naval ship. "Hornblower here will show you to the tactical aerodynes now being raised to the aft flight deck." The OOD indicated a specialized mobile below-decks seabot at his side, a skinny padded assemblage of three legs and four arms with a head like that of a praying mantis.

As the seabot led them aft, all Curt and his two sergeants saw were red-lit corridors, bulkheads, and companionways. At one time the comm system barked forth a message from one of the AI computers controlling the huge vessel: "Now hear this! Cargobots have completed transfer of cargo from the *Foulois* to the tactical aerodynes on the aft flight deck. All personnel lay below. Prepare to launch the *Foulois*. Stand by to launch tac aerodynes when they are manned and ready! Prepare to dive following tac aerodyne launch!"

A hundred years ago, similar procedures would have been used aboard the old surface aircraft carriers, but the threat of nuclear war at sea had caused those huge

80

floating airfields to be replaced by enormous carrier submarines. The carrier subs had become feasible only because of the continuous development of vertical-take-off aircraft, starting with the classic Sea Harrier jump jet and culminating in the new saucer-shaped aerodynes.

Curt never heard the *Foulois* depart. Only when the flight deck was clear were Curt and his two sergeants permitted to ascend to where the two tactical aerodynes, much smaller and more compact than the *Foulois*, waited them.

Curt and Kester boarded the larger one, code named Beauregard, while Gerard went aboard the smaller Pickett, a tactical strike ship that would provide escort cover. Both aerodynes were subsonic craft with the classical round saucer shapes of frisbees. Although Curt couldn't see in the darkness, he knew they were both painted in drab sand-and-shit desert camouflage hues.

Settling into the pilot's seat of Beauregard with Kester in the defense operator's position beside him, Curt removed his sidearm and kit, plugged his linkage harness into the craft, and slowly felt the huge aerodyne become part of him. Suddenly, he "saw" with Beauregard's radar, laser, and infrared sensors. He heard through Beauregard's pickups and pressure sensors. Beauregard was Curt Carson; and he *was* Beauregard. As Henry Kester plugged in, Curt felt the Master Sergeant's presence as well.

Although manual controls and visual instrumentation were available to Curt, he didn't have to touch them. They were fall-back provisions, to be used only if Beauregard's artificially intelligent computer was somehow disrupted or destroyed.

Curt ran Beauregard as if it were simply an extension of himself while the artificially intelligent computer that really was Beauregard controlled the details of running the ship.

Beauregard is ready for lift and departure. Curt didn't say it. He simply thought it. The electrodes of his harness picked up the signals from his nervous system and channeled his thought as a command to the aerodyne's computer.

Pickett is ready for lift and departure, came the signal from Gerard in the other aerodyne.

Beauregard, this is McCain *Flight Ops. Clear to launch. Come to an altitude of twenty meters and hover. Pickett, launch behind Beauregard and follow Beauregard at a distance of one hundred meters.*

Beauregard lifted without further input from Curt. Pickett was right behind them.

Come to precalculated heading for Kuh-e-Taftan, coordinates in data base, Curt telepathed to the Beauregard's computer. *Maintain ten meters maximum altitude. Press to maximum cruise. Enable stealth. Sensors to maximum range and resolution.*

The affirmative reply from Beauregard was voiceless.

The two aerodynes sped swiftly and silently through the air over the Gulf of Oman toward the still hidden Makran coast of Baluchistan.

Behind them, the carrier submarine *McCain* slipped silently beneath the waters of the Gulf of Oman.

I'll drive, Curt telepathed to Kester. *Henry, watch for trouble. You, too, Nick. Heads up here. We've got the Iranian air and naval base of Chah Bahkar off to the west and the Pakistanis at Pasni coast guard station on the east.*

It was like practicing mental telepathy with his two sergeants, though he couldn't read their thoughts any more than they could read his. The ability to keep command and communication thoughts separated from the usual flow-of-consciousness thoughts was second nature to all RI soldiers. It had been part of their training, and had been honed by experience in real and simulated battle, as had their human ability to make decisions on the basis of incomplete data and to come up with solutions to unanticipated problems. These abilities made human beings the master of the extended senses and muscles that were computerized war robots.

The term "warbot brainies" was entirely apropos. These humans were indeed the brains of the warbots.

I'm more worried about the frigging Iranians, Gerard admitted. *We're gonna be penetrating their airspace. They ain't gonna like it if they see us doin' it.*

Radar signal, Kester reported. *From the ground surveillance radar at Chah Bahkar. Signature says it's that French long-range radar the Iranians bought ten years ago. I'm surprised they've managed to keep it working this long. Must be manned by contract technicians . . . Not to worry, Captain. We can pick up their radar pulses, but we're too low for them to discriminate us out of sea-return clutter.*

Unless they've upgraded the electronics suite to include doppler, Curt replied.

Captain, might help to occasionally make like a porpoise, Gerard suggested.

Only if indications show that the Iranians are giving us additional attention, Curt decided.

Ship ahead, Kester reported. In Curt's mind, the visual image of an Arab dhow built up from the rapidly improving infrared data. *No detector pulses from it.*

Coasting trader, Curt remarked. *Bounce up to fifteen meters and go over him. He'll never know what went by. Kester, monitor any possible radio traffic from him.*

Those native ships don't carry anything as technical as radio, Kester remarked.

They don't need it, Curt added. *Those dhows have been sailing this coast line for thirty centuries.*

In the dark of the night, they would never have seen the coasting dhow except by infrared, not even when they went over it and then settled back to ten meters altitude.

The coast came up quickly, and they found themselves flying up the bay where the Dahst River emptied into the gulf.

Except for quasi-visual images from the radars, infrared pickups, and lasers of Beauregard and Pickett, there was no other indication that they'd made landfall. Curt *knew* there had to be roads and villages down there because Beauregard was integrating and overlaying satellite images with the electrooptical data coming from its own sensors. But there were no lights whatsoever. It was pitch black in the visual spectrum. The only indications of possible human habitation were tiny infrared signals from what were probably nomadic campfires. It was very much like coming out of Phoenix en route to Payson on a clear night. Suddenly, the lights of the metroplex ceased and the view ahead was like looking

84

into a black hole. There was one striking difference here, however. Over Arizona, there were always some small points of light from ranches, tiny towns, and highways; over Baluchistan, there was absolutely nothing.

Any probing? Any radar? Anything? Curt asked.

Not a thing, Kester replied. *And nothing out there airborne looking for us, either.*

If the Iranians had a hand in the hijacking, they should have their air defenses up for an incoming rescue mission, Nick Gerard remarked.

The Iranians may not have had anything to do with the hijacking, Curt reminded him. *We'd probably have heard something about it. We've heard nothing, which means there's been no change in the situation except perhaps another videotape. These Jehorkhims are a black-sheep splinter group, remember?*

Hope you're right, Gerard responded.

As the two aerodynes continued to speed northward at treetop level, a few lone palm trees appeared from time to time, near riverbeds and oases, in an otherwise treeless terrain. It would have been utterly impossible to make this flight without the passive use of infrared radiations from the ground and the reflected laser light received by Beauregard after it had been beamed down from satellites and had illuminated the landscape. Except for the two-way exchange of data by tight-beam lasercom between the two aerodynes and the multichannel data link upward with the satellites and thence with Georgie, there was very little electromagnetic radiation being emitted by the two craft. And, had anyone laid a radar signal on them, little of that radiation would have been reflected back for detection purposes because of the radar absorption features and stealth shapes of the two ships.

An increasing number of volcanic cones began to appear as the two ships continued northward into the Asian continent, and evidences of recent vulcanism became more numerous after they crossed the Mashkel River valley.

Finally, at 0330 local time, right on schedule, the unmistakable conical mass of the extinct volcano, Kuh-e-Taftan, began to loom ahead of them, its four thousand-meter summit rearing into the clear night sky.

Curt took Beauregard around the summit, settled down about a hundred meters on the north slope, and began to sweep the locality for a good site.

Can't "see" Zahedan, Kester remarked. *Either it has no I-R signature—which it should—or there's a ridge between our location and the town.*

Nick, ease up vertically ten meters at a time until you can pick up Zahedan's I-R signature, Curt ordered.

After a moment, Gerard telepathed back, *The summit behind us is a false summit. We're on the south wall of the old crater. If you scan to the northeast, you can see that the crater has eroded there. Essentially, we've got a ridge between us and Zahedan.*

Okay, let's move onto that ridge, Curt replied, *and then see if we can't find a less rocky location.*

The north ridge of the ancient crater gave them a direct view of Zahedan about fifty kilometers farther north. Curt surveyed several possible sites while Gerard stayed on guard, higher and behind them. Finally, Curt settled Beauregard to the ground on a gentle slope surrounded by stunted tamarisk and acacia trees.

The wind was blowing steadily from the north, strongly enough to make its presence felt but not strongly enough to blow dust. This seemed strange to Curt. The wind shouldn't be blowing that hard, even at this altitude, in the early predawn hours. But there it was, sharp and gusty.

A long and careful scan of the immediate surroundings with all available sensors convinced Curt that no human presence existed within a kilometer.

Activate camouflage. Switch to chameleon mode, Curt ordered. *Nick, land Pickett. Check minus-x. As soon as dawn light will permit, put up your birdbots and eye-peel our surroundings.*

The three men spent the next two hours getting ready for their reconnaissance of Zahedan, which loomed dully on the northern horizon in their infrared scanners. The capacity of the power packs would allow each birdbot to take only one ratbot into Zahedan, before returning for recharging at the command post in Beauregard. Curt decided to run the ratbots. He put Kester in charge of birdbot transport, and left Gerard in control of additional birdbots to be used for defense scanning and recon over Zahedan.

Once we get the ratbots down in Zahedan, Curt explained, going over the tactical plan, *and the birdbot transports back at Beauregard, I want Kester to join me for ground recon in the town. Nick, continue to handle air recon with all your defense bots set on auto and in report mode.*

What are we looking for? Kester wanted to know.

Defenses first, hostage location second. High-resolution near-view aerial recon will come from Nick's bird-

bots; our ratbots will give the close ground view, Curt explained.

Roger, Captain, Master Sergeant Kester replied. *Getting light in the east.*

Ready here, came Nick Gerard's electronic thought. *Bust our buns, then wait for the sun to come up. Hurry up and wait.*

As the eastern sky continued to lighten, Curt didn't relax. He put out deep sensor probes, trying to gain a better feel for the countryside. Infrared didn't tell him very much except that Zahedan was hotter than the hills in which it nestled. There was no question about the location of the railway terminus; he spotted the heat signatures from two Henschel Diesel-electric locomotive units. There was little else to discriminate in Zahedan's heat signature except the chimneys and fires that slowly grew more active as daylight brightened and people began to stir, to build up their fires for morning cooking, and for warmth. Even in this harsh semidesert climate, the predawn temperature was only a few degrees above zero Celsius.

And when the sun did come up, it did so very suddenly, the first spark of light winking into existence as the rim of the rising sun blinked brightly on a brilliantly clear horizon broken by the rugged outline of the Chagai Hills. The summit of Kuh-e-Taftan was then bathed in crimson light which washed over the two grounded, stealthed, and camouflaged aerodynes. To the north and east, the valleys were still in darkness and a strange, dusty haze.

Animal life began to stir around them. Birds twittered and fluttered from scrubby tree to scrubby tree.

Ground creatures came out of burrows. An Asian fox quickly surveyed Beauregard, decided the aerodyne was harmless and not good to eat, then disappeared.

Curt's view of Zahedan was suddenly cut off by a moving warm body that came between Beauregard's sensors and the town.

Nick. What's out there? Can you see it from your position? Curt's thoughts snapped through the circuitry.

Alert, Beauregard's flat, unemotional computer voice cut in before Gerard could answer. *Living organism, temperature thirty-seven degrees Celsius, range thirty meters, moving in this direction, random course, quarter of a meter per second rate of closure. Now two of them. Now three.*

CHAPTER FIVE

Dammit! Curt thought savagely. He was so surprised that he neglected to mask his fierce thought from the linkage circuit. *I was right. The goddamned Jehorkhims were waiting to bushwack us. Stupid, Carson. Real stupid.*

But by the time Curt's thought burst into Beauregard's circuitry, Kester had reassumed control over the defenses. *Witholding defensive actions until I get an ident on the targets.* There was a momentary pause. *Captain, I think you oughta have a look.*

Curt switched to Beauregard's visual sensors, saw what Henry Kester was seeing, then started to laugh at the same instant Sergeant Nick Gerard reported, *Captain, it's five goats.*

Orgasmic. Hell, we should have remembered that the people around here are nomadic herdsmen. Curt's relief was evident. *Any more goats around? They got a herdsman with them?*

Putting up a birdbot, Gerard broke in. Curt's computer vision showed a huge falcon taking wing from Pickett. It flapped its wings and thrashed into the dawn skies. *Just launched. I'll search the area. Probably won't find a herdsman, though.*

You an old expert on goat herding? Kester asked.

No, but we're close to timberline—in spite of the fact that there ain't much timber hereabouts, the platoon sergeant replied. *In case you haven't noticed, the outside temperature's just above zero Celsius. And this isn't really good grazing land, even for goats. I'll bet ten bucks these are either wild goats or strays.*

Ten bucks says you don't find a herdsman, eh? Kester came back. *Okay, you're on, Nick.*

Curt said nothing. He was engrossed in his own inputs. *Hold the launch of the Zahedan recon mission until we have a complete status report of our immediate surroundings,* Curt told Kester and Gerard. *No sense in getting all the reconbots on their way and then having to switch attention to defending ourselves.*

Gerard reported, *Nothing around here but five goats and a lot of rocks. That damned wind is nasty—right out of the north at about ten meters per second. Tough to control the birdbot.*

Spot any people around? Curt wanted a double-check on this.

Negative, Nick Gerard answered. *I just won ten bucks.*

See me next pay day, Nick. If I wasn't monitoring your birdbot eyes, I'd think you hadn't looked hard enough . . . but I got no problems with your recon.

Captain, now that I'm up here and looking around, I see an abandoned airfield about twenty kilometers east-northeast of us. That ain't Zahedan, is it?

Curt recalled the map of the area. *That's Mirjaveh*

on the Pakistan border. Nick, as we withdraw from the
recon mission in Zahedan, send a birdbot over Mirjaveh
and see if it's in any condition to be used as a staging
base for an airborne assault.

Roger, will do.

Okay, everybody ready to go snooping around Za-
hedan?

Roger.

Ready.

Launch recon mission.

Ten birdbots looking for all the world like gyrfalcons
departed Beauregard. Five of them, those in Nick Gerard's defensive detail, circled high in covering mode
with airborne sensors at the ready. Five others gripped
in their huge plastic talons smaller robots that appeared
to be big gray rats. Neither the birdbots or the ratbots
were as versatile as their living counterparts, but for
a clandestine recon mission, they were perfect. They
were realistic enough, if anyone saw them, to be mis-
taken for the real thing. It would take a hands-on inspection to discover they were machines. And Curt
didn't anticipate letting anyone get that close to them.
If the bots malfunctioned or were damaged, their operator could destroy them. If the data channel went
down without being commanded to do so, the bots
would self-destruct.

Recon bots weren't cheap, especially these. The ratbots were preproduction models fresh out of development. Curt figured that Hettrick had had to call in
some very expensive favors to get them from McCarthy
Proving Ground.

The major problem with a reconbot was its energy

supply, and Curt suspected this might cause some problems on the mission. Unlike a living organism, a reconbot had limited energy stored in its power pack. The RI had put continual pressure on the Ordnance Corps to perfect longer duration power packs, especially for birdbots which were ornithopters whose ancestry could be traced to the successful radio-controlled pterodactyl built by the Smithsonian Institution in the last century. Flying by wing-beating required a very high rate of energy expenditure, and when a birdbot carried a ten-kilogram ratbot as it was doing on this mission, it used wattage at a enormous rate. Kester's birdbots would barely be able to make the trip to Zahedan and return for the necessary power pack recharge. However, the master sergeant had a second wave of recon birdbots ready to go once he'd delivered the ratbots to Zahedan and could turn over to Beauregard the control of the returning birdbots.

The capacities of all three men were stretched to their limits in controlling about five robots each. On the flight into Zahedan, Curt used the optical and infrared sensors in the lead birdbot. These were focused for distance and could discriminate edge effects better. He didn't try to make mental-verbal notes of what he "saw." There wasn't time, and the input was being recorded anyway. He kept the channels clear of chatter so that good, solid, high bit-rate data could flow back to Beauregard.

Except for the railway yard and the terminus buildings, Zahedan looked as if it hadn't changed in five thousand years. The march of civilization had overlooked this incredibly remote and poor backwater through which Taleb River ran in a trickle. Although the data base said that the rainfall was greater than fifteen centimeters per year, taking the region out of the pure desert category, Curt decided that he would rate as "desertlike" the arid, almost grassless steppe and the barren Siahan Range that swung southward in a great loop.

The layout of Zahedan—Curt couldn't conceive of the place as anything but a town although the latest census data showed it had a population of about twenty thousand people—was typical of the Arab towns that sprinkled the land from Morocco to the Indus Valley. A large, ornate mosque was dominant. The few two-story stuccoed buildings were apparently the political headquarters of the regional government. As the town began to stir in the early morning light, most of the traffic was composed of people, camels, and donkeys. Only a few ground vehicles managed to squeeze their way through the extremely narrow streets that wound through the town in no apparent pattern, turning sharply and in places, permitting only a single person to pass. Curt decided it was going to be pure hell to get warbots through those streets.

Set one of my ratbots down by the mosque, he ordered Kester. *I want another one on the ground near the marketplace or bazaar. And a third one in the vicinity of those government buildings. I'm going to put the other ratbots in hiding as reserve.*

He instructed Beauregard to take over automatic control of the grounded ratbots, to keep them moving in sheltered and protected places. He wasn't able to give full attention to all three, so he switched quickly from one to another, catching snatches of incoming data, trying to evaluate the overall picture, and hoping to garner some piece of information that might lead to locating the hostages.

But he didn't understand the patois, a mixture of Arabic and Baluchi, the ratbots were hearing. It took Georgie back in Diamond Point several seconds to integrate the phoneme sounds with the data bank Arabic language information and to translate. Since Georgie couldn't translate the obscure Baluchi language, the computer tried to use its nearest relative, Farsi. The results weren't totally acceptable at first. Curt was able to get only a few words, and the sentence structure was badly distorted. Furthermore, almost two seconds of satellite transmission-path delay took place between Curt's receipt of the sound of a native speaking and the translation that came back from Georgie.

The conversation on the streets seemed to be only local small talk.

The mosque could hold several thousand devout Muslims, but was now empty. If the Jehorkhims were as devoutly fanatic as the data indicated, most of them would be in the mosque five times every day. Curt put a ratbot in automatic guard in the mosque, instructing it to call him if anyone showed up matching the database image of Imam Abdul Madjid Rahman.

Kester was flying recon sweeps over the town, getting data from about fifty meters up.

Gerard's covering birdbots—gyrfalcons—swung slowly in wheeling circles, riding the growing thermal air currents that burbled over the town. Their sensors searched for radar or lidar signals that might indicate defensive military systems.

Nothing.

Nothing to indicate that Zahedan was anything more than the sleepy backwater it had been for millennia.

Nothing to indicate that the town was the headquarters of a fanatical Islamic cult.

Nothing ... until his street ratbot signaled something new and different.

Curt switched inputs. The ratbot in the marketplace zeroed its video and audio pickups on a group of armed men wearing brilliant white burnooses, khaki shirts and trousers, and long white capes. They were armed with short scimitars and compound bows about a meter long. If they carried firearms, these weren't in evidence.

The three armed men appeared to be shaking down a date merchant for a little cumshaw protection. The word "Jehorkhim" turned up in the conversation.

Instructing the ratbot to stay with the three Jehorkhim soldiers, which is what Curt concluded they were, he withdrew his mind from the ratbot circuits to learn how well the mission was proceeding.

Wall to wall data, was Kester's cryptic remark.

Don't try to evaluate it, Curt warned.

No time for that. Kester was almost totally engrossed in monitoring his birdbots, so Curt left him alone to do his job.

An aircraft's landing at Zahedan aerodrome, Gerard reported. *An old Soviet Antonov transport plane. No markings except registration. Let me zoom in on that. Okay, its registry is Iranian: Echo Papa dash Hotel*

Alpha Delta Tango. Georgie can learn its ownership from that registration data. Hold it! Only four people getting out. Three are obviously flight crew. One's a passenger. He's getting something out of the baggage hold. Looks like ... it is. It's a carton of videotape casettes.

Track him, Curt ordered.

Kester joined in the tracking with one of his recon birdbots. The thought-vocal chatter on the link continued as Gerard gave a running narration, *The Orient Express hypersonic transport looks okay. Can't say more than that from scanning it at this distance. But that Antonov transport's seen better days. Got a lot of leaking seals and such. Look at the seeps around the prop spinners and down the landing-gear oleo legs. I'll bet it's an old IranAir ship surplused out with more than fifty thousand hours on the airframe ...*

Georgie's machine voice cut in at this point, *ICAO data show that the aircraft is registered in Iran to a charter carrier, ShirazAir. No direct connection established with the Jehorkhim sect at this time.*

Probably just a chartered plane used to carry those videotapes in and out, and bring in equipment and spares. Georgie, see if you can't get some data on its flight plan. Where did it come from? Curt queried the megacomputer through the long satellite radio link.

Checking.

Gerard zeroed in on an extremely beat-up Toyota Land Rover into which the courier had climbed, holding his carton of videocasettes. *I'll follow him into town.*

Nick, as long as you're in the vicinity of the aerofield, check for air defense installations, Curt suggested.

I did. Zip. Zilch. Nothing that looks like a SAM or an antiaircraft gun.

How about shoulder-launched missiles?

Couldn't see 'em, but I doubt the Jehorkhims have 'em. Captain, remember that the Jehorkhims don't like to use anything that extends the muscle power of a man.

That explained why the three Jehorkhim soldiers in the marketplace carried no firearms, only classical scimitars and bows.

If that was really the case, the rescue mission was going to be a piece of cake, Curt figured.

No data on the flight plan, Georgie reported, *but domestic flight plans aren't filed with ICAO, only the international ones.*

Shit. Well, they had to get those videotapes from somewhere outside of Iran and ship them in. Any way to check incoming cargo manifests? Export documents? Customs declarations?

Blank videocassettes are made almost everywhere and shipped by the billions. Iran has no customs reporting requirements for blank videocassettes, only prerecorded ones.

Struck out again. Georgie, try to find out what you can.

Curt's thought dialogue with the megacomputer was cut short by a signal from Henry Kester. *Captain, I've got wall-to-wall aerial data on the central part of the town. Can I get the hell out of here before some Jehorkhim archer decides to have me for lunch?*

Okay, sweep the outskirts with emphasis on finding military installations, particularly defenses.

Probably a military and customs checkpoint on the railway back at Mirjaveh where the line crosses the border from Pakistan, but I haven't seen anything around the town.

Nick's checking the aerodrome. How's it coming, Nick?

Not even air traffic surveillance radar. And no control tower, either.

They don't need either with the air traffic density here. Maybe one or two planes a day at best. Okay, Henry, make sure the railway terminal and the incoming roads are checked. If they've got any defenses, they're probably deployed at transportation nodes.

Wait until you get a close look at the so-called "roads," the master sergeant reported. *Alexander the Great might get an army of foot soldiers over them, but I wouldn't count on an all-terrain vehicle making it very far without bending an axle.*

The ratbot in the mosque demanded Curt's attention. He switched to monitoring its sensors.

Imam Abdul Madjid Rahman had been somewhere in the mosque and was now leaving with about twenty of his followers.

I'm going to follow the Imam, Curt informed his two sergeants. *He might go to his headquarters or even to where the hostages are held. Cover me aloft, Kester.*

Curt took control of the ratbot and began to slip along walls and gutters behind the group. Kester flew a birdbot overhead to monitor their movements from the air. That turned out to be a good decision because Curt's ratbot lost the Jehorkhims in the winding streets.

99

Notified that the Imam and his party had entered one of the two large white buildings in town, Curt located the ratbot that was monitoring that area and managed to slip it into the building through the large open double doors that led into a foyer with staircases going up and down. The two Jehorkhim guards on the door were far too interested in looking sharp for the Imam and they missed the entry of the ratbot.

Beyond the stairways the ratbot entered a narrow hallway lit by the light of a single electric bulb hanging from the ceiling. The Imam and his party were nowhere to be found.

Henry, they've got electricity, Curt told his top sergeant. *Find out where it comes from.*

No power lines coming into Zahedan. Kester's thought came back. *I've spotted a single telephone land line following the road north to Mashhad and another following the railway east to Quetta in Pakistan. But no power lines. They're using gasoline-powered generators. One's at the aerodrome to run the radios and lights. The other is outside the government building you're in at the moment, Captain. Both units appear to be connected to large gasoline storage tanks.*

Good, Curt thought. That meant they had to transport the gasoline in either by rail from Pakistan, by truck from Iran, or by air. Such logistical support could be interdicted if necessary, cutting off what little electric power existed in Zahedan. It would also be easy to take out their communications, what there was of them. Curt decided they'd better put taps on the telephone lines and have the signals beamed up to satellites.

At the moment, he didn't dare switch for a quick look at the generator outside the building. He was engrossed in staying with his ratbot. He increased the sensitivity of the auditory pickups, hoping to locate people by their voices.

It worked. He picked up the sounds of a strong argument. It was apparently going on in English.

He took a sound level measurement, moved the ratbot a few meters, and took another one. Moving another two meters, he took a third reading and told Beauregard to locate. The command center computer came back with, *Two locations, one more probable than the other, but both very broad because the signal difference between the three locations isn't very great. Go down the hall. The voices are coming from what is likely to be the left side of the corridor in a room. Be on the lookout for the possibility there is a room with a closed door on the right side.*

There was no door on the left, but Curt found the closed door on the right side of the corridor. Unlike many doors he'd seen and passed in Zahedan, this one fit tightly into its jam. He couldn't get into the room by going under the door, but voices were coming from behind it. He turned up the ratbot's audio sensors.

"Abdul, you've *got* to change your approach. The plan isn't working! I told you it wouldn't!" It was a female voice with just a touch of accent.

"You're too impatient, Doctor." The voice of the Imam Rahman. "One of two things is going to happen. Either the American and Japanese governments will accede to the public clamor to stop the torture and killing of the hostages, and will pay us what we ask, or they'll

101

send in military forces. Since I believe the latter is likely, I'm preparing to deal with it. My soldiers will capture the robot soldiers, and they will be held for ransom while you use them for your work. They should be very useful to you, Doctor."

"And how do you think you can capture them? By sending Jehorkhim armed with swords and bows up against soldiers and warbots using the latest weaponry? Your troops will be slaughtered!"

"Dr. Taisha, you don't know about the Mongols under Genghis Khan. They never invaded your country because they didn't get that far. But they came into Iran, and we've never forgotten how they fought."

"That was seven hundred years ago! What has the Mongol horde got to do with the *jihad*?"

"We intend to fight as the Mongols did: with great speed and mobility. We shall simply overwhelm the enemy, one soldier and one warbot at a time."

"You'll be beaten."

"How can you be so certain?"

"Because I haven't perfected my techniques yet. You don't have the necessary control over your soldiers." The female voice, a liquid contralto, paused for a moment, then went on in an exasperated tone. "I can give it to you. That's why you took me into your movement, even though I'm a woman and not a Muslim."

"You forget that I did so *in spite* of the fact that you're a woman and because you were a scientist working in an area that doesn't conflict with the Koran."

"Yes, I know. It was an arrangement of convenience," the female voice replied. "My work is progressing well. I will soon be able to control human beings with computers. I will make them perform superhuman feats of speed and strength and endurance. They'll perform exactly as I wish right up to the limits of their physical abilities.''

"Yes, and you've killed a few of my Jehorkhim troops trying to do that," the Imam replied.

"But I've shown you what's possible. I've already indoctrinated your troops so they'll follow your orders without question. Still, that's not enough. If you won't use modern robotic weapons because you believe controlling machines to extend people's natural abilities is wrong, your soldiers will have to be supermen to outfight high-tech soldiers and robots. And I'm not to that point in my work where I can guarantee to produce such supermen for you. Without them, you can't win. You acted prematurely in hijacking that airliner.''

"It was necessary to get the money I need for military supplies and *you* need for new equipment. You agreed to the plan. You backed me," the Imam reminded her.

"Because I needed the equipment and because I hoped to use some of the hostages as experimental subjects," the woman called Dr. Taisha snapped back. "I can't rely solely on experimental results derived from your Jehorkhim soldiers or the rebellious peasants they capture for me.''

"What's wrong with using nonbelievers and rebels? I don't mind if you kill them. It saves my Jehorkhims the trouble of beheading them.''

"I need to experiment on sophisticated and intelligent people with complex minds educated in advanced high-tech cultures. I'm not getting my part of the bargain, Imam. You're killing off the valuable hostages one by one."

"I know of no other way to get the results we want quickly," the Imam told her flatly.

"What you're doing won't work in the long run. It might have if the American and Japanese governments had immediately offered to ransom the hostages. But they haven't. They want to talk. They know what they're doing. Psychology is my field of expertise, and a psychological principle called 'overload' is now operative. People are growing tired of being revulsed by the daily videotapes of torture and killing."

"What would you want me to do, Doctor?"

"I don't know what you *can* do other than stand by to fight off the whole American army when they get here. I can try to accelerate my experiments. Perhaps I can achieve a breakthrough that will give you *some* supermen. But I'll need unlimited use of the hostages."

"Very well, Dr. Taisha, I'll give you hostages. Where do you want them brought?"

"To the laboratory you allowed me to set up. And please take measures to ensure that the electric power is not interrupted while I'm working."

"But the hostages must be returned to the dungeon when they're not being used in your laboratory. I'll give the orders at once, Doctor."

Curt heard a chair scrape the floor. Someone had stood up. Apparently the meeting was over.

Curt quickly moved the ratbot down the hallway while keeping its visual sensors focused on the closed door.

The Imam came out. He was followed by a short young woman whose figure was partially hidden by white slacks and a lab coat. A dark shawl was drawn over her head and lower face in compliance with orthodox Muslim custom. Curt couldn't see her entire face, but he was immediately impressed by her fair skin and her large, dark, almond-shaped eyes. She was either Oriental or Eurasian.

Curt followed the pair at a distance. In the foyer of the building, they descended the stairway to the basement. At the bottom of the stairs, the Imam opened a heavy, locked door and they moved out of sight as it closed behind them, but not before Curt heard a scream and caught the Imam's testy remark, "They've started without me again!"

Henry, we're pulling out, Curt snapped. *We've found the hostages.*

Shouldn't we stick around to see what that doctor is up to?

That's not necessary. Our mission is to get the hostages out of here fast. We know where the Jehorkhims are holding them. We have information on Zahedan's defenses. We're bugging out now. Curt's telethought snapped back. *Where can we store these ratbots in deactivated condition so they won't be found and we can reactivate them if we need them during the strike?*

Looks like there're some warehouses down by the rail terminus, Master Sergeant Kester reported. *Probably plenty of real rats down there.*

Beauregard, start moving the ratbots to the location Kester points out to you. Nick, cover Henry's birdbots as they return to the aerodynes. I'm withdrawing from

105

*the ratbots now. Henry, let me join one of your birds.
I want to double-check this whole area again from the
air.*

*Take your choice, Captain. I've got four birdbots
aloft.*

Curt's thought suggestion caused Beauregard to
switch the company commander's sensory inputs to one
of the recon birdbots returning from Zahedan.

After the Imam's reference to Genghis Khan and the
Mongol horde, Curt knew what the Imam's tactics would
probably be: Occupy no defensive positions but move
rapidly, opportunistically, and, using the element of surprise, hack away at individual warbot units, using speed
and shock. Those tactics were well understood in this
part of the world, and they were the only ones that
could possibly by used by a military force whose leaders
didn't believe in advanced sensors or warbots.

Curt felt confident the Imam's planning was flawed.
He knew military history far better than the Imam, and
he thought he could beat these ancient tactics.

He was rudely jolted by a signal from Beauregard.
*Alert. Alert. Two human beings are now within one kil-
ometer of the command post on a path that will bring
them to within fifty meters of our location.*

Withdrawing quickly from the birdbot, Curt extended himself in Beauregard instead, feeling for the
sensor inputs.

He didn't see them on visual first. He picked them
up through the chemical sensors, Beauregard's sense
of "smell." The two humans were obviously upwind
because the sensors detected the unmistakable sig-

nature of chemical molecules exuded from unwashed bodies.

A man and a boy, apparently a herdsman and his son, were clambering up the volcanic slopes.

CHAPTER SIX

Contingency Bravo. Stand by to bug out. Curt activated the fall-back plan. He wanted to keep the recon mission in covert status, but the two humans were close enough to see the departure of the two saucer-shaped aerodynes. So Curt had to figure out how to cut his losses. *Kester, Gerard, can we get the birdbots back before they get here?*

No, sir, Kester telereported without hesitation. *The intruders will be close enough to see us in about four minutes. It'll take us ten minutes to recover all the birdbots. Want us to unlink and let 'em crash?*

No, the Jehorkhims might find the remains. And we won't know whether they did or not. Curt didn't mind dumping ten complex and expensive birdbots in the Baluchistan desert—that was part of the cost of doing business—but he was concerned about Kester and Gerard unlinking from their birdbots too quickly. They'd been in linkage with those bots for several hours now. The mental jolt might be too much without the services of linkage biotechs. He couldn't carry out the whole mission alone.

We can kill 'em when they see us, Sergeant Nick Gerard suggested.

You're sounding like one of Kelly's people. The Companions don't deliberately waste innocent bystanders.

Captain, Master Sergeant Henry Kester broke in *the only thing we can do is stun them and take them with us.*

I don't like that either. They might be missed by someone.

Hey, Captain, this is a rough territory. Losing shepherds to lions and such could be an everyday thing. The Bible's full of stuff like that, Gerard pointed out.

Yeah, but that was more than two thousand years ago, Nick, Kester reminded him. *Damned lion would starve to death today.*

No time to argue, Curt snapped. He had only one viable alternative. He didn't want to kill the two innocent intruders, but he didn't want to risk the two herdsmen reporting to the Jehorkhims.

Looks like about three minutes, Kester warned. *I'm comin' as fast as I can, but I can't get there in time.*

Beauregard, query Georgie about the possible value of these two as data sources, Curt instructed his computer.

Beauregard came right back, *Unable to evaluate their usefulness under the present conditions. They might be helpful because they're familiar with the territory. But they may not cooperate.*

Curt was partial to waiting until the last possible moment before acting. *Okay, let's keep a cool stool. Watch them. They might not see us.*

No, they'll see us in about two minutes, Kester reported.

Although human emotions rarely came through a linkage net, it was pretty obvious that Curt was venting a huge sigh of resignation. *Okay, stand by with the stunner,* he ordered. *What's the estimated arrival time of the birdbots now?*

Seven minutes.

Nick, can you handle all ten of the birdbots?

Yeah, if they're on automatic. I'll put 'em in a wheeling holding pattern and bring them in one at a time.

Henry, give Nick your birdbots. I need you to run Beauregard's weaponry.

The herdsman and his son appeared to be looking for lost goats; they were searching the rocks and bushes quite carefully. There was no chance that they'd miss the aerodynes sitting among the volcanic crags.

The boy saw them first. His eyes opened wide in surprise and terror. Turning to the older man, he called out in Baluchi. The older man scrabbled over, looked, pulled at the boy's kaftan, and started to run back down the slope.

Curt gave the order, *Stun 'em.*

Beauregard's port turret hatch opened, the gun stuck its muzzle out, the two stunner fletchettes full of tranquilizer were fired at reduced charge toward the herdsman and the boy, each hitting its target.

Got 'em. Now, how do we bring them aboard, Captain? Kester asked.

I'm not so sure I want to bring them aboard. Beauregard, give me a sit-guess. If we don't take them with us when we leave, what are the chances they'll report us to the Imam in Zahedan? And if we take them, what are the chances they'll be missed by someone?"

Insufficient data, Beauregard fired back at once.

Give me your best evaluation of the situation based on the available data, Curt ordered the reluctant computer.

This evaluation contains conclusions with an extremely low confidence level, Beauregard prefaced the report. *There is a high probability they will go back to Zahedan after regaining consciousness, if for no other reason than to regale their friends with an amazing story about jinn and flying carpets. In a region such as this, where very little happens and every day is much like the last, anything that creates some excitement is a welcome diversion. It might take the rest of the day for them to get to Zahedan. Thus, the Imam might know by tomorrow at the latest that Zahedan has been reconnoitered. Operation Squire cannot be mounted for another thirty-six hours. If you take them with you, no one will know what happened to them, and their absence will probably not be reported. Even if it were, there will be no indication of what happened to them. Lack of information could lead to speculation and guesswork on the enemy's part, which is preferable to giving him solid data. Therefore, the recommendation is that you take them with you.*

It was the usual rather flat, unemotional, and thorough evaluation that one would expect from an AI battle computer.

Okay, let's bring them in, Curt snapped. In most combat situations, things did not go as planned. That was why humans commanded robots.

Captain, Master Sergeant Henry Kester observed, *we have no transport bots capable of doing that. One of us will have to go out and bring them in.*

I'll go, Curt decided. *I can get out of linkage far more easily than you can. And maybe I won't have to relink if you and Nick can run things.*

Yeah, we can do it, Captain, Kester advised him. *But take it easy, sir, You've been in linkage as long as we have. It'll be real easy to drop into idiot mode.*

I'll take it as slow as I can, Curt reassured his master sergeant. *How much time do I have before that stun wears off?*

One hour, plus or minus twenty minutes.

Shit. Thirty minutes maximum unlink time! Henry, I'm not going to be able to get back into linkage at all again under these circumstances. Not without biotechs to help. You and Nick will have to get us out of here.

Roger, Captain. No problem.

Curt went through the routine of unlinking as rapidly as he dared, being careful to bring himself back to reality slowly, gently savoring the restoration of each new stimulus from the real world around him. He wished Helen Devlin were present. She was a sexy little sergeant, and her ministrations were often a little more than the field manuals called for.

There were a lot of sexy women in the RI, Curt thought. Somehow, women willing to fight alongside men had an allure that Curt couldn't put his finger on. But he liked it. And he liked the women in the RI.

Thinking about sex helped Curt come out of linkage. Computers could accurately simulate nearly every human activity, but there was no sexual attraction be-

112

tween human and machine. No computer had yet been able to accurately simulate human sexuality without using recorded sensory data, and recorded tapes just didn't have the realism, resolution, or detailed accuracy of the real thing.

If there was one unique characteristic humans possessed, Curt thought, it was the infinite variety of ways they achieved satisfaction of the sexual drive. Computers never could know the joy of that.

Within thirty minutes, Curt found himself totally unlinked. He had the usual mild headache, the *lamchevak* or hangover from intense linkage. He rummaged through his medical kit, found the tube of capsules, and popped a pill into his mouth. It would lower his blood pressure and reduce the size of the blood vessels in his brain, thus cutting back on the enormous blood flow that accompanied the intense mental and neural activity of linkage.

He saw Henry Kester, relaxed in the copilot's seat, his eyes closed and his breathing deep and regular. "Beauregard," he vocalized to the ship, "switch command to Sergeant Kester when he asks for it, but maintain verbal contact with me."

"Roger, Captain. He's already got it."

"All birdbots recovered?"

"All birdbots recovered. The mission is now awaiting your recovery of the two stunned humans."

"Henry, can you hear me?"

"Roger. This is Sergeant Kester speaking through Beauregard."

"What's the situation around the aerodynes? Any other human presence detected?"

"No human presence other than the two stunned individuals."

Curt unplugged his linkage harness. It had started to itch, but he wouldn't be wearing it any longer, he thought, and that was a blessing. The sun was already in the western sky and heading for the horizon. In a few more hours, sunset would occur and they could withdraw to the Gulf of Oman.

The lower hatch swung down to make a ramp. Holding his CG-17 carbine at the ready, Curt cautiously walked down it to the ground.

A warbots sense of smell isn't as good as a human's, so the first thing Curt noticed was the awful stench of the slopes of Kuh-e-Taftan.

He knew that every place in the world had its own distinctive odor—the sulfurous coal-smoke stink of eastern European cities, the eye-blistering photochemical smog of American sunbelt cities, the moldering mushroom musk of the deciduous forests of Europe and eastern North America, the piny aroma of high mountains, and the piñion smell of foothills.

But the smell of Baluchistan was different. He didn't like it. The odor seemed to be a combination of burning wood, rotting dung, decomposing organic material, and unwashed bodies, all simmering in the hot afternoon sunshine. He was glad his bots hadn't transmitted it to him. He wanted to make the pickup and get back into the ship as quickly as possible.

Part of the smell came from the two stunned people lying on the rocky ground. Curt slung his carbine over his shoulder and rolled the herdsman over.

The man wasn't very big. In fact, he was wiry, thin,

and looked almost starved. His scraggly, unkempt beard partially hid his decaying, discolored teeth, and his hands were covered with a layer of hardened dust. Whitish salt from evaporated sweat caked his body. It had probably been months since he had had a bath.

Curt decided to recover the herdsman first because he was the heavier and therefore the most difficult to carry. But the man was light. He couldn't have weighed fifty kilograms. Curt got the herdsman over his shoulders in a fireman's carry, vowing that the first thing the man would be told to do was take a bath, and if he wouldn't, Curt would dunk him in the first available water. After carrying the herdsman up the ramp into the ship, Curt deposited him in an empty equipment compartment and locked the door as a precaution.

The youngster didn't smell any better, but he was too young to have grown a beard and his teeth were still reasonably good. In fact, the boy was darkly handsome, and couldn't have been more than twelve years old.

As Curt rolled him over to pick him up, the youngster suddenly came awake. Or perhaps he'd been awake, yet too scared to do anything more than play dead. The boy rolled over and thrashed out with his arms, catching Curt unawares. Quickly he scrambled to his feet, intending to run, but he was thwarted by the folds of his short wool kaftan.

"Oh, no, you don't, you stinking little bastard!" Curt yelled. He reached out and grabbed the boy by his arm.

"Ow! Goddammit!" Curt's yelp of pain came when the boy's teeth sank into the body armor covering his right forearm, not breaking the skin or drawing blood.

That was too much. Curt didn't like to fight with children, but he belted the boy sharply across the side of the head. "Cool it, or I'll cold-cock you!" he shouted.

The boy lunged for the carbine. Curt chopped him over the carotid, and he went limp. After checking to make sure the little hellion was really unconscious, Curt slung him across his shoulder and carried him back to the ship.

There wasn't an empty compartment in which the boy could be stashed during the flight out, and there wasn't room for him in the compartment where the older man was locked. So Curt took the boy to the control deck and strapped him tightly into the unused observer's seat. As a final precaution, he lashed the boy's arms to the seat with two hold-down straps.

It was the best he could do under the circumstances. "Monitor the youngster," he instructed Beauregard. "Let me know immediately if he gets loose. He's as quick and slippery as a fish . . . and he smells far worse."

"Roger, Captain," Beauregard replied. "What are your plans and desires?"

"Maintain stealth and camouflage until sundown. At end of twilight, we lift off for the Gulf of Oman and rendezvous with the *McCain.* Can you understand and translate the Baluchi language for me?"

"I don't have that capability, but Georgie does as a result of the scouting mission. He's had ample time to analyze the verbal data."

"Network with him and stand by to translate between the boy and me when he wakes up. Maybe I can convince the kid I'm not going to kill him."

116

"Are you going to relink with me?"

"Negative! I'm tired and I hurt. And I want to be able to grab this little sonofabitch if he gets wild."

"Why don't you semilink?" Beauregard suggested. "It will make the Baluchi translation easier and I'll be able to perform a little medical therapy on that bite. Does it hurt badly?"

"No, it's just a bruise. My body armor kept him from breaking the skin. I'd like to bust his head for doing that, but I think I can understand his panic."

"Plug in your harness. You won't have to relink. I can perform a little therapy on your arm while we're waiting for sundown."

The youngster regained consciousness at about sunset. He looked wildly around, thrashing against the straps in terrified panic.

"Tell him to calm down," Curt ordered Beauregard. "Tell him we aren't going to hurt him unless he gets violent. Let him know he can't escape."

Beauregard promptly translated this into a stream of fluent Baluchi.

Hearing the intelligent computer's voice through the loudspeaker, the boy froze, looked at the loudspeaker in panic, and vented a stream of words.

"He wants to know if we're *jinn* that came down from the sky," Beauregard translated.

The computer-translated conversation between the company commander and the young Baluchistani went as follows:

"We're not *jinn*. We're soldiers of the United States

117

Army's Robot Infantry, not that it means anything to you at this point. My name is Captain Curt Carson. Your father is in this vehicle. We're taking the two of you with us because we can't risk having you report our presence to Imam Abdul Madjid Rahman in Zahedan."

The boy appeared reluctant to talk freely. However, he finally said grimly, "He isn't my father. He bought me to help him in his work." He suddenly stopped, fearing that he might be telling too much and thus giving this stranger additional power over him. He wasn't sure that these people weren't really *jinn* with awesome powers.

"Bought you? You're a slave?"

"Yes." It seemed obvious to the youngster that Curt had overwhelming power. Feeling he had little to lose, he went on, "He has said he will free me when he is too old to continue his work. It is not a bad bargain because I will have a trade to follow."

"Well, there's been a change in plan. You made the mistake of searching for your lost goats and discovering us."

"We were not looking for goats. We were searching for flint and other gemstones." There was a pause before he added, "And we wouldn't report anything we saw to those crazy people who took over Zahedan."

"What do you know about those people?"

The question was met with silence, so Curt decided he'd get back on a personal level with the boy who didn't seem reluctant to talk about himself. "What's your name?"

The boy drew his lips tightly together and maintained silence.

Curt knew the problem. In many primitive cultures, people believe that if another person or a supernatural being like an angel or *jinni* knows your name, he can exercise complete power over you. Curt said bluntly, "I'm not going to hurt you, and you certainly won't be any worse off if you tell me. I've told you my name. What's yours?"

The boy looked up timidly, his bravado now gone. "Hassan," he said.

"Is that all? Just Hassan?"

"Hassan."

"And your owner's name?"

"He is called Mahmud, the stone merchant."

"Stone merchant?"

"He searches for precious stones, rocks, pieces of copper, and ancient metal things. He sells them to the jewelry makers in Zahedan and Mirjaveh. Sometimes, we have gone as far as Bampur when he has a good piece that will bring better money there. He has told me if I find a good and valuable thing, he will take me on the railway to a real city called Quetta and to a place where we can see water flowing constantly along the ground, not just when it rains."

"Hassan, where do you live?"

"Here on the mountainside."

"Where is your house?"

"We have no house. Mahmud has a tent that we live in and a donkey for carrying loads I cannot handle. We left them down the mountainside."

And they'll stay there, Curt thought. This wasn't an

anthropological expedition. He didn't need to bring back examples of the squalor in which these two lived.

The youngster had lost some of his fright and was beginning to open up a bit more. Curt pressed his advantage, trying to make the best of this opportunity to learn something about the Baluchi people. Hassan seemed to be a bright boy, although he had never seen the inside of a schoolroom. He'd have to be smart and resourceful, Curt decided, to manage to survive in this region.

"Where are you going to take us?" Hassan blurted out. It was obvious from the tone of his voice, though he spoke in Baluchi, that he was frightened and trying hard not to show it. Curt decided that Hassan's bravado was commendable. The boy had sort of brave defiance that made a good warbot brainy.

"You wouldn't understand if I told you," Curt replied. "But I give you my word that you and Mahmud will not be harmed if you do not try to escape. You will be fed, given new clothing, and treated with honor and respect. If you give me your word that you will not attempt violence or try to escape, I'll allow you to stay here where you can see what's going on. And I'll try to explain things to you as they happen. Will you agree to that?" Actually, Curt was bluffing; he didn't know where else in the aerodyne he could put Hassan to keep him out of trouble, but he didn't want the boy to remain restrained in the seat for hours.

"Well?" Curt repeated as Hassan remained silent.

The boy's curiosity overcame his fear. "I agree," he said.

The meal wasn't elaborate. Curt chose a simple menu

with a hot entrée, had Beauregard select the items from the supplies and heat them, and then unstrapped Hassan's arms and presented the boy with the food.

"Don't worry; it isn't poisoned," he declared when Hassan silently refused to touch it. He took a bit of Hassan's food and placed it in his own mouth. Only then did Hassan begin to eat. Although the meal was only Type-S field rations, more of a basic maintenance diet than anything else and the butt of complaints and jokes among warbot brainies, Hassan took tentative bites of each item to assure himself of the taste, then wolfed down the rest.

As the sun set, Curt queried Beauregard again. "Is Sergeant Kester certain that he can handle the rest of the operation?"

"Yes. His physical and mental condition are excellent."

Good old Henry! Hard as nails and twice as straight! "Okay, how about Sergeant Gerard in the cover aerodyne?"

"He's been resting since the return of the birdbots. He reports everything is copacetic for the recovery phase of the mission."

Curt was confident that the two aerodynes wouldn't be detected or attacked by any Jehorkhim air defenses. The recon data from this scouting mission had indicated no such defenses existed. And when the sun settled below the western horizon and the shadows on the land disappeared, the two ships lifted off and retraced their inbound course. This time, however, because of the possibility of fatigue on the part of both Kester and Gerard, Curt ordered a three hundred-meter altitude instead of nap-of-the-earth. It would make it easier on the two sergeants. So the aerodynes sped through the twilight skies, their lights out and stealth procedures in effect.

Although he hadn't communicated with the *McCain*, Curt felt confident that the link through Beauregard to Georgie in Diamond Point automatically meant that the *McCain* would know they were coming out of Iran and would be prepared for the recovery.

Things were going very well, and he took a moment from time to time to explain to Hassan where they were and what was happening. The youngster watched in open-mouthed amazement, hardly believing the miracles he was seeing.

It looked like a piece of cake until the two aerodynes crossed the coastline and headed out over the water.

"Alert," Beauregard suddenly snapped. "Four targets, four o'clock high, range twenty-seven kilometers, converging course, closing velocity Mach two-point-three-five. Passive lidar signature indicates they are Super Gaspard X-wing interceptors recently purchased by the Islamic Iranian Air Force from France . . ."

CHAPTER SEVEN

"Dammit, I've got no choice. I've got to go back into linkage!" Curt snapped. In spite of the fact that it was extremely dangerous to go into deep linkage quickly, this was an emergency. Kester and Gerard would desperately need him. Running the whole show while under attack was too much for two men, even with AI systems taking care of most of the routine activity.

Curt's resumption of deep linkage would have another hairy consequence: Hassan would be left unwatched. Curt told Beauregard to monitor the boy and report any quick movements. Then he steeled himself and gave the commands that put him back into deep linkage. The shock was severe. Curt experienced a momentary blast of extreme disorientation, confusion between his natural senses and the artificial ones of the robotic system. For an instant, he didn't know which sensory data were from his own system and which from Beauregard.

In real time, this situation lasted only two seconds, but Curt felt it took minutes for his mind and nervous system to readjust. Beauregard worked rapidly, searching for proper input signals and attempting to correlate output signals to match Curt's sensory channels.

To Beauregard, it was a self-programming problem. To Curt, it was a madhouse and a nightmare, a bad dream that wracked his body with waves of terror.

Curt had undergone training in simulators to prepare him for just such contingencies. He knew what was going on, and his training allowed him to stay sane while it was happening. But the stress racked him more than usual.

I must be puckered out, he remarked rhetorically to the system. *That hurt. But this is what I get paid for.*

Kester replied, *Yeah, but it don't make up for the hassle. I keep saying I'm gettin' too old for this. Captain, take the defenses. I'll hold course for the rendezvous point.*

Roger. Got 'em. Nick, do you have a make on the incoming targets?

Tally ho. I have 'em. Iranians, all right. But, Captain, we're not in Iranian airspace now.

Iran claims territorial jurisdiction out to a hundred kilometers off the coast, Curt reminded the platoon sergeant. *We're still in their airspace. But where did those humpers come from?*

It was Master Sergeant Henry Kester who thought back, *They popped up from the general direction of the Chah Bahkar air base. Could have been down in ground clutter where we couldn't see 'em. They probably stayed low and slow until they got a gross track on us, then waited until we got over the water so they could get a better look-down return.*

Balls. We let down our guard before the mission was over, Nick Gerard's thought came through as a snarl.

Nothing we could do about it, Nick, Curt told him. *Even if we'd been skimming at ten meters, they could have picked us up on infrared any time they wanted to look. Now, everyone, trap shut while I check the situation.*

Curt would have to act fast. He could because robotic control in linkage was faster than manual control. However, Mach 2.3 and range 37 klicks meant the Iranian aircraft would be on them in less than 30 seconds.

He scanned the sensors to get a reading on weather and sea conditions. Wind was sixteen meters per second out of the north, a continuation of the constant breeze that blew over the highlands of Baluchistan. The sea surface was covered with light chop and three-meter swells, each in a different direction.

Beauregard, tell Georgie to get us some air support, Curt told the aerodyne's computer.

Unavailable, came the answer almost at once.

Why? We have ships in this vicinity. The McCain for one. It's got combat air capability. We need it. Emergency.

Georgie says the Navy won't show sea-launched air support for us because of rules of engagement ordered by Washington. The McCain is in Iranian waters.

Goddamn friggin' Navy ... Curt began.

Not Navy, and not Joint Chiefs of Staff, Beauregard reported for Georgie. *Standing directive from the National Security Authority to all Persian Gulf petrosecurity units.*

Well, hell, we'll have to save our own ass then. Down

to ten meters, Curt told Kester. *Just clear the wave tops. Come to a heading of two-three-zero and back off the speed to one-four-zero klicks.*

Captain, that's a little close to the water. We may hit a wave. And cutting back speed makes us sitting ducks, Nick Gerard complained.

Do it. We'll try to match our speed with multiples of the swell and chop rates, Curt explained. *That'll tend to confuse even doppler radar. If we can't get through using stealth tactics to make us look like part of the background, I'll go to deception jamming and velocity track breaking,* Curt explained.

I can split off from Beauregard by a hundred meters or so, Captain. That would let you run some of that good old cross-eye jamming, Nick Gerard suggested. Beauregard and Pickett could then retransmit the Iranian doppler radar signal with a phase difference at greater signal power, confusing the airborne radars of the interceptors and creating false radar targets.

Worse comes to worse, Kester added, *we can bloom chaff or toggle the high-power interference jammer. We haven't used any of the chaff we brought along, and I powered up the jammer before you took over, Captain.*

Good idea, Gerard's thought came back. *Let's burn the shit out of their receivers.*

Nick, weave back and forth over us with a five-second period. Link your countermeasures to Beauregard, Curt ordered.

How about letting me assume offensive-defensive mode and go after them as they come in? Gerard asked.

Negative, negative, Curt shot back quickly. *Let's not have any tiger error right now. We're too close to the*

126

water. They can't close on us too much for fear of hitting the drink in the dark. And they may not be good enough to do it anyway. Night flying over the water at ten meters has a high pucker factor.

Curt was going to have to make do with what he had and hope it would be enough to spoof the Iranians. He didn't know whether or not his electronic countermeasures would do any good because those Gaspard X-wings might have the latest French avionics suites. He asked for database information on the Gaspard X-wings. Beauregard didn't have the data, but Georgie did, which added a few milliseconds delay because of transmission times. Georgie reported that these were rudimentary interceptors of the simplest sort that had been refurbished by France and sold to the Iranians as "almost new" or "zero-time" aircraft, which they weren't. But perhaps they were the best the Iranians could hack anyway. The data base said the Iranian Gaspards were equipped with primitive look-down shoot-down capabilities from doppler radar signals that were analyzed by on-board computers and reported out to the rest of the attack system only if they were different from other signals in the area. Thus, even the stealthed aerodynes would leave a "hole" in the background signature. Curt couldn't shift the aerodynes' courses and speeds quickly enough to make them look like ocean waves, only multiples thereof. So he'd have to make the surroundings look more like stealthed aerodynes, and thus cause confusion in the Iranians' attack systems.

But he had only seconds in which to play with velocity track breaking.

If the Iranian pilots launched any missiles, he would

count on the fact that their computer equipment might be slightly out of tolerance, thereby causing some of the inbound missiles to miss, but the percentages were small. He'd have to go to jamming and chaff after the missiles were launched and Beauregard got a reading to tell him what kind of missiles they were.

Ten klicks and closing, Nick Gerard reported.

Curt had that data already and was trying to do something about it by using the most sophisticated electronic countermeasures techniques aboard. *No use trying the simple stuff first; there isn't time. We've got to hit them with the best we've got,* he told his two sergeants. *Time to toss out everything, including Polish toilet paper, if we've got any.* That latrine accessory was renown for its excellence as radar chaff. It was hard and brittle, which caused it to break into millions of randomly-sized pieces, and most radars will pick up a return from anything that differs from its surroundings. "Warsaw bun wad" certainly filled that requirement. Some RI troopers who'd run into the stuff in regions where supplies had come from Eastern Europe claimed that the only humane use for it was as radar chaff.

The lead plane launched a missile.

Revanche air-to-air missile, Beauregard identified it, analyzing its propulsion and seeker signatures. Curt saw it coming through a combination of light-amplified and infrared sensors on Beauregard. The missile was a long white pole trailing a brilliant, searing tail of hot flame as its rocket motor burned.

Easy spoof, Kester remarked. *And the Iranians*

launched at the limit of the missile's range. Lots of time for an easy spoof.

Go get 'em, Beauregard, Curt ordered.

It was an easy spoof, for Beauregard's high-speed circuits recognized the incoming missile, searched the computer memory for the proper countermeasures, and acted. Curt watched as Beauregard did things on an apparently instantaneous basis, shifting doppler radar return frequencies to confuse the missile's electronically stupid brain by presenting it with several false targets.

It worked.

The first missile swerved, made a partial high-g turn, wavered, lost velocity rapidly as it reached the limit of its range, and fell into the sea a kilometer to the right of Beauregard.

A second missile was launched by the wingman. It came within four hundred meters and hit the ocean with a splash.

They may have found the key to our countermeasures, Gerard guessed.

Okay, stand by with chaff and jamming when they launch the next two. Curt waited for the third and fourth missiles. The Iranian pilots now had had ample time to figure out what had spoofed the first two and to activate counter-countermeasures, if the Gaspards were so equipped. If the third missile didn't do the job, the fourth one probably would unless Beauregard had some unknown tricks up his electronic sleeve.

The third and fourth missiles were never launched.

The four Iranian interceptors veered sharply west, broke off the attack, and climbed. They reformed at a thousand meters and began to circle in search mode. Curt kept sensing their radar signals as they swept the area, but they were apparently unable to see or lock onto any target.

They've lost us, Nick Gerard reported.

Whatever we're doing, keep it up, Curt said, momentarily relieved.

Thank God they didn't use infrared. We're a lot warmer than the water below us.

They did, Curt told him. *It apparently wasn't working right tonight.*

Then what the hell happened? Henry Kester wanted to know. *They broke off right when they had us by the short hairs.*

Could have been that Navy air support I asked for. Did we get it after all? Curt wondered.

Nothin' else up there. Unless the Navy jocks are spoofing our own equipment and we don't see 'em, Gerard reported.

The answer to their questions and confusion came quickly. *Sergeant Kester, please relinquish flight control to me,* came the request from Beauregard.

Curt protested. *Beauregard, this is no time to . . .*

We are within one minute of rendezvous with the McCain, Beauregard reported. *I have acquired the McCain's approach signals and informed them of our final approach. We're cleared for approach.*

That's it. Curt transmitted the thought. The USS *McCain*, SSCV-17, was one of the newest USN submersible carriers, and had the latest and most sophisticated electronic warfare equipment. The *McCain* had probably detected the Iranians and laid down a blanket of countermeasures that suddenly gave the Gaspards and their missiles a multitude of false targets. This had been a risky ploy because it still left the real targets available for acquisition and attack if they could be discriminated. It was also risky because the Iranians weren't stupid; they now knew someone was down there, on or below the water.

But the Iranian interceptors had another problem. *They're breaking off and heading home,* Curt reported. *Either they're short on fuel or they don't want to tangle ... or both.* Mach-two-plus aircraft gulp fuel, and the Gaspards weren't the new fuel-efficient long-range craft. If they did have enough fuel left to mount a second attack, the Iranian pilots probably have opted not to challenge something they couldn't identify. Or another sortie might be on the way. There could be any number of reasons why the Iranians broke off and headed northwest at supersonic cruise speed.

Then Curt saw the *McCain* surface a hundred meters ahead and sensed the edge illuminators of its fore and aft flight decks. Beauregard slowed to hover and settled gently to the aft deck atop the elevator. Curt watched as Pickett landed on the fore deck.

When Beauregard opened the lower hatch, people began to swarm aboard, even as the lift lowered the ship into the sub. *Biotechs are boarding for delink processing,* Beauregard reported.

As Curt felt the *McCain's* aft lift begun to surge downward, he sensed someone now on the control deck with him. He didn't bother to identify the newcomer but relaxed as Beauregard started to disconnect him slowly from the complex and rapid world of robotics.

131

Curt began to delink and sensed that Kester was doing the same. Kester's mental touch retreated. Very quickly, Curt was no longer able to think to his Master Sergeant or to receive Kester's mental inputs. And suddenly Beauregard was no longer an extension of his mind but a separate entity. It was difficult as usual.

Except this time, glory be, Biotech Sergeant Helen Devlin was there. He sensed her now as he came back to the real world. She'd unplugged his linkage harness. She was already using acupuncture and acupressure therapy to help him get rid of his cramped muscles.

"You're completely exhausted," the diminutive bio-tech sergeant said.

"That's what you think," Curt groaned. He ignored what his body was telling him because his libido was fired up. He lusted for Devlin, but he discovered he couldn't bring his muscles to obey his commands.

"What's the awful smell in here?" the biotech asked.

"A young prisoner of war, Hassan. I had to bring him back with me. Hasn't ever had a bath, I suspect."

"What prisoner? Where?"

Curt quickly turned his head and looked around, then was sorry he'd done it. He had the granddaddy of all headaches. In addition, Hassan was gone from the seat in which Curt had strapped him and then, to allow him to eat supper, had released the restraints on his arms. "Dammit, I *told* Beauregard to keep an eye on the kid and report if he made any quick moves! Helen, get me a circuit back into Beauregard. I've got to find out where the boy went!"

"But you're far too tired . . ."

132

"Sergeant! If you don't plug me back in, I'll do it myself!"

But Beauregard was still monitoring audio in the cabin because Henry Kester had relinquished control and come out of linkage. "Captain, don't worry . . ."

"Worry! Why, you collection of slightly impure crystals! . . ."

Beauregard had enough intelligence to sense Curt's anger and frustration. He quietly told the captain, "Hassan did not make any sudden moves. You were busy with the defense against the interceptors, so I agreed to let him go down to comfort his owner, Mahmud. The *McCain's* Marine security guards already have the two of them in custody. And Colonel Belinda Hettrick would like to see you in the Lion's Den as soon as possible."

Curt sighed deeply. It was unusual for the colonel to want to debrief so quickly. "You're a good trooper, Beau."

"Thank you, sir. I try my best to emulate my namesake."

"You can't see the colonel right away, Captain," Sergeant Devlin warned him. "You're much too fatigued."

"Sergeant, when the colonel wants me for anything, I'd damned well better be there."

"Rank hath its privileges," Helen Devlin muttered. "You really need bed and broad right now."

"I know it," Curt told her.

The lift had lowered Beauregard from the flight deck onto the totally enclosed hangar deck. The huge flight deck doors closed over the aerodyne, and within minutes after recovering both craft, the *McCain* was diving to safety five hundred meters below the surface.

"Kester, are you back among the living yet?" Curt asked his master sergeant, who was still in the pilot's seat, eyes open. "I want you to come with me to see Colonel Hettrick for debrief. You probably saw things I didn't."

"I didn't see anything the birdbots didn't see and the system didn't record, sir." The master sergeant's tone was a tad touchy, and Curt realized that the older man was probably far more fatigued then he.

The mission was over. It was time to go back to formal discipline in order to shut out some of the effects of fatigue. Formal military discipline was by the book. You knew what responses to give in any situation, you knew what to expect from others, and that relieved you of the necessity of having to do a lot of creative thinking. "Very well, Sergeant. But I believe your experience is going to be worth a great deal when we get around to interpreting the data." He rose from the co-pilot's seat and accidentally stumbled as he gained his feet.

"How do you feel?" Helen asked, steadying him.

"Tired and exhausted," Curt replied testily.

"You need rest."

"Undoubtedly. But this is the Army," Curt muttered, gathering up his personal pack and carbine. "Do you certify I'm delinked okay?"

"You're dehydrated and hungry. You need to get out of that harness and armor. A hot shower would do you good. You should have about ten hours' sleep. And you need me. Did you eat *anything* on the mission?"

134

"Only a field meal about four hours ago. Never mind the harness and armor; I can live with them for another hour or so. Sign me off. I've got to see the colonel ass-ap."

"Yes, sir." Helen knew that duty came first to this officer.

"Thank you, Sergeant . . . Helen," Curt said the last softly, knowing that the little biotech really had his best interests at heart and was doing her job.

In spite of Sergeant Devlin's administrations, Curt was still stiff from sitting too long, and his muscles were sore. With Henry Kester, he walked out of the aerodyne onto the flight deck. Sergeant Nick Gerard was waiting for them. The dapper little platoon sergeant was the youngest of the three men and he could recover more rapidly from the long period of linkage. He tossed a quick salute to Curt and remarked, "Sheesh, Captain, I thought we were in for a knife fight for sure when those four Iranian interceptors jumped us! It was pure hell trying to weave back and forth across the top of you. Henry, thanks for holding Beauregard steady."

"Thank Beauregard," Kester told him as the three of them walked off the flight deck. "I just told him what to do. He's a good driver. He was the one who did it."

"Captain, what kind of countermeasures did you lay on there at the last?"

"Wasn't me," Curt explained. "We were actually within range of the *McCain's* ECM suites, but I didn't know it because I was concentrating on the interceptors. The *McCain* whizzos down in combat ops probably

135

spoofed both the missiles and the planes to hide the fact that the *McCain* was nearby."

"Vulnerable."

"Bloody Navy went high-risk for us," Kester remarked.

"Yeah. Ready for debrief?"

"I guess so. I'm stinking from thinking. I could use cleaning up and showering down. As a matter of fact, sir, we all could," Kester said diplomatically.

"Okay, the colonel realizes that we're going to stink. Let's get this over with before we forget something."

"Speakin' of stinkin', what happened to those two stinkin' Arabs?" Kester wondered.

"That's what I'm worried about," Curt admitted. "We've either brought back a heap of trouble or a gold mine of information . . . and I don't know which at this point."

Colonel Hettrick was in the *McCain's* External Combat Operations Center. When Curt and his men walked into the large, tiered room that looked like a miniature coliseum—hence its sobriquet, the Lion's Den—with its holographic projections in the center and its ascending banks of terminals and operating positions, he didn't immediately see his superior officer in the deep red lights. He finally asked the Marine stationed at the entrance and was directed to the top tier about ninety degrees to the left.

Hettrick saw them coming and got up to greet them. She looked fit and trim in her Type-B field uniform, and she returned their salutes with a sharp snapping motion. Curt sensed something wrong. The colonel was upset.

136

"Come with me, please, Captain. Sergeants, you're dismissed," she said curtly.

Kester glanced querulously at Curt, but his look told the company commander, *We're with you, Captain, whatever the problem happens to be. Call on us if you need us.* Then he said, "We'll wait for you in the Cub's Cupboard, sir," meaning that he and Gerard would be in the rest and relaxation cafeteria right off the Lion's Den.

Colonel Hettrick led Curt to a side room with a table and chairs in it. She sat down but didn't ask Curt to sit. "Report, Captain!" she said formally.

At least, Curt thought, she had the good sense to do whatever she was going to do in private and not embarrass a subordinate by dressing him down in front of the troops. Colonel Hettrick might be upset, but Curt knew she would never be unfair.

"Mission completed successfully, Colonel," he told her stiffly.

"You took prisoners." It was a statement, not a question.

"Yes, Colonel, I did."

"It's contrary to operational policy and doctrine to take prisoners. Regulation forty-three-dash-seven: 'Noncombatant humans encountered in operations will not be seized and held against their wills, but will be released back to their respective organizations.' "

"I'm aware of the regulation, Colonel. I acted under the provisions of Reg nine-dash-three: 'The officer in command of an isolated unit in action bears the sole responsibility and the ultimate accountability for the safety and integrity of his command and may take whatever action is necessary to save lives even if, in his judgment, his actions may be contrary to these regulations.' I took the prisoners to save lives—those of the hostages."

Colonel Hettrick absently tapped the table top with a fingernail. "Were you in danger from those nomads?"

"At the time, we were not," Curt replied bluntly. He knew he'd done the right thing under the circumstances and according to regulations, and he also knew that Hettrick would put up with no excuses or boot licking. When Hettrick said nothing, he went on to explain, "We had no way of knowing whether or not they'd report our presence to the Jehorkhims. If they'd reported us, a scouting mission might have had a major negative impact upon Operation Squire. Therefore, since we couldn't withdraw before being seen, I had the choice of killing them or making them, de facto, prisoners. I won't kill in cold blood. Therefore, I elected to exercise the second choice."

Colonel Hettrick said nothing for a moment, "Captain, I won't overrule the personal judgment of an officer who made a decision in action. I wasn't there and I mustn't second-guess you. I'll forward your verbal report upstairs along with mine."

"Thank you, Colonel," Curt said when she paused. He knew she'd have to file a report to General Knox concerning Mahmud and Hassan, and he also knew the questioning session was pure regulation and undoubtedly had been requested by a higher officer—unquestionably General Victor Knox. The colonel was the one saddled with the demand for a report.

She softened and allowed a smile to play around the corners of her mouth. "And, Curt, I don't believe disciplinary action or even a verbal reprimand is in order. You did an outstanding job and got excellent information."

"Thank you, Colonel," Curt repeated. There was little more that he could or should say at this juncture.

"Please sit down, Captain."

Curt did so, and the woman officer said, "The Geneva Modified Convention requires us to return these two to the government authorities in their homeland. Do you have any suggestions regarding this?"

"I believe the Convention isn't specific regarding time," Curt recalled. "It says we must do so within a 'reasonable' time. I recommend that we return them at the conclusion of Operation Squire. Otherwise, we could indeed jeopardize the mission."

The colonel thought about this for a moment, then replied. "I concur."

"In the meantime, if they're willing to talk, they can undoubtedly flesh out the information we obtained on the scouting mission," Curt suggested. He wondered why Hettrick wanted him to stay after she'd carried out the primary task of querying him about the prisoners. He was getting more weary by the moment. The linkage harness and the body armor were beginning to irritate him, and he longed for a hot shower, some food, some sleep, and some sex.

"Are they willing to talk?"

"I think so. Hassan seemed cooperative. He told me about himself when I questioned him, and even gave me some information I didn't ask for."

139

"Have you spoken with the man?"

"No, I put Mahmud into a cargo compartment, and didn't get the chance to speak with him. I don't know whether he'll cooperate or not. In fact, he doesn't even know who I am. Mahmud was unconscious when I carried him into Beauregard."

"Please interrogate both of them, Captain."

"Certainly. But may I request two things first?"

"What are they?"

"Mahmud and Hassan should be taken down to sick bay, bathed, dressed in clean clothes, and given a physical exam. I've put up with their terrible stink long enough. I don't think they've ever had a bath; it's time they did. And we should make sure they don't bring any contagious diseases into our midst, especially any they're immune to and we're not."

"When Marines complain about the smell, it's bad. I've given the necessary orders. Anything else?"

"I've been in action for nearly thirty-six hours, Colonel. I'm bushed. I'd like some sleep so I don't make a dumb mistake and blow the whole interrogation."

"No problem."

"May I go now, Colonel?"

Her tone shifted from the formal, disciplined voice of command to a more personal lilt. "Is there anything else?"

Curt didn't know whether or not she was throwing protocol out the window and extending veiled offer to ask her to bed—which was her prerogative, provided she did it as she had. But it didn't appeal to him because he suddenly discovered that the raging fires of his postlinkage libido had gone out ... and it wasn't because Hettrick wasn't an attractive woman. He was exhausted. Driven almost to his physical and mental limits. Wearily, he told her, "No, Colonel Hettrick. But thank you."

"Very well. Dismissed. Good job! By the way, the rest of the Washington Greys are aboard, including your Companions."

"That's good. Glad they made it." Curt nodded, stood, and saluted. He was just too tired to do much of anything else. He managed to say, "Colonel, you weren't really upset with me about the prisoners, were you?"

"No, but I couldn't buffer you as I usually do."

"General Knox upset about it? Care to tell me why?"

She nodded. "Prisoners weren't in the plan. The general wants this operation run by the book and according to plan, Curt. It may be his last one, and he doesn't want to take chances. If he goes by the book, he's always got a way to cover himself."

"That's putting it kindly. Well, I guess we'll just have to muddle through to victory anyhow. I'll try not to make life too difficult for you ..."

"You're not the cross I have to bear."

Leaving the conference cubicle, Curt went through the Lion's Den to the Cub's Cupboard, found his two sergeants, and told them to get some rest and then report to Lieutenant Alexis Morgan in ten hours. Kester was looking haggard, but Nick Gerard appeared to be bright and alert except for the deep, dark circles under his eyes.

The ship's quartermaster had already assigned quarters to them, and Regimental Logistics had seen to it that Curt's compartment contained toilet articles and fresh uniforms. He didn't need any help peeling out of the body armor and linkage harness. A hot shower made him feel a little better, and he ate the hot meal placed on the bedside table by the service robot, then turned out the lights, and fell into bed.

Later, Curt awoke to find someone warm and soft in bed with him. He thought it was Helen, but he was far too tired to inquire. He was off duty and Rule Ten didn't apply, so he relaxed and let nature take its course.

CHAPTER EIGHT

"'O Captain! My Captain! Rise up and hear the bells . . .'"

Someone was doing something nice to Curt and it felt good. "Helen, you she-devil!" he muttered sleepily.

"Sorry, Captain. Sergeant Devlin left before I got here. But you're pretty damned good even when you're alseep!"

He realized that Lieutenant Alexis Morgan was whispering in his ear. "The hell with it!" he growled, and put his arm around her. "The world will run without us. I'm staying in the sack . . ."

Alexis didn't resist, but she did whisper, "Colonel Hettrick wants you to interrogate the prisoners."

"They won't go anywhere," Curt observed.

Alexis Morgan didn't respond but she suddenly became colder. "Curt, the Jehorkhims killed another hostage last night."

"Goddamn it! Why'd you have to remind me of that?"

"Because the world goes on running without you."

"I find it strange you don't want to dally a bit."

143

"We've dallied already. You probably don't remember, but I'm dallied out. You've been in the sack for thirteen hours. The colonel's been leaving insistent messages for you on the comm console, but she's too much of a lady to come down here and roust you out."

Curt's stomach was growling. "I'm hungry," he admitted.

"Does the captain desire me to procure rations for him?" Alexis asked in semimocking tones.

"Naw, I'll be vertical shortly; then we'll go get some chow."

"By your command . . ." She rolled out of bed, threw on a robe, and told the comm console that Captain Carson had just awakened and would report to the *McCain's* sick bay to interrogate the prisoners in one hour.

"You don't give me much time," Curt told her as he donned a fresh Class-B field uniform.

"We don't have much time, if you recall," Alexis told him, also dressing. "They promised to kill a hostage every day. And we're scheduled to shove off for Zahedan in about six hours."

"So the Jehorkhims are still killing hostages?"

"New videotapes show up somewhere in the world every day. And always scheduled to make the prime-time newscasts in the States."

The thought sickened Curt, but it motivated him to get powered up. He could relax and enjoy himself once the hostages were safely out of Zahedan. He felt guilty to be living in relative luxury aboard the *McCain* while more than a hundred people were being held in dungeons in a place that was fifty centuries in the past. He recalled the sights and sounds of Zahedan. What an isolated, barren, primitive, impossible backwater!

Now he had to interrogate two people from that place. He wondered if he could establish communications with them. Maybe he could try putting Mahmud and Hassan in linkage and letting Georgie scan their minds. But Curt didn't know what sort of mental blocks the two might have. And he was hesitant to do that because when a person wasn't trained in mind-machine linkage, the session could result in zero information or conflicting data. In addition, there was the possibility of driving the untrained person into insanity. Still, it was something he might have to do as a last resort.

"Alexis, I want you to come with me to the interview."

Even though they were off duty and formal discipline wasn't mandatory, he'd referred to a duty matter, and Lieutenant Alexis Morgan knew that such a request was equivalent to a direct order. However, since they were not under combat conditions, Army discipline allowed her to ask why, which she did.

"Because I want to strengthen the impression that we're not the sort of soldiers who've marched back and forth over their people from time immemorial," Curt explained. "And I want you there because you're a woman."

"Well, thank you, but why? Aren't women second-class citizens in most of the orthodox Islamic nations?"

"Muslim women may not enjoy a lot of male perks, but they've got their own privileges. After all, the Crusaders learned chivalry from the infidels."

145

"So I don't have to wear a veil for the interrogation?"

"Damned right you don't, Lieutenant." He got up and went to the door. "We're now back on duty."

"Yes, Captain," Alexis Morgan said. "Sorry. I didn't mean to be flippant or disrespectful. It's just that occasionally our demands for discipline, our uniformity in dress and in the way we talk ... well, sometimes that gets repressive and ... tedious."

"Yeah, I agree. But it holds the Army together," Curt responded. "Let's go see if Navy food's improved any."

The food on the *McCain* was pretty good, they decided.

The muted heartbeat of the carrier submarine was all around them as they went along the corridors to the sick bay. A quiet-running sub because of her twin-screw turboelectric drive and free circulation nuclear reactors, the *McCain* nevertheless still had distinctive sounds—the quiet turbulence of the water slipping past the composite hull and the sighing of the air system. These sounds—and gravity—reminded Curt that he was in a submarine and not a space station. And the *McCain* was an unreal place. Curt had to work hard to remind himself that he wasn't in a simulator or in linkage.

Mahmud and Hassan were in a private room in sick bay. Both had changed into clean Navy dungarees. Mahmud was sitting moodily on the edge of a bunk. Both he and Hassan had their eyes glued on the television screen, not understanding any of the language but engrossed in the fairy-tale world of the current top-rated soap opera, "Destinies," with its beautiful women, handsome men, and exaggerated personal conflicts.

Mahmud sat up straight when Curt and Alexis came in. His expression and body posture indicated submissive but defiant dignity. Curt knew the signals. The man was frightened but trying hard not to show it.

It was Hassan who looked up, grinned broadly, and said in English, "Hello!" The boy was obviously picking up the language from TV and from listening to those around him in the sick bay.

Mahmud said something sharply in Baluchi to Hassan, and the boy became glum.

Curt showed them both of his hands, open and empty. Alexis took the signal and did likewise. Stepping to the wall comm console, Curt touched it and said, "Put Georgie on line."

"Working!" came the female voice of the *McCain's* intelligent computer.

"Hello, Captain Carson!" It was Georgie, his computer voice clear in spite of a communications link that traversed more than 20,000 kilometers of ocean. At the *McCain's* depth of five hundred meters, ordinary radio and lasercom wouldn't work. Something did, but the tech people always politely dodged Curt's questions about long-range underwater networks, just as they refused to discuss the details of warbot linkage technology: Combat troops didn't need to know.

"Georgie, Lieutenant Alexis Morgan is with me. We're talking with Mahmud and Hassan. Please translate English and Baluchi, one to the other, using your 'mother-voice.' And record this interview." He didn't need to be polite with a computer, but he thought of

Georgie as a remote and never-seen human being who was almost as much of a personal slave to him as Hassan was to Mahmud. Human slavery bothered him, however. Machines should be slaves, not people.

Georgie replied in the calm, caring, contralto voice of an older woman, "I'm ready, Captain."

Curt turned from the comm terminal, motioned Alexis to sit down, and did so himself, facing the Baluchi. "Mahmud, I am Captain Curt Carson, United States Army Robot Infantry. This is Lieutenant Alexis Morgan. We intend to rescue the hostages held by the Jehorkhims in Zahedan. That's why we were on the slopes of Kuh-e-Taftan." He paused to let Georgie translate, then continued, "You and Hassan saw our scout ships. I couldn't allow you to go back and report us to the Imam Abdul Madjid Rahman in Zahedan, so I put you to sleep and brought you here. You're in a very large boat under the sea. You will not be harmed. You've been bathed and given new clothes. We'll see to it that you're well fed. After we've rescued the hostages held by the Jehorkhims in Zahedan, you and Hassan will be returned to where we found you. Tell me: Are you feeling well? May I get anything for you?" He hoped Georgie was translating properly, especially the idioms he'd used, but Georgie had proved equal to the task in the past.

Mahmud listened in stunned silence to what Georgie's voice said in Baluchi. What had happened to him was obviously far beyond his wildest imaginings. In fact, he couldn't conceive of something like the *McCain* or Georgie or any of the miracles he was seeing around him. Had he died? Was this Paradise? Or Hell? Were

148

these two strange beings people or *jinn*? He didn't know. And he didn't know how to react or respond to the situation. In his confusion, he felt he should protect himself by denying that he was involved with the enemy of these people. He blurted out, "I am not one of the *jihad* fanatics in Zahedan!"

"Hassan has told me that."

"Hassan, you are not to speak to this man!"

"Yes, Mahmud," the boy replied respectfully, and returned his attention to the dramatics of the video screen. If they wanted to talk with him, they'd call him, Hassan decided. Besides, Mahmud was obviously displeased by learning that he'd spoken with the strange man with the shaved head and the unusual clothing, so Hassan felt it would be better not to attract attention at the moment.

"I need information from Hassan as badly as I need it from you, Mahmud," Curt interrupted, looking coldly at the nomad.

"He is mine! I shall do with him as I please! And it is my right to beat him if he does not do what I tell him."

Curt shook his head. "Not here you won't. Now, what do you know about the Jehorkhims?"

"I know nothing," Mahmud muttered defiantly. He didn't want to answer the questions of this big, well-muscled man, but he was afraid of what might happen if he didn't. In fact, he wasn't totally certain that the man and the woman weren't *jinn* because of all their magical powers.

"I think you do," Curt snapped. "You mentioned the *jihad* fanatics in Zahedan. Tell me what you know."

"I know nothing," Mahmud persisted, his little eyes blazing.

"If you don't tell me voluntarily, I have other methods ..." Curt didn't have time to waste. Operation Squire was due to push off in a matter of hours. This man obviously had information, and he had been ordered to get it. He remembered Hettrick's caution about the Modified Geneva Convention regarding the treatment of noncombatants. Under the circumstances, the best he could do was attempt to get voluntary cooperation from Mahmud. If he wasn't successful, he'd let someone else worry about abiding by the various provisions of the law of armed conflict. If the intelligence people aboard became involved, the consequences for Mahmud were unpredictable. That bothered Curt, but he reminded himself that other people were being tortured and killed in Zahedan.

Mahmud understood Curt's remark to be a threat of torture, and the nomad wasn't going to submit without putting up a fight. Because he could see no way out of his quandary, he acted in the only way he could, blindly and irrationally.

The little man moved fast.

He lunged off the bunk on which he was sitting and drove hard into Curt's belly, his fists flailing.

Seven years ago, Curt had played first-string offensive running back for West Point. He was seven years older now and hadn't played football since leaving the Academy, but his reactions were still operative. Although the little man took him down to the floor, Curt had tensed his torso muscles and thus hadn't had the wind knocked out of him.

As he'd gone down, Curt had reached out and grabbed Mahmud, taking the nomad down on top of him. Then, he'd rolled, arms around Mahmud, and actually landed on the steel deck atop him. The breath gushed out of Mahmud as Curt's one hundred kilograms flattened him to the floor.

Almost instinctively, Curt lashed out with the edge of his right hand, putting the momentum of his falling body into the short stroke which landed on the side of Mahmud's head right behind the ear.

Suddenly he had a limp bag of meat and bones under him.

Curt quickly felt for Mahmud's pulse at the carotid artery.

There was none.

Scrambling quickly to his knees, Curt straddled Mahmud and began CPR, calling out to Alexis Morgan, "Get the medics! I think I killed him!"

Alexis had acted decisively when Mahmud had thrown himself at Curt. She'd reached out and pinned Hassan in a bear hug. But it was Georgie who'd been most helpful. Sensing that something had gone awry, Georgie had notified the trauma team in the sick bay.

"Goddamn it to hell!" Curt cursed as he pumped Mahmud's chest. "I didn't mean to kill him! He's got information!"

"Wasn't your fault," was all that Alexis managed to get out before the door slid open and the trauma team burst in.

There wasn't really room in the small compartment for everyone. "Captain, Lieutenant, out, please, and take the boy with you," the Navy doctor ordered.

As they stood in the corridor outside while the trauma team worked, Curt said to Hassan, "You'd damned well better behave yourself. I cold-cocked you once, and I've got no hesitation about doing it again!"

Georgie wasn't listening, so there was no translation. But Hassan got the message from Curt's tone of voice. Besides, Alexis Morgan still held him in her powerful grip. Alexis was a small woman, but she was muscular and strong. Hassan told himself that these people were powerful and would brook no nonsense. He might get hurt as he had before if he tried anything sudden and violent. Although the brief encounter between Curt and Mahmud had been almost a blur, Hassan had seen enough of it to know he was effectively outgunned.

"Captain, what did you do?" Alexis wanted to know.

"I think," Curt tried to remember, "I hit him on the side of the head. Karate chop. Don't know where I connected. I didn't have much power behind it, and I didn't land on him that hard." He shook his head remorsefully. "Goddamn it to hell, I should have been ready for something like that. Let my guard down. Serves me right. But I didn't mean to kill the sonofabitch."

Minutes passed, and they could hear activity in the compartment as the trauma team worked on Mahmud. Finally, the Navy doctor came out. "I'll need a statement, Major."

"About what, Doctor?"

"About the death of that man."

"Christ," Curt said slowly. "I didn't think I hit him that hard. What did I do to him?"

"I don't know. Autopsy will tell, maybe. And I must warn you, Major, that what you tell me and what I learn from the autopsy is admissible evidence in any court-martial that may come out of this."

CHAPTER NINE

"Orgasmic!" Curt snorted. "Well, Georgie was listening. He's got the data."

"Undoubtedly. But, as you know, Major Carson, regulations require that I notify the ship's legal officer and the chief police petty officer. I am also required to get your statement," the naval doctor reminded him. He had followed ship's protocol by bucking Curt up one rank.

"Okay, do it," Curt muttered. "But we haven't got much time. We're scheduled for a mission in a couple of hours, and I've got to interrogate Hassan. Time's a wastin'."

"You're being a bit cavalier, Major. Under the Revised Code of Military Justice, you'll have to be placed under arrest."

Curt snorted. Legalistic details! He knew that arrest was different from confinement, that an officer wouldn't be confined to quarters until shortly before a court-martial, and that it would take the wheels of military justice several months to grind toward the actual trial. In any event, Curt didn't feel threatened. He'd acted in self-defense, even if he'd hit the man too hard. "Let's go through the drill, Doctor," he said to the ship's surgeon.

The doctor took them to another cubicle and asked the artificially intelligent computer of the *McCain* to record. Curt requested that Georgie be patched into the net as well so that an identical set of data would exist in the records of 17th Division (RI), and he insisted that the naval doctor refer to him by his proper rank.

Lieutenant Alexis Morgan volunteered to give her statement as a witness. Fanatically loyal to her company commander, she wasn't about to allow any little factor to be overlooked. Killing a prisoner, especially a non-combatant, was a serious matter under the Revised Code of Military Justice.

When it was over, the *McCain*'s officer of the deck and chief police petty officer stepped into the compartment and officially placed Curt under arrest. It was a formality only. When the OOD informed the ship's legal officer over the intercom, he was in turn informed that General Knox had officially requested jurisdiction since Curt had been acting under Army command when the incident took place, even though it had happened on a naval vessel.

"Well, Major," the doctor remarked, "we've done what we're supposed to do. No hard feelings, I hope."

"None," Curt assured him. Sometimes the bureaucracy of the military services kept these huge organizations operating smoothly; in other cases, the procedures were just more hassle. You always had to touch second base or you couldn't make a home run. "But I do have a request. I still have a job of my own to do and a hot mission coming up that depends on doing that job. I'd like to use this compartment for the interrogation of the boy Hassan."

The surgeon looked pensive. "Do you want me to stick around, just in case? Or do you want me to guard a video monitor?"

"Why?"

"The boy could also become violent."

"I don't think so. Hassan knows I'll bust his head if he does," Curt replied.

"Don't hit him too hard; he'll break," the doctor advised. "I was the doctor who checked him over . . . after he'd had a shower."

"So? What's the matter with him? He looks healthy to me," Curt replied.

"The youngster isn't a normal child by our standards. In fact, I've never seen the like of him, even in our worst American slums. He's a case study in everything that a kid shouldn't be, physically speaking." The medical man shook his head sadly and began to tick points off on his fingers as he expounded them. "One: He's undernourished. Probably always has been. Two: He appears to have rickets and various other micronutrient deficiencies. Three: He has a calcium deficiency, and his bones aren't well formed as a result—I have a sneaking hunch that's what I'll also find when I autopsy his father. Four: His adult teeth are starting to rot in his jaw; he needs to see a dentist soon if he's to keep them. Five: He was covered with lice and mites and ticks before the medics ran him through what amounts to a sheep dip, which didn't help the skin sores and lesions caused by those vermin. Six: He's underdeveloped physically and probably mentally as well; his mother obviously didn't eat right during her pregnancy, nor did she feed him properly when he was a baby. As a result, his mind and nervous system may not be thoroughly developed. He *may* be about ten or eleven years old, but he may also be about fourteen or fifteen. In any event, he's got the mind and body of a ten-year-old boy, and there's no indication he'll ever grow beyond that. To put it bluntly, he's been shortchanged by life."

Curt wasn't so sure about the mental part of the doctor's diagnosis. He'd talked with Hassan in the aerodyne, and the boy had seemed rather sharp.

After Hassan had been brought in, the doctor left them alone in the compartment. Alexis sighed. "Poor Hassan!"

"That guy may be a good ship's surgeon, but he isn't necessarily a neurologist," Curt pointed out. "Some of what he said is just plain bullshit. This kid's reasonably smart. I know; I've talked with him. Watch. You'll see." He turned to the comm panel. "Georgie, are you still on line here?"

"Working," came the reply.

"Translate again. Baluchi and English."

"Working." The voice came back, this time in the familiar contralto of the previous interrogation session with Mahmud.

Curt sat facing the passive Hassan and said in a gentle voice, "Hassan, I'm sorry I killed your father."

"He wasn't my father," Hassan said as Georgie translated.

"You uncle, then. Or your relative."

157

"Mahmud was not my relative. My father sold me to Mahmud many years ago when I was very young."

"*Sold you?*" Alexis blurted out.

"Why did he sell you, Hassan?" Curt persisted.

"My family was starving," Hassan explained slowly as though he were dredging up old and unhappy memories. "The rains did not come. Nothing would grow, not even on our best land. There was nothing to eat. He sold the goats we had not already eaten. He then had to sell the camels, my sister, and me in order to buy food."

"That's terrible!" Alexis murmured.

Hassan shrugged. "If he had not sold me, I would be dead now. We had nothing to eat. But Mahmud always fed me. When he was angry with me, he beat me, but he still fed me. Often we didn't eat very much. But we didn't starve."

"I didn't mean to kill Mahmud." Curt didn't know whether an apology would mean very much right then, but he made the gesture anyway.

"I know. I was there. I saw. Mahmud often had a very short temper. I think it served him right. Now I belong to you, Captain Carson."

Wup! Curt thought. *A new faction in the action.* "Well, we'll see about that. We have different rules here."

"I am yours by our customs," Hassan explained.

Curt didn't want to get involved right then in the consequences of owning a slave, nor did he want to spend a lot of time trying to explain to Hassan why the boy might be free, or even what freedom meant. Curt

158

reminded himself that he had work to do. "What can you tell me about the Jehorkhims in Zahedan?"

"I am not a Jehorkhim."

"I believe you. But who are the Jehorkhims and how many of them are in Zahedan?"

Hassan thought about this question for a moment after Georgie translated. He wanted to be somewhat cautious with these people. He didn't fully trust them yet, although he was in their complete control. And he wasn't going to try the same stunt that Mahmud had. "I will tell you," he agreed, but added the caveat, "However, you must understand that I know only about the Jehorkhims from what I learned in the streets of Zahedan." Shortchanged on brains or not, the boy was certainly streetwise.

"I believe you're not a Jehorkhim," Curt repeated. "What have you learned about them?"

"They came to Zahedan last year before Ramadan," Hassan's words tumbled out so fast that Georgie had difficulty in keeping up the pace of translation. "They had been told to leave Iran by the ayatollahs in Teheran. Pakistan would not let them cross the border, so they returned to Zahedan. They took over much of the government. The Imam has many more soldiers than the governor of Baluchistan, so the governor went back to Teheran. The Imam has been very careful. He has not angered the Teheran government. His soldiers collect the taxes for Teheran as well as alms for the Imam and the Jehorkhims. And the Imam is strict, which pleases the ayatollahs. But the Jehorkhims go beyond even our Shiite submission to the will of Allah."

The boy was a hell of a lot smarter than the Navy

doctor had given him credit for, Curt decided then and there. What he'd just told them was a gold mine of information that could have been gotten no other way.

When Hassan stopped, Curt asked, "How many Jehorkhims in Zahedan?"

"Many."

"How many?" Curt persisted.

Hassan paused for a moment then blurted out, "*'takriban alf wa khumsemiyeh*. Almost fifteen hundred."

"Nearly two regiments strong, if they were all soldiers," Alexis observed.

"Hassan, are they all soldiers? How many *askari*?"

Hassan shrugged. "I have not counted them. Many wives and households are with the soldiers. And the Imam has with him many *waliy*." Georgie paused to find the proper translation, then went on. ". . . Chosen companions."

"Does he have any scientists? Engineers? Technicians? Mechanics?"

Hassan spread his hands. "I do not know. A story in the marketplace says that the Imam has the help of a woman who may be a *jinni* from a land in the east."

"Dr. Rhosha Taisha?"

"I have heard that is her name."

There was silence following Hassan's answer, so Curt prodded him, "What does she do for the Imam?"

"I do not know, but it is said she helps him maintain his power and carries out the torture of the hostages. She is much feared in Zahedan because she may be a *jinni* with unknown magical powers."

"What sort of magic does she possess?"

160

"She makes people do things. Some say she uses strange devices to help her. I know no more, so I cannot tell you more."

"Well, that's enough to start with."

"It sure is!" Alexis said almost joyously. "Captain, we need to see how this data meshes with everything we learned on the recon mission."

Hassan looked directly at Curt. "Captain Curt Carson, you are a strange man. I have noticed that you do not treat Lieutenant Morgan as Mahmud would treat a woman. Why? How do you keep your wives and children obedient to you?"

Curt laughed. "Hassan, in our land, we treat our wives and children kindly so they will obey out of respect for us," he replied with a smile, twisting the truth so that this boy from a different culture might understand it. Then he added, "I'm not married yet, Hassan. Nor is Lieutenant Morgan."

Hassan looked back and forth between the two of them. "That is good. It seemed impossible that you did not command her and she did not obey you. But if you are not married, it is more understandable."

"Oh, Lieutenant Morgan obeys me when necessary. We're both soldiers, and she's under my command."

Hassan shook his head. "I do not understand how you can have women in an army."

Alexis sensed an opening and pressed him with the question, "Then the Jehorkhims do not have women soldiers?"

Hassan shook his head. "No, but they have women who serve them. I have seen them in mock battle. Women bring them weapons, food, and water."

161

"What kind of weapons? Do they have any war machines?" Curt was vitally interested in discovering whether or not the Jehorkhims had hidden defenses such as SAM missles, antiaircraft weaponry, artillery, or tactical rockets. Certainly, the quick-look data from the recon mission had revealed nothing, but Curt was skeptical of such totally negative data, especially since he'd be putting himself and his people on the line when they went in for Operation Squire.

Hassan shrugged and shook his head. "They do not have war machines like yours. Some of them ride very fast horses, and a few ride camels. They have some weapons that look like your guns, but most Jehorkhim soldiers carry only the short bow and a scimitar."

When Hassan was silent for a while, Curt finally asked him, "What else can you tell me about the Jehorkhims?"

"What else is there to tell? I have told you everything I know. Jehorkhims are Jehorkhims. Soldiers are soldiers," the boy said with a shrug of his thin shoulders. "Do you want me to guide you in Zahedan, Captain Carson? I am your *khaddam*, your servant. I must do what you tell me."

Curt was surprised, but he answered, "Not this time, Hassan. You must stay here and do what people tell you to do. After we rescue the hostages held in Zahedan, we can decide what you want to do next."

Hassan started to say something but decided not to. As a slave he was forbidden to argue with his master.

Curt's efforts to elicit more military information from Hassan failed. The boy didn't know anything else, so couldn't answer Curt's questions about Jehorkhim troops. He had no idea where they were billeted, how they defended the hostages, how they were organized, or how they communicated in the field.

Georgie finally interrupted with an announcement. "Captain, Lieutenant, the premission operational briefing is scheduled in fifteen minutes. The colonel requests that you terminate the interrogation and join the rest of the Washington Greys."

"Did you get all the data recorded?" Curt asked.

"Yes, but regimental and divisional intelligence staffs say they don't have time to evaluate it before the mission."

"Orgasmic!" Curt snorted in disgust. "We bust our buns, I kill a man, and the staff stooges are too goddamned busy with their frigging paperwork to look at the data. Shit!"

"Colonel Hettrick requests that you introduce that factor during the briefing. But I'd suggest that you temper the language a little bit," Georgie went on.

"Yeah, I'll do that," Curt replied and stood up. "Hassan, stay here and do as you're told. Learn whatever you can. Maybe when I get back, we can figure out something so that we don't have to send you back to Zahedan."

"Yes, Captain Carson. I will do my best to learn everything I can."

After they'd left the sick bay, Alexis blurted out, "Captain! You can't be serious! If it isn't against the regs to own a slave, it's certainly not generally acceptable!"

"Lieutenant, I don't own him. He just thinks I do."

Alexis Morgan realized she might be treading on sensitive ground, so she reverted to formal military proto-col. "Begging your pardon, sir, but if you don't send Hassan back to Zahedan after this is over, are you sure you can keep him? Don't you think you'd better check it out with the regimental adjutant?"

"I will. But I don't want to send him back."

"What's so bad about that? It's the only life he knows."

"He may want to do something else. Besides, he helped us, and returning a favor is a matter of princi-ple, Alexis."

She grasped his arm and stopped walking. He stopped, too. "Curt, just between us, person to person, I think you've let your emotions take over. What are you going to do with a young boy?"

He had never seen Alexis like this, but he hadn't known her longer than the ten months she'd served with Carson's Companions. He'd always thought women soldiers were somewhat more emotional than men, but he was discovering that *this* woman apparently didn't allow emotions to cloud her rationality. He thought a moment about her question, gently removed her hand from his arm, and began to walk again. He finally told her, "I'd send him to school. I'd let him learn there's more in the world than scrabbling over the hillsides and trying to stay alive."

"I thought you were one of the most conservative people I'd ever met . . . except for my father! But you are going liberal and letting all your emotions hang out!"

"No, that's not it," he admitted. "Look, I have an opportunity with Hassan to correct something I think

164

is wrong: human slavery. Maybe I can correct the way slavery has screwed up a pretty good kid . . . and Hassan's a pretty good kid, wouldn't you say?"

"Yes, but can you change his past?"

"Maybe not, but I can probably do something about his future. And I'm not sure I could live with myself if I didn't *try*. I have to try, Alexis."

"You don't know anything about Hassan, do you?"

"Only what I've learned by talking with him. He's a bright kid who'll give it a big try."

"Do you remember what the ship's surgeon said? Hassan may not have the brains to make the change."

"Maybe not. But maybe we should give him the chance. We don't *know* what Hassan's potential is, Alexis."

"You can't buck the medical facts."

"Maybe. But who says they're complete? I'm going to ask Hassan what *he* wants."

"He may not know."

"I've got to try, Lieutenant."

"Very well, sir, but please don't let it distract you from our primary mission. A hostage dies every day we don't get in there and rescue them!"

Curt sighed and nodded. "I know. Let's get to the ops briefing. We're probably late already."

"They can't pull off the mission without Carson's Companions."

"Would you rather see Kelly's Killers get it instead?" He already knew the answer to that question, but Alexis Morgan shook her head anyway.

Compartment Delta-Two-Four was a planning room, a snake pit. It was a miniature version of the Lion's

Den with linkage chairs and terminals arranged around a central holo tank. Colonel Belinda Hettrick was there. So were Kelly's Killers, Walker's warriors, and Manny's Marauders. Lieutenant Jerry Allen arrived a moment after Curt and Alexis stepped in. There was little small talk save for personal greetings.

Hettrick took Curt to one side. "Dammit, Carson," she said, "why did you have to kill that Baluchi?"

"I didn't intend to, Colonel. I just wanted to cold-cock him," Curt explained.

"I know that. I've reviewed the data. But to hold Operation Squire together, I had to call in some favors and get General Carlisle to take it all the way to the top and make it an interservice matter."

Curt sighed. "Colonel, I'll place myself under personal arrest and confinement if you want—"

"The hell you will!" Hettrick was angry, but not totally with Curt Carson. "You're Number One company commander for Operation Squire. Even if you weren't, I wouldn't let these canoe jockeys assume jurisdiction over one of my people. Besides, Carson, it took a lot of maneuvering to allow the RI to get jurisdiction. I'll assign a Temporary Juridical Investigation Officer to the case after the mission, but I can't figure out a way to keep you out of it short of locking you up and throwing away the key."

"Thank you, Colonel, but don't be so sure. I've got new data from Hassan. We might have to change our plan."

"That's a tall order, Curt. Mission planning is already completed."

166

"By the book, I presume?" Curt's tone was only slightly derisive.

"I'll ignore that inference since I'm working under the same restraint as you," his colonel told him. "Sit down. We've got work to do."

After checking to ascertain that her First Battalion officers were present, Hettrick slipped into a linkage chair. "Quiet down and listen up," she told them. "This will be soft comm linkage. Divisional and Regimental staffs are still at Diamond Point. They've gone over the recon data, and we're ready to get on with the ops plan for the mission. Signal when you're in linkage."

It was obvious when linkage began. The image of General Victor Knox took form in another chair, his real body still at the Division's headquarters in Diamond Point.

"Ladies and gentlemen," General Knox began, pompously as usual, "time is of the essence because of the two Army R&D officers being held in Zahedan. Therefore, I must carry out this operation with only one battalion. It would require another day or two to put the full Washington Greys regiment into position. Since we're not facing an enemy strong in manpower or weaponry, we can go in with limited forces because of our superior firepower and low personal vulnerability."

Curt was having trouble believing what he was hearing.

"Therefore, the Washington Greys, will mount Operation Squire with emphasis on surprise and speed. The situation also requires a minor shift in procedure. This is the first time since the current all-warbot doctrine was established that soldiers will be directly and physically involved in action with warbots providing support, a procedure which differs from our normal tactical doctrine in which humans support and direct warbots. But, I'm an old soldier, as are many of you. I've led troops in personal combat without warbots, so I know it can be done. Carson's Companions will wear mobile linkage harnesses but will operate their warbots by voice commands as support elements. Ordnance has supplied the necessary equipment.

"Here's the basic operation plan for Operation Squire. Carson's Companions will be the lead element. They and their warbots will be airlifted into place on or in front of the building holding the hostages; using M-22 urban street battle warbots, they will penetrate the building and secure the hostages who will then be transported from the roof of the building to the aerodrome by multiple trips of the large aerodyne used by Carson's Companions. Manny's Marauders will create a diversion by attacking the western perimeter of the city, thus drawing off the Jehorkhim forces. Walker's Warriors will secure the Zahedan aerodrome with TS-10 strike aerodynes so that the Air Force can land jet transport aircraft which will proceed to airlift the hostages to Dhubai. Kelly's Killers will serve as a mobile reserve and covering element utilizing tactical strike aerodynes carrying M-22 bots for possible ground use. The battalion robot command post will be established in the same position used by Captain Carson during the scouting mission. This RCP will be under the command of Colonel Hettrick. All warbots with the exception of those worked by Carson's Companions will be controlled from the RCP."

The general paused, then went on, "Any questions?"

Curt signaled. "Yes, sir."

"Captain? Problems?"

"Lots of them, General. The whole damned plan is flawed. It isn't going to work."

CHAPTER TEN

"Did I understand you correctly, Captain Carson?" General Knox asked, a tone of disbelief in his voice.

"I'm sure you did, General. It appears that adequate consideration has not been given to the intelligence data my two sergeants and I worked so hard to obtain. On the basis of what we learned on our recon mission, I believe Operation Squire as presently planned has a very high probability of failure." Curt was way the hell out on a limb on this one, but he knew the Washington Greys would be in deep trouble if they went in using the operational plan General Knox had outlined.

"Captain," Knox shot back, his irritation evident. "Gee-two gave your data a quick look. They didn't find anything that was new or that would cause us to change Operation Squire."

"General, they're wrong," Curt Carson stated flatly.

"Wrong? How do you know? On what basis do you make this charge, Captain?" The voice of General Victor Knox was low and angry. This field officer had dared to challenge what might well be his last glorious mission, a hostage rescue strike like the one that had commenced his military career years ago. Knox had every confidence that he knew what he was doing. These young officers had never done this before; he had.

On the other hand, Curt had been to Zahedan. He knew precisely what was wrong with the mission plan. He had to lay its flaws out clearly and concisely because he might not get a second chance to do so. And, if he didn't succeed, Carson's Companions would have to try to carry out an impossible mission.

All officers and soldiers are sometimes forced to obey stupid orders during their careers, yet most of them figure out how to survive. Ten people would suffer if Operation Squire failed: General Knox, Colonel Hettrick, and Carson's Companions. Knox was nearing the end of his military career; he would simply be quietly retired. Colonel Hettrick's career would be dead-ended. Curt and Carson's Companions might end up like Captain Jason Petty and Petty's Patriots, Second Battalion, the Cottonbalers Regiment, 26th Division (RI).

Petty had followed stupid orders and obeyed bad rules of engagement during the Second Kasserine when he'd sent his armored warbots into the pass with his mobile command post not far behind.

At Second Kasserine, the rules called for visual identification of targets before shooting, but the Krik rebels remained hidden, and wiped out Petty's warbots with Soviet AT-66 *Deekeey Kaban* (Wild Boar) antitank weapons. Under extremely heavy fire and left without warbot protection, Petty could either fight it out personally—and his soldiers weren't adequately armed to do that—or withdraw his command post. In the heat of battle, with his troops' physical security in heavy jeop-

171

ardy, Petty forgot to communicate his action to the regimental command post. He was later cited for failing to call for reserves instead of withdrawing. But his real downfall in the minds of higher officers, who, some said, were looking for a scapegoat to save their own stars, was his withdrawal without communicating his actions. One of the outfits on his flank, Marshall's Maulers, was surrounded as a result and forced to surrender, bots and brainies alike. That had never happened before in robot warfare; it wasn't supposed to happen. Human warriors, according to doctrine, weren't supposed to expose themselves to battle risk. The negotiations went on for almost a year before the officers and NCOs of Marshall's Maulers were ransomed.

The ransom wasn't the big issue. The compromise of sensitive technical information was. It had cost the government a goodly sum to develop new linkage networks that would permit command posts to be sited at greater distances from the action and would utilize new and different warbot C-cubed-I (command, control, communications, and intelligence) linkage networks because the old ones had been immediately compromised when they were captured. No one admitted that Petty was under a cloud, and no official reprimand appeared in his permanent record, but the man had been passed over twice for promotion and had been assigned, with his company, to the Mideast PetroSecurity Force conducting endless pipeline patrols.

"I've been in Zahedan—at least, I've been there through the sensors of both recon ratbots and birdbots," Curt began, very conscious of the rapt attention directed at him by the general and his staff. "It is the usual Arab town, with so many nooks, crannies, byways, and alleyways that it's going to be extremely extremely difficult to fight against people who know the place."

"We've fought in Arab villages before," General Knox broke in. It was quite improper and impolite to interrupt another officer, but he was so shaken by Curt's unexpected critique that he simply forgot his manners. "Tunisia ... Yemen ... Sfax."

"Excuse me, General Knox, I wasn't there; that was before I graduated. But recalling the analysis and critique I took part in during my last year at the Point, in those actions the Arab towns were bypassed or besieged or flattened by artillery after evacuation warnings were given. The reports I read said the RI never fought in those rat mazes because of the difficulty of conducting robot warfare there. Am I correct, sir?"

"Ahem ... yes, but there's no other way to get to the hostages. We must go into Zahedan."

"Yes, sir, but we can't fight in Zahedan as we did against the Rotwaffe insurgents in the Münsterlagen operation, which was my first," Curt pointed out. "The streets in Zahedan are narrow, twisting ... a maze. And we'll have to fight in that environment against as many as fifteen hundred Jehorkhims who are suicidal Muslim fanatics."

"Where did you get those force numbers, Captain?" General Knox thought he'd found a soft spot in Curt's argument.

"From my interrogation of the Baluchi boy, Hassan. We brought him back from the recon mission." Curt knew he wasn't making brownie points with Knox, but on the other hand he wasn't about to suck up to any officer, general or field, who proposed or supported an operational plan that entailed an exceptionally high risk for warbot brainies.

Knox cleared his throat. "Captain, it's commonplace for people in these Muslim countries to exaggerate numbers, especially when it comes to troop strength. A hundred soldiers seem like a thousand. No one wants to believe he'd been defeated by anything less than an overwhelming force, so numbers are exaggerated. And you interrogated the boy, I understand, after you'd killed his father."

"That's another matter, General. But Hassan was cooperative."

"Nonsense!" General Knox snorted in derision. "What does a nomad boy know? Based on my own experience and a computer study of the communications capabilities and logistical support facilities of Zahedan—a pure and simple elementary Staff College study by the way—my own estimate indicates there are no more than four hundred Jehorkhims in and around Zahedan with a greatest-probability estimate of some two-hundred-fifty. Zahedan cannot support an additional military population of eight hundred troops, much less fifteen hundred. The agricultural base isn't there. Such a large military force couldn't be fed from local sources, and there's virtually no logistical input by rail or air, none by road. Therefore, the Jehorkhims must be self-sufficient. And they lack communications capability. A military organization cannot be controlled, cannot fight, without communications. Now, Captain, this plan is based on accepted procedures. It's by the book. You can't go wrong following the book."

"General, with all due respect," Curt retorted firmly, "I'm the one who's going to experiment with new doctrine by putting my body and those of my warbot brainies into that primitive hellhole to rescue those hostages. I'd rather overestimate enemy strength than underestimate it. The Jehorkhims may be armed only with the swords and bows I saw them carrying on the streets of Zahedan, but those can be extremely effective against other human beings in close quarters. Armored robots would probably survive attacks with swords and arrows, but my soldiers can't count on that. And I don't think Ordnance has any test data on what kind of swordplay it takes to disable a warbot."

"Captain Carson, what do you want?" It was Colonel Hettrick who broke into the confrontation, possibly to save Curt's butt.

"Pardon me, Colonel?"

"How would you do it? How would *you* organize this operation? What sort of forces would you want at your command? Captain, when an officer reacts to an operational plan as you have, I want to make damned sure something hasn't been overlooked. It's not a good idea to send a critical officer into action without hearing his ideas on how to approach it." Colonel Hettrick wanted to protect her troops. She knew full well that battles had been lost because generals hadn't paid any attention to feedback from officers in the line of fire. Overlord would have been a disaster for the Allies a hundred years ago if von Rundstedt and Hitler had heeded Rommel's assessment of the situation and had transferred troops from the Pas de Calais area to the Normandy beachheads.

"Colonel, we have only one shot at this," Carson pointed out. "If we miss, the Jehorkhims may slaughter the hostages, so we may not get a second try. And there are still too many unknowns. For example, from the point of view of a company commander, I'd like to have a better idea of how the Jehorkhims will fight. We've been told they're zealots and fanatics, but are they suicidal like some Islamic troops and irregulars have been in the past? Do they have any old Soviet AKMS assault rifles? Hand grenades? Antirobot and antitank rocket projectiles? Do they know anything about our warbot weaponry? Do they have *any* laser weapons, even the little portable countermeasures types that can be used to blind our sensors? We didn't see or detect any of these, but since we didn't attempt to exercise the Jehorkhim defenses, I don't have answers to these questions, and I haven't been given them by anyone."

Curt paused for a moment to marshal his facts. "Let's take a look at what the Jehorkhims have going for them and what we *may* run up against when we come head-to-head with them. They may have strength in numbers, which is a critical and timeless advantage in combat. They're in a defensive position, which has been recognized as being a key element of military strength since long before Clausewitz. We may or may not have surprise on our side; we were spotted by Iranian interceptor forces during recovery from the scouting mission, and Teheran may have reported that fact to the Imam. Furthermore, no one has yet mentioned the possibility that the Imam might *expect* us to mount a hostage-rescue mission which would negate the factor of surprise.

176

"And, finally, when we get down in that maze of streets, we're going to lose the advantage of mobility. It's the Jehorkhims' home turf, and only three of us have ever been on it. They know all the back alleys; we don't. The only things we'll have going for us are high-tech, communications, and vertical envelopment. They're not enough to ensure success.

"On that basis, if you really want to know what I'd do, Colonel, I wouldn't hit Zahedan with anything less than a brigade. And I'd hit fast. I'd keep the operational plan simple: Put aerodynes all over that town and shoot anything that moves in the streets." Curt suddenly realized that he was talking like Marty Kelly. Well, maybe Kelly would be an asset in this operation.

"I'd burn a hole through the roof of the building where the hostages are being held, then put people into that building behind assault robots through every possible opening, all at once. I'd lift the surviving hostages directly into a big transport aerodyne positioned over the building, then get out of there fast. None of this staging stuff. None of this diversion crap. I'd concentrate forces and do this as simply as possible. It's complicated enough."

There was silence in the pit for many seconds; then General Knox replied slowly and quietly, "Captain Carson, what you've suggested simply can't be done. The manpower isn't available on such short notice. I want to act fast. The Jehorkhims are already killing the hostages." The general didn't have to say more. It was apparent to every officer present that pressure from above must be growing. Every day, a videotape showing another hostage being tortured and murdered was re-

177

leased to the news media of the world. Some channels were now refusing to broadcast the tapes.

The general went on, "The operational plan is the best that can be put together, considering the manpower and time available. Operation Squire will be launched at sunset tonight. If you object, Captain Carson, I'll simply have to replace you."

Curt said no more. He'd blown his bolt. There was nothing more he could do.

General Knox then pulled an old and unsavory stunt, hoping to shame Curt in front of his troops. "However, do Captains Garcia, Walker, or Kelly have similar reservations?" The general looked directly at the other three company commanders.

There was no reaction. All company commanders sat mutely, even Marty Kelly. Curt couldn't figure out why the man hadn't asked for the Companions' task. Maybe Kelly also saw the potential for disaster. Or maybe Kelly was looking for glory by hauling Curt's company out of trouble.

Knox was visibly pleased. He hadn't expected Curt Carson to behave as he had. Insofar as the general was concerned, the young captain of Carson's Companions should have jumped at this chance to exhibit valor, courage, and combat capability because this operation would undoubtedly earn him a promotion, a decoration, a citation, and a reputation that would follow him throughout his military career.

Knox wondered whether or not robot warfare had really caused young, new officers like Carson to become cowards who didn't want to engage the enemy in combat. Knox was an old soldier who'd been through many campaigns. He'd survived the great military revolution that had been created by technology, but he was still a combat soldier. "The Last Grunt," some nameless officer had once called him one night at the Club. Victor Knox knew what it was like to be shot at, but now he was beginning to believe that soldiering had been irretrievably changed by military technology.

"Any questions?" Knox asked.

Colonel Hettrick responded. "General, is there no alternative to conducting the operation as briefed?"

"Under the circumstances, the answer is no."

"What are the consequences of a two-day postponement in order to get more units involved, sir?"

"The consequences? Two more hostages' lives. They've already killed four of them, including the one that will be murdered at sunset today. By going in tonight, we can hold it down to six deaths. A two-day postponement means at least eight."

Hettrick persisted, "General, what's the estimated casualty count of the present operation?"

"We expect to lose fourteen percent of our robots. That's a high casualty rate, but acceptable under most military guidelines."

"General, how many *human* deaths are estimated for my outfit?"

"Eh?"

"General, since this all boils down to saving human lives," Hettrick said, "suppose Operation Squire is delayed for two days. The delay will mean that two to three more hostages will be killed by the Jehorkhims. If we go in tonight, we may save them. But how many of our own RI people will die in the process? I know

179

from personal experience during a short leave in Manhattan—some punks thought two female cadets would be easy to mug—that someone will probably be hurt or killed. General, has the trade-off of hostages' lives for troopers' lives been considered?''

General Knox didn't answer at once. Then he said testily, "My staff hasn't considered that because they have no procedures for doing so. But I did, based on *my* experience in prewarbot days."

"Human deaths, General. How many?"

General Knox replied strongly. "Colonel, no program exists for calculating that, but if carried out as planned, I estimate that Operation Squire won't cause anyone to buy the farm."

Curt didn't understand the general's reference to a farm, but he suspected that it had something to do with a soldier's being able to buy a retirement farm with his disability insurance if he was "killed" in action and given a medical discharge. He didn't see that that had anything to do with actually being killed in hand-to-hand combat.

"No further questions? Very well. Carry out Operation Squire, and it will forevermore be a credit to the glory and valor of the RI. Dismissed!"

It hurt when Curt suddenly got to his feet and broke soft linkage. The sensors and effectors in the chair hadn't been attached to his skin, but the neural pain of breaking off so quickly caused him to stagger momentarily. Only his anger kept him from doing more than wincing. Motioning curtly to his two officers, he started to storm out of the briefing room.

But Marty Kelly stepped into his path. With a twisted

sneer on his face, Kelly taunted Curt, "Well, Captain Chicken, any time you and your troops get scared and want to save your asses, give Kelly's Killers a call!"

Curt suppressed the urge to hit him. "Easy for you to say, Kelly. You'll be sitting on your own ass back in the RCP, safe and happy. If I need anything in Zahedan, I'll need you without your robots. Willing to come in with us when it's really hot?"

Hettrick stepped between them. "Kelly, report to your company. Carson, I want to see you . . . now!"

"Won't do any good to chew me out, Colonel," Curt told her bluntly.

"Kelly, move it!" Hettrick snapped when the beefy company commander didn't react. "I'm not going to chew you out, Carson. You did what you felt was necessary." Pulling him off to one side, she looked up at him and asked, "Do you really think it's as risky as that?"

"Colonel, I wouldn't have laid myself out for slaughter otherwise."

She looked around quickly, then admitted, "Frankly, I agree with you and what you said. What can I do to help head off a possible disaster?"

"Forget all this complicated crap about diversions and such," Curt told her. "Secure the aerodrome, of course. But otherwise, put everything you can in the air over me. Shoot at anything that moves."

"I don't have many strike aircraft."

"Then get Manny's robots in through those streets as fast as possible and concentrate their firepower around where we are," Curt suggested. "This diversionary crap is a waste of time and firepower. We're

181

going to be outnumbered, and in the middle of a mess. Firepower will count."

"I'll do the best I can without screwing up the whole operation."

"Yes, Colonel, I know you will. Now, if you'll excuse me, I've got to detail-brief my company."

Curt collected his two lieutenants and had Sergeants Kester, Gerard, and Sampson paged. A few minutes later, all of Carson's Companions stood around the suit-up compartment assigned to them in the *McCain*.

"Henry, did the three of you monitor the briefing as usual?" Curt had given standing orders to his people to engage in discrete monitoring of any operational briefing involving the Companions. He didn't want to waste time repeating the details.

Master Sergeant Henry Kester nodded. "Yes, sir, we heard it all."

Curt looked slowly around the room "This mission is new, difficult, dangerous, and possibly lethal. If we're careful and if we use our bots properly, we might pull it off. But we could be killed. Really killed. Damned good chance of it. Any one got a problem with this?"

Alexis Morgan raised her chin proudly. "Captain, as your second in command, I've already evaluated the risks. I'll follow you."

He had expected that of Alexis Morgan. He looked at Lieutenant Allen.

"Captain, have the Companions ever started out on a mission anticipating failing?" the new lieutenant asked.

"No."

"Then we shouldn't begin now. When orders are

182

given, I carry them out. They taught me about duty, honor, country. This involves all three. What are your orders, sir?"

Again, the expected response.

"Master Sergeant Kester?"

The older man obviously had thought the situation over quite thoroughly. "When I joined the United States Army, no one ever promised me I wouldn't be killed. When we started working with the first war robots, they told me it would be less dangerous. I never believed 'em. I'd rather be killed, really killed, than suffer what the poor bastards go through now when they lose their last bot, go catatonic, and are written off as missing in action. I'll fight with you, Captain."

"So will I, Captain," Sergeant Gerard added quickly. "If I can't stand up to those Jehorkhim soldiers we scouted . . . well, I wouldn't be much of a platoon sergeant, would I?"

Curt knew Gerard would be scared stiff, but he would never reveal it. Platoon Sergeant Gerard was too proud a man to do that.

"Sergeant Sampson?"

Although Edith Sampson had shaved her head like all other warbot troopers, there was no disguising the temperament that had not been cut off like her flaming hair. Sampson didn't mind hand-to-hand combat; she'd decked Curt several times in training workouts, usually coming up off the mat when another would have called the match a loss. "I don't like the odds, but I don't have any choice. Give me two assault bots with Mod Four AI, and I'll cover you, Captain."

"Okay, but can all of you handle this?" Curt went

on. "Can we actually go in there and control our support bots at the same time we're trying to fight in person? We haven't had any practice with that." Curt knew that what he was asking of them was extremely difficult.

"Sampson's right," Alexis said. "With Mod Four artificial intelligence levels in our bots and verbal command protocols, we don't even need linkage. Warbots are still stupid in comparison to brainies. They do what they're told, they don't argue, and they report if anything goes wrong."

"Do we have any time for simulator practice?" Jerry Allen asked.

"Operation Squire departs at twenty hundred hours local," Curt reminded them. "Two hours from now. There isn't enough time to do much of anything. We'd better spend those two hours getting ready and checking equipment."

"Twenty hundred hours local time. That's about when they murder another hostage, isn't it?" Alexis observed.

"Just before supper," Nick added.

"Well, Captain," Master Sergeant Kester said quietly, "if we do our jobs right and don't screw up too badly, they won't kill any more hostages. This will be the last one."

"We'll be doing what we get paid for," Edith Sampson added.

Young or old, experienced or green, man or woman, Carson's Companions were soldiers Curt could be proud of. He looked carefully at each one of them. Tomorrow, they might not all be sitting around a table and indulg-

ing in gallows humor. Some of them might go home to
Diamond Point in a plastic bag.

"We won't screw up," he promised. "I'll buy the
drinks for everyone when we get out of Zahedan and
back to Diamond Point."

"We'll hold you to that promise, Captain," Henry
Kester said with a smile.

"You can tell the high brass that Carson's Companions are ready, Captain," Alexis told him.

"I'll do that," Curt promised. "In the meantime,
we've got two hours to put our act together. This mission is different from any we've been on before, so I
want you kitted-out for it. Each of you *will* carry a personal firearm just as Henry, Nick, and I did on the
recon mission. It should be a close-quarters people-stop-
per, not a battle rifle. Take all the ammo you can carry;
I don't want anyone running short. Also carry a non-
firearm personal weapon—a knife, if you know how to
use one. Other details: Wear body armor, especially
around your torso and on your head. Night vision
equipment: Wear i-r specs, and carry a pair of all-vision
binocs because it may get dark inside that building.
Also carry a hand flashlight, xenon beam, with emergency strobe and fresh battery. Pack a couple of kilos
of plasticex-B around your waist with six timed initiators, separated from the plasticex-B, just in case we
have to blow up something. Everyone in sunscreen makeup: nongreasy night color, face and hands, even though
I want you to wear gloves. Nick, have some Navy files
get us six heavy-duty bolt cutters. Each of us will carry
one. And everyone carries a Class Five MediKit.

"We haven't trained with this equipment. Some of

us haven't used it since basic training or since we left the Academy. You've got two hours to familiarize yourself with it again and a four-hour flight to catch up on anything you feel shaky about.

"But before you get all wound up," Curt concluded, "I want this unit fit and ready with a cool stool and a hot pot. Chow down, hit the latrine, check with the ship's padre if you want, and I'll see you on the flight deck for final equipment checks in thirty minutes. I've got to give the colonel the word that Carson's Companions are ready for anything. She's counting on us, and she won't let us down. So we'd better not let her down. Let's move out!"

CHAPTER ELEVEN

Carson's Companions lined up for departure inspection in front of their warbots in the aft flight hangar of the *McCain* which was still cruising five hundred meters beneath the surface of the Gulf of Oman. Curt hitched his CG-17 carbine over his shoulder and walked slowly in front of them, looking them over, trying to assess in his mind precisely how each of them would behave in the upcoming fracas.

Lieutenant Alexis Morgan looked at him dispassionately. Gone was her soft demeanor; she was in her fighting mode. The skin-tight body armor covered her young body. Dark camouflage makeup blurred the softness of her feminine features. A CZ-380 submachine carbine was slung across her chest. Alexis had been through several insurgency operations with Curt. He considered her a good officer. Although she performed with logical and precise coolness during a fight, she'd never been on a remote operation such as this, nor had she ever been in the thick of it physically—as all of them were likely to be before the sun set again. Curt didn't honestly know whether or not she'd hang together if things went to slime, but he'd count on her until and unless she reached a breaking point.

Jerry Allen, fresh out of West Point, carried a Department-issue Hornet machine pistol and a NYPD billy stick at his waist, wearing his personal battle gear with the familiarity of recent use. Academy training included personal physical combat without robots. Jerry had come through it recently, whereas such things were seven years in Curt's past. In spite of the fact that this was Jerry's first combat mission, and a very unusual one at that, Curt wouldn't have to worry about him. The young lieutenant might be inexperienced and unblooded, but he was as full of zeal and enthusiasm as Curt had been those years ago.

And the commanding officer of Carson's Companions didn't worry about Henry Kester, either. Curt briefly reflected, that perhaps one of the reasons why Carson's Companions had been selected as point unit for this operation was Kester's twenty-two years of service and his expertise in the forgotten art of personal combat. Henry was an old hand who'd crawled on his belly through the mud with live rounds snapping inches above him. He'd transitioned to robot warfare, not without some difficulty, because he was a soldier, would always be a soldier, and would therefore keep up with the march of military technology regardless of its speed or direction. The master sergeant's concession to the past was the small but potent MAC-10 .45-caliber submachine gun hanging from a strap around his neck. Henry Kester carried other personal weapons as well, but they were discreetly concealed.

Nick Gerard, in spite of his flamboyant nature and

impulsive reactions, was also a professional soldier, albeit not as experienced as Henry Kester. Carson knew he could be counted upon to be where he was supposed to be when he was supposed to be there doing what he was supposed to do. Gerard was a hundred percent reg, although his battle suit and body armor were perhaps too well fitted, an indication of the man's preoccupation with personal appearance. Curt didn't mind. That didn't compromise Gerard's combat integrity. He allowed his people a certain degree of choice, especially on this mission in which they were actually laying their own lives on the line.

But Curt Carson was concerned about Sergeant Edwina Sampson who was sudden, positive, and violent with her bots, and often impulsive. He would see to it that battle control over her bots was maintained when the company was in linkage, but he was worried about how she'd react in a face-to-face combat situation. She had no experience in personal combat so far as he knew, and that lack was reflected in her choice of a personal weapon: the Beretta nine-millimeter automatic pistol holstered at her waist.

"Sergeant," he told her, "you're the one who's got to live with your choice of a personal weapon, but I'd be happier if you'd chosen something other than a pistol."

"I can hit with it, Captain."

"Undoubtedly. But my personal weapons' instructor at the Academy once told me that in his entire combat career he'd seen only ten men killed by pistols . . . and nine were from accidental discharges."

She shook her helmeted head. "Not this trooper, Captain."

189

"Let's hope not." He'd accepted Edwina Sampson into the Companions on the recommendation of Henry Kester who'd known her father. But Curt now wondered if he'd actually agreed to accept her because of the continual pressure for gender equalization in the Army, and because of his own belief that it hadn't been ethical for armies of the last century to allow women to serve in posts where they could be killed while denying them the right to defend themselves. Curt had no doubt about Sampson's fighting capabilities, but he often wondered how they could be better directed.

The bots were powered-up and standing for inspection. With a slight toss of his head, Curt motioned for Master Sergeant Kester to accompany him.

Twelve of the warbots were M-22 stair-climber and rubble-runner assault bots. None of these resembled human beings. Technology required that they be simpler and much more specialized. Each M-22 warbot had a pair of continuous treads, but also sported six robust "feet" that could be extended from its barrel-like body for climbing stairs and rubble piles, where treads might not suffice. The M-22s looked like elongated oil drums, and were about the height of human beings; but they had no heads. Sensors were arranged around the tops of the drums, providing redundancy in case one or more sets were put out of action. Their rounded shapes indicated heavy, layered armor, once called "Chobham" but later refined to multilayered, extremely tough, composite plastic separated by layers of velocity-attenuating closed-pore foam. Most of their bulk was due to the power packs and quick-charge units that allowed them to back up to aerodynes or other power sources and get fast pick-ups.

The "brains" of each warbot, an AI computer, would fit easily into the palm of a technician's hand, and it was located deep inside the barrel-like bot.

The "arms" and "hands" could be retracted into the armored bodies, and one of the "arms" was nothing more than an antipersonnel fletchette gun. None of the warbots used on this mission carried satellite relay equipment; General Knox had vetoed that because it was new and he didn't want it to fall into Jehorkhim hands. Curt doubted that the Jehorkhims could keep such advanced electronic devices working, much less duplicate them, but an order was an order.

"All these bots have Mod Four AI installed?" Curt asked.

"Yes, sir. And verbal command with remote radio link enabled. As you instructed, we disabled the direct human-to-warbot linkage capability but didn't remove those modules because of time constraints. They'll operate on voice commands but we can direct-link with them if we have to."

"What are those bots in the second rank?"

Kester smiled. "Something Sergeant Sampson dreamed up while you and I were on recon," he explained. "Lieutenant Morgan had them flown out from Diamond Point with the rest of the Companions. We worked on them most of the day. Uh, slight nonregulation modification, Captain, but under the circumstances I felt it was justified."

"What did you do to them?"

"Well, the six of us can't carry a hundred hostages

191

out of that building for pickup, not if we're fighting off the Jehorkhims. So Sampson—she's a whiz at bot mods, Captain, and we didn't know it—she figured out how to modify and reprogram an ambulance litterbot to haul two people at a time up to where we'll airlift them."

Curt inspected the bots. They looked like ordinary two-level hospital gurneys that could be folded into back-to-back wheelchairs on a single stair-climbing chassis with rotating treads. It paid to have good people, he decided.

There was no need to inspect or exercise the bots; Curt knew they'd be in top condition. And there was no need to discuss how they'd be deployed. Since they had the most advanced Mod Four artificial intelligence multiprocessors installed, these bots would accept orders, carry them out, or modify them according to the conditions; and they would report compliance, inability to comply, or trouble. Curt knew he'd have to check up on them occasionally, but they were far more automatic than most commercial bots.

The personnel and warbot inspection finished, Curt looked up at the disk-shaped aerodyne above them. "Sergeant," he said to Henry Kester, "what happened to the inlet screens and filters?"

"The Navy types removed them under instructions from General Knox," the master sergeant reported with just a touch of resentment in his voice.

Curt knew that General Knox was a micromanager who liked to use communications to direct tactical operations down to the platoon level. He was counting on Colonel Hettrick to counter that, but he couldn't do anything about the general's modification of the aerodyne. "We're going into a semidesert environment. We should have screens on those engine inlets," he observed.

"The Navy mechanics say the aerodyne is overgrossed with the six of us and the warbots," Kester explained. "The engines can't pull enough power with the screens cutting down the inlet flow. I guess the general saw some computer analysis that showed the removal of the inlet screens would increase mass flow and thrust enough to do the job. So the inlet screens were removed."

"I'm not sure I approve of that," Curt stated.

"I questioned it, too, Captain. I was told that the general had approved the modification. I couldn't argue with that."

Nor could Curt. He didn't think the removal wise, but he was forced to give the general the benefit of the doubt, make one of the compromises entailed in conducting an emergency operation.

Strangely, in spite of that, Curt felt reasonably confident about the operation now. His confidence might merely be premission hype. How much of it was real, how much subjective? There was no way he could sort that out, nor did he want to. He only wanted to go into Zahedan, do the job, and get out.

Aboard the aerodyne, which Curt had christened with the code name Trajan after the famous Roman military commander and emperor, they settled in while the autopilot brought the craft up to the ready for engine start.

The operational plan called for Carson's Companions and their warbots to use an armored transport aerodyne stripped of everything except the Mod 3 AI autopilot which required human monitoring. The Killers, the Warriors, and the Marauders would come in on ten additional aerodynes to emplace the RCP, put the robots around Zahedan, and run air cover and recovery. The Robot Command Post would be sited on the slopes of Kuh-e-Taftan in one aerodyne, code name Napoleon, from which the warbot brainies would operate their bots in Zahedan.

The other three companies and the regimental staff will be operating under normal doctrine, Curt thought glumly, but the Companions are the sacrificial sheep who have to put their bodies on the line.

He decided he'd better review his standing orders, his "contract" with his troops. "Lieutenant Morgan and Sergeant Kester," he was speaking to the soot-smeared woman riding behind him and to the old soldier in the copilot's seat beside him, "let me repeat the contingency plans. Lieutenant Morgan is second in command, with Sergeant Kester as third in command. Lieutenant Allen, I'm not slighting you; you haven't been with us long enough, and Sergeant Kester is far more familiar with our operating techniques than you are at this time."

"Yes, sir. No problem, sir. I'm the new kid in town," Allen replied quietly.

"Good man! Additional order: the loss of two Companions is cause for the initiation of a retrograde operation. In short, if two Companions are put out of action for any reason whatsoever, whoever is in command at that moment will get the Companions out of

194

there immediately regardless of the hostages' situation. Understood?"

Kester merely nodded assent.

"Captain, if command falls on my shoulders, I won't leave any Companion there," Alexis Morgan stated flatly. "Alive or dead, six Companions will come out of Zahedan!"

"Lieutenant, you will follow the standing orders," Curt snapped, his precombat tension beginning to mount. "I will not have the company jeopardized by trying to get dead bodies out! If I catch it, I'd rather you got a live hostage out of there instead of my useless body. Recovering a dead Companion could cause another Companion to get killed. It's just plain not worth it! Understand?"

"Yes, sir," Alexis Morgan replied glumly.

The fact that a soldier might actually be physically killed was a new and sobering consideration, one that the RI had not had to think about for decades. Curt reflected that the whole war game had changed.

"Okay, I'm going into linkage with Trajan now," Curt remarked. He felt the ship's computer respond to his command as he began to make the aerodyne an extension of himself. But his linkage procedure was interrupted with startling suddenness. Even through the aerodyne's hull, the grating *whoop-whoop-whoop* of the emergency alarm could be heard.

Fire reported on the flight deck, Trajan said unemotionally.

The aerodyne was suddenly engulfed by water.

Fire control has been triggered, Trajan reported.

Sheets of water cascaded down on the transparent

canopy of the aerodyne, and ran off in rivers from the upper surface of the craft. Curt remembered something. *Doesn't the fire suppression system on a submarine use salt water?*

Affirmative.

As suddenly as the deluge had begun, it stopped. The flight-deck bull horn was heard, "Hear this! Hear this! Fire emergency on aft flight deck is concluded! False alarm! False alarm!"

Curt still wasn't in total linkage. He looked around at Trajan's exterior surfaces in the dim red light. Sea water was everywhere. It ran off the aerodyne's lift surfaces, dripped from every protrusion on the aircraft's saucer-shaped hull. It might also have run in through the many openings in the hull. This bothered Curt. He knew that next to acid, nothing is quite as corrosive as sea water. *Trajan, did you take any sea water aboard during the deluge?*

A few leaks here and there, Captain. I'm not fully sealed as a Navy aerodyne would be. I was not designed to operate in a maritime environment. But I've checked all my systems and there seems to be no problems at this time. All systems are go.

Kester looked around and noticed drops of water falling from the bottom edge of the main control panel. He shook his head. "Man, I hope so!" he said. He wasn't in total linkage yet, either.

Curt didn't want to depend on hope. "Sergeant, don't trust any machine that tests itself and reports it's okay, especially after an accident that could have damaged its brains. Get into linkage with the aerodyne.

196

Punch up the documentation and let's run the manual check list. I'm going to test every critical item myself."

He got only a short way through the multipage document that scrolled up on the aerodyne's control panel screen, for the *McCain* arose from the depths and the huge hangar-deck doors opened above them. Even over the Gulf of Oman, the air was so clear that millions of stars could be seen.

Stand by to launch aerodynes, came the call from the *McCain*'s Air Ops computer.

"Negative! Negative!" Curt yelled both aloud and through the aerodyne's communications system. "We haven't finished running the check list!"

A human voice, that of the *McCain*'s Air Ops Officer, came back, "Major Carson, we can remain on the surface here only long enough to launch the Operation Squire aerodynes. Are you aborting, sir?"

"No, but I want to check things myself after that bath!"

"Does the autopilot self-check, sir?"

"Affirmative! But I don't trust it!"

"Then I must ask you to launch *now* or to abort."

"Dammit, we're depending too much on computers! I want to check everything before we commit to launch!" Curt replied savagely. "I may have to put this thing in the drink if something isn't working."

"We'll stand by to pick you up if you do."

That stupid sonofabitch wouldn't get his butt wet, and he wouldn't have to claw his way out of a sinking aerodyne. Curt controlled his anger. Well, maybe Trajan's self-check was okay. He hoped so because he'd

197

have to trust it this time. *Trajan, spool-up and prepare for lift,* Curt ordered.

Roger, Captain. Spooling up. Immediately, the blowers began to spin-up with an ascending whine. A white vapor, probably steam, gushed out of one lift slot, then dissipated.

Prelift checks complete. Turbine seven shows ninety-five percent power. All other systems are within operational tolerances, the autopilot reported.

Is your total power within specs and adequate for the mission?

Affirmative.

Report ready for lift.

Roger. Ready for lift.

They never heard the digital lift-off command that passed from AI computer to AI computer. With a vertical surge and an increased turbine whine, the aerodyne lifted off the exposed deck of the *McCain.* Almost as quickly as deck contact was broken, Trajan slewed to the course heading, moved about a hundred meters from the carrier sub, and hovered at an altitude of ten meters, waiting for the other aerodynes of Operation Squire to formate around it.

Ten other aerodynes could dimly be seen through the darkness as they took positions in the air. There was no radio contact between them save for the brief forty-millisecond burst of digitized data from the command center aerodyne, Napoleon, to the other autopilots. Together, the ships took up the course heading and moved off to the north, coming to cruise speed with Napoleon in the center of the formation. Each autopilot maintained its position by means of tight-beam laser ranging.

As the coast of Baluchistan showed up ahead on the passive lidar display, Trajan spoke, *Warrior Three reports hydraulic problems. Warrior Three is aborting. Warrior Three is unable to maintain flight. Warrior Three is ditching into the ocean.*

Curt quickly reviewed the mission rules. The loss of one of the Warrior aerodynes meant one less ship would be available for securing the Zahedan aerodrome, but the operation was still a go. The order came from Colonel Hettrick in Napoleon, *Killer Boss, detach an assault aerodyne to Warrior Boss.* She'd moved one of the reserves from Kelly's control to Edith Walker's command.

Even though the radio transmissions were at superhigh frequency and microseconds in length because of digital coding and compression, Curt knew that radio silence had been broken. Stealthed or not, Operation Squire had momentarily revealed its presence in the sky. The formation was a radar and infrared black hole, a volume of airspace that would return no signal, exhibit no signature. This anomaly could be recognized by advanced detection systems. Curt knew that the Iranians and the Pakistanis had such things, but he hoped they weren't working. Much of the military equipment in the Middle East wasn't. Flying up the border as they were, the ten ships might be vulnerable to attack from either nation's air-defense forces. The two countries did not get along, although both were Islamic states. They were squabbling about who owned Baluchistan. As a result, Curt knew from his previous recon mission, air defenses were emplaced about a hundred kilometers behind the border.

Alert. Alert. Trajan barked. *Eight targets, nine o'clock high, closing at Mach two. Signatures indicate Iranian Super Rafael interceptors.* The autopilot was simply vocalizing the microsecond data burst from Napoleon.

Curt's palms began to sweat. The ten-ship formation was a bigger and juicier target than the two recon aerodynes had been. Obviously, the Iranians had been alerted by Curt's previous flight and were ready to pick up Operation Squire as it came in.

Had the Iranians also notified the Jehorkhims in Zahedan?

If so, they were heading for a warm welcome.

And one aerodyne was down and out already! Curt had the sinking feeling that they were dashing madly into a monumental screwup. He watched the diplay Trajan picked up on its passive lidar sensors and displayed on the panel screen.

We're in for a fight, Curt thought.

Have aerodynes ever tangled with Super Rafaels? Alexis asked.

In the Tunisian operation, yes. It was a stand-off. No clear winner. Not like it was when the old Harrier jumpjets first tangled with supersonic interceptors over the Falklands.

Wonderful, Alexis responded tersely.

Sitting ducks. It was Kester's observation.

Not yet. Curt indicated new targets on the screen.

Alert. Alert. Ten targets, two o'clock, same altitude,

200

converging course. Signature analysis indicates Pakistani Soviet-built Kadishev Ka-21 air-defense aerodynes.

Any radio communication between them yet?

No, but they undoubtedly see one another. I am receiving their radar sensing bursts and replies. They are looking at each other right now.

Are they going after us or each other?

That cannot be determined at this time. It was a flat reply from the AI autopilot. *The Iranian formation has slowed and come to a parallel course with us. So have the Pakistanis.*

Are we countermeasuring?

Only stealth at this time. No active countermeasures in use.

Curt didn't want to break radio silence, so he sat there with sweaty palms and waited.

He tried to work out the military situation and options. If they'd been spotted—why else would both air-defense forces have scrambled?—would the information be passed along to Zahedan? Or had the Paskistanis scrambled on the Iranians who had originally scrambled on unambiguous black-hole radar returns from Operation Squire inbound over the Gulf? Had the Iranians lost the ten aerodynes in increased ground clutter once the Operation Squire force was over the coast?

He commanded a view around Trajan, slowly sweeping the enhanced-vision night sensors horizontally.

And he saw what the Iranians might have spotted. He commanded a switch to infrared sensors, and looked again to confirm what he'd seen in the dim starlight.

One aerodyne at ten meters didn't have enough downwash to stir up any dirt and sand, but ten aerodynes blasting across the countryside in close formation at ten meters blew up a rooster tail of sand and dirt behind them, marking their course precisely and locating them within meters. Furthermore, the dirt and sand couldn't be stealthed; it was glaringly evident on even the most primitive radar screens.

Curt disobeyed orders and broke radio silence. *Napoleon, this is Trajan. We're kicking up a dust trail. Suggest bounding up to thirty meters at once.*

There was no reply, but the whole formation suddenly surged upward.

The dust trail diminished and then disappeared.

Curt checked the display. The two air-defense squadrons were no longer following. Either they'd lost track of the formation or they were now more interested in each other. At any rate they were standing off and circling on opposite sides of the border.

They've lost us, Alexis remarked, relief in her voice.

Yeah, but will we have a reception committee in Zahedan? Curt asked rhetorically. He told his Companions, *We must be prepared to fight our way in. If we take incoming on the way down to the street, we'll back off and let the Warriors come in for a fire sweep.*

Seventy-five kilometers south of Zahedan, before they'd drawn abreast of Mirjaveh, the formation broke apart on command and by design. Napoleon headed for the north ridge of Kuh-e-Taftan while the three ships of Manny's Marauders spread out in a skirmish line ahead of Trajan. The three aerodynes left with Walker's Warriors cutting right to skirt the east side of Zahedan and get to the aerodrome. Somewhere in the dark predawn sky, a transport aircraft was winging its way in from the Air Force base in Yemen, equipped to evac the hostages from the Zahedan aerodrome once Walker's Warriors had secured it.

Curt and Henry Kester came out of their "soft" or partial linkage with Trajan, unplugged their mobile linkage harnesses, and took over verbal and manual control of the saucer-shaped aerodyne.

So far, so good, Curt thought. If everything went right, and if they hadn't been reported to the Imam, they might pull this one off.

"Alert. Alert," Trajan advised in verbal mode. "Shutting down turbine seven. It's running a high lubricant temperature and out-of-tolerance upper-shaft bearing temperature."

"Can you hold altitude?" Curt suddenly saw them having to fight their way in Zahedan afoot, which wouldn't work. The mission rules said that if Trajan quit, the operation was scrubbed.

"I've burned off several hundred kilograms of fuel, so I can hover in ground effect if I use one-oh-three-percent power on the remaining turbines. I have advised Napoleon. I have received no change of plan."

"If you do, let me know at once."

"Roger."

The plan called for Manny's Marauders to dump their ground-assault bots on the west side of town as the first diversion, then for Walker's Warriors to hit the aerodrome. Until the Marauders were on the ground with their warbots and the Warriors were engaged at the aerodrome, Curt had to keep Trajan in hover outside the town. As the first light of dawn broke over Zahedan, Curt saw that the operation was moving according to schedule. There was no longer any necessity to maintain communications silence, and the comm channels suddenly came alive with combat chatter which the Companions, being out of linkage, heard as computer-transformed audio data.

"We're setting down to drop our bots," Captain Manny Garcia's voice announced. "Hold it! Where'd they come from? Couple hundred Jehorkhims camped out in tents! Napoleon, I need help! Can you send Kelly in to cover me while I'm putting bots on the ground? I can't fight my aerodynes and my bots at the same time."

"Are you picking up fire?" Hettrick's voice asked.

"Just started. Our downwash woke them up. By God, they've got firearms! Thought they had only swords and bows!"

"Killer Boss, get in there and conduct a fire suppression strike," Hettrick ordered.

"Take me a few minutes to get there," Marty Kelly told her.

"Then expedite!"

"Moving! Get the Marauders out of the way! Have them move somewhere and hold so we don't hit 'em!"

"We're shifting out of rifle range," Manny Garcia replied. "Okay, we're clear."

"Trajan, hold position until the Killers do their job."

Napoleon, I want to go in *now!*" Curt snapped. "They're still confused down there."

"Negative! Direct order from Knox! Hold and hover!"

Curt detected the frustration in Hettrick's voice. General Victor Knox was trying to micromanage the battle from the safety of Diamond Point halfway around the world. He put Trajan into hover mode and held position. "Roger," Curt replied sourly, and remarked to Alexis and Kester, "Troops, be prepared for this whole operation to turn into slime very quickly. Things are beginning to break down too early, and we're short-handed by one 'dyne."

"Napoleon, this is Warrior Boss! We're on the aerodrome. No resistance. But the main runway has a herd of cows on it!"

"Get airborne and stampede them off," Hettrick ordered.

"We'll kill a few."

"So I'll buy the steaks when we get back."

"We gotta get them off the runway first. Got no way to haul a dead carcass out of the way of the transport plane . . ."

Trajan's autopilot suddenly reported, "Trouble. I can't hold in hover. I'm fourteen percent shy of power. I'm going to have to keep moving to maintain some dynamic lift by air speed."

"Dump fuel!" Curt ordered.

The robot autopilot exercised the primitive judgment qualities built into its artificial intelligence processors. "If I dump any fuel at all to lighten load, I can't make it back to the *McCain*. Best course of action is to get down in ground effect and cut wide circles."

"Can you get back out of ground effect again?"

"Not with my present load and available power."

Curt made the critical decision. He took manual control of the aerodyne, headed it toward the center of Zahedan, and brought it to forward cruise speed. Then he called Hettrick, "Napoleon, this is Trajan Boss. We can't hold. We're going in."

"Negative, negative!" Hettrick's voice replied. "The orders are to hold position."

"Combat commander's prerogative: I'm overriding orders and going in." Curt turned to his Companions. "Stand by to debark as quickly as we get in there."

"We're ready, Captain," Alexis told him.

"Hot to trot, sir!" was Jerry Allen's comment. He sounded a bit shaky.

Curt heard the sound of a submachine-gun bolt being pulled.

They were over the outskirts of Zahedan.

The streets were swarming with people. Some were heading toward the mosque for early morning prayers. Others were spreading prayer rugs on the ground.

Curt had no trouble seeing the two-story building in which the hostages were being held. He steered toward it, pushing Trajan to maximum forward speed, aware that he might be overstressing the engines. Trajan cleared the low, flat roofs by only meters.

"I'm losing turbines three and four. Overheating from overboost. Turbine two is losing flow rate," Trajan reported tonelessly.

"Hang in there," Curt told Trajan as well as his Companions. "I think we can make it."

However, as the flat roof of the building that held the hostages' loomed in front of them, Kester reported, "Rifle fire!"

A slug slammed upward through the thin shell of the aerodyne in front of the windshield canopy. Curt felt other rounds hit the craft, which was a huge target in the sky.

"Morgan! Allen! Kester! Gerard! Open the bottom hatches! Try to give us fire support from your personal weapons as we go down!" Curt ordered.

"Weren't suppose to have firearms," Gerard muttered.

"Or tents in the field or cows on the runway," Kester told him as he crawled out of the copilot's seat.

"Trajan Boss, this is Trajan! Turbines three and four are gone. Shutting them down."

It's going to slime! Curt thought viciously. "Abort! Abort! Trajan, get out of here!"

"Unable! I cannot maintain altitude or even climb."

Fighting furiously to remain in the air, Curt tried to bring the heavy aerodyne slowly on to the roof.

He was only partly successful. Trajan had marginal lift capability left. The landing was hard.

As one of the landing pads touched the roof, the weight of the overloaded aerodyne broke through, and with a ripping, grinding sound, the craft came to rest, one landing pad jammed through rafters and beams, the whole ship tilted at a crazy angle.

CHAPTER TWELVE

Rifle slugs hit the aerodyne, the sounds peppery and sharp, intermingled with brisant bursts of return fire from the Companions.

"Bots out on the roof! Cover us!" Curt ordered, using his helmet communication pack to broadcast on the tactical radio channel to his brainies and warbots. He was a little shaky; he hadn't actually been under fire since he'd been at West Point. So he used a trick that Henry Kester had taught him; he dropped his voice an octave to a near growl.

He didn't expect confirmation from his bots. Bots programmed for nonlinked independent action didn't normally report receipt of or compliance with orders because they were expected to do what they were told. If any of their AI systems didn't understand the order or if they detected a conflict in their programming, they asked for clarification.

Sensing the stress in Curt's voice, Henry Kester gave him a terse but reassuring reply, "They're moving!"

Curt knew he had to move fast, too. He didn't know how long it would take for the Jehorkhims to realize what was going on and to begin to slaughter the hostages in the basement.

But he also had to worry about getting out of there once the mission had been completed. He turned his attention to the ship. "Trajan, can you lift off this roof? Can you get us out of here?"

"Negative. Four of my turbines are out of commission. If two of the turbines aren't badly damaged, once they've cooled off, I might be able to lift with fifty-percent load."

"Not good enough! Napoleon, this is Trajan Boss!" Curt snapped, calling Hettrick, "plan for contingency evacuation of hostages and Companions from this rooftop."

"Get the hostages to the roof," Hettrick replied. "We'll organize an aerodyne lift out to the aerodrome once the battle situation stabilizes and we gain control of the situation."

Which means, Curt thought, that the mission is going from bad to very bad.

They might not get out of Zahedan. But working out those details wasn't his job; that was why Hettrick wore silver eagles. Or, in this case, why Knox rated the star on his shoulder, if the general was really micromanaging this mess.

Curt got busy on his end of the mission.

Six of the M-22 assault bots unloaded. They swept the roof with fletchette fire, mowing down the four Jehorkhim riflemen who'd been standing guard at its corners. Six more assault bots were out now, and heading for the stairway that ran down the side of the building.

The building on which they'd landed was taller than

the one-story structures around it except for the two-story government building a short distance away. "Bots Alpha and Bravo, defend the roof. Keep that other two-story building under surveillance. Don't let anyone get onto the roof or the top floor and place us this roof under fire," Curt snapped out the orders. "All other assault bots, go down the stairs. Shoot any person who attacks you. Check all rooms on the floor below. Report human occupants of these rooms to me, verbally, as you find them. Move! We're behind you. Transport bots, follow us."

The assault bots didn't reply but began to do what they were told.

Thinking that perhaps he might be able to use a dead Jehorkhim's firearm, Curt stepped over the prostrate form of a sentry and picked up an old Soviet-made AKMS. This particular "ultimate insurgency and assault rifle" had seen better days. Curt hoisted it, aimed it at the nearby government building, and squeezed the trigger. It fired two rounds before it jammed—and there was no way to quickly clear the jam. With a modicum of maintenance and a minimum of care, these Soviet Kalashnikov rifles were durable and reliable, but this one had received neither. Curt didn't want to rely on it, not even as a backup weapon. He unslung his Winchester CG-17 carbine, slipped a clip of fifty caseless rounds into it, cocked it, and began to follow the six bots down the outside stairway, calling to his brainies, "Follow me!"

A Jehorkhim soldier, scimitar in hand, tried to come up the stairs as the first bot started down. A bot-launched fletchette caught him in the chest as he drew

210

back his arm to swing that curved piece of steel. Blood gushed from the wound as the white-turbaned man pitched over the solid balustrade and fell to the street below.

Curt had not been under fire since those early days at West Point when his instructors had made him experience it as part of his military education, and he'd never expected to be in that situation again. He was more scared than he had ever been in robot combat, but there was no time to think about it. And he wasn't alone. Adrenalin was pumping hard through all of the Companions. Combat in which people were actually trying to kill them was a new experience, except for Henry Kester. It gave them an accelerated high, and made the stink of battle even more pronounced.

Curt knew the sensations he was experiencing were very different from those fed to him by Georgie as he worked warbots through linkage. And a tiny part of his mind kept reminding him that if he got killed in action this time, it wasn't just a bot that would get greased. That made a difference. Judging by the intensity of the other five Companions, they also were very aware of it.

Step by step, they descended the stairs, personal weapons at the ready, not knowing when they might meet a deadly situation. Kester kept his MAC-10 pointed down into the street below. When he squeezed off a three-shot burst at a Jehorkhim—easy to recognize because of their bright white turban—who poked his head out of a doorway, the brisant report of the .45 caliber submachine gun made Alexis jump. "Easy, Lieutenant," Nick Gerard advised.

"It's loud."

211

"Yeah. Always is."

Splat! Pop! A rifle round hit the building above their heads, followed by the crack of its shock wave. Shards of soft mortar and dust rained down on them. Someone in the other government building had ranged them. They instinctively ducked behind the solid balustrade. Jerry Allen was white-faced but grim. Alexis was shaking slightly.

Crouched behind the balustrade Curt brought his CG-17 into firing position. He waited until he saw the telltale flash of an AKMS at a window. Then he squeezed off a three-round burst. It ripped out of the carbine at 6,000 rounds per second, so fast that the burst sounded like one report. His aim was good. He'd sighted-in that CG-17 properly. No more rifle fire would come from there.

"And that, Sampson," Curt remarked to the sergeant carrying the Beretta, "is why I don't like toy pistols. Move out, everyone, before another sniper takes over there."

The six of them and the assault bots got through the door onto the second floor, not a moment too soon. A hail of steel-tipped arrows rattled against the outer wall and came through the opening to scatter across the floor.

The assault bots were moving rapidly down the long hallway toward the staircase at the center of the building, checking into each room as they passed it. The offices were empty.

As the bots went down the main staircase to the ground floor, there was scattered firing from below. They immediately returned it. Then came silence. When

Curt and the troops got to the head of the stairs, two bots were guarding the front entrance, two were at the head of the stairway to the basement, and two more were heading down that stairway.

Curt recognized the location. He'd "been there before," in linkage with the recon ratbot.

Screams and shouts suddenly came from the stairway to the basement. Curt stuck his head over the railing and managed a quick look.

The heavy door at the bottom of the stairs was open, and panicked hostages, some of them in pretty bad shape, were being pushed up the stairway by those behind them.

"Don't shoot!" Curt yelled at his warbots. "Come back up the stairs! Make way for those people!"

It was an old trick. The Mongol hordes had used it centuries ago. There had been no "rules of war" then, and the ruthless Mongols had driven captured hostages ahead of them when assaulting a town or moving against an army in a strongly defended position. The reluctance of the opposing soldiers to shoot at their own people allowed the Mongols to operate behind a screen and to outmaneuver the enemy. Occasionally, the Mongol light cavalry would charge right through the hostages, trampling them while secure in the knowledge that they probably wouldn't be fired upon by the archers and pilum throwers of the enemy.

But Curt knew that trick, and he knew how to counter it. "Come on! Come on!" he yelled at the screaming, shoving hostages. "We're American Robot Infantry! Come on! Move!"

The countering tactic involved getting as many hos-

213

tages as possible out of that basement and under the protection of the Companions. By absorbing the hostage mob into them, the Companions could rescue them and expose their Jehorkhim captors to fire.

Coming up the stairs were males and females of all ages. They were shocked, hurt, and dazed, but they recognized the sand-and-spinach camouflage uniforms and the distinctive RI battle helmets.

Perhaps thirty of the hostages made it before Henry Kester suddenly opened fire with that hand cannon of his. The .45-caliber slugs he aimed at the open basement door behind them found at least two targets wearing white turbans.

Alexis Morgan grimaced as one of those slugs tore a man's head off and drove his decapitated body backward.

The second Jehorkhim suddenly had a gushing red hole where his chest had been.

All of Carson's Companions were quickly initiated into the bloody world of personal combat, which was unlike robot warfare where machines simply destroyed other machines.

Below, the heavy door slammed, shutting off the flow of panicky hostages. But about thirty had streamed up the stairway, some carrying others.

Curt reached out and grasped one of the hostages, a man of about his own age. He was dirty, dry-lipped, and haggard but he didn't look as dazed as some of the others. "I'm Captain Curt Carson, U. S. Army Robot Infantry. How many more hostages and Jehorkhims are in the basement?"

The man was obviously nearly out of control. "Thank

God! Oh, thank God you've come! There must be another hundred down there. And a dozen of those sadistic devils! Listen, will you kill those bastards for me? Will you? I had to watch them torture and kill my wife!"

"I'll take care of it. Now save yourself. Go up the stairs to the roof." Curt clapped the man gently on the shoulder and gave him a gentle push in the proper direction. He then turned to Alexis. "We've got some of them, at least! Thirty people they won't torture! Bring the transport bots down. You're in charge of hostage evac. Get these people up to the roof. Have the transport bots take them up there if necessary."

"How are we going to get them off the roof and out to the aerodrome?" Lieutenant Morgan wanted to know. The operational plan had gone to worms. Originally, the hostages were to be loaded into Trajan, twenty at a time, and lifted out to the aerodrome. Now, Trajan couldn't lift.

And the mess could be blamed on a monumental screwup. Curt knew he should have aborted when Trajan had gotten soaked with sea water on the *McCain*. But the disaster was also the fault of political pressure, numerous failures in intelligence analysis and operational planning, and an intolerable amount of micromanagement by General Knox.

Curt took no pride in the knowledge that he'd been right and General Victor Knox had been wrong. It seemed that nothing had gone right with Operation Squire, but there was no time to try to figure out why. They had to get as many people out of this mess as they could. At the moment, wrong might mean "dead wrong" for Carson's Companions.

215

Time to call for help. "Napoleon, this is Trajan Boss. You read me?"

"Down in the mud, but readable, Trajan Boss," Hettrick's voice came through his earphones.

"We've got the first thirty or so hostages. Lieutenant Morgan is taking them to the roof. Where are the aerodynes to transport them to the 'drome?"

"I'm detaching two assault aerodynes from the Warriors, one from the Marauders. They're coming! I've got to hold the two Killer aerodynes in reserve. Get the hostages to the roof!"

Assault aerodynes had limited people-carrying capability. Each one would be able to take only three or four people at a time. It would take a long time to lift a hundred hostages out. "Colonel, dammit, I need every 'dyne I can get! I don't know how long I'll be able to operate here before the Jehorkhims attack. To hell with reserves! Our prime objective is to get these hostages out!"

Hettrick's reply was quick, sharp, and angry. "The general has ordered the two remaining Killer aerodynes to be held as reserves."

"Reserves for what?"

"Captain! Do the best you can with what you've got! That's all you're going to get!"

"Shit!" It was the same old story, old as the Army, old as soldiering. Follow orders, get your ass in a sling, then figure out a way to save yourself. And don't forget to carry out the mission while you're doing it.

Well, the Companions had rescued the first thirty hostages. Now they had to get the rest of them.

That wasn't going to be easy. The others were in the

basement dungeon along with an unknown number of armed Jehorkhims.

He swung his arm. "Sampson, get around behind the stairwell. You too, Allen! Gerard, take the head of the stairs with Sergeant Kester but keep under cover. Bots Three and Five, down the stairs to the door. Put one kilo of plasticex on each hinge and latch. Set initiators for fifteen seconds and retreat up the stairs!"

It didn't take long. The bots moved fast. "Initiators set!" squawked a bot from the bottom of the stairs.

Master Sergeant Henry Kester hit the floor. He was the only one who really understood what would happen when several kilos of plasticex blew.

The stairwell attenuated the blast wave somewhat. It didn't bother the drumlike M-22 assault bots who'd gotten beyond the top of the stairs and had moved out of the way. The shock wave just rolled over them, but it blew the front doors of the building off their hinges and into the narrow street with such force a cloud of dust surged up the stairs.

And it caught Sergeant Nick Gerard and blew him backward from the head of the stairwell, ripping his helmet off.

"He's hurt!" Kester yelled. Blood was coming from Gerard's ears and nostrils, and he was unconscious. Kester quickly went to him.

Curt couldn't take the time to check on Gerard. If he didn't take immediate action and exploit the shock and confusion caused by the explosion, he'd lose an important advantage. "Bots Three and Five! Down the stairs! Through the door! Open fire on white-turbaned Jehorkhims. Don't shoot hostages!" As they disappeared into the pall of dust that filled the stairwell, Curt motioned to the two Companions standing by. "Allen! Sampson! Uh ... Jerry, you okay?"

The young lieutenant was shaking his head. "Yeah ... yes, sir! Didn't realize there'd be that much of a shock wave."

"Sampson?"

"Okay, Captain."

"Follow me!"

He plunged into the stairway, feeling for each step. Even when he flipped the all-vision optics in front of his eyes, he was unable to penetrate the smoke and dust.

He heard the bots firing in the murk ahead of him, but as he reached what was left of the doorjam the firing ceased.

Curt stopped in his tracks. He wasn't about to go through that opening without being able to see what was beyond. Allen and Sampson ran into him. "Wait," Curt told them.

The dust was settling quickly. Through the haze, Curt's eyes picked out what appeared to be five dead Jehorkhims sprawled on the floor before him, apparently victims of the blast. Farther back in the basement, however, silhouettes began to take form against the lights. Curt brought his carbine up, then saw what was going on.

"Don't shoot! Please don't shoot!" The female's cry was quickly echoed by the voice of a young man.

He knew why the bots had stopped firing.

"Hold fire!" Curt yelled to Allen and Sampson.

Seven Jehorkhims wielding scimitars in one hand and

short yataghans in the other were facing him, each holding a razor-sharp yataghan to the throat of the hostage positioned in front of him as a shield. As the dust cleared, the Jehorkhims began to move forward, pushing the hostages before them.

There was no way to get a clear shot at them.

This was a variation on the tactic they'd tried a few minutes before. But now it was working.

Curt knew the assault bots were probably useless in these close quarters. They wouldn't fire for fear of hitting friendlies and brainies. The judgment circuits in their Mod Four AI multiprocessors were good and fast, but their overriding programming prevented them from taking the slightest chance of hitting human beings they hadn't been instructed to shoot at.

This was going to be a hand-to-hand fight. "Spread out!" Curt ordered, hoping the helmet-mounted compak would get the message through in spite of the screaming and yelling in the basement. Allen and Sampson moved to opposite sides of him.

This movement separated the three of them. The Jehorkhims took advantage of it. Two of them pushed their hostage shields aside and charged at Sergeant Edwina Sampson, the smallest Companion present.

She put two rounds from her Beretta into the first Jehorkhim. That slowed him momentarily, but he kept coming. Curt cursed himself for failing to insist that she carry a more potent sidearm. He swung his carbine's muzzle about and mowed down both attacking Jehorkhims with one burst before they reached her.

In the confusion thus generated, the remaining Jehorkhims charged, screaming and yelling wildly.

Jerry Allen hesitated to fire. He was afraid of hitting the hostages who were left standing.

But Curt didn't pause. He managed to get two more Jehorkhims before he took a glancing blow from a scimitar on his left shoulder and upper arm. The blade shattered upon contacting his densely woven body armor, and he wasn't cut. But the force of the blow staggered him.

As the Jehorkhim warrior closed on him, Curt deflected the yataghan blade with the carbine and managed to club the man in the face with the butt.

At that instant, in a flash of recognition, Curt saw that the man was the torturer he'd seen on that first videotape. The Jehorkhim, a huge and burly man, went down with blood all over his face. Curt didn't want to worry about him later and he didn't think such a man should be allowed to live anyway, so he directed a three-round burst at the man's face.

That made him feel better for an instant.

When he turned to help Sampson, he saw that she'd learned her lesson about the Beretta. She stopped the Jehorkhim charging her by shooting him directly in the face. A nine-millimeter bullet might not stop a charging fanatic if it hit him in the torso, but it did its job when it landed right between the eyes.

Jerry Allen was down. But before the Jehorkhim could swing his scimitar or thrust that yataghan, Curt blew the man's white-turbaned head off with a burst from the carbine.

It was over. It had seemed to take a long time, but only ten seconds had elapsed since they'd entered the door to the basement. Apparently no Jehorkhims were left alive in that dungeon and torture chamber.

Curt's injured arm suddenly began to hurt. Badly.

Jerry Allen's lower left arm was bleeding, and had a strange angle to it. The young lieutenant was writhing with pain. "Goddamn it to hell! He got my arm! Oh, shit!" Allen dropped his submachine pistol and crumpled to his knees.

"Sampson?" Curt called, straightening up and looking around. The throbbing in his arm was beginning to spread up to his shoulder.

"I'm okay," she replied in a shaky voice. "Shook, but okay."

"Give the lieutenant a painkiller. Then see if he's able to walk upstairs." Curt wasn't so sure he could use his own left arm now, and he wondered if there were more Jehorkhims in the basement.

He heard a ripping sound as the sergeant opened a sealpak from her MediKit. "Right away, Captain!"

Two of the hostages used as shields had been wounded by stray bullets during the fracas.

"Henry!" he called to his sergeant on his helmet comm. "Get the transport bots down here!"

"I need some help up here," Kester's voice came back. "They're coming in the windows, the doors, everywhere."

"Call in air cover!"

"Kelly's Killers at your service, buddy!" came Captain Marty Kelly's voice. "But we're busy! Dammit, Carson, I hate to say this, but you were right! That intelligence guestimate of force strength was wrong. Really wrong! There must be nearly a thousand Jehor-khims out here! It's a neat fight!"

"Yeah, you sonofabitch, you're sitting on your ass safe and sound back at the RCP! Just shut up and give us some help instead of killing Jehorkhims," Curt snapped angrily, then tried to get back to the business at hand, though his arm was hurting more every minute. "Assault bots Three and Five! Up the stairs! Report to Sergeant Kester!"

The transport bots were coming through the blasted doorway.

Curt called out in a loud voice that echoed through the basement, "We're United States Army Robot Infantry troops! Rescue mission! Anyone who can walk, get out the door! If you can't walk, call for help! If you're locked up, holler and we'll take care of it!"

The place became a bedlam of voices crying, calling out, screaming, moaning, yelling.

"Sampson! Get a transport bot for Allen. Then get out your bolt cutters and help me!" Curt snapped, slinging his carbine over his shoulder and bending over to search the dead Jehorkhims for cell keys. His left arm was nearly useless now. "Kester! Can you come down here to help us?"

"Negative, Captain! We're holding off a couple hundred Jehorkhims!"

Damn! Curt thought. The fucking operation was undermanned! But they hadn't listened when he'd told them. Now they might lose the hostages and Carson's Companions.

He and Sergeant Sampson found about sixty hostages in various areas of the basement. Some were

222

shackled and chained. Others were locked inside primitive cells. Curt had Sampson cut the chains and break the locks. His left arm was throbbing painfully.

He found Dr. Robert Armstrong and Colonel Willa Lovell. They were chained to the wall he'd seen them on on the videotape. The bloodstained and -spattered torture area was nearby. Dirty and scarred, both officers were standing in their own filth. Through cracked lips, Willa Lovell managed to croak, "Water! Water!"

Curt removed his canteen from his belt and held it up to her lips, saying, "Glad you're alive! We'll cut those chains and get you out of here. Can you walk?"

Dr. Armstrong was breathing hard. "I think so. I've been chained up so long I don't know whether I can move or not ... Who are you?"

Curt told him and passed him the canteen once Lovell was finished with it. "I can get a transport bot to help you."

"Use them for the hostages who are injured," Willa Lovell replied.

"I think I'll be all right once I can move around a little bit," Armstrong remarked. "I'm surprised to see you, Captain. I didn't think the Army would mount this kind of a mission because of standard operating procedures."

"Well, Doctor, there was no other way to get in here and get you out."

"We won't forget the risk you've taken. How many bots do you have?"

"Doctor, it's best that you don't know."

"Eh?"

"This operation could still fail, and what you don't know, they can't torture out of you."

"Oh ..."

"If you did it with less than brigade strength—"

Curt interrupted Colonel Willa Lovell. "We had to. We didn't have brigade strength available."

Edwina Sampson came over and cut their chains, but she couldn't remove the shackles around their wrists, necks, and ankles.

"It's going to be a difficult operation, then," Willa Lovell remarked, stretching her stiff arms.

Armstrong stretched also, then bent down to pick up a Soviet AKMS rifle that a Jehorkhim guard wasn't going to use any longer. "Never fired one of these before, but I guess I can learn. How about you, Willa?"

"Never done it before either, but I'll damned well learn fast!"

"Pick up any additional bandoliers or clips of ammunition you can find," Curt advised them.

Edwina Sampson looked at him. She ripped open another MediKit and injected a painkiller into her commanding officer. "Captain, you need that, but you wouldn't ask for it." Before he could argue with her, she handed him her Beretta pistol and said, "You can shoot this with one hand. You can't use your carbine now, except to scare people. Give it to me. I'll make it talk."

And she had to do that. As they shepherded the sixty people up the stairs, some being carried by transport bots, they discovered that a fire fight was going on in front of the building.

One assault bot was down, its top blown off, and the

224

three trying to keep the street sanitized had been hit by bullets which hadn't penetrated their armor. Master Sergeant Kester was the only Companion there.

"Captain, the situation is becoming untenable. Suggest we all move up to the roof where we can hold the Jehorkhims off, take advantage of air cover, and be lifted out ... You're hurt, sir."

"A Jehorkhim whacked me on the arm with his sword. Body armor saved me. No bleeding, but it might be broken. I'm still vertical and still nasty," Curt told him, though he was beginning to feel a little weak and the painkiller was making him woozy. "Where's Allen? Gerard?"

"On the roof. Gerard's okay. Shook up a tad. But Allen's hurting."

"How many operative assault bots left?"

"We've lost two."

"Okay, move the last of these hostages up to the roof ass-ap! Have the remaining bots cover our retreat." He toggled his compak. "Morgan! What are the conditions on the roof?"

"Crowded!" Alexis Morgan's voice responded. "And serious! Trajan can't lift off. Too many turbines out. Got Warrior and Killer aerodynes here now. Some of the Killer aerodynes jettisoned their M-22 assault bots in the streets, just let 'em crash on the Jehorkhims like iron bombs. They're lifting three or four people out at a crack now and making it to the aerodrome."

"Are you taking any fire on the roof?"

"Very little. Mostly arrows. High-angle trajectory stuff. Can't see where they're coming from. We're using Trajan as a cover, a shield to get under. But some

225

people have taken arrows. Hope the rescue transport has medics aboard.''

"It does.'' Colonel Hettrick's voice came through for the first time in many long minutes. "Captain, we're going to try to get some more fuel in for the aerodynes.''

"What's that?'' Curt asked.

"Some of the 'dynes are running low on fuel because of their use as people transports. The Jehorkhims are putting up a stiff fight at the aerodrome, and we've had to reposition as many of the assault bots as possible to cover the transport craft.''

"Colonel, are you going to be able to get everyone out of here?'' Curt wanted to know.

"We think so. It's going to be close.''

Whole damned operation has been run too fucking close to the ragged goddamned edge of failure! Curt thought. "Okay, we're evacuating the first floor, up to the second, and coming onto the roof! Colonel Hettrick, I've got Dr. Armstrong and Colonel Lovell with me. Kester! Sampson! Bring those bots up behind us to cover us! Let them take the fire! With any luck at all, we might make it to the roof!''

CHAPTER THIRTEEN

The roof of the building was full of people, most of them jammed together in the shade of Trajan's twenty-meter shape. Some hostages had picked up Jehorkhim rifles and were sniping over the roof ledge at white-turbaned soldiers who made the mistake of presenting targets in the streets below. Others who'd managed to get Jehorkhim rifles had the other government building under fire.

But the rooftop was windy and growing hotter by the minute as the bright sun climbed higher into the clear sky.

Lieutenant Alexis Morgan pulled Curt into the shade of Trajan's hulk. "You're wounded," she told him.

"Yeah . . ." It was all he could muster at the moment.

She put her canteen to his lips. He took one gulp and then shook his head. "Alexis, go easy on the water. A lot of people are up here on this roof. Unless we get them off pretty damned quick, we may run out of water—and everything else. What's the situation?"

"We've gotten twenty-seven hostages off the roof and

out to the aerodrome," she reported, wiping his forehead with a cloth dampened with water from her canteen. "The Jehorkhims don't appear to be attacking us here. They're just making life miserable for us instead."

"What's the situation elsewhere?"

"I don't know. But we're working with seven to eight aerodynes for the airlift."

"Seven to eight?"

"Kelly diverts one occasionally to make an air strike against a target of opprtunity."

"Bastard is going to get shot down and lose that aerodyne," Curt growled. "What the hell is Knox doing? Thought he was running the show. Can't he keep Kelly under control?"

"Everyone's hands are full, Curt. Some people are running as many as six warbots. Aerodyne pilots can't do anything but fly aerodynes."

It seemed to Curt that everything had gone to slime since they'd started down into the basement and lost situational awareness. He was wounded, but still in command. And he was responsible for all the people still on the roof of the building. He had to know what was going on. He keyed his helmet compak. "Napoleon, this is Trajan Boss. We've got all the hostages out of the basement and onto the roof. How fast can you get us out of here?"

The voice that came back belonged to Georgie at faraway Diamond Point. It was a flat, unemotional voice that sounded out of place in the midst of this battle. Georgie went through a dispassionate and brief report: "The Jehorkhims are resisting strongly around the aerodrome. Walker's Warriors are heavily engaged. So are Manny's Marauders, on the west side of town. The Jehorkhims have few firearms and no artillery, but they're mounted. They move so much faster and there are so many of them that the bots have had to give up pursuit and form a defensive perimeter. Their swords and bows are very effective against bots. No air support is available because the eight aerodynes are engaged in evac. Each aerodyne can carry three to four people. A round trip from the aerodrome requires a minimum of thirty minutes. There are a total of fifty-eight more people to evacuate. The operation will be completed at thirteen hundred hours local, if we can refuel the aerodynes quickly enough from the Air Force transport now on the ramp at Zahedan."

"Are the aerodynes running out of fuel?"

"Affirmative. This is an energy-intensive situation. To carry the maximum loads, the aerodynes are flying with partial fuel loads. This requires that they refuel more often. The strong wind was not accounted for in the planning. The evac is therefore taking more time and fuel than estimated. I am forecasting a fuel-critical situation in one hour."

Curt looked at Alexis. "Someone is probably going to get left here, Lieutenant," he told her flatly.

"Can we fight our way out to the aerodrome through these streets?" she asked.

"I can't." He looked down at his left arm which was throbbing, useless, and probably broken. "Neither can Jerry Allen."

"We've lifted the lieutenant and Sergeant Gerard out to the aerodrome already."

229

"Dammit, Lieutenant, the hostages come first!"

"I wasn't told that. Standing orders state that wounded always have first evac priority."

"Shit! I won't argue with you. Too late, anyway. Can we hold out here for five hours?"

"I don't know."

"Well, find out, dammit!" Curt snapped. "Sorry, Lieutenant. This whole damned thing is a master screwup! What are the critical items? How much water in our canteens?"

"Water isn't the critical item," Alexis Morgan told him. Beads of sweat were making runs in the dark camouflage makeup on her young face. "Trajan has about three hundred liters of demineralized water aboard for power boost. And the craft's fuel cells probably have some more in the holding tanks."

Curt sighed. "Thank God for that! It's going to get damned hot and dry here before they lift all of us out. How's the ammo situation?"

Alexis shrugged. "Hard to say. We don't know how many Russian cartridges were picked up with the AKMS rifles. Maybe a hundred rounds per weapon. Whether or not it's adequate depends on how many times the Jehorkhims try to storm the roof."

"Okay, put the bots to guarding the stairway. Keep the other building under surveillance and fire. Getting out of here is first priority, not killing Jehorkhims. We're going to hold up here, lift hostages out, and conserve our water and ammo," Curt instructed. Then he began to snap out orders. "Those hostages along the parapet are getting even for the past couple of days, but be sure they conserve their ammo. Also get them

230

out of that rain of arrows; we don't have the facilities here to treat them if they start looking like pincushions. Conserve our ammo to provide fire cover when the aerodynes show up to load."

"Right!"

Curt had to sit back against the metal leg of one of Trajan's landing struts. He was getting even more woozy from the painkiller and the heat, plus the stress of personal battle. No wonder warbots had been welcomed with open arms when they'd become available! "Lieutenant, I'm having troubles. Keep this operation moving."

"Roger, Captain! Will do! If we can organize this and maintain some discipline, maybe we'll have a chance of getting everyone out alive." She got to her feet and moved out from under the protection of Trajan.

Curt was trying to save the situation. He knew he had only three choices: hang on and be rescued, surrender, or actually be killed defending the rooftop position. He didn't relish thinking of the latter two, so he concentrated on the first. He was the commanding officer on the site, and it was up to him to do whatever he could to salvage the operation, screwed up though it was. He wasn't the first officer in military history who'd found himself in deep trouble because of what his superiors had done or failed to do.

This fracas was a classic example of a poorly planned and executed military operation. Intelligence data, obtained at great risk and expense, had been either ignored or poorly evaluated. And prejudice had been allowed to influence the final assessment, which turned

231

out to be wrong on important particulars: enemy strength, weapons, and capabilities. The operation had been rushed. As a result, it had been undermanned and underequipped.

Another two days—only two more days—would have made a lot of difference. The harried intelligence people would have had a chance to look more carefully at the data. The operations people would have had more time to think through their unnecessarily complex plan. And there would have been time to bring in additional forces.

Colonel Hettrick might even have had a better opportunity to short-circuit General Knox's micromanagement of the operation from the safety of Diamond Point.

Curt thought he knew what had happened to the military thought process: Warbots had made the life of an individual human soldier far too valuable for the high command to even consider risking it in action. In a way, the human soldier had become like the battleship or the aircraft carrier—too expensive to risk in combat.

The prevailing logic was simple: Robots with artificial intelligence could do it all, take the deadly risks and save human lives. Therefore, doctrine now said: Don't risk the human being.

The pendulum had swung since the twentieth century when generals had sent five hundred thousand soldiers in waves into No Man's Land, into the sheet of bullets from well-placed machine guns. Or when the Soviets had stormed Berlin and lost sixty-five percent of their forces in the process when every military planner knew that losing ten percent of a force meant the battle was lost.

Because of this recent doctrine of the "sanctity of human life," someone in Army's command loop—maybe most of the colonels and generals—had allowed the possible killing of two more hostages to sway the decision on when to initiate Operation Squire. The brass had their priorities confused. So now the lives of the remaining hostages and of the six people in Carson's Companions were threatened.

And the poor brainies out in the field under fire were going to pay for the brass being wrong ... as always. Curt didn't like the idea that he'd be one of them.

But, if such were indeed the case, he'd be the last of Carson's Companions to leave Zahedan. He knew Alexis and Edwina would have evac priority over Kester and him, although he couldn't have justified why he'd come to that conclusion. Peace or war, he'd always believed in "women and children first," even if the women were fighting alongside him. He and Henry could stick it out, but he'd order Henry to take the last aerodyne out if it came to that.

Should he be captured and manage to live through captivity, he'd be helped by the thought that the Companions who managed to get out of Zahedan would make life so difficult for the high command that there might be hope for a quick rescue mission. Carson's Companions looked out for their own, and so did the Washington Greys. Furthermore, the Army couldn't possibly stand the bad publicity caused by abandoning its warbot brainies in action.

These thoughts ran randomly through Curt's mind

as he was progressively overcome by the pain in his arm, which the painkiller wasn't cutting down much, the growing heat even in the shade of the aerodyne, the incessant hot wind that gusted over the rooftop, and the occasional cracking of gunfire or the rattle of arrows on the aerodyne above him.

Curt was therefore surprised when Lieutenant Alexis Morgan told him in matter-of-fact tones, "Well, you won't have to worry about surviving this operation, Captain. With that banged-up arm, you can't fight so you're automatically classified as wounded. You're being evacuated on the next aerodyne out of here."

"The hell you say!" Curt roared. He waved Sampson's pistol. "I can still shoot with my other arm! And I'm not leaving here until we all get out!"

"But—"

"That's a direct order, Lieutenant! I am *not* relinquishing command! But I am counting on you to keep things organized and running smoothly so that we *do* all get out of here! No more bot flush about evacking your CO until the job is finished! Understood?"

She saluted. "Understood, Captain. Excuse me, but if I've got to hold this fracas together, I've got a lot of things to do in a hell of a hurry." And she was gone.

Colonel Willa Lovell picked her way through the crowd of hostages seated in the shade of Trajan, and sat down in front of him. She was pale and the iron shackles were still around her bruised wrists, neck, and ankles. She was cut and dirty, but there was one thing different about her here than on the videotape Curt had seen those long days ago in Diamond Point: She had hope in her eyes now. "Thank you, Captain, for putting your life on the line for us."

"Colonel," he told her with a dry throat, slurring his words slightly, "I saw that first videotape. I was someone who could do something to stop it. So here I am."

"That wasn't required of a warbot officer," Willa Lovell observed. "What happened to all the warbots? Where were they?" She was far more attractive than on the videotape, Curt thought, even with her shoulder-length auburn hair in wild disarray and no vestige of cosmetics on her smooth face. She had a strong, broad face with high cheeks and a lower lip that pouted slightly below straight white teeth. Curt wondered what her smile was like. The ragged clothing she wore, mere remnants of what had once been a stylish business travel suit, didn't hide the fact that she had a full and mature body. Whether she'd taken advantage of biocosmetics to maintain her appearance was irrelevent; she was a handsome, striking, and alluring woman simply because of the way she acted and carried herself. And because of her attitude. Although she'd undergone several days of unspeakable horror, she still appeared to be rather indomitable.

"Colonel, I know you're an expert in robotics, but we're in a situation where bots can't cut it. Could any warbot have come into that dungeon and done what three human soldiers did?"

"Probably not," Lovell admitted.

"Damned right! The best a robot can do is support what we poor, puny humans do because we can." He shook his head slightly. It hurt, and the pain was creeping up his neck now. "Down there in the basement, assault bots with the latest AI circuitry didn't even shoot because they might have hit one of the hostages the Jehorkhim guards were using as shields. Their basic programming wouldn't permit them to do anything that might harm a human identified as 'friendly.' So they locked up and did nothing.''

"It'll be different when you get the Mod Fives."

"We haven't got the Mod Fives, whatever they are. And we've been told things would be different every time a new mod came out. Sorry, they haven't.''

"You're hurt.''

"Yes, Doctor, I'm hurt. If that scimitar blow didn't break my arm, it probably tore some tendons.''

She brushed her hair out of her face, and Curt saw her eyes, eyes that had seen nearly a week of horror unknown in the high-tech world in which she moved and lived. There was now a brightness in them, though they were rimmed with fatigue. "Please let me have a look,'' she offered, reaching out. "I'm an M.D. in addition to being a robotics specialist.''

Curt was in no condition to argue. But his arm hurt when she took it in both of her hands and began to explore it with sensitive fingers. "You're wearing body armor,'' she said.

"Yes.''

"That probably saved your arm. Can we cut the armor off so I can check the damage?''

"It can't be cut,'' he reminded her. "And I can't roll it up.''

"Well, a doctor often has to make do with the situation at hand,'' she muttered and began to probe and explore his left arm. The muscles of his upper arm were so tender, it nauseated him when she touched them, but she bent his elbow without causing joint pain. And as she manipulated the arm, she quickly came to the conclusion that there were no broken bones and told him so.

"Then what the hell hurts so goddamned much?" he wanted to know.

"I think the blow tore some tendons in the region of your elbow or simply traumatized the muscle mass so badly that there may be hundreds of small hemorrhages in the muscle tissue. They're called connective hemorrhages. They're very painful. I can't tell without radiography and ultrasound tomography, but I don't think it's anything too serious. If we have to, I could go in there surgically and relieve some of the edema."

"Not here," Curt told her.

"No, not here, of course. But when we get where there's a surgical facility," she explained.

"You seem to think there's going to be no problem from here on."

"You got us this far," Willa Lovell reminded him.

Curt decided he wouldn't burden her with his pessimistic outlook on the operation, but he feared that damned few of them would get out. He tried to grin as he told her, "That's what we came to do. And we'll finish the job. By the way, you went through a couple of days of pure hell yourself, Colonel. I'm the one who should be asking about you. Are you all right? Did they hurt you?"

"Oh, they hurt me. But I'll get over it," Willa Lovell admitted with a toss of her head. "We'll both spend some time in the new clinic where they can carry out

237

whatever surgery is necessary or even run some bio-electronic programming to heal whatever's wrong with your arm. You'd be surprised, Captain, by what we've been able to accomplish. We're doing in humane ways, the sort of things that Dr. Taisha wants to accomplish for her own warped purposes."

It occurred to Curt that Lovell probably knew a great deal more about the Jehorkhims than many others, including Division G-2. After all, she'd been with or near them for about a week, and he was certain she was the sort of person who would notice little things. She might have some information that could pull this whole mission out of the mire. "Who *is* this Dr. Taisha? I ran into her on the scouting mission, but I didn't get the chance to find out what she was up to. Or the Imam either, for that matter. Why are the Jehorkhims doing this, anyway? What the hell do they stand to gain?"

Willa Lovell shrugged. "Captain, the Jehorkhims are religious zealots, fanatical followers of a violent revelatory religion. Anything the Imam wants them to do can be justified with one simple statement: 'It is the will of Allah!' And the Imam interprets the will of Allah."

"Yeah, okay, but *why* are they striking out against anything they believe is an extension of human beings—like television or cybots? They're using television to promote their cause with the torture videotapes."

"Oh, are they releasing those videotapes to the world?" Lovell asked in surprise.

"Sure are, and demanding ten million in gold bullion for each hostage."

Willa Lovell sat down next to him in the shade. The hot wind from the north was still blowing gustily over the roof, but the *pop-pop-pop* of rifle fire and the rattle of arrows had again temporarily ceased. "I'm not sure I fully understand it myself. But the Islamic religion prohibits any idols or any representation of the human form in any sort of art. Well, the Jehorkhims under the Imam Rahman have taken that to the extreme—as many sects from all types of religions do. Mohammed wanted Islam to be a *human* religion, so he even outlawed bells as a call to prayer. The Imam Rahman believes that loudspeakers shouldn't be used by meuzzins." She paused for a moment, "In America, there's an analogous Christian sect, but only partly analogous. They don't believe in telephones, radios, television, electricity, tractors, or automobiles. The Plain People, the Amish or Mennonites hold much the same beliefs about modern technology."

"But they aren't aggressive about it!" Curt objected.

"That's the big difference," Willa observed, shifting the shackles on her wrists to keep them from further irritating bruises and cuts.

"When I was on recon a few days ago, I heard Taisha tell the Imam something about machine control of people," Curt said, hoping he could lead the robotics expert into telling him more.

"Well, that's another difference between the Jehorkhims and all the other fanatical Islamic *jihad* sects. The Imam Rahman has borrowed something from the Protestant Christians: the concept of the inherent imperfection of mankind."

"What does Dr. Taisha have to do with that?"

When Colonel Willa Lovell looked at Curt, there was a coldness in her eyes. "Taisha has taken our work with human control of machines—the basic principles of robotic linkage—and turned it around. She believes that people can be made to do what machines tell them. And the Imam buys that because it not only gives substance to his religious concepts but it assures that he'll have absolute power over his disciples."

Curt was very quiet for a few moments. A small fire fight started up on the outside stairway to the roof. Apparently, some Jehorkhims were trying to storm up the stairway. The two M-22 assault bots posted at the top of the stairs managed to beat back the attack with a hail of fletchettes. Then one of them withdrew, signaling to Alexis Morgan and Henry Kester that it was out of ammo. Sampson opened the bot up and began reloading it with rounds from the supply stored on Trajan, while Kester repositioned another M-22 at the head of the stairs.

"Did they use any of Taisha's techniques on any of the hostages?" Curt asked the attractive colonel.

"Yes, but I don't know what happened to the three hostages she took."

"Was that the reason the Jehorkhims took so many hostages, Doctor?"

She moved the iron band around her throat so that it chafed the bruises less. "I don't know. We were never told. Dr. Armstrong and I talked about the reasons behind the hijacking, but we could never figure out a rational reason for it."

"Sure as hell, the Imam doesn't think the way we do!"

"Anyone who takes hostages rarely thinks the way we do," Lovell pointed out to him. "You say he was openly asking for ransom. Could be that he needs money to buy weapons. I don't know what he wants to do with them. Who does he want to conquer?"

"The world, probably." It had been a long time since a dictator like Hitler had surfaced.

Lovell nodded. "Megalomania. Or maybe Allah told him to do it. This region of the world is known throughout history as being a place where God in his many forms reveals himself to selected acolytes."

"I can't figure out what the hell Taisha was doing here either. There must be an easier way to get human experimental subjects for her work." Curt was still puzzled by the strange alliance between the religious leader and the scientist. It didn't make sense to him.

"I can't really talk too much about some of the things we're doing at Fort McCarthy," Lovell admitted in a low voice. "But experiments using computers and robots—to help paraplegics, for example—have been going on for decades. The computer/robot can be programmed to make human muscles operate. The RI depends upon computers to activate soldiers' nervous systems to produce the sensations of sight and hearing. We've tried to control living organisms with computers—not because we want human beings to be slaves of machines. We believe we have to find out what the problems and techniques are, in case someone else manages to do it. So we'll be able to develop countermeasures."

"Have you?" Curt asked.

"Have we managed to achieve computer control over a human being? Well, to some extent, yes. But not all the way. That's all I can tell you, Captain."

241

"Kills people, doesn't it?" Curt suddenly asked.

Colonel Willa Lovell was silent for a moment before she replied simply, "Yes. But only intelligent people."

"And that's what Taisha wanted: Intelligent people for use as experimental subjects. Colonel, I think the Imam's ransom demand was a red herring."

"So do I. He stopped the daily torture killing of hostages yesterday. But Taisha used the hostages instead. We never saw them again, of course."

Curt said no more, but he thought to himself: Great! We suckered ourselves right into this without adequate intelligence data! If we'd known yesterday what Willa just told me, we could have mustered enough strength to do this job right in the first place!

At the moment, the job wasn't being done. The rescue mission was teetering on the brink of failure. Two of his Companions had been hurt, and he wasn't exactly feeling great himself. They'd expended bots and 'dynes and ammo. Perhaps they'd killed people unnecessarily. And they might not get off this roof alive.

But Curt knew the operation wasn't over yet. He had to continue to try to make it work. Certainly, he wasn't going to sit on his butt in the shade of an aerodyne and let things go to hell. He trusted Alexis Morgan, but he was the commanding officer. He bore the responsibility for his part of the operation.

Captain Curt Carson had what many people call a "second wind." He had reserves of strength. He called them up. Painful arm or not, he was going to see to it that everyone got off that roof alive.

Staggering to his feet, he motioned for Colonel Willa Lovell to remain where she was. "Stay out of the sun," he told her. "I may be hurting, but you and the other hostages have been hurting more ... and for a longer time. Let me see if I can't speed up things."

The sound of gunfire began to increase. Over the tops of the houses to the north came the pancake shapes of eight aerodynes, moving fast to make themselves poor targets. The flat rooftop became a wind-blown melee as, one by one, the 'dynes hovered with doors open to expose their empty weapon bays while Alexis, Henry, and Edwina pushed and lifted and squeezed hostages into them. Curt helped organize things by keeping hostages from rushing the 'dynes, overloading them, and bringing them crashing to the roof.

When all eight 'dynes were disappearing northward toward the aerodrome, Curt called Hettrick. "Napoleon, this is Trajan Boss. Hey, Colonel, lemme make a suggestion. It may be easier if you spread out those 'dynes rather than have them all cluster over the roof here at the same time. When they're together, they draw lots of fire. If Edith and Manny can keep them coming at more or less regular intervals one at a time, we can load faster and keep the pipeline to the aerodrome full. It will also keep the Jehorkhim troops in the streets from regrouping and reloading while they wait for the next formation to fly over."

"Can't do it, Curt. We have to concentrate on defending the aerodynes when they're at the aerodrome and fight off Jehorkhims with ground warbots when they're not. We've got real trouble out there."

"What's going on?"

"The Jehorkhims have shifted the main body of their forces," she reported. "Looks like they've got only to-

243

ken strength involved in holding you on the roof. Seems they don't like urban fighting, but prefer to maneuver in the open around the aerodrome."

"Can't Manny's warbots be redeployed to the aerodrome?"

"No airlift. Besides, what's left of them is pinned down west of town in a date-palm grove."

"What have the Jehorkhims got that makes them so effective?"

"Light cavalry."

"What? Horses can't stand up against automatic weaponry!" Curt objected. He was voicing accepted beliefs. Burned into every soldier's mind was the picture of the Polish cavalry valiantly attacking German Panzer units in September 1939. Everyone "knew" that the old horse cavalry was obsolete.

What they didn't remember was the Soviet cavalry surging through the deep, cold Russian snow to overwhelm frozen Panzers in retreat.

"We're fighting a lot of Jehorkhims and they've got a lot of small horses," Hettrick's voice reported in Curt's headphones. "They keep moving until the horses get shot out from under them; then they fight on the ground in ditches and gullies until other Jehorkhims bring a string of ponies out in defilade. They remount and move again. They're so mobile and so many that they're overloading out data channels! There must be at least a thousand of them moving around the aerodrome right now!" She didn't mention that G-2 had estimated before the operation got under way that only two to three hundred Jehorkhim soldiers were billeted in Zahedan.

"Okay, we'll do the best we can."

"You'll have to. We all are."

The temperature continued to rise. The wind increased. The sun beat down relentlessly on the flat roof.

Finally, the call came from Colonel Hettrick. "Trajan Boss, this is Napoleon. Can you possibly make it on the ground to the aerodrome in the next thirty minutes?"

Curt looked at Alexis Morgan and Henry Kester. All of them knew what the message really meant. "Napoleon, this is Trajan Boss. Negative, negative! We can't control the streets, and we'll be cut down if we try to get out on the ground, even with aerodyne cover!"

"Trajan Boss, we're in deep trouble at the aerodrome. The intensity of the Jehorkhim attacks threaten to overwhelm what bots we have left on defense. We've also lost two of the Killer 'dynes. How many people left on the roof?"

"Four Companions and thirty-four hostages, including Dr. Armstrong and Colonel Lovell."

"I'm handing you a tough decision: Pick thirty people for the last recovery which is now on its way in."

"Goddammit, Colonel, *one more* beyond that will get all of us out!"

"Sorry, Curt, we just can't do it without risking everyone we've evacked to the aerodrome thus far. We're running out of aerodyne fuel and warbots. The warbots we have left are running out of ammo. We'll have to abandon warbots and aerodynes just to get the hostages and the RCP out of here."

Curt said nothing for a moment; then he asked, "How long before you can get a backup mission in here to

245

pick us up? How long would we be expected to hold out until you could make another try for us?"

"We're working on it?"

"Are *you* working on it, Colonel? Or is it being micromanaged by General Knox?"

"I cut the general's link from Diamond Point about an hour ago," Hettrick revealed. "I'm trying to salvage this mess. How long can you hold out on the roof?"

"I don't know. We might be good for another twenty-four hours. Maybe. Maybe not. If the Jehorkhims don't mount an assault on this roof once the transport aircraft leaves the aerodrome and frees up some of their troops, we could make it through the night. Maybe. Can you hack it within twenty-four hours?"

"Captain Carson ... Curt ... *I don't know*! I can't give you an answer."

"So you want me to hold on?"

"Damned right!"

Curt turned to look over the remaining people. Which thirty would go?"

And who were the four who would stay?

He had to make the decision. Who were the ones he'd select and thereby force to face certain death or a continuation of this torture and perhaps worse?

CHAPTER FOURTEEN

Captain Curt Carson found himself in a position he
didn't like. He was the one who would have to deter-
mine who would live and who might very well die in
this hellhole in the middle of nowhere.

He knew that, left to their own resources, the hostages could become a mob. No military man has ever
forgotten the television pictures of the Saigon evacuation. Curt knew he'd have to take charge and that he'd
be supported by his disciplined Companions. But making a life-and-death decision involving civilians was a
task he didn't relish.

He hadn't wanted to go on this mission at all and
had argued against it. He could be stashed safely in the
command post on Kuh-e-Taftan with the other company
commanders, letting his warbots take the fire. But, no,
he'd been noble.

Well, there wasn't much he could do about that now.
He was on the roof and he might not get off. But thirty
people would. Which ones?

Curt made up his mind right then that three categories would have priority: injured, women, and civilians, in that order.

He motioned Lieutenant Alexis Morgan over to the shade of the aerodyne. "How many wounded are left on the roof?"

"Counting you?"

"No, not counting me!"

"We've got most of them off already except those with minor bruises. Most of the hostages have injuries of one sort of another, but they're ambulatory."

"How many hostages left on the roof?" Curt repeated.

"Thirty-four."

That really cut it! Thirty-four people who, by rights, deserved to be given priority for the final evac, but only thirty slots available. That would leave four hostages and four Companions on the roof.

Curt cursed and shook his head. "Lieutenant, the next airlift from here is going to be the last one for eight hours or more." He tried to make it sound better than he believed it was, but he tried not to lie. "The 'dynes can take out only thirty more people because of Jehorkhim pressure at the aerodrome. And we've got thirty-four hostages who *must* be evacked. How do we select them? Got any suggestions?"

She looked him squarely in the eye and replied, "No, sir, I don't. I don't think I'm capable of making that decision."

By this time, the conversation between the two officers had been overheard by Colonel Willa Lovell, Dr. Robert Armstrong, and several of the remaining hostages.

248

Colonel Lovell broke in to ask, "How long will we have to hold out here before we can expect another rescue effort?"

"Eight hours. A day. I don't know right now. I haven't been told," Curt admitted. He knew it would be contrary to doctrine to give them an expected arrival time for any future mission; if they were captured by the Jehorkhims—and this was a ninety-nine percent probability—they wouldn't have any information that could compromise the surprise element of a follow-on mission. But Curt knew that the second rescue mission to Zahedan couldn't be mounted before the next day at the very earliest. Which meant at least thirty hours on the roof—if they could hold out that long.

Dr. Robert Armstrong spoke up. "Captain Carson, there's only one fair and equitable way to choose the thirty people who'll be lifted out."

"What do you have in mind, Doctor? And make it fast. The last aerodyne flight is coming in from the aerodrome now."

"Draw straws."

Curt shook his head. "Forget it! This is a military mission, and I'm in command! It's my decision, and I can't duck it."

"But, Captain, the only fair method is to depend upon the laws of chance," the Army scientist observed. "No one will harbor second thoughts or recriminations if we draw straws. Otherwise, the blame for selection, right or wrong, is going to fall on a single individual's shoulders, and later that could cause a great deal of trouble."

A murmur ran through the hostages gathered under

249

the bulk of the damaged aerodyne. Some people merely shook their heads, but a few comments could be heard:

"Best way to do it!"

"Why bother? We're all dead anyway!"

Curt did what he knew he must. Grasping Trajan's landing strut with his good right arm, he hauled himself to a standing position. With great effort, he lifted Sampson's Beretta so that all could see it. Without a word, he looked at the crowd of people. The expression on his face caused the hubbub to subside. When it was quiet except for the wind blowing around the grounded aerodyne, Curt said in a loud, low voice of command, "This is a military mission. I'm responsible. I'll make the decisions. If you don't like them, and if I get back, we'll see what happens then."

He pointed toward the remaining female hostages. "First of all ... you eight women. You're going." He glanced down at Willa Lovell. "You, too, Colonel."

"No," she said simply. "Civilians first."

"You're being evacked, Colonel," Curt told her.

"The hell I am! You'll have to tie me up and physically throw me into that aerodyne."

Curt didn't like her reply. "Colonel, you may be the real reason the Imam hijacked the Orient Express in the first place. You know things that Taisha would like to know."

"If that's the case, then Dr. Armstrong is the one to be evacked," Willa Lovell declared.

"Willa, that's ridiculous," Armstrong responded.

"Is it, Bob? We think we know what Taisha is trying to do. So tell me: Who had the most critical information insofar as she's concerned?" Lovell looked at Curt and went on, "Captain Carson, get Dr. Armstrong out of here! I'm only a superadministrator with an M.D. and an Army commission. He's the one who's got critical robotic linkage data in his head. Taisha doesn't know that yet, but she *must not* be allowed to get that information by torture or whatever other means she's got."

"Dr. Armstrong, you go," Curt said simply.

"What if I won't?"

"You will. Get out of here and use whatever clout you've got to get that follow-on mission in here as quickly as you can. Stop arguing. I made it this far, and I'll make it the rest of the way!"

Reluctantly, Armstrong handed Lieutenant Jerry Allen's Hornet carbine to Colonel Lovell, and said, "Willa, save one round, one last round."

She took the carbine, slung it over her shoulder along with the AKMS she already had, and replied, "If there's only one round left, I'll save it for that bitch Taisha!"

Looking around, Curt sized up the hostages. He had to make his selection. He decided selecting nineteen men who were older and looked more sickly than the others. Finally, he pointed out each of them. "You ... and you ... and you ..."

Finally, he pointed to Lieutenant Alexis Morgan and Platoon Sergeant Edwina Sampson. "And you two."

Lieutenant Alexis Morgan stared directly back at her commanding officer. "With all due respect, Captain, I'm a fighting soldier and I respectfully decline to leave helpless civilians under fire and in danger of death. If we get out of this alive, you may discipline me for refusing to obey a direct order. But in the meantime, I'm staying!"

251

"So am I!" Sergeant Edwina Sampson declared. Then she added, "Sir!"

"Listen!" Curt snapped. "You two *are* Carson's Companions! I don't know how long Allen and Gerard are going to be out of action, so I want someone to organize the second rescue strike. I need Henry here; he's had experience in personal combat. Lieutenant, you're second in command; you go. Sampson, you're de facto master sergeant in Henry's absence; you go, too. I don't want any shit out of either of you! Do as you're told!"

Lieutenant Alexis Morgan had made her point, but she'd lost the argument. She knew better than to buck her Captain. She held out her submachine carbine to Curt. "You'll need this, Captain."

He gently pushed it back toward her. "No, you'll need it at the aerodrome. There's fighting out there. Protect these people. That's your job. You've done it well, you're doing great now, so keep on doing it." He turned to Sergeant Sampson. "The same goes for you, Sergeant, so shut the hell up! I expect both of you to be in the first wave of the rescue."

"It shouldn't end this way," Alexis Morgan said in a low voice.

"Who said it's ending, Lieutenant? What did I just tell you? Get the hell out of here and get that second wave organized! I'm counting on you and Sampson . . . and Allen and Gerard when they get patched up."

"Wait a minute!" The shout came from a large, middle-aged man standing near the rear of the hostage crowd. "I've put up with as much as anyone here!"

Another hostage plucked at his arm, said, "Elliot, shut the hell up!"

"What's with you, Chip? This guy's got no right to evacuate his two army women ahead of civilians."

With his right arm, Curt lifted the Beretta and pointed it in the general direction of the man. "I've got all the right in the world, buddy, and it's here. Sit down and shut up! I'm running the show!"

The roar of approaching aerodynes was heard over the wind. There was little time left, and certainly no time for argument.

The man knew it. He raised his captured AKMS rifle toward Curt. "Only as long as you're alive . . ."

Curt shot without taking careful aim. He didn't have time to do anything else. He pulled off three shots as fast as he could, and he didn't see Master Sergeant Henry Kester take action. Henry was too quick.

The wiry old sergeant literally threw himself at the hostage, and the shots from Curt's pistol caught both men. Curt saw the hostage jerk and fall backward as a bullet hit him, and with amazement, he saw Henry Kester spin around as he took a bullet also intended for the troublemaker.

Most of the hostages dropped to the roof instinctively at the sound of gunfire.

"Jesus, Henry! That was a goddam stupid sonofabitching thing to do!" Curt yelled, not really aware of what he was saying, but yelling out of frustration because he'd accidentally shot his master sergeant.

Lieutenant Alexis Morgan leaped over people to get to Henry Kester's side, pulling her medical kit from her bandolier as she did so.

Sergeant Edwina Sampson had an AKMS directly out in front of her, ready to fire. "Nobody moves!" she snarled. "Lieutenant, how's Henry? It bad?"

Alexis Morgan didn't look up from the master sergeant. "Don't know. I think he took a round in the belly. Hard to tell. Body armor."

Henry Kester's voice was full of pain. "Yeah, lower torso, near hip. Goddamned lucky it was only a nine-millimeter. Couldn't have done much damage . . . but I gotta admit it hurts like hell."

Curt was still frozen in the position he'd assumed when he'd seen Kester leap into the line of fire. He didn't drop the muzzle of the Beretta. "Shit!" was his only comment.

His stupefied hesitation was suddenly broken by the thunder of the eight aerodynes now hovering around the building. No time for recrimination. No time to figure out what happened. Henry Kester was wounded. He'd go out with the last flight. "Colonel! Sampson! Get these people aboard!" he yelled.

Edwina Sampson didn't hesitate. She knew that her slot in the last evacuation had gone to Kester, but she exposed herself to a hail of sporadic rifle fire and arrows as she shepherded the selected hostages to each aerodyne.

Curt had his hands full commanding the remaining hostages and the defending warbots. His job was now straightforward: Do whatever possible to supress Jehorkhim ground fire and get those eight aerodynes out of there without serious damage. The aircraft were taking hits from rifle fire. To some extent, they were armored against it, but there was always the chance of the lucky shot, "the golden BB," that might hit a critical point and bring down an aerodyne.

There was no time for farewells. Jehorkhim rifle and archery fire filled the air. The Jehorkhims knew better than to launch arrows at the aerodynes; they fired instead in high-angle trajectories that allowed the arrows to fall on the roof. Rifle fire wasn't as intense as before.

The evacuation was as orderly as possible under the circumstance. Curt never saw Alexis Morgan or Henry Kester board an aerodyne, but suddenly the aerodynes were disappearing over the rooftops of Zahedan, heading toward the aerodrome to the north.

Curt found Edwina Sampson on one side of him with an AKMS and Colonel Willa Lovell on the other with an RI Hornet. "Hold your fire!" he yelled over the wind and the sound of sporadic firing. "Save your ammo! Get under the aerodyne! Take cover! Warbots, shoot anyone who tries to come up those stairs. Don't fire at anyone in the street or in the building across the street unless someone fires at you."

He now had to organize the last stand on the rooftop. He still had communications with the RCP on the faraway slope of Kuh-e-Taftan. "Napoleon, this is Trajan Boss." He spoke into his helmet compak. "Colonel, the last airlift just departed."

"Roger, Trajan Boss. Listen, Curt, we're doing the best we can to regroup. We're going to try to get you out of there. How long can you hold out?"

"I don't know," Curt admitted. "When can we anticipate the next evac?"

"Can't tell you. In fact, I don't want to tell you." That meant Colonel Hettrick didn't want to take the slightest chance of compromising sensitive tactical information. Or maybe she really didn't know. Curt wanted to believe it was the first reason. He felt strung out, with everything exposed. Hettrick probably sensed that, because she told him, "Marshal your available forces and establish the best defensive situation you can. Don't report details to me; the Jehorkhims might be bugging this channel because they've pulled plenty of surprises already. But get your situation organized to your satisfaction and report to me that you've done so. We're staying here on Kuh-e-Taftan to support you."

Knowing that helped a little. But Curt decided he'd get busy and stay busy. That would keep him from brooding over how bad the situation really was and how much his left arm was hurting in spite of painkillers.

He took stock of what he had. Basically, eight people, including himself and Edwina Sampson, were left on the roof. He had eight M-22 assault bots and six of the lash-up transport bots left.

The bots could be used as the first line of defense. The transport bots were useless as fighting machines, but they would be useful as decoy targets or as a wall of inorganic mass the Jehorkhim soldiers would have to pass around or climb over. Curt decided to use them as his primary passive defense. As such, they wouldn't need fresh power packs. They might be able to function at low level for a long time on whatever power they had left. The M-22 assault bots, on the other hand, could be used to backup the transport bots as an active defense with their fletchette guns, grenades, and explosives. But he had to know how the assault bots' power reserves stacked up for what might be a long job. He ordered Sergeant Edwina Sampson to checkout each of them, drawing one out of the line at a time.

Then he looked over the rest of his irregular command.

Actually, these people weren't officially his to command. He could lead them only if they chose to follow. Except for Colonel Lovell and Sergeant Sampson, they weren't Army. They were civilians he'd been sent to rescue.

Seven people were more than he'd ever led in battle. With the advent of robot warfare, the number of humans in a combat RI company had been drastically reduced from about a hundred to six. He didn't know how he'd organize his irregular force. But maybe he wouldn't have time, and maybe it couldn't be done anyway.

His remaining manpower was armed mostly with old Soviet AKMS semiautomatic rifles taken from dead Jehorkhims. Each person seemed to have between thirty and seventy rounds of the fat, truncated brass-cased ammunition for those rifles. Some of the civilians didn't know how to shoot very well, but they could point guns, pull triggers, and scare Jehorkhims in the process.

Curt thought it was a good thing that the old AKMS was the sort of gun even the most ignorant peasant could operate. Of the remaining hostages, all were males. Some were mildly injured but all were ambulatory, intelligent, American and Japanese businessmen. In a pinch like this, they could shoot the AKMS well enough to cause the Jehorkhims to keep their heads down or, if the Imam's men attacked, to reduce the attackers' numbers. Curt figured it would be an expensive matter in terms of men for the Imam to attempt an assault on the roof.

He and Sampson were still carrying several kilos of plasticex and initiators. If worse came to worse, they could blow the external stairway off the building, and that would make it more difficult for the Jehorkhims to storm their bastion.

Behind the cover of assault bots, he and the sergeant installed plasticex in critical areas at the head of the stairway. They armed the charges with initiators, but didn't activate them. Blowing away the stairway also meant destroying their only way to get off the roof. They might need it. And he didn't need to blow it away just yet; he would catch some Jehorkhims on it when he did blow it.

When Curt got back to the shade of the aerodyne, he found Willa Lovell examining the 7.62-millimeter Hornet machine pistol that Jerry Allen had once carried. "Know how to use that?" Curt asked.

She looked darkly back at him. "No. I've never had a gun in my hand before today. They used to frighten me. Now this doesn't scare me at all, certainly not as much as those Jehorkhims and that bitch Taisha." She turned the Hornet over in her hands, studying it with almost academic fervor.

"You've never shot a gun before?" It seemed impossible to Curt that an Army colonel had never done so.

"Never. I was commissioned out of med school. Noncombat designator code," she explained. "I assume this is like any gun I've seen on television: point it at someone you want to kill and pull the trigger."

"That's the general idea. Can you do it?"

"What do you mean, can I do it?"

"Some people can't pull the trigger when the gun is pointed at someone else," Curt told her bluntly. "What type of person are you?"

Without the slightest hesitation, Willa replied coldly, "I've already shot Jehorkhims today. So if I'm pointing it at a Jehorkhim, I won't have the slightest hesitation about pulling the trigger. And if I miss on the first shot, I'll keep firing until he goes down."

"I hope so." Time would tell. He believed she'd do it, but it was hard to know for certain. Despite his years as an officer in the Robot Infantry and the robot combat he'd seen, Curt had never personally killed a human being with a firearm before that day. He'd often wondered whether or not he could do it. But when it had become a matter of saving his own life, he hadn't even thought about it. He'd pulled the trigger. Still, some people weren't that way, especially in cultures where such raw, naked violence was shown only on television and rarely experienced in person.

A firearm is an extremely violent weapon, and Curt had been surprised to learn that some people weren't afraid of them but cowered at the sight of a bare blade. It might have been helpful had these old Soviet weapons been fitted with the bayonets which had once made some firearms deadly close combat weapons. Swiss pikes. But bayonets had disappeared from military arsenals years ago.

"What do I do when it stops shooting?" Willa wanted to know.

"A Hornet ejects the empty magazine forward. You'll

see it and feel the additional recoil. When you do, take one of these preloaded box magazines and simply slide it into the front end of the piece until it clicks into place. The magazine can be inserted only in one direction: the proper direction. The first cartridge will be chambered automatically. The gun is then ready to shoot another fifty rounds."

"Sounds easy enough. Good design."

"It had to be. It was designed for use under very stressful conditions," Curt explained.

"How much ammunition do we have?"

"Not enough. Probably some more in the aerodyne, but I haven't looked."

"Speaking of this aerodyne"—Colonel Willa Lovell looked up at its brooding hulk—"why won't it fly?"

"Because someone who didn't know any better had the sand filter screens removed from the engine inlets in order to get additional power to lift the load we carried," Curt explained in an irritated voice. "Overboosted the engines and allowed foreign objects to get into the bearings. And the craft took an accidental sea-water bath just as the mission began."

"Have you tried to start it?"

He shook his head. "I've been pedaling as fast as I can."

"Pardon me?"

"Sorry. Old RI joke. I'll explain it someday when we're not under the gun."

"Try starting the aerodyne. Maybe it'll lift."

Curt grimaced. "I don't think so, but I'll give it a try. Maybe it'll get us as far as the RCP on Kuh-e-Taftan." He turned to Sampson. "Sergeant, I'm going to try firing up Trajan. If anything lights off, he may blow a lot of air around."

"Couldn't blow things around any more than this damned wind," Sampson growled.

Willa Lovell looked around the interior of the ship as the two of them went aboard. "You know, we could hold out in here if worse comes to worse."

"Eight people? In this tin can? It'd be more than a little crowded."

"Yes, but the Jehorkhims would have trouble getting in, and that might allow for a little more delay."

"Thanks for the suggestion. The only thing that worries me about it is the very simple way the Jehorkhims have of getting us out."

"What's that?" the robotic expert wanted to know.

"They'd simply light a fire under it."

"And burn down the building?"

"Ever build a campfire on a wooden floor?"

"No, but—"

"Put down a couple inches of sand—there's plenty of that around here—then build the fire on top of that."

"Oh. It wasn't such a good idea. If you can get this ship started, can't you blow out the fire?"

"I don't know. But I don't want to risk it. We could get fried."

"Yes, it is pretty hot in here."

"Aerodynes get damned hot in the desert sun. I wouldn't sit in the copilot's seat if I were you. It's a ball burner—in your case, a check burner. And don't put your hands on any surface that's been hit by the sunlight shining through the canopy." Curt slid into the pilot's seat. It was hot, but he was wearing body

261

armor and battle dress. He flipped the master switch. Stand-by batteries should have kept Trajan's AI unit active. And they had.

"Trajan, report the status of your engines," Curt ordered.

"Four of seven are out of action," the aerodyne reported. "Preliminary analysis conducted after three and four cooled off showed foreign objects had infiltrated the upper spool bearings. I have determined it was the result of operating without inlet filters and screens. Engine one overheated the hot section and may have scalloped turbine blades. Engine five suffered accelerated corrosion damage due to the presence of sea water and subsequent lift-off and operation before drying out the compressor section. The sea water getting into the working parts should be rated as a Contingency One mission abort condition."

Too late to worry about that. It was just another screwup that resulted from pressure to get the mission off. "What's the best lift-off power you can generate?"

"By short-term overspeeding, I can give you forty-six-point-seven percent power."

"Is that enough to lift?"

"Negative! I need sixty percent power to lift my empty weight plus the weight of the fuel on board at this time."

Curt scratched his chin where the stubble of a beard was beginning to itch. "Assume an eight-person load and enough fuel dumped to permit you to lift off with available power. What's your range under those conditions?"

"Range isn't a factor. Time aloft is. I could stay up about three minutes under those conditions."

"Nice try," Willa Lovell muttered.

Curt nodded. "Well, the ship will roast in this sun, but there's water here. And I can always use Trajan as a last resort."

"How's that?"

"Load everyone aboard and run the engines up. The down-blast over the roof won't lift us, but it will sure as hell make it tough for anyone to stay on his feet out there. Or to get that fire going under us. As a last ditch defense and delaying tactic, that might gain us an hour or two until the Jehorkhims figure out that we can't lift."

He told Trajan to stay alive and ready, and the two of them debarked onto the roof. With the gusty wind blowing, it was a bit cooler on the open roof than inside the aerodyne.

Curt's pain-numbed mind suddenly generated an idea. He called Hettrick on his helmet compak. "Napoleon, this is Trajan Boss. Did the transport get off the aerodrome okay?"

"Roger, Trajan Boss, it did."

"Where are the aerodynes that were deployed out there? Can they airlift us to your RCP?"

"They're out of fuel. And I've got a tough situation on my hands. The Jehorkhims are regrouping and moving. They've wiped out most of the Marauders' warbots, and we've had to abandon the Warriors' bots at the aerodrome."

That was bad news. The Washington Greys of the 17th Division (RI) were taking a beating.

263

But they weren't beaten yet. Not as long as one of them had the ability to resist.

Curt needed to know how many Jehorkhims might be available for an assault on the roof. "What about the Jehorkhim casualties? Have we hurt them any? How many Jehorkhims are left? And please give me a reasonably accurate count, Colonel, not another Gee-two estimate."

There was no sharpness in Colonel Belinda Hettrick's reply although she knew full well what Curt meant. "Rough count indicates about eight hundred to a thousand Jehorkhims left."

"Crap!" Curt breathed when he heard those numbers. "I never dreamed my career would end in the modern equivalent of Custer's Last Stand."

"What was that, Captain?"

"Never mind, Colonel."

The Guard dies but never surrenders! Those were fighting words. But how closely could he follow that ancient battle cry of the Napoleonic wars? They had been fought a long time ago in a different world and against a different enemy, one that might treat captured soldiers and officers with honor and dignity if they surrendered. Curt doubted that the Imam and his Jehorkhims would pay the slightest bit of attention to the Modified Geneva or Manila accords, and he didn't relish the idea of fighting to the death. But he resigned himself to the possibility of doing so, especially in light of the way the Jehorkhims had treated the Orient Express hostages.

The blazing sun was at the zenith, and the roof became hotter and hotter. Had it not been for the very dry, gusty north wind, it would have been unbearable. As it was, several men began to turn beet red from sunburn, and Curt had to order them into the shade. Field rations for eighteen man-days were found in Trajan, and Curt saw to it that these were divided up equally among them. It wasn't very much but it would last for another couple of days at least.

Water could become a problem however. Even though there was a supply aboard Trajan, one Golden BB into the boost water tank could dump it all onto the roof in short order. Willa Lovell figured it out: Everyone would require between three and four liters of water per day, more if the fighting got active. With what was available in Trajan, they had about six days' supply left.

Curt figured the enemy's estimate would be on the low side, because they didn't know of the additional supply in Trajan. The Imam just might try to wait them out, knowing that the longer he waited the less resistance his troops would meet.

But Curt also knew the Imam hadn't counted on the assault bots which didn't need water.

According to Curt's sit-guess, the first attack would come shortly after sunset.

Colonel Willa Lovell wanted to know why.

Curt explained to her, "The Imam knows we've been up here all day. He can figure out that we're very hot, wind-weary, maybe thirsty, and probably exhausted. He'll have his Jehorkhim troops make an assault about an hour before sundown. Look for it just after a prayer session in which they've made their peace with Allah."

"Okay, I'll buy that." Willa Lovell looked up at Curt and asked, "What do you intend to do, Captain?"

"Fight like hell. You know our doctrine and code of honor as well as I do," Curt pointed out to her.

"Well, I remember something about it, but I've never paid much attention to it because I didn't have to," Lovell admitted. "I'm with you, Captain. I don't relish the idea of what the Jehorkhims might do to us if we surrender."

Curt's compak chimed. It was Colonel Hettrick in the RCP on Kuh-e-Taftan. "Trajan Boss, this is Napoleon. Something's happening. A contingent of about two hundred Jehorkhims is heading back into Zahedan. About seven hundred more are mounted and moving rapidly in squadron-sized units toward the riverbed south of town. Looks like they're going to bivouac for the night down by the river where forage and water exist for the animals. Have you detected any increased level of Jehorkhim activity there?"

"None," Curt reported. "It's pretty damned quiet ... like the Jehorkhims were waiting for reinforcements. You say they're on their way ... Maybe. Did you say about eight hundred of them were mounted and heading south?"

"That's what our sensors are seeing."

Curt Carson suddenly asked, "Colonel, do you know how fast a mounted unit can move? Light cavalry squadrons used to be able to travel about ten kilometers per hour under forced march conditions. If I were you, I'd be on the lookout for an assault by those mounted troops. They could be at Kuh-e-Taftan by sunset!"

"Ridiculous! They don't know we're out here!"

"The Jehorkhims know the general direction our 'dynes came from earlier today; they were up and getting ready for morning prayers when we moved in. And they've got someone who knows something about robots, an Indo-Chinese scientist known as Dr. Rhosha Taisha. I don't know whether or not she's got the equipment to receive and pinpoint our communication," Curt reported. "But don't automatically assume that they haven't been tapping our tactical command net. And even if they don't know exactly where you are, they'll send those light cavalry units out on a scouting mission. Cavalry has always been good at that. I think that's what they're doing. When do you plan to mount a rescue mission to get us out?"

"Curt, we can't do anything before dawn tomorrow, provided Division can scrape together some reinforcements tonight and get them in here."

"Colonel, what are *you* going to do if that Jehorkhim light cavalry scouting mission shows up late this afternoon?"

"The only thing we can do: Conduct a retrograde operation. We haven't got enough warbots left to defend the RCP," his commanding officer pointed out.

In plain English, they would retreat, leaving Curt and seven people stranded on a rooftop in Zahedan.

CHAPTER FIFTEEN

It had been a very bad day. And Curt could see no way out of the bad time to come. He didn't know whether the Jehorkhims wanted to wipe them out or capture them alive.

Still, there was nothing he could do but wait, which made it even more difficult.

He was honest with Sergeant Edwina Sampson when she crawled across the roof to the shade of the aerodyne during a lull in the sporadic fighting and asked him bluntly, "Captain, what are our chances?"

"Of what?" Curt asked in return, though he knew full well what she meant.

"Of being rescued."

"Right now, not very good. Tomorrow, maybe better."

"Come on, Captain, don't fence with me. I'm in no damned mood to play games. I'll put it straight: What are our chances of getting out of here alive?"

"Not very damned good, Sergeant."

"That's what I thought. Hell, I'm glad you didn't try to pep-talk me," she replied with equal candor, nodding her head under her helmet. "What do the Jehor-khims do to soldiers they capture in battle?"

"I don't know whether or not these religious nuts follow the Hague and Geneva Conventions or the Manila Compact ... or if they even know a damned thing about them," Curt admitted, not really wanting to tell her that he believed the rooftop contingent was facing slaughter or slow death by torture. "Would it help if you knew, Sergeant?"

"Not much, except I might be a little more mean and nasty when we got right down to the final fight, depending." She looked thoughtful for a moment, ran her hand along the butt of her AKMS. It was obvious she wanted to say something but didn't know exactly how to phrase it. "Uh, Captain, I know that discipline counts when things go to slime." She hesitated. "But I'm the only sergeant left here, so you don't really have to call me Sergeant. Knowing what might be ahead of us ... it would make me feel a little better if, uh, you'd call me 'Edie' until this mess gets settled."

"Hell, yes, Edie. Why not?"

Her camouflage-smeared face, though beaded with sweat, suddenly seemed a bit brighter, and her greenish eyes took on a bit of sparkle. Curt had upped her morale, and that was something they all needed at the moment. With the hint of a smile playing around the corners of her thin lips, Sampson told him, "Thank you, Captain. We might not see another sunset together."

"Bullshit! We will!"

"Well, if we do, then I'm Sergeant Sampson again. But it's nice to know that I'm Edie for a little while ...

269

just in case things don't work out. After all, we've been through a few fur balls together."

"We won them, too, don't forget."

"Yes, sir! And with some luck and a little guts, we'll get out of this one too." She touched her helmet visor with the fingers of her right hand in an informal salute. "I'll go check out the initiators on the stairway explosives again. Just want to make sure . . ."

There was a clink of metal as Colonel Willa Lovell sat down next to him, crossed her arms, and brought her wrist shackles into contact with one another. She got right to the point. "Why did General Carlisle send human troops in here?" she suddenly asked.

"General Carlisle didn't. General Knox was in command of this operation," Curt informed her.

"Knox? Oh, yes, I remember him."

"Yeah, an unforgettable character."

"Whatever in the world was he thinking about when he planned this mess? Or was he thinking at all?" When Curt didn't answer, she went on, "Sorry, that's not a fair question. But I can't understand why such a straightforward mission like this could get botched up to the point of failure."

Curt had to remind himself that Colonel Willa Lovell had a noncombat designator code. She wouldn't understand how a complex mission could go tits-up because of bad planning and the unexpected vagaries of combat. So he simply said, "Because the RI and the Army have become victims of the same sort of thinking that's plagued military people since the dawn of time."

"What do you mean?"

"Every time the military gets a new type of technology, we tend to treat it in three sequential ways," Curt pointed out. "When we first hear about it, we don't think it will work or affect what we've already got and how we fight; so we ignore it until it gets used against us or becomes much better than what we've got. In the second phase, we cautiously try it out in the most conservative way with doctrine that doesn't match its technical capabilities, usually under the goading of a Billy Mitchell type, and we end up using it the wrong way or incompletely and therefore ineffectively. Finally, when we find it works just great, we build the whole damned military establishment around it. We forget a lot of what we learned before and depend too heavily on this new technology. And that always leads to the same consequences."

"Oh? What consequences?"

"We get caught short by our dependence on a new technology and on the doctrines, strategies, and tactics we develop for it. Always. Never fails. That's exactly and precisely what happened in this operation."

"You're trying to tell me that doctrine screwed it up, not people?" Willa asked in an unbelieving tone. "Excuse me, Captain, but General Knox's reputation is widely known."

Curt shrugged. "I'm sure it is. But we've all got to share the blame a little bit. We really didn't know how to do a hostage strike and rescue mission like this one without warbots. We haven't done anything like it in a couple of decades. People like General Knox remember the glory of such action; others, like Master Sergeant Henry Kester who crawled on his belly through the mud, weren't asked. So we went into personal combat with

271

warbot doctrine. A hundred years ago, a battalion of United States Marines would have known how to get in here and get everyone out with minimum losses."

"We haven't needed personal combat troops for a long time," Colonel Willa Lovell pointed out. "Warbots have been perfectly good extensions to the capabilities of human soldiers."

Curt nodded. "Yeah, I thought so, too. I'm a military officer who was educated to fight in every way known to man. But after I graduated from the United States Military Academy, I was trained as a warbot brainy to fight through my warbots. So was my company, my regiment, and the Seventeenth Division, Robot Infantry. But in this operation, we had to improvise. And we did it wrong. In the dumb, stumbling process of slapping this operation together with half-assed intelligence and the wrong goddamned approach, we failed to do simple things that any twentieth-century soldier would have pulled off. So here we are, too little and too late, without the right weapons, and with weapons we haven't employed properly. Furthermore, we were forced to meet an arbitrary and unrealistic schedule despite equipment failures that damned well should have caused us to abort the mission early in the game."

"You're being pretty harsh on the Army. And yourself," the robotics expert observed quietly.

Curt sighed. "Well, Christ, what the hell else can I say, Colonel? We blew it! We screwed it royally! And that's the way I think the mission critique will go. But I may never live to be raked over the coals for the mistakes I've made or for someone else's."

"I prefer to take a more positive view," Willa replied

after pausing to think about what Curt had told her. "We'll make it. And when we do, I'd like to get you detached to Ordnance R&D so you can help work out some of the bugs in the present equipment."

"Hell, Colonel, the problem isn't bugs in the equipment," Curt declared. "It's the way warbot brainies and staff stooges and even you science types *think*. The big, unquestionable, undebatable belief right now is simple: The warbot is the answer to riskless warfare. It ain't. Zahedan is proving that. We don't like it. At least, I don't like it."

He didn't tell her that he didn't want to waste his time trying to convince science-boffos what it was really like to be engaged in warbot or personal combat. If he got out of this, he wanted to go back to Carson's Companions, his own outfit. He wanted to make some changes in the training schedules and methods so that if they ever had to do anything like this again, they'd be prepared for it and they could hack it. To hell with doctrine and tactical procedures worked out by staff stooges; he and his Companions would work them out for themselves. Let the science-boffos come to see *him!*

The long afternoon passed with only occasional sniping or raining arrows. It was obvious that the Jehorkhims were running short of ammunition or were conserving what they had for an assault. Occasionally, one of the M-22 assault bots fired a few fletchettes down the stairway. Assault bots didn't waste ammo, so Curt knew a Jehorkhim soldier had been hit when he heard a bot shot. That was the only advantage in having warbots on a personal combat mission. Warbots could draw and absorb fire that otherwise would be aimed at people.

Curt reflected again on the old saying that most of a soldier's time is spent waiting for something to happen. He tried to rest in the shade of Trajan, but his arm had swelled up under his body armor, putting pressure on the tissues and increasing his pain and immobility. He took more painkillers and wished that Willa Lovell had inserted some acupuncture blocks; but his body armor had made that impossible.

He knew that this mission was going to lead to some major changes in doctrine for the Army. Much that was known about personal combat had been forgotten or ignored in the years since robot warfare had become predominant. Now it had been learned and relearned.

But Curt decided he didn't like personal combat. It was too dirty, too exhausting, and too intense.

Still, he was a soldier. He had work to do, even if it involved only the ancient art of preparing and holding a defensive position against impossible odds. His plan was straightforward: Hold out as long as possible, minimizing casualties and conserving water, food, and ammo. The longer he held out, the better the chance a rescue mission would get to them.

But he had strong doubts that he could hold out long enough. He knew the situation, knew how long it would take to get forces to this isolated part of the world. The entire resources of the 17th Division and even those of the RI itself were probably being marshaled in order to redress this costly rescue mission, he was certain of that.

And he wasn't going to surrender. The code of the

American soldier required him to fight until there was no way left to resist. He was going to hang on by his fingernails as long as he could.

But he didn't have many resources—only a motley collection of businessmen, some of whom had never fired a weapon before, others who'd been trained in the oriental martial arts, and a couple who were so frightened that he really didn't know whether or not he could count on them. There was no time to train these men, and some of them couldn't have undergone military training anyway; they were too individualistic and undisciplined.

Curt and his seven people, plus a motley array of warbots could be outnumbered and overwhelmed with relative ease even if the stairway was blown away with plasticex to prevent its use in an assault. The Jehorkhims could certainly scale the seven-meter wall and parapet using wall-climbing pikes, Lucerne hammers, grappling hooks, ladders, and other equipment. Guns wouldn't even be needed. For the hand-to-hand fighting on the roof, Jehorkhim bows, crossbows, lances, and scimitars would be perfectly adequate. And if a sunset assault didn't work, the Jehorkhims had the manpower to try again during the night or at dawn. Sooner or later, Curt and his mixed force would be worn down or reduced in numbers. Then they would have two choices: surrender or fight to the death. Curt wouldn't surrender, but he didn't like to think of the alternative.

There seemed to be no way out. Curt knew Hettrick couldn't mount a rescue mission with the limited equipment she had available. Rescue, when it came, would be at least twenty-four to forty-eight hours in the future. And that was a long time off.

About an hour before sunset, his helmet compak chimed to draw his attention. He had the sinking feeling that the worst was happening even before he heard Colonel Belinda Hettrick call, "Trajan Boss, this is Napoleon!" There was a note of urgency in her voice.

"Go ahead, Napoleon. Trajan Boss is listening."

"Trajan Boss, you were right, dammit! We've been discovered by the advance elements of about seven hundred mounted Jehorkhim troops. Attack has just started." There was no panic in Colonel Hettrick's voice, but he knew she was concerned and upset because he'd warned her of this possibility earlier. "Sorry, but I'm initiating an immediate retrograde operation."

It was bound to happen, Curt told himself. "Can you divert to Zahedan and pick us off this roof as you withdraw? Got enough room?"

"Negative, negative! We're abandoning our warbots and even our tactical aerodynes! I've gotta get us out of here! We're not equipped for personal combat. Sorry, Curt, but we'll be back! We'll get you out! That I promise you!"

Well, maybe she would, Curt thought, recalling another commander who'd withdrawn with the dramatic words, "I shall return!" He had. But a lot of people had been killed while he was gone. "Okay, but I'm going to keep my helmet compak on as long as it works. Maybe one of the satellites can pick it up and maintain communication with you. In any event, have someone monitor it so you'll know what's happening to us!" The compak was powered by Curt's body heat; it would go

276

dead only if he were killed or if someone took his helmet from him.

"You're being monitored through Diamond Poi—" Suddenly, the transmission from Hettrick ceased. To Curt, that meant one of two things: Hettrick had been KIA or she'd been actually killed. He tried to reestablish contact. He couldn't.

Curt didn't tell anyone. Only Edie Sampson knew about the command post on Kuh-e-Taftan. No need to upset her with the news that it was being abandoned, and they were now stranded in Zahedan. She was ready for that, but he didn't want to destroy the final thread of hope for rescue that might be holding his irregular contingent together.

He wondered if the Jehorkhims were monitoring the tactical command frequency between Curt and Hettrick, for the Jehorkhim assault on the roof began almost at once.

Every window of the nearby two-story government building suddenly seemed to sprout two or three rifle muzzles. The covering fire that swept the rooftop was intense. Everyone had to take cover behind the parapet facing it.

"Jehorkhim soldiers are coming up the stairs!" came the report from one of the M-22 assault bots.

"Blow 'em, Edie!" Curt yelled.

When the plasticex detonated, the masonry building rocked and shook, and it seemed for an instant that the whole side would collapse and let the roof fall into the interior.

One of the assault bots didn't get out of the way in time and was thrown off the roof and dashed onto the street below. One quick look told Curt that the bot hadn't been a total loss; it had landed on about four Jehorkhim soldiers who wouldn't be taking part in the roof assault.

No Jehorkhim soldiers charged up the stairs because they were no longer there. But Curt and the others were pinned down behind the parapet.

Arrows began to rain down on them, fired from the street on the other side of the building. They took their toll. One man was struck in the leg, and another in the side. The man who went to help them took an arrow in the fleshy part of his lower torso.

Curt felt the shock wave before he saw the results. The opposite side of the roof erupted in an explosion. Roofing lumber, and plaster dust flew into the air. The hostage who'd been covering that side of the roof was picked up and thrown, like a limp rag doll, over the parapet and into the street.

Now only Curt, Edwina Sampson, Willa Lovell, and one hostage were capable of fighting.

The Jehorkhims had set explosives on the second floor ceiling, probably a shaped charge or Limpet mine, and had blown an access hole to the roof large enough for one or two men to scramble through at a time.

But when Jehorkhim soldiers showed their heads through that hole, they became perfect targets. Willa Lovell was the first to shoot and got her man. Edie Sampson wasn't far behind her in getting off a burst that also found its target. The only hostage who wasn't wounded turned out to be an excellent marksman, too. As long as those who could fire a weapon had ammunition, no Jehorkhim was going to climb through that hold onto the roof.

After only two minutes of frenzied action, everything went quiet again. Even the devastating rifle and arrow fire ceased. Either the Jehorkhims were low on ammunition or they were regrouping for their next assault.

"What next?" Sampson wanted to know.

"They may try blowing the roof over on this side," Curt guessed. "Everyone spread out along the parapet. That way, one explosion isn't going to get all of us."

But no explosion came.

More than twenty minutes went by, and nothing happened.

Then, incongruously and incredibly, a white cloth tied to a broom handle slowly came up through the hole in the roof and was waved back and forth. A loud voice called, "Cease fire! May we have a temporary cease fire? I offer you negotiations under a flag of truce!"

"The Imam!" Willa Lovell breathed.

"Why in the hell does he want to talk under a white flag?" Edie Sampson wondered. "Are you gonna parley with him, Captain? Can we trust the bastard?"

"I don't know. If he wants to talk, let him show himself . . . unarmed."

"Captain, if he comes up on the roof to parley, he'll be a sitting duck if he tries anything," Edwina Sampson whispered.

"He's under a flag of truce, Edie," Curt pointed out.

"Bullshit. If I kill him, court-martial me."

"If you kill the Jehorkhim leader, there's no telling what those crazies will do," Curt told her. "It's better to confront someone who's in charge than to face a

279

frenzied mob or a vengeful successor. Besides, I want to buy some time. I'll parley, but I won't give him a goddamned thing. Keep me covered," Curt said. Then he called out, "Very well! We agree to parley under a flag of truce. Come up to the roof through the hole . . . slowly . . . unarmed . . . and alone."

The Imam Abdul Madjid Rahman was so confident of his control of the situation that he crawled up onto the roof bearing the white banner. But he didn't move away from the opening.

"You're a good soldier, sir," the Imam observed levelly, when Curt stepped out from under the aerodyne and faced him. "May I have the honor of knowing your name?"

"Curtis Christopher Carson, Captain, United States Army, serial number 60-299-716-96, date of birth March—"

"Ah, yes, the Geneva Convention. Well, don't worry, Captain Carson. I don't need military information."

"And you would be? . . ." Curt knew, but he wanted the Imam to go through the same protocol.

"Abdul Madjid Rahman, Imam of the Jehorkhim Muslims by the grace of Allah the Beneficent, the Merciful." The Imam spoke in perfect, fluent academic Oxonian English. "You and your people have put up a valiant fight, Captain Carson."

"We don't give up if we can still fight," Curt told him briefly.

"That is obvious. But your situation here is quite untenable," the Imam pointed out, unnecessarily. "We can storm this roof and kill or capture all of you at any time we wish to do so. If we don't do it within the next

280

few hours, we will certainly do it within the next day. Your food, water, and ammunition won't last forever. But if you persist, more people on both sides will be killed or wounded. This is unnecessary, Captain. And it would be a pity to have to slaughter such good soldiers."

"I have no intention of surrendering to you, Imam," Curt told him firmly. He was tired and feeling mean so he added. "Not as long as I have the means to resist. We may all be killed up here, but that's sure as hell better than being tortured in your dungeons. I don't think you'd pay the slightest goddamned attention to the Hague, Geneva, or Manila conventions."

The Imam smiled. "You're right. I have no intention of adhering to those flawed agreements. I follow the Koran and the laws of the Prophet. They are much more stringent and explicit with regard to treatment of opponents captured in battle after a valiant fight."

"Bullshit!" Curt was deliberately using rough language. "You sure as hell didn't show the Orient Express hostages any decent treatment!"

"Ah, but they were not valiant warriors!" the Imam fired back. "They were sheep, mere bleating animals who made no attempt to defend themselves! Such people deserve whatever the victor decrees." The contempt in the Imam's voice was quickly replaced by a conciliatory tone. "A warrior is treated differently by Jehorkhims. Those of you on this roof have put up a valiant fight." The Imam paused, then went on, "To surrender in the face of such great odds is no disgrace. If you surrender to me now and disarm yourselves, you will be confined as prisoners, of course, and you will be held

281

for ransom in accordance with our tradition. But we will not torture you.''

The Imam shrugged. ''Otherwise, we shall continue the battle at great cost to both of us.''

In spite of the assurances of the Imam, Curt knew that he would never surrender and turn six other people over to this fanatic who'd already shown himself to be utterly brutal in his treatment of prisoners.

''I won't surrender as long as I have the capability to fight,'' Curt stated flatly.

The Imam looked around at the hard-faced men and women on the roof, all armed and apparently far more deadly than those he'd had in his dungeons. Some were badly wounded, but they still seemed defiant. ''It's surprising how quickly one can become a fighter,'' the Imam observed. ''But, Captain, half your people are wounded. Do you have medical services available to treat them?''

''I have a doctor,'' Curt replied.

''But no adequate medical supplies,'' the Imam went on smoothly. ''I offer to take your three wounded men and provide proper medical treatment for them.''

This offer stopped Curt. He said nothing for a moment, then asked, ''Why do you make this offer?''

''Because they will die without more medical care than you can give them on this rooftop. And because I am basically a compassionate man; I do not like to see valiant warriors suffer. The Koran instructs me to care for the sick, the wounded, the hungry, and especially the valiant wounded, enemy or no.''

''These wounded men aren't under my command; they're hostages we came to rescue,'' Curt observed.

"I'll ask them what they want to do." He turned his back on the Imam and walked over to the parapet, deliberately standing tall and presenting an obvious target for the snipers in the other building. He knew there was a chance he'd be shot, but he was hoping his body armor would stop or slow down a Soviet bullet. Still, if the sniper was a good shot and hit his unprotected area, he'd never know what had happened.

He was really testing the Imam's sincerity; either the religious leader would operate under the white flag, or he couldn't be trusted.

Curt spoke to the wounded men, one of whom was nearly unconscious. "Gentlemen, the Imam has offered to care for you as wounded warriors. Apparently, he makes a distinction between you as hostages and as warriors who've fought the Jehorkhims. I don't know what sort of medical capability he has, but it's got to be more than what I can offer. If you continue to fight with us, you're likely to die from those wounds. Or you can decide to let the Jehorkhims take care of you. Gentlemen, what will it be?"

One of the wounded was Japanese. He was badly hurt, an arrow was lodged in his left side. He was in pain, yet he was doing a magnificent job of refusing to show it. "We have not forgotten the code of Bushido," he said slowly. "Give me a rifle. I will die fighting. Banzai!"

A wounded American, a young man in his late twenties, was bleeding, for he had deliberately wrenched the steel-barbed Jehorkhim arrow from his leg. Breathing hard, he croaked from his dry mouth, "I heard what he said. I also know what he did to my friends, and to

283

the other passengers." He still had shackles on his wrists, and he held them out. "I'd rather die up here than go back to those dungeons and torture chambers! I don't want to watch another person tortured to death!"

The older American who was wounded in the upper leg spoke up. "Captain, why don't you just give up? There's no hope for any of us."

Curt was blunt. "I'm a professional soldier. I don't surrender as long as I can still fight. But you're not in the Army. The Imam has offered surrender terms which I cannot accept. But he's also offered to care for the wounded. You heard him. You're free to take him up on his offer if you want."

"Fuck him," the young American said. "We've got him to the point where he's willing to talk under a white flag. That means we're giving his troops a real hard time. I'm tired and dirty and hungry and hurting like hell. But, shit, as long as we're hassling him and as long as I can get a painkiller so I can continue to shoot, let's keep it up."

"Don't you want to get out of here alive?" the older American asked.

"Yeah, but not as a prisoner. Being a prisoner of this bastard sucks."

"I'm throwing in the towel," the older man said. "I've had it. He said he'd treat us with respect as worthy opponents. I believe him."

The younger American spat on the ground. "I'll see you in hell."

The older man was engulfed in pain, the steel-tipped arrow having penetrated his left side just above the hip.

"Just get me out of here, please. This hurts so damned bad . . ."

Curt turned to Edie Sampson. "Help me get him over to the Imam. Colonel Lovell, please take care of the other wounded men." Curt indicated the Japanese and the young American.

He turned and walked back over to the Imam. "One of the wounded men has decided to take you up on your offer."

"A wise move. I suggest you might consider it as well, Captain."

"Sorry, not this year . . ."

The Imam stepped aside, dropped the white flag through the hole in the roof, and then gestured for two armed and white-turbaned Jehorkhim soldiers to climb up and help the wounded man. One of the Jehorkhims grabbed the sling on his old AKMS and hitched it around his other shoulder.

What happened then occurred so fast that Curt never really knew what went on until he talked with everyone much later and patched it together.

"Lyin', cheatin' bastards!" Edie Sampson screamed and shot the Jehorkhim who'd touched the rifle slung over his shoulder.

The Imam must have simply stepped back and dropped through the hole in the roof. He was suddenly gone.

But out of that hole came armed Jehorkhims.

And other armed Jehorkhims suddenly streamed over the parapet around the rooftop. Curt had been right in his guess. The Jehorkhim troops storming over the parapet carried no rifles, only scimitars and clubs.

Curt now realized what the Imam had done.

The Jehorkhim religious leader was smart and wily. He'd taken no chances. If Curt and the six others wouldn't surrender under the flag of truce, the Imam had Plan B. While he parleyed, his Jehorkhim soldiers quietly scaled the walls around the building, and they were ready to mount an assault the instant the white flag went down.

The Imam had dropped the white flag to allow his Jehorkhims to assist in lowering the wounded older man through the hole in the roof. Other Jehorkhims had seen the white flag disappear. Then Sergeant Edie Sampson had reacted in a trigger-happy way to the innocent move of a Jehorkhim.

Curt didn't see the Jehorkhim who hit him hard from behind.

CHAPTER SIXTEEN

Captain Curt Carson began to regain consciousness slowly. A bright light was shining in his eyes.

Oh, shit, the goddamned bright light-in-the-face bit! The Jehorkhims are torturing me! Bastards went back on the Imam's word, he thought.

Even without opening his eyes, he felt that the torture had already started. His left arm hurt like hell, and his head and right shoulder were throbbing with pain. He didn't open his eyes. Nor did he voice his next thought: Whatever the bastards are doing to me, it's already goddamned painful . . .

He could hear strange cries. Apparently the Jehorkhims were torturing someone else as well.

But when he became a bit more lucid and decided to open his eyes, he discovered that the brilliant sunlight of Baluchistan was shining on him through an open window.

The strange cry that reached his ears was coming from the minaret of the nearby mosque. A muezzin was calling the faithful to morning prayer.

It took a moment for the pieces of the puzzle to fall into place inside his throbbing head.

He wondered where the pain in his head and shoulder came from? He vaguely remembered being hit from behind.

Then the final moments on the roof came back to him.

In utter disgust, he said aloud, "Aw, shit, the goddamned Jehorkhims hit us when we weren't expecting it." He'd let down his guard, even though he'd known the Imam might not honor a flag of truce. Yet, parleying under a flag of truce didn't prevent either side from consolidating its forces in preparation for what might happen afterward.

He'd become too used to fighting through warbots. As a combat soldier, he should have been more wary, should have taken steps to prevent what had happened.

But what real chance had he had? His command, such as it had been, was reduced to Colonel Willa Lovell and Sergeant Edwina Sampson, the only two military people left on the roof, plus one sharpshooter civilian and the wounded.

Now, for all intents and purposes, he was a hostage. He couldn't be a prisoner of war in a conflict which didn't really exist. The United States Army wasn't fighting a declared war; the adversary wasn't a country, only a fanatical religious sect.

Curt didn't really know what his status was, or if the Geneva and Hague conventions meant a damned thing. Reality was different from what international lawyers talked about over green felt tables.

He'd have to play it by ear.

He took several deep breaths and came to the conclusion that he was still a soldier, whether he fought personally or through warbots. And long years of training made him pause and take stock.

First, he was still alive.

But he'd been stripped of his body armor. His mobile linkage harness had also been removed, along with the catheter and fecal bag. He was dressed only in his loose, sand-dappled desert-camouflage coverall. Being rid of the body armor helped; he could move a bit more freely. He was glad to be out of that piece of equipment.

But in view of Dr. Rhosha Taisha's experimentation, he was worried about his mobile linkage harness. It wasn't classified, but few people outside the RI really knew of its existence; most commercial robot operators used different forms of linkage equipment. Had Taisha seen anything like it before? Was she studying it? Thinking about how to apply it to the inverted technology that would put people under the control of computerized machines?

In fact, how the hell was Taisha working that reversal out? Curt took it for granted that machines were to serve people, and he couldn't understand how a thinking human being could allow a machine to take over and control him.

Well, he decided as his mind became more clear, he'd run through the first part of the drill. He was alive. He'd been stripped of his mobile linkage harness, his body armor, and the weapons he'd stashed on his person. He'd been totally disarmed. Whoever had stripped him, however, had also redressed him in his loosely woven coverall.

How about the rest of him?

He looked down at his left arm and discovered, much to his surprise, that the swelling wasn't as bad as it had seemed. It still hurt, but it wasn't as painful as it had been yesterday on the rooftop. Although the pain was dull and throbbing and distracting, he could move his fingers a little now. And he could flex his wrist, slowly. His left elbow was still extremely sore, but he could bend his arm a little. His triceps were the most painful part of his arm, and that pain ran down to his elbow. Tendon damage, he surmised. He rolled back his left sleeve to take a look, then wished he hadn't. His arm was black and blue, and yellow streaks ran through the bruises.

"Good God, that looks lousy! I'd better see if I can get some medication for it," he said to himself. It wasn't an open wound and probably wouldn't become gangrenous, but its nasty coloration worried him. Maybe the Jehorkhims didn't use medication. On the other hand, he remembered that ancient Arabic medicine had been more advanced than that in medieval Europe; the Crusaders had brought back a lot of Islamic medical knowledge.

The Jehorkhims may have already treated his arm. As his senses slowly reawakened, he noticed a strange, semisweet smell to the skin of his left arm. Apparently, someone had covered it with some sort of salve after he'd been captured.

The right side of his skull hurt; so did his right shoulder. But not as badly as his left arm. Pulling back his coverall, he saw that his shoulder was bruised where it had taken the glancing blow which had knocked him out of action. Well, he thought, that isn't as bad as some bruises I picked up in back alleys.

His face was covered with stubble and so was his head. He hadn't shaved either in more than—how long had it been?—at least thirty-six hours.

He checked himself over. Everything still seemed to be present and accounted for—spectacles, testicles, wallet, and watch, as the old inventory had it.

He hadn't been beaten or tortured. The Imam had kept his word about that ... thus far. And he wasn't chained or tied.

Okay, he was a prisoner. But he wasn't totally incapacitated.

He knew what to do.

The words drilled into him at West Point echoed in his memory: *If I am captured, I will continue to resist by all means available. I will neither accept parole nor special favors from the enemy.*

Okay, where the hell was he and how could he get out?

He let his eyes roam slowly around the room. It was an extremely plain place—no wall decorations, a high ceiling on which a single light bulb burned in a socket, and a single large window laced with ironwork. The brass bed was lumpy—he'd slept pretty well in spite of that—and there were no covers, nothing with which he could fashion a rope.

Two dead insects—they looked like huge roaches—were floating in the water pitcher on the floor near the head of the bed.

Also on the floor was an empty earthen pot. He decided it was about time he took a leak. Besides, urine could be thrown in a guard's face if he decided to try to escape.

Escape to where? He was in Zahedan, a primitive town in the Baluchistan province of eastern Iran, damned near a thousand kilometers from anywhere. Suppose he did get away? Could he find Sergeant Edwina Sampson, Colonel Willa Lovell, and the others? How could he get them all out of here?

He didn't know, but he decided he'd keep thinking about it. Planning an escape was one way for a POW to keep from going nuts.

As he urinated into the pot, he began to order his priorities. He ticked them off in his mind.

One: Escape.

Two: Find personal weapons.

Three: Find Edwina Sampson, Willa Lovell, and the others.

Four: Release them.

Five: Get the hell out of Zahedan.

He had a solution for only the fifth priority: He might be able to steal an airplane at the aerodrome *if* an aircraft he could fly just happened to be there. Or he might try to get aboard a train to Pakistan *if* a locomotive came to Zahedan. What happened next would be another matter; he had no idea how the Pakistanis were reacting to this American hostage-rescue mission because he didn't know if they'd scrambled their air-defense equipment against the mission or against the Iranians during yesterday morning's fly-in.

Or was it yesterday? He seemed to have lost a few hours somewhere.

As for the other four items on his escape priority list,

292

he didn't know how to achieve those. But because he'd now developed a rudimentary plan, feasible or not, he would keep his eyes open for ways to make it work or ways to modify it so he might take advantage of any opportunity that might present itself.

He stepped over to the window and looked around. The room was on the second floor. Therefore, he had to be in the building where he'd made the stand on the roof or in the two-story building that had been next to it. Beyond the iron filigreed bars was a sea of one-story structures.

He could see no way to get the iron grillwork loose. Even if he had, it was a four-meter drop to the street. He could injure an ankle jumping, and he had nothing with which to fashion a rope.

The door to the room opened and an armed, turbaned Jehorkhim brought in a bronze tray. On it was an orange-brown fruit a little smaller than an orange, with a waxy skin. There was also a bowl of what looked like mush, and a small cup which held some of the heaviest, darkest, most aromatic coffee he'd ever encountered. The Jehorkhim said nothing, didn't take his eyes off Curt, put the tray on the floor, and left. Curt heard a bolt being secured from without.

Well, at least they were going to feed him reasonably well. He sat down cross-legged on the floor and fell to.

Curt had never tasted a kumquat before. He decided that was what it had to be because it wasn't like any other citrus fruit he'd ever eaten. He remembered that according to the sexual lore of West Point cadets, a powerful aphrodisiac called rahadlakum was made from kumquat rind. A cadet had claimed that he'd found the

293

recipe in *The Arabian Nights*, but another had said he'd gotten the idea from an old Broadway stage show. Curt really didn't care about the aspect of kumquats on this morning since there didn't seem to be much opportunity to test the fruit's aphrodisiac characteristics. But he found the kumquat bitterly sweet, and it tasted strangely good to him, probably because he hadn't taken the time to eat for about twenty-four hours or so.

The mush wasn't very good, however. It was tepid, not hot, but it helped fill his stomach. He had no idea what it had been made from because its taste was new to him.

As for the thick, muddy coffee, it was strong enough to crawl out of the cup and wrestle him two falls out of three. Given Curt's condition that morning, it would have probably have won, but its bitterness helped him shake the weariness out of his brain.

Although he'd been on a low-residue diet for combat purposes, that had pretty well run its course, and Curt had to make up his mind whether to try the pot, a poor excuse for a bed pan, or thrill the Zahedans by mooning out the window while playing "bombs away." He chose the former. He really didn't want to take the chance that some zealous Jehorkhim might react adversely and shoot his ass off.

It was shortly thereafter that he was honored by an escort of four armed Jehorkhims who simply came in, blindfolded him with a black rag, and then roughly led him through doors, along corridors, and up and down stairs until he was thoroughly confused.

When the black blindfold came off, he found himself

294

in a large room with open windows through which the constant north wind of Baluchistan blew, providing a sort of natural air conditioning. The Imam, Abdul Madjid Rahman, was seated cross-legged on a Persian carpet that would have been worth a small fortune in New York City.

Seated in a more occidental fashion on an ornate wooden chair nearby and dressed in clean, well-tailored white slacks and a high-collared linen jacket was Dr. Rhosha Taisha, her beautiful Eurasian face brightly spattered with the patterns of sunlight that filtered through the intricately designed screen beside her. She was sipping tea from an exquisite gold-inlaid cup that was almost as delicate and exquisite as she.

Curt thought for a moment that the old story about the kumquat rind might have been right. Taisha was certainly twelve on a scale of ten, the sort of woman who rightly deserved the title of "crasher" because he was certain if he'd seen her walking down Sunset Boulevard he'd have crashed his car.

He decided that she was one hell of a beautiful, exotic woman. In another place and another time, under different circumstances, he would have laid on the macho rush just to see whether or not the feeling might be mutual.

But at the moment, he didn't think it was. Taisha was an absolutely gorgeous woman, but she wasn't radiating sexiness. In fact, he didn't like the way she was looking at him. There was something evil about this woman. It didn't show on her face, but it surrounded her like an aura. She was as deadly as a beautiful but hungry leopard.

"Good morning, Captain Carson!" the Imam said pleasantly. "I don't believe you've met my associate."

Curt didn't let on that he had met her remotely by means of the recon ratbot days ago. "I haven't had the pleasure," Curt replied. He was wary, but he felt it wouldn't hurt to play the role of officer and gentleman. The Imam had been well educated, probably in England. Although he might be a fanatic, it was obvious to Curt that the man wasn't a simple peasant. He extended polite courtesies, even to a prisoner.

"This is Dr. Rhosha Taisha," the Imam Rahman went on. "She is my technical advisor."

Curt bowed slightly but did not take her hand and shake it in the American fashion or kiss it in the European style because Taisha didn't offer it. She merely inclined her head slightly in a semioriental bow.

"Indeed?" Curt replied gallantly. "And what is your specialty, Doctor?"

She looked at him boldly with her large almond eyes, and replied with great coolness, "I am a neurologist specializing in human-machine interfaces."

"Really? I find that rather strange, knowing what I do of the Imam's religious beliefs," Curt observed, still standing rather awkwardly before them, his left arm dangling helplessly at his side.

"It's not at all strange," the Imam put in. "The holy book tells us not to use devices which mimic or improve upon the human being. Robots are extensions to human capabilities."

"Excuse me, but your troops used old Soviet AKMS assault rifles against us," Curt observed. "Isn't that as much an extension of human capabilities as the short bow your cavalry uses? Both extend the capabilities of the human arm to throw a rock."

The Imam waved his hand. "Not at all. The Soviet rifle is merely an improvement on the bow which was used in the time of the Prophet. In view of the fact that we do have several hundred Soviet rifles, it was my interpretation that they were necessary to our *jihad* and could therefore be considered improved bows."

Hypocritical sonofabitch! Curt thought. But the Imam was empowered by his religion to make such interpretations. Curt was now very wary. The man had shown his willingness to interpret things to his own advantage. Where was the dividing line for this opportunistic religious leader? Thermonulcear explosives? Curt knew he was up against a man who would rationalize in order to accomplish what he personally wanted to do. And it was becoming obvious that the Imam probably wouldn't stop at anything less than attempting world conquest.

In fact, Curt knew that was exactly what the word *jihad* meant.

Every so often in history, a person comes along with the charisma to match a desire for world conquest. It had been many years since such a one had surfaced. Curt watched and studied the Imam very carefully, searching for signs that might confirm whether or not this religious fanatic was a modern megalomaniac.

Curt knew the Imam was lying and using his religious belief to rationalize the lies. Curt also knew that he was in no position to argue. The only thing that would really make a difference to the Imam was a bullet in the heart. Curt hoped he'd be able to put one there before this man turned his madness loose on the world, perhaps through the technical developments of Dr. Rhosha Taisha.

But, in the meantime, the Imam continued to behave politely. Curt didn't know why. He figured he'd learn soon enough. "Would you care for coffee, Captain?" He didn't ask Curt to sit down.

Since Curt had regained some of his strength, he took the relaxed stance of a sentry who must remain standing at his post for hours, a trick he'd learned back at the Point where cadets were still required to stand guard, even alongside robots. Curt could stand that way for hours if need be.

He replied to the Islamic sect's leader, "No, thank you. Your coffee is a bit strong for my taste. However, all that aside, I find it fascinating that you have a robotics technical advisor. You certainly had no warbots in your military force."

"No coffee? Pity. It's exceptionally good coffee this morning, Captain. However, as you wish . . ." The Imam shrugged and Curt thought his pleasantness belied his inner zeal. "As for war robots, I would like to have them for special operations, but I do not need them. Properly trained and motivated men will fight far more effectively than robots. Dr. Taisha's job is to see to it that they will willingly fight to the death if necessary."

"I thought the true Islamic warrior fought to the death because of the promise of ascending into Paradise," Curt observed. "Do you now have to send men into battle with suicidal orders?"

"Not at all. Our religion requires that they win. They do not have to be given orders to do that. If they are killed while attempting to win, then that is the will of of Allah, the Beneficent, the Merciful. However, the Iran-Iraq war showed that far too many soldiers surrendered when, according to their Islamic religious teachings, they should have fought on."

Curt didn't press the point. He wanted to keep the Imam talking and to get Dr. Taisha to talk a bit more. He did not want to ask questions which might result in the Imam cutting off the dialogue and questioning him.

But Curt had to ask one thing, "How are my people? Sergeant Sampson? Colonel Lovell? The wounded men?"

The Imam waved his hand and replied diffidently, "The reports I received from my lieutenants after morning prayers indicated that three of the men were gravely wounded when we got them off the roof. They may have been wounded before or during our final assault; I do not know which, and we will never know for certain. I am sorry to report that they died during the night. In view of the fact that we have no way to preserve their corpses, I have ordered them buried."

Curt objected. "They must be identified and returned to their families."

"That is not possible under the circumstances."

Curt decided to settle that matter later. He was far more interested in the living. "And the others, including the women?"

"The one former hostage is unharmed, but he is not being cooperative. The women are in good health and are confined to suitable quarters for women."

"Imam, those two women are members of the United States Army," Curt pointed out. "They are equal in all ways to male soldiers. They must be given quarters equal to mine."

"We do not treat women as equals," the Imam told him flatly. "However, we will treat them with decency and respect, as is our custom. In fact, I believe you Europeans learned that from us and called it chivalry."

"The Hague, Geneva, and Manila conventions require equal quarters for captured soldiers, regardless of sex," Curt told him stiffly in the most formal manner.

"We spoke of that under a flag of truce on the roof yesterday, I believe," the Imam reminded him. "I do not follow those modern and inadequate rules."

"But I do, and so does the rest of the world. I suggest you do the same," Curt told him. After he'd said it, he realized he shouldn't have. The Imam had succeeded in making him lose his temper.

The Imam sensed this and retorted sharply, "You are my prisoner! Just who do you think you are?"

"I know who I am, and you know it, too. Last night, I gave you my name, rank, serial number, birth place, and birth date. That's all I'm required to tell you under international law. Do you wish me to repeat that information?" This confrontation was evolving into an interrogation, albeit one skillfully carried out. Curt wanted to learn why the Imam had ordered soldiers to bring him there. It wasn't just for polite, diplomatic small talk. What was really in the back of the man's devious but intelligent mind?

The Imam waved his hand. "That's quite unnecessary. I do, indeed, know who you are. And, incidentally, I would suggest that you forget international law, as I've told you many times. It means nothing here. I fol-

300

low far more ancient traditions. Even if I did not, an actual state of armed conflict doesn't exist between us and the United States of America ... or any other infidel state opposed to the will of Allah. And we don't follow recent customs. Our code of warfare is ancient. We Jehorkhims are not fighting a European gentleman's war, Captain. We are engaged in the ancient *jihad* which predates present conventions of warfare. Therefore, no international agreements apply insofar as I'm concerned." The Imam stopped waving his hand and held it up to cut off Curt's rejoinder. "However, I promised that you and your people would not be tortured if you surrendered. You did not do so. Our final assault was triggered by one of your own soldiers foolishly breaking the truce, so I am no longer bound to keep my word not to torture you, Captain. What I will permit my Jehorkhims to do to you is therefore at my pleasure."

Curt silently cursed Sergeant Edwina Sampson's impulsive behavior; though, as he recalled, she had only reacted to what appeared to be a violation of the truce on the part of the Jehorkhims. But he was far more worried over the fact that the Imam was one of those zealots whose religious fanaticism permitted him to break whatever rules he wished or to retract whatever agreements he'd made always under the rationale of divine guidance—in the Imam's case, the will of Allah.

"However," the Imam went on, a strange, twisted leer on his face, "torture may not be desirable. I have other uses for you. You see, Captain, you are an educated man. I have not had the opportunity to talk with gentlemen since I left England many years ago, and

301

frankly, I miss the stimulation of intellectual discussion.''

"You can forget intellectual discussions," Curt snapped. "My commission may state that I'm an officer and a gentleman, but I'm really just a gravel-crunching field soldier. All you'll get from me other than meaningless small talk is my name, my rank, my—"

"Imam, he is obviously a well-trained and greatly experienced warbot officer. He is just what I've been looking for." Dr. Taisha was becoming impatient with the Imam's protracted discussion.

She went on, ice in her voice. "Furthermore, these robot soldiers were doing something quite different. In attempting to rescue the prisoners, they used a totally new technology of robot warfare, something I haven't learned about in spite of my extensive study of all available literature.''

Dr. Rhosha Taisha's large eyes looked directly at Curt as she asked, "Captain, how were you able to engage in personal combat while running robots at the same time?''

"I don't know what you mean," Curt replied slowly. He was glad that she was on the wrong track, and he wasn't going to set her straight. She probably wouldn't believe him anyway. It would be difficult for anyone to conceive that the RI had screwed up so badly or had used such a lash-up of personal and robotics combat.

"Do not play games with me!" Taisha's tone was cold, menacing. Coming from a woman with her stunning, exotic beauty, it was jarring. "You had warbots on the roof with you. However, there was no indication that you or your soldiers were in linkage with them,

302

even though you wore mobile linkage harnesses. So they must have been operating under unusual new circumstances, and depending upon their artificial intelligence circuitry for more independent robotics activity. How did you accomplish that?"

Curt decided to tell the truth. It wasn't classified, and he wouldn't be believed in any case. "The warbots used their AI capability to carry out orders we gave them verbally. There was no linkage."

Dr. Taisha's expression became hard and vicious. "You are not telling the truth, Captain. I inspected your equipment quite thoroughly last night. I even had the opportunity to dismantle one of your assault warbots and to look into the workings of your artificially intelligent aerodyne."

"Did you find anything interesting?" Curt suddenly asked.

"I am asking the questions!" Taisha did not raise her smooth voice or allow any anger to creep into her reply. "Whether you answer them or not, I will eventually learn why and how you were conducting this mission under such a strange variant of your operational doctrine." She was quite calm and composed as she spoke. Her hands were folded gracefully in her lap, her posture was straight and correct. But Curt could sense that there was unbelievable violence in her mind.

He knew that, except for the linkage technology which he didn't know anything about, the warbots, aerodynes, and computers brought into Zahedan during Operation Squire contained no sensitive, classified equipment other than the up-graded Mod Four artificial intelligence units. But he did not know how they

303

worked or how they differed from the Mod Three AI units, so he didn't worry about what Dr. Taisha would learn about them from him. Colonel Lovell might pose a different problem.

"In any event," the beautiful Eurasian neuroscientist continued in her surprisingly unemotional way, "I don't need verbal answers to my questions about these and other matters. I will discover the answers because they are already in your mind, and I can get to them with or without your cooperation."

She turned her head to look at the Imam, not moving her body, which was obviously voluptuous despite the white smock and slacks she wore. "Your excellency, I would like to begin my investigation with this man. He is experienced in linkage operations, and he can be most valuable in acquiring the data I require to perfect our ultimate warrior concept."

"You would rather use Captain Carson than his sergeant who's also trained in these procedures?" The Imam asked.

"If I kill him in the process, his sergeant will serve as a backup. However, I will also investigate her because she will give me the female reaction to my techniques. I have never had the opportunity to utilize a female robotic operator as an experimental subject before. It could be very revealing . . ."

"And Colonel Lovell?" The Imam reminded his technical adviser of the robotic specialist.

"I do not want to kill her first. She may know far more than these basic combat soldiers. I had always planned to conduct experimentation on her last, once I had perfected my techniques on lesser people."

"Dr. Taisha, how long will your investigation of these three soldiers take?" the Imam suddenly asked.

"I cannot tell you."

The Imam sighed. It was obvious to Curt that the religious leader put up with a great deal from this beautiful, evil woman in the hopes of a better chance at world conquest and perhaps some more personal reward. "Doctor, I'm not establishing any deadlines on your work. However, it's entirely within the realm of possibility that the Americans may mount another rescue operation very soon," Imam Rahman pointed out. "I need your assurance that in the next few days you won't require resources I'll need for overcoming the next assault."

A slight smile played around the right corner of Dr. Taisha's sensuous mouth. "Imam, I have all the resources I need. Thanks to the failure of the United States Army yesterday, I have acquired the equipment I need from the warbot materiel captured around Zahedan."

"I was thinking of your use of electrical power. Our generating capacity is limited."

Dr. Taisha shook her head. "My measuring equipment requires very little power. As for the electrical requirements of the experimental equipment, I have told you many times that I am dealing with millionths of a watt at a small fraction of a volt. Only a modest amount of electricity is required to produce profound effects on the human nervous system. For example, I could use ordinary batteries for electroshock procedures."

"Just a minute!" Curt interjected loudly. "Whether or not a de facto state of war exists, my people and I

305

are prisoners of war. We didn't have to surrender. Article Thirteen of the 1949 Geneva Prisoner of War Convention specifically states—"

"My *profound* apologies if you still believe I intend to follow flawed and unworkable international agreements which we Muslims had absolutely no part in formulating," the Imam shot back. "Doctor, if you wish to begin your experimentation on this man now, the guards are waiting just outside the door."

CHAPTER SEVENTEEN

"You spoke of Islamic respect for valiant fighters," Curt protested.

There was no humor or rancor in the Imam's response. "That I did. And it has absolutely nothing to do with this. I gave you my word that neither I nor my people would torture you if you surrendered. You did not, so nothing prevents me from using you, a prisoner, to further my own cause. Before this meeting, Dr. Taisha convinced me of your enormous value in perfecting some of her most advanced work in machine control of human beings—in short, creating more perfect soldiers by putting them under the direct and constant command of infallible machines. She is engaged in *most* fascinating work, the perfection of human control by machinery." He turned to smile at her. "As your demonstrations last night more than amply proved, Doctor ..."

"I, too, am pleased that everything went so well."

"You're just about as hypocritical as they come, Imam!" Curt snapped. "You refuse to allow your followers to use remote extensions to their senses, yet you're encouraging the artificial control of humans by computers."

"There is a great deal of difference, Captain . . . as you will see!" Dr. Taisha assured him. "Imam, may I?"

"Of course, Doctor."

The door to the room flew open and the same four Jehorkhim soldiers who'd brought him to the Imam suddenly appeared. Curt couldn't fight them. His injured left arm was an enormous hindrance. One was now at each side of him, a third held a drawn scimitar edge-up between Curt's legs as he stood in a sentry's stance, and the fourth quickly placed a blindfold around his eyes.

They didn't take him far—down a flight of steps, along an echoing corridor, and through a doorway into a room that smelled vaguely similar to the linkage compartments of Army command centers and simulators.

The blindfold was whipped off, and Curt found himself standing in a laboratory. No wonder it smelled like a linkage command post! It contained many of the same pieces of equipment, and the smell came from the nonallergenic electronic contact paste used on sensors and electrodes when the very best linkage connection was required.

The room was slightly cool, which told Curt it was probably in the basement of one of the two-story government buildings.

While two Jehorkhim brawnies held him, two others stripped off his light battle coveralls, leaving him stark naked. A man untrained to undergo the rigors of interrogation would immediately become more tractable in this state. The first thing a professional interrogator does is to strip a person in a room that is just a few degrees too cool. This lowers the will to resist because it makes a person feel exceptionally vulnerable in a world where everyone else wears clothing. Curt knew this. He'd been through Personal Survival 404 at the Point, the course in which a cadet had to stay alive in the wilderness with nothing more than his bare hands; it had also taught him how to survive under interrogation.

So being stripped naked only bothered him for a moment. Then his trained mind took control.

He prepared himself for the next step in the procedure, which was designed to strip him of his self-respect and then of his values: Taisha and her Jehorkhim helpers would do something that would cause Curt to lose bladder or sphincter control. Fortunately, Curt had urinated and defecated in his quarters before being summoned to see the Imam. In any event, making him break toilet training, one of the oldest and most deep-seated of all childhood imperatives, wouldn't bother him. Not after he'd survived Personal Survival 404, and had had a couple of close calls in combat linkage. In fact, most warbot brainies crapped in their pants quite often, which had led to the humorous call when a warbot brainy came out of linkage after a difficult mission: "Pass the paper!"

But the one thing he could not control—most men couldn't—was what was euphemistically termed in official Army parlance "the gallant reflex."

Dr. Rhosha Taisha noticed it and remarked with frigid objectivity, "It is interesting to note that a warbot officer is still a normal human being in that regard, Captain.''

Curt replied with equal coolness, seeking some glimmer of female response behind Taisha's glacial facade and finding none. ''Well, Doctor, it not only proves that human instincts are deeply rooted but that you are a very desirable woman. Under different circumstances—''

''Which do not occur unless I decide that they will, Captain. And they won't, I assure you. You are a fine specimen, but I have other plans for you.'' Taisha turned and busied herself with several racks of electronic equipment.

She was as sensual from the back as from the front, Curt decided. Dammit, there had to be something behind this woman's cold scientific demeanor! He suddenly felt it would be a real challenge to unleash it.

''I find it hard to believe that you have that much control over yourself,'' the warbot officer remarked. He knew he could excite women; he'd done so many times in the past. The rules of war said that as a prisoner he should use every capability at his disposal. If he could divert this icy woman from her single-minded search for scientific data, he might make things a little bit easier for himself, and learn a few things. Or doing so might lead to some avenue of escape. It was worth a try. ''Most women as attractive as you deliberately maintain their appearance for specific reasons.''

''Of course. I know precisely what I'm doing.'' Taisha was maddeningly matter-of-fact. ''My appearance gains me the attention of both men and women. It makes men far more tractable and eager to please, and it makes

310

women envious and anxious to know how I do it, which lowers their resistance. Everyone feels more comfortable around an attractive person. Whether I'm requesting support from powerful people or experimenting on subjects from whom I'm trying to gain information, my pleasurably attractive female appearance elicits a far greater degree of cooperation than being perceived as an ugly witch would."

Which you probably are, Curt thought. He was getting nowhere with her. It infuriated him. Someday, a very powerful man was going to dull the sharp edge of Dr. Rhosha Taisha's aloof superiority and pierce the veil of her exotic inscrutability.

But not right then. Four Jehorkhim soldiers picked Curt up as easily as if he were a child. He couldn't even struggle; the Jehorkhim who'd grasped Curt's swollen left arm had done so in a most painful manner. Curt gritted his teeth to keep from crying aloud. By the time he got himself under control and waves of pain no longer washed over his mind, he was lying face down on a bare, cold, enameled table while the Jehorkhim strapped his wrists and legs to it, leaving him in a spread-eagled position on his belly. Curt took a sharp breath when they stretched out his left arm to shackle his wrist.

Dr. Rhosha Taisha was standing next to the table, a gleaming, ancient straight razor in her hand.

Curt said nothing, although he was fully aware of what she could do with that razor.

"Allow me to compliment you, Captain," she said levelly, waving the razor slightly so that it glinted in the light. "Most men would be sniveling, trembling children by now."

Curt looked up at her as best he could, and replied with equal candor, "I'm lying on my belly. So you'd have a hell of a time turning me into a eunuch. Besides, I don't think you want to neuter me just yet. You can cut me and hurt me, but I've been cut and hurt before."

"Captain," she said coolly, "I have it in my power to hurt you if I so desire. But I am no sadist."

"The hell you say? Willa Lovell told me you supervised the torturers."

"I was asked for my scientific expertise regarding how to best affect the human nervous system. I did not carry out the torture," Dr. Rhosha Taisha insisted. "But, be that as it may, it is not in my best interest to harm you. You are the first specimen I've worked with who has experience in human-computer interface linkage. I can see it has been several days since you engaged in linkage because you haven't shaved your head. Therefore, I urge you to lie quietly and cooperate while I do so."

Never argue with a person holding a razor! That was the humorous jibe favored by cadets and recruits when their heads were shaved prior to initial experience in linkage. Curt didn't think it was so funny now, but he held very still indeed while Dr. Taisha carefully shaved the stubble from his head and then ran the razor down the back of his neck and his spine. It was very sharp.

But Dr. Taisha's hands and fingers were soft and very warm, and she was extremely gentle where she touched him. This surprised Curt. He would have suspected hands as cold as her voice, and rough treatment from a woman who apparently had little empathy with other human beings.

What kind of woman was this Rhosha Taisha, Curt wondered? She was certainly stunning with her Eurasian features, and her small body was extremely nubile, even when shrouded in lab attire. She should be exuding an enormous amount of sensuality, more than she already did. Yet, she seemed to be cold, aloof, almost frigid.

When she'd been with the Imam a few minutes ago, there had been a veiled exchange about the past night, and Curt began to wonder if this strange woman could somehow turn her sexuality on and off the way she controlled her laboratory equipment.

He had known many women, and those that acted as Taisha did usually have some deep-seated problem. What was hers? Was she afraid? Of what? Or whom? And why? Or was a psychopathic monster hiding beneath her exquisite female facade? Was she somehow the personification of pure but beautiful evil?

Curt didn't believe in good and evil in the black-and-white, either-or sense. He always operated on the theory that all people had something good in them, even the enemies he fought and the stupid officers who gave him stupid orders. He believed that something drove people to do what they did, evil and degraded though it might seem to others.

What the hell was driving Dr. Rhosha Taisha? he asked himself.

He didn't get an answer to his question right away. She installed a linkage harness along his spine and up and around his shaved head. It wasn't exactly the same design as the Army-issue RI mobile linkage harness he'd been wearing yesterday. It didn't fit as well, seemed to be crudely made, and had fewer sensors and electrodes. The multicontact connector that attached the cable between the harness and the lab equipment was located between his shoulder blades, a difficult place to reach even if he'd been unshackled.

As Rhosha Taisha began to turn on and adjust various pieces of electronic equipment, including something he recognized as a very high-level, multiprocessor, artificial intelligence unit probably more powerful than the Mark Four, Curt began to understand what she was about to do.

She was preparing to utilize much the same technology developed for industrial robots and warbots operated as remote extension of human beings by means of direct nonintrusive linkage between the human nervous system and computer circuits.

Except she was going to reverse the system.

Instead of allowing the human being to control the machine, she was preparing to permit the computers to control Curt's nervous system.

If the programming and artificial intelligence circuitry was adequately designed, machines would run his nervous system by electronic command, turning *him* into the automatic robot!

In the back of his mind, he thought he remembered that this had been tried before, somewhere, sometime, by somebody . . . and it hadn't worked very well. In fact, it had almost killed people . . . but he couldn't remember the exact circumstances.

Well, Curt Carson knew a few things about human-machine interfaces and about how to keep a machine from killing him. He'd learned to block certain areas of his central nervous system to prevent them from responding to any external commands, including his own. The training of an RI warbot brainy included yoga and various other mind-over-body techniques, some of which allowed poorly garbed Bhuddist monks to sit motionless in subfreezing temperatures and remain alive.

However, whatever Dr. Rhosha Taisha had developed did, indeed, seem to be very powerful. He could begin to sense the effects of her equipment as she began to adjust controls and enter programming commands on a key pad.

Furthermore, her techniques were not primitive. No tingle of sensors or other electrodes, the usual precursors of amateur efforts at human-machine interface, alerted him to what was happening to him.

"Now, Captain, I want you to tell me what you feel is happening to you," Dr. Rhosha Taisha ordered.

"Hell, Doctor, you ought to be able to see that for yourself on your readbacks!" Curt snapped.

Suddenly, he seemed to be outside his own body.

He could see. He could hear. He could feel. He knew what was happening. He knew what was going on around him. But it was as though he were a paraplegic with no voluntary control over his arms and legs. In fact, he discovered he no longer had conscious control of himself.

Disconnected mentally from his corporeal self, Curt retreated into a small portion of his mind. The entity, Curt Carson, was now located right between his eyes and about thirty centimeters back from the front of his forehead. That was where he "existed." That was what was left of his ego, his soul, himself.

"You have very strong neural systems, Captain Carson," Dr. Taisha remarked, a touch of admiration in her otherwise cool voice. "It is quite obvious to me that you are thoroughly experienced in the command of warbots through remote computer-enhanced linkage. I should warn you that I have full control of your heart muscles and your breathing. In fact, I have taken over control of most of your autonomic nervous system. Your life is literally in the hands of my computer. However, I am leaving your vocal centers and larynx under your voluntary control because I want you to tell me about your subjective feelings and sensations as the experiment progresses."

Curt deliberately didn't reply. His breathing took up the rhythm it normally would assume for talking, but he didn't say a word. Perhaps with misplaced gallantry, he wanted to show her that he could retain some control over himself in spite of what she and her machines did to his nervous system. This was very difficult because he wanted to tell her to go to hell in the Mandarin Chinese he had learned at the Point; he believed she might speak it fluently.

Surprised by Curt's silence, Dr. Taisha checked some instruments and studied a display on a screen. Then she said, "Captain Carson, I want you to speak to me."

Curt kept silent. He had no intention of cooperating with her, and he got the feeling that Dr. Rhosha Taisha didn't yet have the sort of complete machine control over a human being that she believed she might have or that she wanted to have. Maybe she'd been working only with Jehorkhim soldiers who might respond differently to computer commands. In any event, he decided he'd learn a great deal more about what she was trying to do and how she was trying to do it if he didn't play her game. In addition, by being uncooperative, he might make her question her confident assumption that she had all the answers.

Taisha was obviously displeased by Curt's lack of response, and concerned about it. "I am certain that I have not disabled the vocal mechanisms. I believe you're deliberately resisting me. Captain Carson, when I have control over a person as I do over you, that person does not resist me for long without suffering the consequences. Very well, I shall try to activate your vocal cords."

Curt felt his throat tighten and he heard an unearthly, inhuman croaking sound coming from it. He tried to reduce his breathing so his vocal cord would not make sounds even if they were under Taisha's control. But it was almost impossible to do so, because he was trying to overpower the signals Taisha's computers were feeding into his nervous system. After the first whispery, throaty squawk, he was silent, although he felt his throat tightening in spasms. He couldn't inhibit the breathing-cycle signals coming from her computer, and he finally had to begin breathing again, in gasps, as his own control was overpowered.

She turned to look at him, arms akimbo. "You must stop resisting me, Captain. I shall have to elicit some cooperation from you by isolating you until you decide

317

that it's better to cooperate than to be one of the living dead."

She made adjustments and reentered instructions into the large computer complex which included a high level of artificial intelligence.

Curt noticed that his vision was beginning to dim.

Slowly, he went blind as his vision grayed-out to the nothingness of no sensation. Blindness is not merely seeing blackness; it's seeing nothing. His eyes still functioned. So did his optic nerves. But his brain was being commanded by Taisha's computer not to process and recognize the signals coming from his optic nerves. He was now totally blind.

Her voice came to him in cold, petulant tones, "Captain, that is just a sample of what I can do to you if you do not cooperate with me. If I do not immediately get your enthusiastic and willing participation in my experiment, I shall slowly take away your sensory perceptions one by one until you are left with no input from the external world. I have blocked your ability to see. I will soon block your ability to smell, then to feel and to hear. After I have eliminated all your perceptions of the external world, I shall block your internal perceptions one by one. Soon, your mind will be totally isolated from your own body. After a surprisingly short period of being completely isolated within your own mind with your own devils and demons, you will be so eager to cooperate with me that you will be surprised at what you are willing to do for me."

She paused for a moment, then gave a short laugh. It was the first time Curt had heard Dr. Rhosha Taisha laugh. She was deriving some perverse joy from doing

318

this, partly because she seemed to know exactly what she was talking about when she spoke of internal demons and devils. "This is the way I handle recalcitrant Jehorkhims who do not willingly undergo the religious indoctrination I am perfecting for the Imam. Eventually after a short time in their own personal hells, they become eager to succumb to what they believe is the will of Allah, which is really *my* will. And they are formidable fighters, are they not, Captain? We shall have little trouble overcoming warbots or individual soldiers such as yourself once I perfect these techniques."

Again she paused as if she were making some slight adjustment. Curt could hear the clicking of the key pad on the computer as she gave it fresh instructions. "Or I could decide to let you torture yourself with as much pain as you believe you could never endure . . . without once having laid a hand on you. Pain is such a subjective thing. Hypnotists have known this for years. Therefore, let me show you that it is perfectly possible for you to generate all the pain necessary to torture yourself—like this."

Curt suddenly had an extremely sharp and painful cramp in his right leg. He wanted to curl up and knead his calf muscles. But he couldn't move. Then the cramp was gone as quickly as it had come.

"You did feel that, did you not? I saw it in your instrument telltales here on the control panel." Dr. Taisha's voice began to rise in pitch and her words began to tumble out faster and faster as she went on, "So I know that you are deliberately remaining silent! I do not like to be defied, Captain! People who defy me will end up being totally controlled by me because

I will soon have the technology to make them do exactly what I want! I will never again have to negotiate with them, wheedle, beg, or crawl on my knees! I will never again have to be a sexual toy for them! My machines will make them my slaves! They will turn the Jehor-khims into the most powerful human soldiers the world has ever seen! And they will be more versatile than your most advanced robots! I will be able to do what the greatest tyrants of old failed to accomplish! By instructing my machines to exercise total control over human beings, I will make people totally predictable and controllable! And *I* will control them. The Imam will think that he is doing it, but I will be controlling him!"

She stopped and Curt heard her hard breathing. Her voice then came softly to him, "And men will do for me and to me exactly what I want exactly when I want. The Imam believes that his performance last night was in accordance with the will of Allah! He does not know that it was in accordance with the will and the knowledge and the power of Dr. Rhosha Taisha!"

After a short pause, she said, "I may even see if you will please me, Captain. But ... first, let me hear you speak! Voluntarily! If you refuse, I will force you to speak!"

When Curt stayed silent, his breath soon began to come in short gasps, apparently at the command of Taisha's computers.

"You will speak!"

Curt did his best to overpower her signals. More croaks came from his throat.

"Very well, I shall isolate you from your world. You

will soon be begging for my voice, my commands, begging to do as I bid."

Her voice faded out.

Slowly, all feeling in Curt's limbs faded away. He became numb.

Then everything was gone.

He was suddenly in limbo, totally isolated from any sensory inputs.

It is, Curt thought, like dying.

But he'd been there before!

Suddenly, in a flash of recognition, he knew exactly what this total isolation from the world of ordinary sensory input paralleled.

This knowledge was going to permit him to withstand anything Dr. Rhosha Taisha could do with her fiendish machines, and thereafter it would help him win over this beautiful, evil woman who dreamed of controlling people's minds and bodies.

CHAPTER EIGHTEEN

Captain Curt Carson seemed to be floating in never-never land. He was alone with only his thoughts.

But being isolated from the stimuli of the external world—sight, sound, taste, feeling, smell, and internal or kinesthetic muscle sense—seemed very familiar to him.

Curt knew exactly what Dr. Rhosha Taisha had done to him, and it didn't bother him.

But Dr. Taisha didn't know that. This was her first mistake.

As an experienced combat soldier, a warbot brainy, and a field commander, he'd been there before.

The situation in which he found himself was almost identical to being "killed in action" when controlling a warbot. However, it was a little different and a lot easier.

Being KIA meant losing all sensory input within milliseconds, all at once, *whammo*, like turning off a switch. But Taisha had taken away Curt's sensory perceptions slowly and deliberately, letting him know as she eliminated each one. That was her second mistake.

He'd been "killed in action" twice in actual combat and many times in simulated combat, and he'd been trained to handle the traumatic shock of suddenly losing all contact with the external world. He knew how to survive in total mental isolation.

Nearly any person will become insane if placed in it. The human mind *needs* sensory input. If it can't get any, it fabricates input in the form of hallucinations, and very quickly, an isolated person begins to live in a personally created world. This was what Dr. Rhosha Taisha was counting on, Curt creating his own living hell.

Captain Curt Carson found himself in something like the half-awake semidream state that everyone experiences when going to sleep at night or waking up in the morning, although most people have no conscious recollection of it. He wasn't frightened. It was familiar. So he just went to sleep. He had no trouble; in sleep, his conscious mind was isolated from the surrounding world anyway.

And he deserved the rest. He was still suffering from cumulative fatigue, but Taisha's computer-enforced mental isolation had eliminated the throbbing pain in his left arm.

It was only just that he'd let Taisha worry for a change. He'd been willing to bet she'd never had an experimental subject go to sleep on her before. It was perhaps the best insult he could have managed.

He didn't know how long he slept. He only knew that he was suddenly and rudely awakened, as if by a drill sergeant going down a line of cots at reveille, whacking sleeping posteriors with a swagger stick to roust out recruits.

"What did you do?" Dr. Rhosha Taisha was screaming, and her beautiful face was twisted into a mask of rage and confusion. She was kneeling in front of the table on which Curt was shackled belly-down, and looking directly into his face. "I should have suspected it! You have a highly trained and disciplined mind! How did you do it?"

"I don't really know," Curt replied, trying to act sleepy. "You put me in some sort of a suspended state where there was nothing for me to do. So I decided to get some sacktime."

"No one has *ever* done that before!"

"Oh? Maybe you haven't been working with real soldiers. I've never known a trooper who wouldn't grab sacktime at the slightest opportunity."

"Not even Jehorkhim soldiers have done what you did!"

"What have they done, Doctor?"

"I'm asking the questions!"

"True. Are you getting any answers?"

"I will get them!"

If Curt could have shrugged, he would have done so. "Maybe. Sometimes the only way to get answers is to get cooperation first. Isn't that the way they teach you scientists to work with the universe?"

She stood up. "A little pain may create cooperation . . ."

Although Curt could handle a limited level of physical pain, doing so took a lot of energy. In his fatigued condition, he might not be able to handle very much.

The pain in his left arm had returned, but he didn't know what his pain threshold was right then. Taisha's induced leg cramp had told him it was quite low. Maybe Taisha could establish very low pain thresholds for him. He felt it was a hell of a time to find out, so he tried to redirect Taisha. "Come on, Doctor! Is that the best you can do? Don't you know that warbot soldiers are trained to shut off pain when they have to?" Curt was bluffing. While it was true that it was "painful" to be linked to a bot when it got hit or damaged, that pain was different from actual body pain. All robot operators learned how to handle that sort of "pain."

"You lie!" she almost screamed the words. "I generated a cramp in your right leg. You reacted!"

"Sure, I reacted! But how can you be sure that I didn't mentally shut it off?"

"The neural electrical signals in your brain were recorded. They told me you felt it!"

"But how do you know that I consciously experienced the sensation as pain, Doctor?"

"Well, I shall see how much pain you can withstand!"

"Why waste your time? You really want to know how a trained warbot officer thinks and operates. Heavy pain signals will mask the very brain signals you're looking for. You should know that some people can cross-connect so that pain becomes pleasure. Hells bells, any masochist can do that!"

Curt didn't know the first thing about what he was saying. He was just shooting from the hip. He had the feeling that Dr. Rhosha Taisha was momentarily confused because she'd run up against a new and unexpected reaction. He was also betting that she wouldn't and couldn't discover that he was conning her. He doubted that she could detect this from her instrument readings. A con job is a very creative act carried out at the highest levels of the brain.

Still, he wanted to get out of this situation as quickly as possible. He'd discovered that Dr. Rhosha Taisha was obsessed, neurotic, and damned dangerous. She might very well kill him, with something as crude as electroshock therapy introduced through the linkage hardness, or something as simple as causing his heart to stop.

Dr. Rhosha Taisha stood up, put her hands on her hips, and pursed her sensual lips. "Very well, if I can't manipulate you because of your training, I'll just have to go deeper into your mind. Right back down to the basic level of belief. I had hoped to be able to get inside your head easily and quickly, but it appears that I shall have to start at a more basic level."

She suddenly smiled. "You come from a Judeo-Christian culture in America. Your religion shares many of the same symbols and legends as Islam. It will be interesting to see how you react to the indoctrination I give to Jehorkhim soldiers. You should react in the same way to those images and symbols. That may make you more tractable. At least, it cannot be as harmful as things stand. It has been *extremely* successful with the Imam's Jehorkhim troops."

Taisha wasn't getting anywhere with Curt, but now he was going to get somewhere. He was going to find out what the Jehorkhims really believed.

Curt already knew something about that. Dr. Taisha

had started with men who believed the teachings of a fanatical sect of a revelatory religion. They'd been promised everlasting paradise if they willingly died in battle against the unbelievers, the infidels. For over a thousand years, Islamic soldiers had gone to their deaths with that promise in mind.

Any people who believed such a promise, backed up only by a "revelation from God" made through a human spokesman, were perfect starting points for someone who wanted to develop the human counterpart of warbots: machine-controlled human warriors. Their religious belief could easily overwhelm the most powerful of all the instincts, that of self-preservation. Psychotic, experts might argue, but history showed, that it worked, not only among Islamic warriors, who'd come within a whisker of conquering Europe several times, but among the Japanese as recently as the last century.

So Curt waited to learn what the Jehorkhims were "taught" through Dr. Taisha's equipment.

When she started to run the program, he felt as though he were again in the battle simulator. He knew deep down inside that what he was experiencing wasn't real, which is the major drawback of all simulator training, though it can make a person sweat pretty hard.

Taisha's Jehorkhim indoctrination program was hallucinatory in nature. And to someone who hadn't spent long hours in warbot linkage, it would have seemed totally real, and been frightening as hell.

Curt's mind was assailed by strange images that were oddly distorted as in a dream. He seemed to be in the open desert near Zahedan. A huge whirling column of sand and dust was approaching him. While not a deeply religious man, Curt had been exposed to the Bible as a child. He knew what he was "seeing."

But the voice from the whirlwind spoke in Baluchi.

Then the scene faded, and Curt guessed that Dr. Rhosha Taisha had made another mistake: She'd forgotten to have her computer translate the sound track from Baluchi to English, which Curt spoke and in which he thought.

The woman might be brilliant in her warped fashion, but evidently her hang-ups prevented her from being a first-class thinker and scientist. That didn't mean that Dr. Rhosha Taisha wasn't a formidable enemy, especially when she had him strapped belly down on a lab table and wired up like a multifunction industrial bot.

When the whirlwind hallucination began to play in Curt's mind again, he felt like he was watching a poorly-made Grade-C television show intended for the amusement of ten-year-old children on Saturday morning.

The computer-translated sound track didn't pick up all the nuances and meanings of the original Baluchi dialogue or the computer was so poorly programmed as a translator that most of the audio sounded strange, stilted, and actually funny. As his second language at West Point, Curt had studied Mandarin Chinese, which he could still read, understand, and speak fluently. Therefore, he knew full well that many Chinese classics, Bhuddist and Taoist religious tracts as well, simply couldn't be translated into English without losing a great deal of their original meaning and impact. Obviously, the same held true here, and the disparity was probably compounded because much of the monologue sounded vaguely like the Koran, which meant that what he was hearing had undergone translation from Arabic to Baluchi to English. No wonder it didn't sound right!

The Jehorkhim mental indoctrination was short, simple, and to the point, the voice out of the whirlwind, apparently supposed to be that of Allah, exhorting the individual to fight infidel unbelievers in *jihad* as the way and the means to salvation and entry into paradise. The voice also commanded the Jehorkhim subject to follow the leadership of the Imam Rahman, one of Mohammed's successors, who had received the Word of Allah, the Benevolent, the Merciful.

To a person from an advanced culture, the hallucination was neither rational nor believable. Curt could easily pick out the inconsistencies and illogical elements.

Furthermore, he immediately spotted the subliminal messages and the use of subsonic "scare" frequencies coming from the whirlwind hallucination. Dr. Rhosha Taisha knew some dirty tricks to play on the human mind, but she'd tailored them to the Jehorkhim mind, not to Curt's.

He had experienced far more linkage than any Jehorkhim, and he'd also watched more television, movies, and the three-dimensional holographic presentations or "hollies." And he'd seen those all his life. Special effects, brain-wrenching visual-auditory surprises, and simplistic, hard-sell, scare-tactic salesmanship were nothing new to him.

What he was experiencing was amateurish. He'd seen better and more creative material and performances come out of American elementary school media communications classes as annual school plays. Even the

Kaydet Minstrels at West Point were far more sophisticated in terms of both dialogue and content. What the Imam and Taisha really needed for the Grade-C production was a good rewrite done by a Madison Avenue pro who knew how to sell ideas, concepts, and products.

But he realized that this computer-generated hallucination would strike fear into the mind of a barely literate farmer from Baluchistan. Its subliminal messages would drive such a man to fight ferociously while following orders, but they would prevent him from doing the sort of individualistic thinking upon which success in modern battle, even with warbots, so often depended. Taisha was trying to turn human soldiers into organic warbots; Curt knew it didn't work, and why.

No wonder the Jehorkhim troops had kept up the wasteful rifle and arrow attack on the rooftop; they'd been told to do it. And when they'd encounter warbots on the aerodrome or in the fields outside Zahedan, they'd simply attacked in wave after wave, unaware of the deadly nature of warbots, until they'd overwhelmed the machines. Their tactics had worked only because of superiority of numbers and ample reserves of horses.

As Curt carefully analyzed the Jehorkhim motivational training film being projected into his nervous system, he figured out how to throw absolute and complete panic into any Jehorkhim force.

But he didn't know how he could get this information to the Washington Greys and the 17th Division (RI) so it could be incorporated into the tactics of the forthcoming rescue mission. Nor did he know how he should react to Dr. Taisha's third-rate hallucinatory message which had apparently worked among the Jehorkhims.

Would Taisha expect the same result from him in terms of unquestioning compliance?

Could he turn this into an advantage for himself and the other captives?

Having been exposed to the Jehorkhim beliefs and commandments in a way that caused other men to become fanatics, could he feign enthusiastic acceptance of the Jehorkhim creed to gain her confidence and that of the Imam so that he might be able to open up an avenue of escape? Or could he soften them up in a way that would permit a second rescue mission to succeed?

Could he fool Dr. Rhosha Taisha? She might be a very sophisticated judge of human nature, a superlative psychologist able to spot what he was trying to do. If she was, how could he get her to let down her guard? Could he run a super con job?

Well, he had to try.

He'd lie like hell. But in a way that Taisha's instruments couldn't detect.

He hoped that Belinda Hettrick and Alexis Morgan were putting together the second rescue mission. But whether or not they were, he had to act as if it was being planned and launched. If they didn't come, he'd play that card when it was dealt. But he didn't want them to show up and find him unprepared to take advantage of their strike.

When Taisha brought him to full conscious control of himself and her laboratory took form around him again, he began his super con job by simply saying,

"Why didn't someone tell me what the Imam Rahman was really trying to do? A world of brotherhood under one God is a worthwhile goal, even if one has to die to help achieve it."

This was a statement of belief that was widely accepted in most of the world, including the United States. Curt wasn't openly lying; his tactic was to tell the truth and nothing but the truth . . . but not the whole truth. He had no difficulty actually believing that the brotherhood of man was probably a good thing. But, in the meantime until everyone thought that way, he also believed it was a good idea to keep his warbots powered-up.

A quick smile flickered at the corner of Dr. Taisha's lips. It was the first display of pleasure Curt had seen on her face.

Had she been successful in converting a trained warbot officer to the Imam's cause? It sounded too good to be true! Something insider her told her that it was. Her emotionless, logical scientific self told her to be wary. She knew this American officer was hard as nails, smart and wily, and amazingly strong both physically and mentally. Furthermore, he was tricky; his rapid conversion could be a ruse.

But Dr. Taisha was a human being. She wanted to believe she had succeeded, and she desperately wanted to secure her situation with the Imam. In fact, she wanted to control him, first with her mind-machine techniques and then by her own talents. But machine control came first, because she believed she could permanently imprint and reprogram a person's mind, whereas she wasn't certain that her feminine wiles would work as thoroughly or as permanently. After all, she'd been spurned once, and she hadn't liked that.

Her stock with the Imam would go up immensely and she would be able to demand everything that the traffic would bear if her computer-driven direct-linkage indoctrination and motivation proved to be so powerful that it could change the mind of an experienced soldier such as Curt. In fact, if it could work on such a sophisticated soldier, it was apparently far more powerful than she had thought.

Maybe she already had the answers to human control.

"Ah, so!" she breathed out, trying to keep her excitement out of her voice. "The indoctrination has opened your mind?"

He chose his words carefully so that he wouldn't be lying. Taisha might be able to spot any lie with her instrumentation. "I learned a hell of a lot," he replied, using soldier language in the hope that it would confuse the instruments as well as Rhosha Taisha. "Hey, I'm ready to sign up if the Imam follows the ancient principles of the *jihad*. Will he accept other believers in God as participants?" Curt remembered that historically the *jihad* had been directed against unbelievers. However, Christians and Jews were considered merely to be followers of earlier one-God doctrines which predated Mohammedanism, in spite of the fact that most Muslims thought the Christian trinity to be slightly polytheistic.

It worked. "You are not lying," Taisha stated, studying the bank of recording instruments.

"Hell, no! Why should I lie about something as important as this?"

Dr. Rhosha Taisha hesitated. She knew she had to be certain that she'd managed to get into the critical areas of Curt's mind, not only to change his beliefs but to render him capable of being controlled, although she didn't know that her human-control techniques were still very primitive. However, the possibilities of what she might have done overwhelmed her caution. With this man available—and perhaps his female colonel and sergeant as allies rather than resistive prisoners—there seemed to be no limit to what she could discover about more sophisticated techniques, and very quickly.

As a researcher, she was excited. This caused her to overlook some critical and important factors. She wasn't the omniscient and superrational scientist she projected to the world. She was emotionally involved with what she was trying to do, and this warped her judgment.

Curt was counting on that, plus the fact that Taisha desperately wanted her project to succeed. He thought he'd found the one switch that would turn her on: self-interest.

And he knew that if he could pull off this scam, he might even be able to figure out some way to screw up the command and control structure of the Jehorkhims before the RI mounted the next rescue mission. Dammit, it had to come! His comrades wouldn't leave him stranded in Zahedan.

Taisha tried to regain her composure. As a precaution against Curt's trying to escape, she loaded her neural stun program into her computer and primed it to trigger at a verbal code call from her. That done, she felt she could free him from the restraints and carry out some controlled-response tests.

She began to unbuckle the straps holding Curt to the table, saying as she did so, "I must make certain tests of your physical responses to computer commands, Captain. That is why I am releasing you. However, I should also explain that I have programmed my multiprocessor to stun you if necessary."

"I've been stunned before," Curt told her. Every West Pointer underwent a neural stun so that, as an officer he would have an appreciation of the mildest reaction to a type of malfunction of a linkage AI. "I don't like it. So don't worry."

When she'd freed him, she told him, "Sit up on the table, please, with your legs dangling from the edge."

It seemed likely to Curt that Dr. Taisha was going to see whether or not he'd react to computer commands by gross muscle activity. Knee-jerk reaction, for example. As a trained warbot brainy, he knew exactly what to do to keep a warbot from driving his muscles through the feedback loop from the bot. Therefore, he also knew how to relax and let it happen. His West Point and on-the-job training had been extensive in this regard; the Robot Infantry didn't like the possibility of losing humans to some glitch in computer hardware/software or to some malfunction in a report-back channel signal from a warbot.

So Curt relaxed, let his beta activity go, and disarmed his delta-blocking.

Taisha was so excited and so anxious to have her tests succeed that she missed seeing those little signals on her instruments.

His knees jerked when commanded. His ankles rotated. He let his torso twist on command. But he cried out when she commanded his left arm to strike out suddenly, because the muscles were still extremely swollen and sore.

"Sorry," he apologized. "I took a sword blow there yesterday. Body armor saved me, but the arm swelled up anyway."

"Yes, I know. I gave that left-arm command deliberately. My tests were extremely successful. This has been a very productive session." Dr. Taisha was even more excited now. She began to remove the linkage harness from Curt's head and back. "I must speak with the Imam. In the meantime, I want you to return to your quarters and rest."

At that moment, free of the linkage harness and of the possibility of being stunned by her computer, Curt could have reacted by grabbing her, taking her prisoner, and making the first move to get out of here.

But he didn't. He didn't yet know where he was or where Edie Sampson and Willa Lovell were. He'd carried out the con game thus far. It was working. He now had some degree of freedom. But it was too early to act.

"I don't know where my quarters are," he pointed out. "I've been blindfolded every time your Jehorkhim troops moved me."

She looked up at him triumphantly. "You will not be blindfolded any longer. I will have the guard outside the door escort you."

Inwardly, Curt breathed a sigh. He'd been right in

choosing to feign cooperation. He was still being guarded, but hopefully the Imam and Taisha would soon have enough confidence in him to remove the guards.

CHAPTER NINETEEN

Operation Squire had been a disaster.

In the snake pit aboard the *McCain* three hundred meters beneath the Gulf of Oman, Colonel Belinda Hettrick gathered her company commanders—Edith Walker of Walker's Warriors, Manuel Garcia of Manny's Marauders, the impulsive and irritable Marty Kelly of Kelly's Killers—and the complement of Carson's Companions now on the *McCain*, three of them recovering from wounds. She had only one thing on her mind.

The wounded Companions were in surprisingly good condition. In spite of robot warfare in which people weren't suppose to be hurt, military medicine had kept pace with other areas of the healing arts. Since naval personnel were often subjected to physical accidents because of the nature of the machines they operated, there was a modern hospital on the *McCain*. Its surgeons and biotechs were experienced in repairing physical damage to human bodies. Aboard were computers that could read the human nervous system and induce sensations into the human brain. These could also eliminate pain, help the body utilize its immune system, and accelerate many of the natural healing processes.

Master Sergeant Henry Kester had undergone ten hours of intensive electronically enhanced healing under the care of the *McCain*'s shipboard computers, doctors, and biotechs. Curt's bullet had missed his hip and pelvis, and it had perforated the lower bowel only once before exiting his body through his butt. Henry Kester limped a little, he looked pale, and he couldn't sit down comfortably. But he'd signed himself out of sick bay and rejoined his unit as soon as he could walk, claiming he'd been hurt worse and kept fighting with his outfit back in Java ... and everyone aboard knew how long ago that was. But the crusty master sergeant would brook no humor about how difficult it was for him to sit down. And was madder than hell that Sergeant Edwina Sampson has taken his place.

Lieutenant Jerry Allen's broken arm was on the mend. Healing enzymes and electronic ion flow across the break had all but knitted it. The young officer wore his arm in a partial sling, but vowed he'd take it off to handle a Hornet on the return mission.

The physical damage done to Sergeant Nick Gerard was minimal. Surgeons agreed to put off the repair of his shattered eardrum; the other one was bruised, but was healing. Gerard was nearly his old self again.

Lieutenant Alexis Morgan, the only uninjured member of Carson's Companions and the temporary commanding officer, was somewhat overwhelmed at suddenly having the command on her shoulders. But she worked hard not to show it. She wasn't about to accuse the top brass of causing the massive screwup the

Companions had been through, but the firm set of her jaw and her narrowed eyes indicated that she wasn't going to sit back and let General Victor Knox take the easy way out by covering his anatomy.

Nonetheless, she restrained herself. Colonel Belinda Hettrick had met her in the snake pit just before the debrief and had told her, "Morgan, you went through pure hell. But keep your cool. I'm mad enough for the two of us. I've got the eagles, so let me do the ass-chewing unless I call on you for a first-hand account."

It was supposed to be a standard mission debrief, but it turned out to be more than that. Everyone in the snake pit was surprised when the holographic image from faraway Diamond Point took shape in the center of the room. It showed not only General Victor Knox but also General Jacob O. Carlisle, the trim commanding general of the 17th "Iron Fist" Division (RI). Carlisle was one of them, a warbot brainy who had evolved, like Henry Kester, out of an old-line infantryman. Both generals were visibly upset, but Knox was doing the best job of disguising his feelings. However, it was obvious that Carlisle had taken charge and was going to run this conference.

"This is supposed to be a debriefing," Carlisle announced in a low but distinct voice, "so I want to make sure that everyone understands what I intend to do. Operation Squire has been the worst military disaster in the Army's history since the Second Kasserine. I've run the tapes; they told me what the computers observed, but not why people did things. I intend to learn why. I want a brief report from each commander involved, and I want to hear from Master Sergeant Henry

Kester. I want quick summaries, not detailed formal reports. I do not intend to fix blame; that's the job of the review board which I shall appoint and convene at a later date."

"General!" It was Alexis Morgan, and her voice was shaking with emotion. "Can we afford to sit around and rehash a godawful failure? We know what went wrong. But we abandoned my company commander, a platoon sergeant, and six other people in Zahedan! They're in big trouble! May I suggest that we go back there with every available brainy and bot without wasting time?"

Carlisle knew Alexis Morgan was out of line, but she'd just come out of personal combat . . . and a losing fight, at that. "Lieutenant Morgan, if we don't find out what went wrong, we could send brainies and warbots in there to be cannon fodder. And you didn't lose that fight. Don't belittle yourselves. You carried out your orders. You rescued all but six of the living hostages. What's at stake now is far more important. Everyone in the world must know that we *never* abandon our own people and we *never* abandon anyone else! We keep at it until every person is accounted for, even if only *one* person is left! There will be no MIAs!" He paused, then asked, "Hettrick, what went wrong?"

Belinda Hettrick's report was brief, terse, and unemotional. "A hell of a lot. To start with, General, I could have devoted more manpower to the operation itself if the Iranian and Pakistani air-defense forces hadn't spotted us going in. We managed to spoof them with ECM, but I had to commit a lot of AI power to maintaining air surveillance on Kuh-e-Taftan because

341

we were in Iran, and I didn't know if or when we might come under air attack.''

General Victor Knox cut in. ''There was no need to worry about that, Colonel, and I told you so. I followed procedures by the book, and notified the Iranians that we would exercise our option under the Manila Compact to enter their sovereign airspace and territory to rescue hostages if they were unwilling or unable to do so.''

''How were the Iranians notified?'' General Carlisle asked.

''Through normal diplomatic channels, according to protocol.''

''Which means,'' Carlisle observed, ''that you notified the Joint Chiefs who in turn notified the State Department who in turn minuted the Maldive embassy in Tehran, which handles diplomatic affairs for the United States there. The Maldivians probably haven't even received the dispatch yet. Hell's dangling balls of fire, here we are in a world of light-speed communications, and diplomats still pass notes in pouches as they did in the eighteenth century!'' General Carlisle grumbled. He knew he'd have to ask the pentagon and State to get on the horn to the biggest nabob they could locate in Teheran, express apologies, and state they were going back for a cleanup mission. It wouldn't be easy. On the other hand, he reflected, there rarely was an easy job.

But he was glad the Administration still followed the Teddy-Ronnie policy: Some of your people have got some of our people; you can't or won't get them released—we don't care which—so we're going in with military force to do the job. Please stay the hell out of the way unless you want to get hurt.

Carlisle asked if Colonel Belinda Hettrick had finished her report, to which she replied, "No, sir. There's a lot more. The Companions had M-22s, which were perfect for what they had to do. But we didn't have the right warbots and had to use Mark Ten Mod Five antipersonnel defensive units. Solid as the rock of Gibraltar, and just about as maneuverable. Shoot up a storm, but can't get out of their own way. Designed to handle massed linear robot assaults. Robotic Napoleonic wars stuff. I'll defer to Captain Walker's report of how she had to contend with the sort of tactics the Jehorkhims used against these robots."

"Captain Walker?"

Edith Walker, a young captain not yet a decade out of the Point, had a growing reputation for tenacity and doggedness in defense, which was why Hettrick had assigned Walker's Warriors to cover the aerodrome. She was very good at multiple operations. Although a human being can do only one thing at a time, Edith Walker had an extremely fast scan which made it appear that she could control several bots at once. Furthermore, she'd been able to teach this ability to her troops. "My running battle reports are in Georgie," she said bluntly, a tiny crack in her thin voice. "Intelligence said I'd be up against lightly armed infantry. But we ran into a horde of Jehorkhims mounted on small Asiatic ponies. No data base had that information. No one considered that mounted troops could survive these days against automatic weapons. Well, the Jehorkhims did! My God, they moved fast! Do you know how hard it is to hit a man on a moving horse—or even a moving horse? My warbots can hit a fast-moving tacair strike craft because they engage it out where angular rates are low. But ground targets moving at high angular rates at close range were something my warbot computers and my brainies weren't prepared to handle. And when we'd shoot a pony out from under a Jehorkhim, he'd fight on foot until a new mount could be brought up for him."

There was a moment of silence before General Carlisle reminded her, "We have the sort of warbots that can handle such tactical situations, Lieutenant."

"Yes, General, but we didn't have them at Zahedan."

"Captain Garcia, you were pinned down on the outskirts of Zahedan. Same problem?" Carlisle asked the next company commander.

"Yes, sir, General, and there was something else that made it tough to fight there," Garcia admitted.

"What was that?"

"I was fifty kilometers away in the command center. I had to depend upon the sensors in my bots."

"Those should have been adequate."

"No, sir, they weren't and they aren't. They were designed to fight other warbots. They couldn't handle fast-moving mounted troops, or the sheer number of available targets." Captain Manny Garcia was tired and angry so he lapsed into brainy slang. "We were all overloaded, and lost damned near all our warbots to mounted cavalry, for crissake! Shouldn't have happened. The Marauders *and* Warriors were goddamned lucky to get out of Zahedan without suffering a double-lobed Lebanese systolic stroke in the process."

"Aw, bullshit, Manny!" It was Marty Kelly. "You acted like you were on a weapons range, selecting targets and all that crap. When the Colonel took over from General Knox and turned me and my Killers loose, we just shot at anything that moved. Didn't have any fucking trouble killing those Jehorkhims. When we shifted over to aerodynes—"

"Why did you shift to aerodynes, Marty, if you were doing so damned well with your warbots on the ground?" Manny Garcia asked quietly. It was a rhetorical question. Manny Garcia knew the answer, but General Carlisle didn't.

"You needed air cover."

"As you said, bullshit, Marty. Your warbots ran out of ammo and got greased by mounted Jehorkhims. That's what really happened," Garcia shot back. "All you had left to run were your aerodynes. But instead of helping me out of the hot grease, you decided to be a hero and smear a bunch of Jehorkhims on the aerodrome road. They just happened to be armed with Soviet AKMS rifles, and you caught a Golden BB. So you wasted an aerodyne that was critical to the hostage evac. The one you wasted on what you thought were helpless ground targets, that aerodyne could have lifted out the last eight people. If you hadn't played tiger, we would have gotten out of Zahedan with enormous material losses but with all of our people."

"Goddamn it, Garcia, the whole Zahedan thing turned into a big, disorganized squirrel cage!" Kelly complained. "When that happens, every warbot brainy has to switch to the head-mounted computer."

Captain Edith Walker's small, hoarse voice remarked, "Sure, Marty, but we were there to rescue hostages, not kill Jehorkhims. Give him his oak leaf cluster, Colonel, and let's go get Curt Carson out of Zahedan."

There was silence for a moment as General Carlisle let his officers blow off steam. He was learning more than he would from a formal report. Finally, he asked, "Is that all, Captain Walker?"

"Yes, sir. As I said, the sordid details are already in Georgie's memory."

"Captain Garcia?"

"The same, sir. We got greased at Zahedan. We shoudn't have."

"Lieutenant Morgan, can you report for Carson's Companions?"

Alexis Morgan was still angry, and used this opportunity to spill it. She told the general in a defiant but dispirited voice, "Yes, sir. It was a bloody goddamned sonofabitching job. We went in with people untrained for this sort of mission, the wrong weapons, inadequate intelligence, insufficient strength, and equipment that was malfunctioning from the start. I don't know what else could possibly go wrong with a mission, General."

"Lieutenant, thank you for your candid remarks." General Jacob Carlisle had been in personal combat himself before warbots had become accepted equipment. He knew how utterly terrifying and debilitating it could be, and he understood this young woman's feeling of exhaustion and failure. But he didn't feel he'd heard the final word. He turned to an old colleague who was sitting next to the young lieutenant. "Master Sergeant Kester, do you have something to add?"

"Yes, sir. I got no argument with Lieutenant Morgan, except she's too soft in her critique of the biggest fuck-up I've ever seen—and I'm not asking you to excuse my language. That's just what the whole goddamned screwed-up operation was." Master Sergeant Henry Kester normally would *never* have spoken that way before an officer and he would have done so only under the most trying circumstances with other NCOs. He'd seen a lot of combat in his Army career, including some with a smooth-faced young Lieutenant just out of West Point, Jacob Oscar Carlisle. Kester had very definite opinions about Operation Squire, and he wanted to tell them to his old friend in blunt terms. Furthermore, he, too, was teetering on the edge of fatigue. "I can forgive Lieutenant Morgan's reluctance to get down and dirty with her critique because it was her first experience in physical combat. But I been through lots of it, some of it with you. I don't like it because it's easier to let a warbot get its pan shot off than to take a round yourself, which I was dumb enough to do, which should give you some idea of how screwed up things got."

"Why was it screwed up, Sergeant?" Carlisle asked the critical question.

Kester put it absolutely straight as Carlisle expected him to do. "Hell, General, any of us who was in Zahedan can tell you, but some are reluctant to criticize the high brass. I could get court-martialed for what I'm going to say, unless you want me to hang up my stripes and harness first."

"Henry, you've never weaseled with me. You've still got your stripes. What the hell went on?" Carlisle came as close as he could to giving a direct order to a man who ought to be wearing stars instead of stripes.

"Sir, Operation Squire was fucked up because an old, forgetful, hero-type general officer tried to micromanage the total operation, down to the individual warbot-brainy level, by sitting at his desk in Diamond Point and running the show himself ... until his incompetence threatened the lives of his subordinates, so they took over and tried to save their asses and the mission."

Jacob Carlisle looked at Victor Knox. "You reported a communications-link failure, General."

Knox cleared his throat. "That's true, Jake."

"Was it cut from the other end?"

"Uh, yes."

"Why didn't you report it?"

"It could have been caused by enemy action. I didn't want to accuse my subordinates of assuming command before I had all the facts."

In a loud voice so that all could hear her clearly, Colonel Hettrick announced, "General, I cut communications. I told General Knox I was going to do it. The records show that. Sergeant Kester wasn't in the command post at the time, but his report is absolutely correct."

"Colonel Hettrick, why did you cut General Knox out of the command loop and assume responsibility for the operation? Did he approve of this?"

"No, sir. He wouldn't approve it. The last order I received from General Knox said, and I quote, 'You will not abandon the Kuh-e-Taftan command post. Withdraw all functioning warbots from the Zahedan area to defend you. The 17th Division, Robot Infantry, must not capitulate against the modern version of the Mongol hordes.' How the hell could I obey that order? The Marauders were pinned down and lost their warbots. The Warriors couldn't withdraw past Zahedan to the command post. The Killers had abandoned their warbots. I couldn't defend the command post, and I reported this. General Knox wasn't in the RCP; he was sitting back at Diamond Point micromanaging the entire operation and, with no sense of how the battle was going, giving conflicting orders. It was my opinion that he'd lost situational awareness. Under those conditions, General Carlisle, it was within my authority to take command of the situation to save what I could of it."

"Colonel Hettrick, you then withdrew from Kuh-e-Taftan and left Colonel Lovell, Captain Carson, and six other people in Zahedan. Why?"

Colonel Belinda Hettrick was tired, and she was shaking with fatigue. "I had no way to get them out. If I'd waited, I'd have lost what was left of the whole Regiment. I had no defenses and no reserves; General Knox had taken Kelly's Killers away to help the Marauders. I was under attack when we got the command-post aerodyne out of there at the last possible moment."

"General Knox? Comment?" The commanding general of the 17th Division (RI) now fixed his stern gaze on the other man.

Knox replied diffidently. "Operation Squire went bad from the start, Jake. I had a lot of low-level foul-ups in the field. I couldn't handle all of them. And I was outnumbered. When it got to the point where there wasn't a hell of a lot I could do to salvage things, I allowed Colonel Hettrick to attempt to save her command."

"General Knox"—the razor-sharp edge to Carlisle's voice let his subordinate know in no uncertain terms that the social familiarity of the Club didn't extend to this meeting and that military discipline was in effect—"why were you outnumbered?"

"Intelligence data and ops analysis said there were less than a thousand Jehorkhims in Zahedan," Knox explained coolly. "It's always been my policy to use as much force as can be mustered for an operation. However, I couldn't get what I needed. On short notice, I could assemble only the Washington Greys."

"Why the big rush?" Carlisle wanted to know.

"The Jehorkhims were killing a hostage every day, Jake. I wanted to get in there as quickly as possible and bring them out before too many were killed," Knox reminded him. "I suspected you had heavy political pressure on you from topside and from the media, so I implemented Operation Squire with whatever I could pull together on short notice. It might not have been adequate, but we had to try."

What General Jacob Carlisle had heard, he did not really want to acknowledge, but he had to heed the criticisms that had come from his fighting troops and from the old comrade he trusted. There was only a brief pause before the commanding general of the 17th Division (RI) said quietly but firmly, "General Knox, I am hereby temporarily reassigning you to the office of General Dunworth, the division's adjutant general. Colonel Hettrick, you will assume temporary command of the First Brigade." Carlisle was surprisingly easy on his subordinate, not because Knox was an old comrade but because there was really little else he could do. Short of ordering a general court-martial, and Carlisle had no hard evidence that would justify doing it, the best the commanding general of the 17th Division (RI) could do to get a subordinate general officer out of the way was to temporarily reassign him.

Carlisle looked at his battle-weary troops. "We're going back to Zahedan. Even if only one warbot brainy or one hostage is left alive there, we're going back! Colonel Hettrick, you're in command. Let me know what you need from the 17th RI and anywhere else. Do it as quickly as you can. My staff and I will join you as fast as we can, but only to back you up. You have the mission, Colonel."

"Yes, sir!" There was some relief in Hettrick's voice, but everyone could tell she was bone weary. They all were. There was a long silence while men and women prepped themselves for a second try.

"General Carlisle," Kester broke the silent tension, "before we put our asses in a sling again, why don't we use the intelligence data we had our hands on but were told to ignore?"

"What are you talking about, Sergeant? Do you know something I don't?" General Carlisle recognized Henry

351

Kester as one smart old warrior. He had often requested him for his operational staff, but the master sergeant had always refused to accept a staff position. Refusing reassignment was one of the prerogatives of an experienced NCO warbot brainy because there were so few good ones.

"General, we had one of the best intelligence sources we could possibly ask for, and we weren't allowed to use him because the command structure wouldn't trust this information. So we let him stew in his quarters on the *McCain* while we went out and tried to be heroes. It's Hassan. Captain Carson captured the kid along with his slavemaster during the recon mission."

"Carson killed the man, didn't he?"

"Sonofabitch panicked and attacked Carson. The Captain hit him once and busted his neck," Kester explained. "Carson could go up on a general court for it."

"We'll see . . . Want to talk with the boy, Sergeant?" Carlisle asked.

"No, sir, this calls for the woman's touch. Let Lieutenant Morgan do it. She knows Hassan. Might be a good idea to have Lieutenant Allen with her, just in case. I'm gonna have my hands full—so will Colonel Hettrick—getting as many brainies and warbots lined up as we can possibly find in this part of the world. But Hassan's certain to tell us something, and maybe we can even get him to guide us back into Zahedan so we're the ones who kick a little ass for a change . . . namely the Imam's."

Carlisle's image looked at the tired face of Lieutenant Alexis Morgan. "Young lady, can you hack it?"

A smile flickered over Alexis Morgan's tired face. "Yes, sir!"

"Do it now!"

She got up and motioned to Jerry Allen. "Come on, shavetail, earn your rations for a change."

CHAPTER TWENTY

Hassan had been truly enjoying himself for the first time in his twelve years.

He discovered that these people weren't going to hurt him. They'd killed Mahmud, but Hassan had considered the older man a fool. He was secretly glad that Mahmud would no longer boss him around.

And to the slave boy from the slopes of Kuh-e-Taftan, the standard lot of the U.S. Navy swabby was royal treatment because even the spartan amenities of the *McCain* recalled to him folk legends of the riches of kings and princes. The existence of indoor plumbing wasn't a novelty, he'd seen it in Zahedan, though it was something of a luxury even there. What impressed him most was the extreme cleanliness of the *McCain*—the freshly laundered sheets, the soft beds, swabbed decks, the absence of dirt and grime—and the food.

It was apparent from Ship Security's records that Hassan had spent a lot of time looking at TV. He was fascinated to learn of worlds he'd never imagined. He watched children's shows. Adult shows bored him after a few minutes; they were beyond his comprehension.

But Hassan had learned much from the TV. And he'd added things up in his mind. Mahmud was dead and he didn't have to worry about him any longer. But Captain Carson seemed very reluctant to take over as Hassan's slavemaster. And these people didn't have slaves.

Hassan didn't really understand personal freedom, but he was getting a taste of it, and he liked it. He didn't want to go back to Baluchistan, Zahedan, and the volcanic slopes of Kuh-e-Taftan.

He wanted to become a part of the miraculous world in which he now found himself.

But how could he do it?

He'd been trained by Mahmud as a merchant trader. He could thank his former master for that much. He'd use what he'd learned.

He needed to figure out this new world he was in; he decided he could do that too.

And he decided he'd been selling what he had too cheaply.

Lieutenants Morgan and Allen decided that their approach to Hassan would be different from Curt's. Allen suggested that they act as they would on a public relations visit to an elementary school, presenting the United States armed forces in terms of adventure, excitement, and protectiveness—things which could be understood by even the youngest child. The purpose of such school visits, of course, was to motivate young people to plan on making careers in the armed services.

They showed Hassan the videotape, "Robots Fight For Your Freedom," in the Arabic language version.

Frankly, the tape almost made the two young officers gag. The motivational material was so primitive and so corny that they felt far above it. Neither of them remembered that years ago they'd each seen a similar videotape which had convinced them that someday they would be soldiers. And neither could have traced the course of this idea to the point of application for admission to West Point.

Georgie didn't have to translate. Although Hassan spoke Baluchi primarily, he was fluent in Arabic as well.

The fifteen minute videotape, carefully edited to that length because of attention-span research, was full of warbot action. Assault bots spit fire, aerodynes made tactical strikes, transport bots removed injured people from earthquake rubble, aerodynes lifted people off the roofs of houses in flooded areas, and emergency bots went into hazardous areas where human rescue teams would have been killed. Animated sections showed how human soldiers commanded warbots. While it was exciting and violent and full of action, the videotape subtly emphasized the humanitarian activities of the Robot Infantry. The recruitment pitch was very subtle.

When the tape was over, Hassan appeared to hold back.

"That's who we are, Hassan. Now, will you help us rescue the rest of our people from the Imam in Zahedan?" Alexis Morgan asked. "We need to know many things that you can tell us."

Hassan was no fool in spite of his age and his lack

of formal schooling. Madmud had taught him that knowledge of the places where good stones and gems were to be found was as valuable as the stones themselves; thus, information was a valuable commodity. He was not stupid enough to give it away.

He didn't speak to Alexis Morgan, but directed his remarks to Jerry Allen. "I have learned to provide things that other people value. For example, if I find a nice piece of chalcedony and if a jewelry maker believes it to have value, he will buy it from me and put it into a beautiful necklace that some rich merchant can then take to a place where someone else will pay money so he might place that necklace around the neck of his favorite wife."

Jerry Allen wasn't used to the bartering mercantilism of the Middle East, and he didn't realize that information had value. It had always been there when he'd wanted it; he didn't realize he paid for it in a million subtle ways. Furthermore, he still looked upon Hassan as an uneducated young nomad. "So? We can probably find lots of gems for you to trade, Hassan."

Hassan sensed that he had a live one on his hands. "You do not understand, *effendi.* I know many things about the Jehorkhims and Zahedan. Is this information valuable to you?"

"Information will help us rescue our people from Zahedan, Hassan, but why should I pay you for it?" Allen asked innocently.

Hassan looked away and replied almost absently, "If what I know is of no apparent value to you, then I will just have to wait and hope that you will return me to where you found me ... if you succeed against the Jehorkhims."

"Aw, to hell with it!" Lieutenant Jerry Allen snapped, and he got up. "Alexis, this kid isn't going to talk unless we pay him off first!"

Alexis Morgan reached out and put her hand on the young officer's sleeve. "Hold on there, Jerry boy! Don't delink that quickly! You've got your threshold set too low. And you've never shopped in the Bazaars in Baghdad or Tunis, have you?" Although she was somewhat surprised by Hassan's sophistication in matters of trading, she knew what he was talking about and how to handle him.

On the other hand, she had a major obstacle to overcome. By choosing to talk with Jerry Allen, Hassan had shown that he didn't want to negotiate with a mere woman. Or had he? Was that part of Hassan's facade? He was a budding young merchant trader. He still had a lot to learn, but he already knew a lot. Alexis realized Hassan was smart in ways American kids weren't, but she felt that she understood how he thought. She'd haggled in marketplaces for as long as she could remember. Originally from El Paso, Texas, she'd learned at an early age to strike a bargain in the *plaza de mercado* across the Rio Grande in Juarez. She figured that she'd at least give it a try with Hassan.

"Hassan, my most esteemed young merchant-trader friend," she told him, piling it on high and thick while using words that Georgie would translate in the most polite way, "my companion is younger than I and therefore new to the ways of the world. On the the other hand, I am willing and ready to bargain. I realize that

358

value must be returned and that a gift must seal the exchange. I would like to know what you think your information may be worth. Perhaps we can strike a deal and make an agreement. As you are obviously aware, we do not lack money."

"Hey, Alexis, cool it!" Jerry whispered to her. "You haven't got the authority to commit funds! And you even offered him a bribe!"

"Jerry, shut the hell up and let an expert handle this!" she whispered back. "Even as a lousy plebe, you couldn't manage to keep your mouth shut and stay out of trouble! Don't forget: I know your number and I outrank you." She paused, then pressed him further. "Or do I have to remind you about an incident during your second year when a certain slightly raunchy porno disk from Singapore got smuggled into the Phillips Hall sim labs, where you even had the guts to charge admission? Value received, my aching buns!"

"How did you? . . ."

"Never mind! I did. And it was pretty bad, too. Not worth the price of admission." She turned back to Hassan. "A thousand pardons, but I had to inform my companion that he was acting in an improper and impolite manner. Now, what do you think your cooperation is worth to us?"

Hassan thought a moment, then replied and Georgie translated, "Mere money will not buy my cooperation. What I can tell you is far more valuable than gold and silver."

Uh-oh! Alexis suddenly wondered what she'd let herself in for. But Hassan was a haggler, so she pressed on. "Please tell me what you want."

"I could ask for and probably get from you a thousand thousand rials ... or even that many Pakistani rupees," Hassan went on. "But when you returned me to Kuh-e-Taftan and I took the money into Zahedan, people would want to know where I got it. The government would become interested in me and would take most of the thousand thousand rials in taxes. And where would I spend the rest? In Zahedan? For what? No, *el-sitti*, you can give me something that is far more valuable to me."

"Well, what is it?" Once Alexis knew, she could start to haggle.

There was no hesitation in the boy's reply. "I would someday be a warbot officer serving with the Washington Greys of the Seventeenth 'Iron Fist' Division, Robot Infantry," he replied proudly, enunciating the words in English.

That preliminary recruiting video must have been *really* powerful, Alexis thought. What she didn't know was that the video had confirmed what Hassan had already decided on.

"I can't promise you that, Hassan."

"You can make the arrangements. I do not wish to go back to Baluchistan. I want to learn how to be a robot officer like you."

"I can only tell you that you'll get the chance to try. You have to do it yourself."

Hassan shrugged. "So? I will work hard. I will learn your language. I have already begun to do so with your story box on the wall. But I cannot do it alone. I need the help of the United States Army Robot Infantry."

360

"You'll have to learn many new things."

"I will learn what needs to be learned."

"You'll have to give up your own ways of doing things."

"I will do that. This is a better way."

The youngster showed spunk. Alexis believed that, given a chance, he'd probably make the grade. If so, she thought, Hassan might someday serve in her own command ten to twelve years down the line. If not, his youthful experience of an ignored part of the world would certainly make him a valuable intelligence expert . . . perhaps a better one than the Army now had.

So Lieutenant Alexis Morgan looked at Hassan and put out her hand. "Then the deal is done."

Hassan hesitated a moment because he had never concluded a deal before, much less one with a woman. But he was well aware of the fact that this woman with the insignia of rank on her uniform obviously had the power to negotiate. Hassan put out his hand and took hers. "You bargain too easily," he told her. "It is easy to talk and give information."

Alexis shook her head. "No. What I agreed to do will be easy. It only seems difficult to you. You bargained your information to save the lives of our people, and I bargained to allow you to change your life. We came to an agreement. You got what you wanted, and I got what I wanted. What else is there?" Then she said to her fellow officer, "Jerry, see if the quartermaster has a set of uniforms that will fit Hassan."

"What? It's against regulations to allow civilians to wear Army uniforms!" Jerry complained.

"Those uniforms will mean a lot more to Hassan

than you think. He's never had any clothes except rags. And they amount to the Army's little gift that seals the deal."

"That's bribery, Alexis!"

She shook her head. "No Jerry, it's *baksheesh* and it's been a way of doing business in this part of the world since the days of the Sumerians more than fifty centuries ago. Hassan expects it, and it would be impolite for us to overlook it. Whatever did they teach you in comparative cultures classes at the Point, plebe?"

Jerry Allen sighed. " 'When in Rome, shoot Roman candles . . .' "

"That's right! Glad you learned something at Playland on the Hudson."

But Jerry Allen feared that they'd overstepped their authority. "Alexis, where the hell are we going to get the money to put him through military prep and all the rest? And I don't have the pull to get him US citizenship, much less an appointment to the Academy."

"Lieutenant Allen!" Alexis was kidding him, and the tone of her voice revealed it. "If this kid gives us the kind of information that gets three Army types and a bunch of civilian hostages out of Zahedan after Knucklehead Knox failed, don't you think Carlisle or Hettrick or someone could find some discretionary funds or some scholarship money? To say nothing of declaring him some kind of *persona sine patriā* and giving him citizenship in place of a hero medal."

"Uh, yeah, I guess so. But it isn't regulation."

Alexis Morgan snorted. "Jerry, when are you going to learn that the regs tell you what you *can't* do. Now, please have the quartermaster get this show on the road.

362

That's a good boy." Alexis felt relieved when Jerry called Sergeant Nick Gerard on the comm and asked him to secure a set of uniforms for Hassan. The young man might learn to delegate and thus become an officer, a leader, and even a gentleman, she decided. She felt qualified to make that judgment, since she'd graduated two years ahead of Allen.

She turned to Hassan. "Now, while we're taking care of some of the details of our agreement and a little gift is on its way here for you, let's get some information. What about the Jehorkhims? Who are they?"

"The Jehorkhims are fanatics. They believe that Allah speaks directly to them because of what the Imam has done."

"Oh? How?"

For the first time, Hassan hesitated before he answered. He wasn't sure he'd be believed. "Jehorkhim soldiers have tried to get Mahmud and me to join them. They told me that it is easy. All we would have to do is experience the revelation that the Imam Rahman received from Allah."

"What's that?" Alexis asked. "How do they experience it?"

"Each Jehorkhim soldier sits alone in a chair with his head draped ... and he sees the vision that the Imam experienced," Hassan explained. "They have told me that it is real. They see it. They feel it. They hear it."

"Ah-ha!" Jerry Allen brightened. "Alexis, do you remember that part of Curt's recon mission record where the ratbot listened to the Imam and a woman scientist talking?"

"You bet I do!"

"Are you thinking what I'm thinking?"

"Damned right! I want to go back and review that data, but I think Hassan's trying to tell us that the scientist—Dr. Taisha, wasn't it?—may be using something like our linkage techniques to brainwash Jehorkhim soldiers," Alexis turned to the boy. "Hassan, have any of the Jehorkhim soldiers told you anything about the revelation from Allah? What's it like? What happens?"

Hassan replied, "To each Jehorkhim experiencing the Imam's revelation, Allah appears hidden in the midst of a whirlwind and speaks, telling the soldier to give his life in the *jihad* against the unfaithful, promising him an immediate place in paradise."

"Sounds familiar," Alexis muttered.

"But many Jehorkhims believe it may not be Allah speaking. They are afraid it is only the *jinn* who speak out of the whirlwind," Hassan ventured to add.

"*Jinn?* I didn't think the Islamic religion involved any supernatural being except Allah," Jerry asked.

"Mohammed revealed the word of Allah in the Koran, but the *jinn* were never banished or destroyed," Hassan explained. "The *jinn* are still around, doing both good and evil things. But I fear the Jehorkhims far more than I fear the *jinn*. Do you want to destroy the Jehorkhims?"

"No, we just want to get Captain Carson, Sergeant Sampson, and the rest of the hostages out of Zahedan. We don't have any orders to destroy the Imam or the Jehorkhims," Alexis explained.

"Will you be using your flying devices?" Hassan asked.

"Yes."

"Then I can tell you what to do if you wish to make the Jehorkhim powerless to stop you from rescuing your people . . . our people."

Alexis thought she knew, but she wanted to hear it from Hassan. I might as well be getting my money's worth, she told herself.

Hassan told her. She was right.

CHAPTER TWENTY-ONE

As Curt Carson lay on the lumpy brass bed after the Jehorkhim soldiers took him back to the barren room with the barred window, he didn't congratulate himself on what he'd accomplished in Dr. Rhosha Taisha's laboratory. It was too early to know what the consequences might be. He stared at the bare ceiling with its single light bulb, and tried to figure out how he could parlay the opening move of his con game into an escape ploy. His mind was busy; Taisha's experiment seemed to have stimulated him to think. He kept running over all the possibilities and potentialities, almost obsessed with working his way out of this mess.

First of all, had he really conned Dr. Rhosha Taisha? He believed he'd found a vulnerable spot in her otherwise formidable personality. She'd gotten so excited when she'd been successful that she'd thrown caution to the winds. But could he also con the Imam? And could he somehow confuse or soften up any Jehorkhim resistance to a second rescue mission?

He was bothered by the thought that Hettrick might not mount a second try. Maybe her losses had been too great during Operation Squire. From his barred window, he'd watched Jehorkhims hauling remains of various warbots down the street, probably to Taisha's laboratory.

Hettrick had told him she'd be back, and he knew she'd come after them with whatever she could put together . . . if Knox would let her.

Curt didn't know what was going on at command level. Knox had disappeared from the command loop during the mission, and maybe—praise be to the high brass who occasionally did something right—General Victor Knox had been removed from command of Operation Squire.

Without a rescue mission, what were the possibilities for escape? Insofar as Curt could tell, he sure as hell couldn't get himself and three other people out of this backwater in the hills of Baluchistan, not unless he could take over an aircraft at the Zehedan aerodrome. The only aircraft he'd seen there were the old Soviet Antonov An-24 and the Orient Express hypersonic transport, neither of which he'd been checked out in; he could probably wrestle that old Soviet ship into the sky, but he sure as hell couldn't fly that hypersonic transport.

How about the railroad? One train a week came into Zahedan from Quetta. Within twenty-four hours, it went back. The chances of getting out of town on that train were remote.

He might be able to salvage some of the surviving warbots, but they couldn't help four people cover several hundred kilometers to safety.

There were too many maybes, and too many long shots.

He'd have to depend upon a rescue mission.

And in order for that to succeed, he had to get everyone together and keep them that way until the mission arrived. Was it the Imam's plan to keep them separated? In the past, terrorists had done that to make rescue attempts unfeasible. Maybe he should try to convince the Imam that a second rescue mission was unlikely.

But maybe the Imam wasn't as smart as Curt was giving him credit for. The Jehorkhims had held all hundred Orient Express hostages in one place. Looking back on it, Curt didn't think that had been too smart.

On the other hand, the Imam and his Jehorkhims might have been just as inexperienced at the hostage game as the Army had been in trying to run a rescue attempt. Curt dismissed that thought; he didn't like to attribute unsubstantiated weaknesses to the enemy. Doing that had gotten everyone in trouble on the first rescue mission.

He wanted to get his hands on some of the warbot materiel that the Washington Greys had abandoned. Maybe the power packs were dead. Maybe not. Perhaps he could establish some sort of communication with Hettrick if he and his robot wizard, Eddie Sampson, could get their hands on some warbots.

The ratbots! Curt suddenly remembered the operable robots he and Henry Kester had left in Zahedan at the end of the recon mission.

But he didn't get the chance to follow that line of thought. By this time, it was shortly after noon prayers, and when a single Jehorkhim soldier opened his door, Curt noticed that it hadn't been locked or otherwise secured. The soldier simply indicated that Curt was to follow him.

There was no blindfold this time.

Curt kept careful track of where he was led.

He also kept his eyes moving, trying to pick up clues as to the whereabouts of the other three people.

The Jehorkhim soldier took him downstairs and across a very narrow street, waving the local people out of the way. Not surprisingly, Curt was led to the government building where the hostages had been held. From its roof most of the hostages had been evacked the day before. He could still see the aerodyne parked at a crazy angle up there. Too bad it didn't have the power or the fuel to lift off and go anywhere. But, if he could get to it, maybe he could salvage something to use in his con or an escape.

On the first floor, there was a lot of rubble from the battle the day before. A few unenthusiastic old women, black shawls covering their heads, were slowly picking up pieces of it, and sweeping dust and debris into little piles on the tiled floor.

It was obviously a government-type building, but Curt saw no one working in the various offices they passed. Of course, the place was still pretty much of a mess after yesterday's battle.

Curt could now see that the Imam was established on the second-floor in a corner room at the opposite end of the building. Curt and his bots hadn't looked around there yesterday because they'd been too preoccupied with getting the hostages out of the basement under fire.

Two guards were posted outside the Imam's door.

He either enjoyed such ceremonial use of people or he was seeing to his own safety. Maybe the Imam wasn't firmly in control. Maybe that was why he had made the compact with Dr. Rhosha Taisha for the indoctrination of his soldiers.

The Imam Abdul Madjid Rahman looked noncommittal as he sat crossed-legged on the carpeted floor. Dr. Rhosha Taisha sat in a chair next to him, drinking tea. She looked extremely pleased.

This time, Curt was asked by the Imam to sit before him, which he did. Again, the Imam offered him coffee. Curt was playing a different game now, so he politely accepted and thanked the Imam.

The coffee was strong, bitter, and very thick, just as it had been at breakfast.

Although the Imam Abdul Madjid Rahman looked noncommittal, there was a certain amount of disbelief and distrust in his expression as he sipped his thick coffee and remarked to Curt, "Dr. Taisha tells me that you've undergone Jehorkhim indoctrination and have decided to become a believer in the will of Allah, the Merciful, the Beneficent."

"No, Imam, not exactly," Curt replied, attempting to maintain his facade, but quickly adding, "I'm not a believer in the will of Allah. But your God isn't very much different from my God. I happen to be Christian myself—actually a Sojourner of the Order of the Turtle."

"I am not familiar with that Christian sect," the Imam admitted coolly.

Curt shrugged. "We Christians have our sects just as you Muslims do. A lot of them, as a matter of fact.

370

My sect is very similar to that of the Jehorkhims. It's a military group which meets every Friday evening when possible." Curt was making this up out of whole cloth as he went along. He was indeed a Sojourner, but the rest he'd dragged out of Friday night Happy-Hour tradition.

"I am not certain that qualifies you to join us in our *jihad.*"

Curt hadn't paid a lot of attention during those long-ago classes on comparative religions held in the granite building on the banks of the Hudson. But he dragged something up from the dim recesses of his mind and decided that, even if it wasn't exactly correct, it might be close enough. "My teachers once taught me Muslims required that a person believe in only one God, that it didn't make any difference if He was Allah or Jehovah, provided taxes were paid to the caliph. My own religious beliefs don't differ too greatly from yours, so I'm not really interested in becoming a Jehorkhim Muslim if I can serve you in a military capacity."

"You are certainly going to great lengths to ingratiate yourself with me, Captain. It leads me to suspect that you wish to be trusted so you won't be guarded and can then escape," the Imam pointed out. "It won't work."

"Of course it won't work!" Curt told him, "Where am I going to go? The troops of Alexander the Great might have walked out of this place, but how far do you think I'm going to get with two women and a civilian . . . and no supplies?" Curt didn't mention the possibility of hijacking an airplane or playing hobo on the railway to Quetta. Nor did he say anything about

371

the assistance he might get from the surviving warbots, if they could be made operable.

The Imam chuckled for a brief instant, then became serious again. "Iskander's troops didn't have airplanes or railways." He took a sip of coffee, then went on. "I can't afford to accept you as a mercenary. I need to hold you and the three others for ransom."

Curt didn't like to say it because it might just be true, but he managed to laugh ironically, "Ransom? Hah! Only three soldiers and one out of more than a hundred hostages? That's considered to be an acceptable military loss. I know the Army, and they won't consider it to be cost effective to come back and get us. The United States has probably written us off. You want ten million bucks in gold bullion for each of us. Do you know what we're really worth on a cost-accounting basis? The Army can train my replacement for less than half a million! And they turn down thousands of applicants every year! So why the hell should I sit on my ass waiting for a rescue that's never going to come when I could be earning my keep by fighting with you? Why do you think I'm talking to you like this?"

The Imam thought about this for a moment. He decided this captive was right. He could continue to squander resources guarding and feeding his captives, now reduced to four, but was that really worth doing? The request for ransom might be ignored by the Americans or it might precipitate another rescue mission, this time with stronger forces, which would further decimate the Jehorkhims. On the other hand, if Carson and his companions cooperated fully with Dr. Taisha, she might, indeed, be able to exert complete control over his Jehorkhims on the battlefield. His men would then become far more powerful than robots.

"And what do you think you might be able to do to 'earn your keep,' as you put it? What could you do for my already powerful Jehorkhim forces?"

Curt played his trump card. "The Jehorkhims will probably do reasonably well against manned armies of smaller countries. But your *jihad* is also directed against world powers committed to robot warfare. You know this or you wouldn't have Dr. Taisha working with you. I'm a soldier, and I know the doctrine and strategy of robot warfare. You've heard of something called 'countermeasures'?"

"Countermeasures against warbots? Why would I need such a thing? I did very well against warbots yesterday."

"You lost too many men." When Curt said that, he could see the immediate reaction on the Imam's face. The losses worried the Imam. "It took fifteen hundred of your best Jehorkhim soldiers to rout a small force of about fifty warbots. The United States isn't going to let that happen again. You'll come up against American-equipped robot infantry forces when you move out of Zahedan to Quetta and try to take Pakistan."

"Who told you I was going to do that?" the Imam snapped.

Curt immediately knew he'd hit on another piece of sensitive information. "No one. I can read a map. The Indus River valley is your easiest objective, and it's mostly Muslim, so you won't have overwhelming religious problems. That's the best direction for you to move to gain resources." This was all pure guesswork on

373

Curt's part, but he sensed he'd hit the right button, thanks to his knowledge of thousands of years of military conquest. If he got away, he now had the hot intelligence on the Imam's next move . . . and on why the Imam had stupidly grabbed hostages—to collect ransom money for more equipment.

Although the Imam had made a stupid move, he was smart and amitious. But, like other would-be world conquerors of the past, he didn't realize how large and diverse the Earth really was. The Imam was thinking of Pakistan, then India. Even if the Jehorkhims got that far, Curt felt certain they couldn't handle the Chinese . . . or the Russians if the Americans let the Russkies in on the deal.

"And you won't be able to use those old Mongol cavalry tactics when you do. They won't work against the automatic weapons of a stronger warbot force. If you lost more than a hundred Jehorkhims yesterday against a small warbot contingent, you'll be clobbered in your first engagement against a full RI brigade, much less a division," Curt went on quickly. "Any commander who loses ten percent of his forces in an engagement has effectively lost the battle. So you're going to have to fight smarter and beat the warbots by knowing and exploiting their weak points."

"What are the weak points of warbots, Captain?" the Imam asked.

"Command and control links," Curt lied. He didn't know a damned thing about their design. That way, if he were tortured, he could never reveal that information.

The beautiful Dr. Taisha asked the critical question.

"Captain, those command and control channels, do you know how they work?"

Curt shook his head. "No, I don't. But I don't *need* to know in order to use warbots or keep them from working. I don't have to know why a radio works or an airplane flies in order to screw up either one with countermeasures."

"How can I be sure of that?"

Curt shrugged. "Try me. Get me as many of the warbots as you can salvage from yesterday's battle. Let me work with my people. Colonel Lovell knows a lot about robots. And Sergeant Sampson is my best warbot technician. I don't know the surviving hostage, but we'll put him to work." Curt looked directly at Taisha and said as coolly as possible, mimicking her without making it obvious that he was doing it, "Then you'll have some robots and operators to work with, Doctor. With your help, your knowledge, and your equipment, we can learn enough to develop countermeasures that will put warbots out of action when we run into them again." Turning back to the Imam, he added, "If you don't do something like this, your indoctrinated warriors will just be mowed down."

What Curt said was true, but he had absolutely no intention of enabling Taisha to develop countermeasures. He wanted Colonel Lovell, Sergeant Sampson, and the male hostage, along with whatever warbot materiel the Jehorkhims had captured. Even if he had only voice command over the M-22 warbots from the rooftop, that was a start.

The Imam cocked an eyebrow. He looked over the rim of his tiny coffee cup while he slowly sipped its thick contents, his eyes leveled at Curt. The American officer, so different from the foreigners he'd met while in school in England, had him slightly confused. It was obvious that this man was well educated; he'd spotted the problems and shortcomings of the Jehorkhim army on his own, problems with which the Imam had wrestled for years before finally deciding they could only be solved by more modern equipment, which cost money, which could be obtained only by taking and ransoming hostages. The Imam needed Curt's expertise, and he knew it. But why was the American officer suddenly becoming a turncoat, a mercenary? That bothered the Imam, so he did what usually go him results: He asked a direct question.

"Captain, I am very suspicious of you. Yesterday, you fought hard and valiantly on the roof. You refused to surrender. Now you wish to change sides. I do not understand this. Why do you wish to do this?"

Curt recalled everything he could about a man he hated: Marty Kelly. This was just the sort of thing Curt could see Kelly doing. Marty would be a perfect soldier of fortune. Curt had spent three years being hazed and goaded by Kelly at West Point. He detested the man, but he had to get inside Kelly's head and act like him.

"I joined the Army because I'm a fighter. They made a glorified machine operator out of me. It isn't very satisfying, if you know what I mean."

"No, I don't. Please explain."

"I fight by sitting in a nice clean room somewhere, wired up to robots."

"So? That's quite safe, isn't it?"

"Yeah. Too damned safe."

"What do you mean, too safe?"

"Well, I didn't understand it until I went into actual physical combat yesterday. It made a difference—a lot of difference." Curt hesitated. He wanted to make the warp and woof of his con job convincing. "Knowing that I could actually be killed made combat more . . . more exciting."

"No, I'm not sure I know what you mean. Tell me," the Imam pressed.

"Well, maybe I used the wrong words," Curt said. He decided to slip into Army slang. He wanted to appear intelligent enough to work on robot countermeasures but not smart enough to develop a complex con scheme to divert the Imam. "The Robot Infantry's a good job. Not too dangerous. I can't get killed in battle. Worse thing that can happen is to have a warbot shot out from under me; no big deal. Fighting? Hah! It's like playing video games! Then I tangled with your Jehorkhims yesterday. They're fighters! When Dr. Taisha put me through your indoctrination program, I learned why. They fight for a spiritual reward, win or lose. Serving you, I might get killed, but if I've got to go, that's the way I want to do it. It's a religious thing. I won't go to the Muslim paradise, but in my religion I'll go to a place called Fiddler's Green."

"Is that a portion of the Christian Heaven?" the Imam asked.

"No, only civilians get to Heaven. Soldiers usually end up on the road to Hell." Curt was stretching the truth again, and hoping, if there was a God, He wouldn't strike him down.

377

The Imam smiled. "I think I understand." And he broke into poetry:

> "God and the soldier, we adore
> In time of danger, not before;
> The danger passed and all things righted,
> God is forgotten and the soldier slighted."

"Yeah, we get a lot of that. The United States doesn't fight big wars anymore, only little stuff. So soldiers always get hind tit. That's why we military people have our own paradise." Deep into his con job now, Curt spoke with conviction.

"Tell me about Fiddler's Green," the Imam prodded.

The Imam himself had just demonstrated an affinity for poetry, so Curt recalled an issue of the cadet newspaper, *The Pointer*. He had to work hard to keep a straight face as he began to recite an old soldier's beer-hall ditty:

> "Halfway down on the road to Hell
> In a shady meadow green,
> Is a place where all dead troopers sit
> Around a good old-time canteen;
> And that eternal resting place
> Is known as Fiddler's Green ..."

"Strange. I haven't read that in your Holy Bible," the Imam pointed out.

"Probably not. From your accent, I'd guess you spent

378

time in Great Britain, where you probably studied the King James' version," Curt responded.

The Imam nodded.

"Well, that verse comes from something like the Islamic *Hadith*. It is a folk interpretation." This was about the tallest tale Curt had ever spun. But he was counting on the fact that no man, not even the Imam, was totally familiar with the details of all the religious sects in the world, especially the sect Curt had made up out of whole cloth and old soldiers' lore.

The Imam Abdul Madjid Rahman thought about this for a moment. He was well aware that he might be taking a great risk by bringing this American into his circle. But he was at risk if he didn't. He was eager, ambitious, and impatient. And he had confidence in the capabilities of his scientific advisor who'd already voiced her enthusiastic approval of Curt. The Imam set down his petite coffee cup and said to Dr. Taisha, "I like this man."

"What did I tell you?" she replied.

"Do you still agree?"

She nodded. "Yes. I can use his help, especially after what he said."

Sonofabitch! First Base! Curt thought gleefully to himself. He'd conned the Imam intellectually, and he believed he'd conned Dr. Taisha physically.

He was wrong, of course.

The Imam rearranged his Kaftan. "Very well. Captain Carson, I will not offer you a position of command in the Jehorkhims until you prove yourself to the doctor and myself. You must understand that only Jehorkhim Muslims can possibly rise beyond the most minor command position in our *jihad*. Furthermore, you cannot take part in any Jehorkhim ceremonies."

"I find no problem with that, Imam, just as long as you honor our religious activities." Curt had some very definite ideas concerning the nature of his new "religious activities." He would insist that the reestablishment of some kind of linkage with the remaining robots was extremely important, and he wanted to talk with Colonel Willa Lovell about how they could make some modifications to permit secret and privileged communications between the three Army people. "If I'm going to do the proper sort of a job for you, I want my people with me. We're a team. They're experienced robotic engineers and technicians. No one of us knows everything about it; together, we can combine our know-how. Dr. Taisha knows what it means to have a technical team that can work together on a problem," Curt insisted.

"That would be a good idea," Taisha concurred, rather surprisingly. "As I told you, all the technical expertise that I can get will be helpful. Especially concerning the warbots' remote command and control systems." But there was an edge in Dr. Taisha's voice, something that told Curt he shouldn't trust her completely. She might not have believed the malarkey he'd just fed the Imam, but she probably didn't offer any objections because a team would contribute to her research and, eventually, to her power over the Jehorkhims. Dr. Rhosha Taisha was an opportunist, and she was interested only in exerting power over people in the new way.

Curt knew that she was a highly experienced electroneurophysiologist; she'd certainly proved that by the way she'd been able to use her computers to program his nervous system. But it was now apparent that she didn't understand the entire linkage principle used in robot warfare. He'd have to make use of that.

Then Dr. Taisha did something Curt Carson hadn't expected. "Imam, it would be of enormous benefit to my work, and it would further confirm that Captain Carson's people are, indeed, working with us if I were to subject them to our Jehorkhim indoctrination. I would learn something more about the reaction of experienced robotic technicians to my human-interface control, and the technicians would learn more about the motivation of the Jehorkhim *jihad.*"

Curt didn't foresee anything wrong with that, at least right then. He knew Edie Sampson would laugh at the material used. He wasn't sure what response Colonel Willa Lovell would have. As for the other young hostage, he knew nothing about the man; he couldn't even guess what would happen there. But he felt confident that all of them were more sophisticated than mere Baluchi herdsman and nomads.

He was wrong, but he didn't know it at the time.

"I expect that the doctor will want to run some experiments on us from time to time," he quickly declared. "We're all experienced in robotics work. But, Imam, you've got to show your good intentions. I've offered to help you. You accepted. The next move is up to you, not me." Curt was skating on thin ice, but he felt sure he could maneuver his way through it.

"What do you mean, Captain Carson?"

"First of all, stop treating us like hostages. The four

of us must be isolated; we've got to be able to talk together and work together."

"Do I have your word that you will do what you say you will?" the Imam replied.

"We'll begin working on warbots as soon as we're together and as quickly as we have available whatever warbots you can salvage," Curt promised. "Your Jehorkhim indoctrination has nothing whatsoever to do with our agreement. If Dr. Taisha wants to do it, we'll go along if it's considered an experiment. Remember, I'm fighting here for a different thing than the will of Allah. I'm a soldier, not a preacher or a holy man."

The Imam nodded. "You four will be quartered together and be allowed to work together. Doctor, I'll assign a detachment of Jehorkhims to bring some of the abandoned warbots into your lab."

Warily, the Imam looked at Curt. "We have struck a bargain, Captain. I still do not trust you completely. I feel the same may be true in your case. Let us hope that it is the will of Allah that we find more in one another as the days go by and we proceed on our *jihad*."

CHAPTER TWENTY-TWO

If Curt Carson had thought that conning the Imam and Dr. Taisha was tough job, the next task that faced him—bringing the captives together and keeping them together—was even tougher.

He *had* to give them a group identity. If their captivity became prolonged, that could mean the difference between survival and being broken in body, mind, and spirit. He had no illusions about the situation; they were prisoners. He had no intention whatsoever of helping the Imam, but he had to con the religious leader. And he considered that was a tall order because he felt that most religious leaders were accomplished con artists. Who else could promise everything after death, yet never be in a position to be held accountable for what happened or didn't happen?

The Imam kept his word; he released them all from solitary confinement and put them in adjoining rooms above Dr. Taisha's basement laboratory. They were together; Curt intended to keep them that way, using military discipline if necessary. By early afternoon, the four captives were seated on the floor of a somewhat larger room on the ground floor of the Imam's building. The black-shawled women had done a desultory job of cleaning up the place, there were still little piles of rubble here and there. Curt reflected that a martinet would make his troops clean the place up, but he had other things on his mind right then.

He had one big problem. Colonel Willa Lovell outranked him. However, this was a combat situation, Curt was the combat commander and Colonel Lovell was a prisoner he'd failed to liberate. Furthermore, she had a noncombatant research-rated position code. Touchy situation. It would have to come to a head very quickly. He didn't think Willa could lead the group, and if she couldn't, things would quickly go from worms to slime.

He could count on Sergeant Edwina Sampson. As for the lone remaining civilian hostage, Curt considered him to be a total unknown.

He decided he'd tackle the unknown first.

"We've been released from solitary confinement," he began, "because I insisted we were a military outfit and I couldn't guarantee any cooperation from you unless a responsible officer was in command."

"What do you mean, cooperation?" Lovell broke in.

Curt held up his hand. "Our first job here is to survive, Colonel. We've got to do it together. Back about a hundred years ago in Korea, the Chinese broke prisoners by destroying the chain of command in captivity. But they never broke the Turks. Do you remember why?"

"I'm not an expert in leading and commanding

troops, Captain," Lovell admitted. Curt had hoped she'd say that.

"The captured Turks always had a leader. They followed his orders, and he kept them together as a unit," Curt explained. "The Chinese would remove the leader from the compound, whereupon the second in command would take over. Then the Chinese would remove him. When they finally got down to only two Turks, they discovered one of them was still in charge. In the meantime, all the other Turks were over in another POW compound where they'd reorganized. American losses in the Chinese POW compounds were tragic, but the Turks came out at the cease-fire with their morale high and no postcaptivity syndromes."

Curt paused and looked around. "And we're going to do the same thing in Zahedan. This is a detached platoon of Carson's Companions. All of us are Regular Army—except you, sir. I don't even know who you are."

"I'm Owen W. Pendleton, Junior," the young man said hesitantly.

Curt looked carefully at Owen Pendleton. The young man had elected to stay on the rooftop and fight rather than be airlifted out. He was spare, clean shaven, and in his late twenties. Tall and lean, a "beanpole" ectomorph, he nonetheless moved smoothly and was in full control of his gangly body. Thinning brown hair fell in an unruly shock over his forehead, and he seemed extremely shy and introverted.

"Pendleton, I don't know a thing about you, except you fought like a regular up on the roof yesterday. Damned good job. Real professional. You didn't get wounded, you seemed to know how to act under fire, and you knew how to handle a firearm. Are you a contract vet?" Curt thought the remaining hostage might be one of the young men who'd signed a multiyear enlistment contract and had then gone on to do other things after military service.

"Two year ROTC at Deseret University," Pendleton explained haltingly.

"Mormon?" Curt asked.

"No, sir."

"How come only two years?"

"Accident in summer camp. Maneuvers," Pendleton explained dispassionately in his hesitant, tongue-tied manner. "Warbot went dead on me. Nobody was expecting any trouble, so I lay on a linkage couch KIA until the exercise was over. I was in therapy for eight months. The PMS&T wouldn't let me risk finishing the full ROTC course, so I got aced out of a Reserve commission."

"You okay otherwise?"

"Yes, sir. Didn't disable me mentally. I make my living as a self-employed AI mentor," Pendleton admitted, using robotics slang.

"Mister, you're a gold mine!" Curt told him gleefully. Mentors for artificial-intelligence computers were programmers and component engineers of these machines. There were very few of them, and they were a breed apart because they'd learned how to think like a computer. "Can you program warbots?"

"I did the basic mentoring for the industrial AI package that became the Mod Four military AI unit."

"You were the one?" Willa Lovell asked. "My, that

was an excellent job! Were you heading to that meeting in Osaka?"

"Yes. We didn't get there, did we?" Pendleton replied.

"Pendleton, as I explained just now, I need a military team here so we can survive," Curt explained. "Want a brevet commission to temporary Second Lieutenant?"

Owen Pendleton smiled for the first time. "Yes, sir!"

"Okay, we can cover the paperwork later," Curt explained, "or you can resign when we get out of here if you want."

The quiet, introverted robotics programmer simply replied, "I won't."

From memory, Curt recited the appointment oath and had Pendleton repeat it: "I, Owen William Pendleton, Junior, having been appointed an officer in the Army of the United States in the grade of second lieutenant, do solemnly swear and affirm that I will support and defend the Constitution of the United States against all enemies, foreign and domestic, that I will bear true faith and allegiance to the same, that I take this obligation freely, without any mental reservation or evasion, and that I will well and faithfully discharge the duties of the office upon which I am about to enter, so help me God."

Curt breathed a sigh of relief. He'd eliminated the tag-end problem of a civilian in the middle of his team. Now he had one last hurdle to jump. He paused for a moment, then said, "Now, listen up, everybody. Here's what we're going to do."

Colonel Willa Lovell had watched the proceedings.

"Captain, you can't take command of this outfit. I'm the senior officer present," she pointed out.

Curt was ready for her. "Colonel, I am the commanding officer of Carson's Companions, which is Company A, First Batallion, Washington Greys Regiment, Seventeenth 'Iron Fist' Division, Robot Infantry. Sergeant Sampson and I are the only two members of the company here, *but it is still a functioning military unit under my command!* I have been given command authority, and I cannot relinquish it to you, regardless of your rank. Am I right, Colonel?"

"I don't know."

"Then check the ARs. They're quite specific on the matter."

"I don't have a copy of the Army Regulations," she admitted.

"Do you have a combat-rated position code?" Curt was referring to the Army personnel qualification which determined what a person could and could not be assigned to do. He knew she was a noncombatant, officers in the Medical Service Corps were assigned to their specialty during their entire military careers.

She sighed. "No, I'm just a doctor; I've never led troops."

"Then I can't step aside and let you assume command, Colonel."

"Very well. I'll follow you. This is no time to fight among ourselves. But you could be wrong, Captain." Colonel Lovell capitulated gracefully, but she left open the possibility that she might take future action if Curt couldn't cut it.

"If I'm wrong, you can nail my hide to the wall for

388

insubordination," Curt said quickly; then he added, "*Maybe*. But we've got a job to do, and I can't explain all the whys and wherefores of it to you at the moment. Listen to me, listen carefully, and *think!*" He paused, looked around, and slapped his cheek with his palm. "Goddamned place is infested with bugs!" He cupped his hand to his ear, then pointed around the room with his finger.

Platoon Sergeant Edie Sampson caught on right away. "Yeah," she replied, "all the bugs in Zahedan might not be natural."

"Oh!" Pendleton suddenly remarked.

Colonel Lovell looked a bit bewildered.

But Curt believed the other three had gotten the message that what he had to say to them was also for the benefit of any Jehorkhims who understood English and were listening.

"First of all," he explained, "I've told the Imam that the Jehorkhims don't stand a chance in hell if they go up against even a regiment of warbots unless they develop some countermeasures. Dr. Taisha is an expert on computer control of human beings, but she doesn't know beans about the flip side: human-controlled robots, especially about warbots and their command and control links. So I asked the Imam to bring in all the abandoned warbots he could find so that we can get some discrete human-warbot-human communication flowing through their AI systems. Then ..."

Curt hadn't expected an outburst from Colonel Willa Lovell. "Carson, have you gone out of your mind? You're aiding and giving comfort to the enemy! Why, you're nothing but a traitor!" She was livid.

389

"Colonel, with all due respect, m'am," Edwina Sampson tried to placate the older officer, "I don't think you understood exactly what the Captain said. Let him finish. He's in command, he's done pretty well so far, and we ought to listen up." She guessed that her company commander had something up his sleeve. She didn't know what it was, but she *knew* Curt Carson wasn't a traitor. She respected and trusted, and in some ways loved, her Captain.

"How could I possibly do anything to help people who've tortured me for days?" The colonel obviously wasn't listening carefully, and she seemed a bit confused, undoubtedly as a cumulative result of days of captivity, torture, fighting, fear, and loneliness.

"Colonel," Curt said quietly, "I notice that the Jehorkhims have removed the iron shackles from your wrists, ankles, and throat. Does that tell you anything?"

Lovell rubbed her wrists. She had to admit to herself that it felt good to be rid of those shackles, although it had been uncomfortable when the Jehorkhims had cut them away. "That doesn't make a damned bit of difference. You know what the regs say. You *know* you can't assist the enemy."

"It's not a reg. It's a Code of Conduct. Do you remember what it says, Colonel?" Edie Sampson suddenly intervened.

"I . . . I haven't read it in years," the colonel admitted. "Medical staff people don't worry about being prisoners."

"Well, you're a prisoner now," Curt reminded her.

"I'm not doing anything nonreg. Since you don't know the Code, follow my orders."

"I'm not going to do it. I refuse to cooperate," Willa Lovell said adamantly. "I'll even disobey a direct order. The Nuremberg precedents are on my side."

"Bullshit!" Edwina Sampson exploded frustrated by the behavior of a woman she felt should react better if only because of rank. Her red-head's temper burst forth from Army constraints. "Lady, maybe you don't really know what the hell is going on, but we're a thousand kilometers from anywhere and in the hands of a fanatical religious warlord. Maybe the Captain shouldn't have risked his life going into that dungeon for you yesterday. Maybe he shouldn't have let Dr. Armstrong be evacked instead of you. Dammit, this officer you're hassling is a goddamned good leader. You said yourself you've never led troops, so try following for a change! Listen *very* carefully to what your commanding officer has to say, then we'll get busy and do what he tells us." She paused for a moment, suddenly aware of what she'd said and of the possible consequences. Her anger still overwhelmed any logical thought processes, but she did try to smooth things out a bit by adding, "I'm not going to argue with you; you're an officer. But I'm going to tell you what a drill instructor once told a recruit who was bitching during training: 'Soldier, shut up and soldier!' " Edie Sampson didn't reveal that these words had been directed at *her*.

Colonel Lovell was still recoiling from the initial power of Sampson's explosive outburst. She was a doctor, and didn't like to take orders. In her work in Army research and development, she gave the orders, even to generals. No one in the Army, especially no NCO, had ever talked to her like that before. She was shocked right down to her core, totally overwhelmed. This behavior wasn't part of the neatly compartmentalized world she'd managed to sustain in her mind, even during the days of captivity. Her first reaction was anger and resentment. Then the dam broke and she began to sob.

Not surprisingly, Edie crossed the floor and sat down next to her. Putting an arm around the Colonel's shoulder, she said, "Sure, dearie, I know. It's been a lot rougher for you than me. You got hijacked, and I went into this with my eyes open. Go ahead and bawl. Lot of people have used this shoulder; it's certified waterproof. And don't worry: Some things we girls never tell."

But there was more to Lovell than stubborn superiority. She pulled herself back together with an astounding if subdued display of sheer will power. She choked back her sobs, dried her dark eyes, tossed her hair out of her face, and sat up ramrod straight. When she spoke, her voice was completely controlled. "I'm sorry, Captain. I apologize for my unprofessional behavior."

Curt had seen supermacho male cadets come apart under fire in field exercises when instructors were teaching, with live ammunition, the ancient tactics of no-robot warfare. Willa Lovell was stronger than many of those long-forgotten former cadets. "You all right now, Colonel?"

"Yes, sir."

"Sure?"

"Yes, sir. What do we need to do, Captain?"

Curt went on, again carefully choosing his words and

392

accentuating them as he spoke. "The Imam has accepted my offer to *help* him develop countermeasures against warbots. Dr. Taisha has developed an electroneural programming system that will allow her computers to control human beings. What they want us to contribute is our expertise on remote robot operations. But neither Taisha nor the Imam know anything about human-warbot *communications*, especially the sort of *secure* communications needed in remote robotics. So here's what we must do. As quickly as Taisha and the Imam get us some of our warbots to work on, we'll don linkage harnesses and *communicate* via the warbots. It'll be secure. You read me?"

For the first time, Willa Lovell smiled. "How many linkage harnesses will we have?"

"Sampson and I were wearing them," Curt recalled.

"Does Dr. Taisha have any sort of a linkage harness?"

Curt nodded. "But it's different from ours."

"Any spares in that aerodyne on the roof?" Willa Lovell asked.

Now Edie Sampson understood what Curt Carson was trying to do! A mode of supersecure communication was possible—electronic thought transfer from one person in a linkage harness to another person in a linkage harness. "Normal equipment includes a couple of spares," she responded. "That gives us four harnesses. And, Captain, the aerodyne that flew us in here—code name Trajan—has the proper modules already aboard. I can pull 'em out and bring them to the lab, probably even be able to talk to Georgie."

"Now we're getting somewhere! How about our helmet compaks?"

"I don't know where the Jehorkhims put them after they took them off us," Edie admitted. "But we can manage without them. I'll need some help."

"Lieutenant Pendleton, can you help Sergeant Sampson pull the necessary units out of the aerodyne?" Curt asked his new officer.

The young AI expert wasn't used to being addressed by his military title. "Huh? Oh! Don't know what you've got in the aerodyne."

"Lieutenant, what I need at this point is a strong back and a weak mind," Edie told him lightly. "You don't qualify for the latter, but you can sure as hell help me pull equipment out. You might even learn something about warbots in the process."

Owen Pendleton nodded slowly. "Okay. It may be some stuff I did for the RI under contract ... I hope."

Curt looked around. This was suddenly a different outfit. The four of them had responded to his leadership. They knew what they were going to do. Curt didn't know exactly where their efforts would lead, but he'd taken the first step.

He had command of the situation.

Until he saw Rhosha Taisha standing quietly and enigmatically in the doorway. "I have been listening," she said coolly.

"We've made some progress," Curt told her.

"So I hear," she said cryptically. "We have salvaged some of your warbots. The ones we managed to carry have been brought into my laboratory downstairs. Some of the tracked robots were much too large to get through the streets, even if they'd had power, which they didn't."

"We're going to pull some hardware out of the aerodyne on the roof," Curt explained. "We've got a lot of very sophisticated robotics equipment at our disposal now."

"Undoubtedly," Taisha remarked. "I must compliment you, Captain Carson. You have organized your team quickly and well. I would like to begin indoctrination as quickly as possible. The Imam is becoming impatient." The hint of mistrust in her voice revealed that she was still suspicious of Curt's motives, and was anxious to run his three people through her Grade-C motivational show.

But Curt didn't want that to start until he'd gotten his secure communications net established. He wasn't sure what their reactions of the others would be, and he wanted to warn them first. In particular, he was worried about Colonel Willa Lovell. The woman had shown herself to be strong willed, but she was just about at the end of her emotional rope.

"Look," he told the beautiful Eurasian scientist, "we're on a thrust here. We think we've worked out a way to indoctrinate everyone at once."

"You've got a technique for multiple projections into several nevous systems simultaneously?" Taisha was surprised.

"Warbots have to run with multiple and parallel channels," Curt explained. "Especially aerodynes with more than single pilot. So we're going to hack together a lash-up and see if it works. Colonel Lovell's going to

395

locate some more of our linkage harnesses; they match our equipment, but yours don't. Sergeant Sampson and Lieutenant Pendleton are going to salvage equipment from the aerodyne. When we get it all together, Lieutenant Pendleton is an AI mentor, a real expert; he wants to check the bitstreaming and look at the channeling and pin-outs to be sure that all the equipment is compatible. Give us an hour or so to see what we can some up with by doing a little gadgeteering."

Taisha looked quizzically at him. "I didn't realize that Owen Pendleton was an Army officer," Taisha commented. "He was a civilian hostage."

"He's accepted a field commission from me, Doctor. Or doesn't a Jehorkhim officer have the prerogative to recruit and promote people in his unit?"

"I do not concern myself with military matters. I am a scientist."

A little over an hour later, Curt wriggled himself into his smelly, sweat-stained mobile linkage harness. This time, he didn't have the expert help of Sergeant Helen Devlin, but Willa Lovell checked to ensure that all the electrode pads were properly positioned. Then, in turn, they helped one another into harnesses.

Dr. Rhosha Taisha watched with interest. She was relieved to discover that they wouldn't be using the warbots; the mobile units which filled one corner of her lab still had weapons—fletchette guns and grenades and strange electronic devices she didn't recognize. She had a small detachment of Jehorkhims within hailing distance just in case, and she was fascinated by the level of technology of the Army warbot equipment. She'd studied the mobile harnesses when they'd been taken

396

off Curt and Edie, and there'd been no question in her mind that she couldn't come close to duplicating the intricacy and small size of these high-tech items.

The procedure was going to be a snap, Curt knew, but he had to act like it was an experiment with unpredictable results. He didn't want to reveal to Taisha that what they were doing was a straightforward application of standard warbot technology.

"First," Curt said, "we'll just see if we've got it working. I volunteer, and I need a partner."

Edie Sampson held up her hand. "Yo, Captain!" She was an experienced warbot brainy, and she knew this was no experiment. If it had been, her commander wouldn't have let anyone else become a subject until he'd tried the equipment first.

Curt had given everyone some sort of job to do, whether it was really necessary or not. "Pendleton, can you monitor the datastream okay?" Curt asked.

The gangly young man was furiously adjusting some of Taisha's equipment. "Yeah, yeah. I can't tell what's really going on, but I'll be able to find out if it's working or not."

"If it's not, and if we don't withdraw ourselves," Curt told him, "pull the plugs on our harnessess."

"Curt, that could be like getting killed in action!" Willa Lovell warned.

"Which is why I want you standing by," he told the doctor. "Did you find enough stuff in the medikit in the airodyne?"

"Barely. I'll make do, but I might not be able to save anyone who goes catatonic in rapid withdrawal if the harness plug is pulled."

"I won't go cato," Edie Sampson promised. "I been through a double-lobed Lebanese systolic stroke before. Don't like it, but I'll make it."

This was all new to Rhosha Taisha, and she was trying hard not to show it while attempting to learn as much as she could. Some of her distrust had disappeared. If these people were really putting themselves in danger, maybe they could be trusted after all.

"Okay, let me see if I can contact the AI computer," Curt said. "Pendleton, if it looks like I did it okay, let Sampson try. If that works, I want you and Lovell to plug in as well."

The possibility that something might go wrong with all four of them in linkage panicked Taisha, but she didn't show it. She'd try to do what she could to save them in that event. If she couldn't, she was totally prepared to let them die because she had her high-speed high-resolution recorders going. She'd be able to replay what had happened. In time she would understand it.

It was a soft linkage. Curt deliberately didn't let himself lose total contact with his real surroundings. He might have been flying the aerodyne, except he wasn't in the ship. He found himself thinking to Trajan.

What happened? Trajan asked. *I don't have my aerodyne around me now.*

Test and maintenance, Curt told the computer. *Are you reading me?*

Brightly. I've been on standby and working well. No problems except with the aerodyne itself. What's the purpose of this maintenance check?

Human-to-human discrete communication through

your circuitry, Curt explained. He then "felt" Edie Sampson's "presence" in the intelligence amplifier as she came on line. Since it was a soft linkage without deep probing and monitoring on Trajan's part, Curt could only sense Edie's direct thoughts to him and to Trajan.

It works, Captain. Edie's thought came through.

Technology triumphs again. I've still got actual visual on our surroundings, but I'm reading both Trajan and you.

Good enough for our first shot, Edie admitted. *But there wasn't anything to it, Captain. Just plugging stuff together. I'm not sure I know all of our capabilities at this point.*

Just so Taisha doesn't catch on. Let's see if we can get Willa in the loop with us.

Colonel Willa Lovell was suddenly there, but she was fuzzy and intermittent.

Willa, how long since you've experienced linkage? Curt asked her.

About a year. Shows, doesn't it? Going to take me some time to readjust, the colonel decided.

Where's Pendleton? Curt asked.

Monitoring, Willa pointed out.

Get him in here. I've got some things to tell everyone.

Let me back out a little bit and plug him in, Edie remarked.

When the young man's presence manifested itself in Trajan's AI computer, it was even more indistinct and fuzzy than Willa Lovell's. *Whole new system,* was the almost-garbled comment from him. *Got to get used to it.*

Pendleton, do you read me? Track me? Understand me? Curt wanted to know.

Yes. But keep it slow, please. Helped mentor this system a couple of years ago. Long time. Forgot how to think some of it.

Will do. Listen, everyone, I couldn't talk openly. Now I can. Taisha can't decipher this message channel, Curt began.

But she's monitoring it, Pendleton warned.

She knows it works, period. She can't tap it or bug it, even though she's recording it. It will take her days, maybe months, to work out the language, Curt assured the AI mentor.

Right. But I can add a few little tricks now that I'm in here. In the meantime, this is your show, Captain.

I want to let all three of you know that no matter what I may appear to be doing or what I might say to the Imam or Doctor Taisha, I'm running a super con job. Thus far, it's working. Curt was relieved about that.

I thought so, was Edie Sampson's comment.

Then what's behind your offer to help the Imam with robotics countermeasures? Colonel Willa Lovell was still having trouble believing Curt. *What's your plan?*

Colonel, you're a doctor and a scientist and a robotic expert, a fact I haven't revealed to the Imam or Taisha, Curt explained. *From your comments earlier, I'm sure you don't have a dishonest bone in your body.*

A medical doctor has to be honest, Captain.

I like to think so. But there's nothing in any rule, regulation, or code that keeps me from lying to the enemy . . . or from doing anything that might get us out of here with our hides intact, Curt went on. *We now know we can get into comm linkage when we need to. We'll run lots of so-called experiments. Trajan reports he can contact Georgie if Edie puts the right modules in place. So we'll do it. I want to find out when the rescue mission is coming.*

Are you sure we're going to be rescued, Captain? Pendleton's blurred thought came through.

Damned right! I'm trying to convince the Imam that it won't happen, but I know the Washington Greys. They'll come, but I don't know how or when. So I've got to play this whole thing in a very opportunistic manner, and you've got to go along with me. Curt paused before he went on thinking to his three troopers. *I've got to warn you about something the Imam has insisted you do. I've already done it, so it's nothing to worry about. In fact, you may get a laugh or two out of it.*

Taisha has developed an indoctrination program for Jehorkhim soldiers. It's the initial step in her overall plan to control human beings by computers in order to eliminate human error. Yeah, I know she's not only nuts but chasing rainbows; it's the human factor that wins wars, not machines. But this Jehorkhim indoctrination program is set up to project religious revelation into the minds of the Jehorkhims to make them fight like devils. You may find that the revelation has parallels in your own religious training. What you'll "see" and *"hear"* is Allah *"speaking"* out of a whirlwind. It's nothing to be frightened about.

"What's it like? Willa Lovell asked.

They were citizens of one of the most advanced cultures on Earth, one in which various forms of direct linkage were used to play games and, in some cases, for intense forms of entertainment. In places like Las Vegas and Singapore, a person didn't even have to hire a hooker anymore; the best ones had been recorded and the total sensory input was available through linkage which provided nearly total sensation—at a considerably lower price and with suitable royalties going to the original performer.

So Curt simply replied, *Like being in linkage for games or entertainment. In fact, treat it the same way you'd handle a Saturday morning kiddie-viddie show. After all, it's intended to impress and brainwash Baluchi nomads, which makes it seem damned stupid to us. At best, it's an amateur effort. Real crapola. All of us are subjected to far more powerful stuff in everyday advertising. But don't laugh at it. Regardless of what you think, say you believe it. It'll save your life. If you have religious qualms about lying, at least you'll live to make amends when you get home. I've gone through it, and it didn't hurt me at all. But I wanted to warn you about it beforehand. If anyone has any objections to undergoing this indoctrination, please grin and bear it. It can't hurt you.*

You're sure of that? Willa Lovell asked.

It won't bother anyone whose head is screwed on tight, Curt promised.

Well, Owen Pendleton's thought came through, *it's*

*probably an experience. Something I can tell my grand-
children about ...*

And you will, sir, Curt promised him.

*Especially when Operation Cyclone gets to
you.*

Curt had the unmistakable feeling that Master
Sergeant Henry Kester had transmitted this thought to
him.

CHAPTER TWENTY-THREE

Henry, is that you? Curt silently asked through the robot linkage channel.

There was no question that it was Master Sergeant Henry Kester. Curt could recognize him just from the way the old soldier phrased his thoughts. *Yeah, Captain, it's me. Georgie was monitoring the linkage environment of the Zahedan area, and we've been monitoring Georgie. Happens to be my watch. Georgie notified me when he picked up the signal from Trajan.*

We're not in Trajan. We pulled his linkage modules and set up in the basement of the building where the hostages were being held.

They got you in the dungeon?

No. We've conned the Imam into thinking we're renegades who've joined his cause. So we're as free as possible under the circumstances, Curt explained. *Four of us in linkage here—myself, Edie Sampson, Colonel Willa Lovell, and one of the hostages who's now Lieutenant Owen Pendleton, an AI mentor.*

Captain, can you give me a report in accelerated linkage time? Kester wanted to know if Curt could speed up his thinking process as warbot brainies were taught to do. This would quickly dump a lot of information through the channel for recording at Henry's end.

Not under the circumstance. Where are you? When will you be here?

Can't tell you anything. Someone might be snooping. How long can you stay in linkage?

Not much longer. Taisha is watching us. This is supposed to be our first experiment to help her with machine control of human soldiers. Can't stay for more than another minute or so.

Okay, Captain, Georgie has you located. So we'll have to use one-way contact to you through the ratbots. You remember the ratbots we left in Zahedan, don't you?

Damned right. I was trying to figure out some way to use them.

We already have. When you see an active ratbot trying to give you instructions, that's me. My job on this mission.

Henry, are you okay? Did my shot wing you bad?

Nothing the medics couldn't fix. More about it later. Hang in there, Captain. We're coming to get you.

Suddenly Master Sergeant Henry Kester's "feel" was gone from the linkage.

Was that what I thought it was? Owen Pendleton wondered.

You bet. Contact with our robot infantry outfit, the Washington Greys, Sergeant Edie Sampson replied. Her relief was evident even through the relatively emotionless linkage channel.

Willa, did you catch it? Curt asked.

I did.

Okay, let's get out of linkage before Taisha gets suspicious. Remember, if any of us can get back into linkage at any time, Georgie will put us through to Hettrick or Kester. But the RI is coming back to get us, and that's the best news I've had all day. Curt was relieved, too. He knew that the RI wouldn't poor-boy the fracas this time. Standard doctrine: If at first you don't succeed, hammer 'em harder when you get a second pass.

But even Curt had no conception of how much force had been laid on in terms of people and bots, or of how quickly it had been done. Now there wasn't just one robot command post on Kuh-e-Taftan, several of them were hidden in the hills around Zahedan. One RCP couldn't handle all the people controlling the warbots involved in Operation Cyclone. Communications flashed quietly at the speed of light between RCPs as darkness drew its veil down over the barren hills around the isolated town.

Hettrick had moved so quickly that General Carlisle hadn't had time to get to the action site from Diamond Point, but he was there in linkage through Georgie. So Hettrick was in actual command of the main RCP on Kuh-e-Taftan because she'd been there and she was highly motivated. *Colonel Hettrick, did the Iranians put up any glitch-makers?* Carlisle wanted to know.

No, sir. We kept our part of the bargain. We've held dead-nuts to flight plan and stayed nonstealthed. So they haven't scrambled on us, but they've sure kept track of us. Likewise the Pakistanis and the Russkies. But we've given no one any heartburn over this. Hettrick's thought traveled half the world through computer-enhanced communications channels.

And we won't if they stand clear and let us get our people out. General Carlisle had arranged for reserve air and land forces to stand by on red alert in Oman, Bahrain, and Kuwait. He didn't want to use them unless absolutely necessary. Even the White House was antsy about this, especially with pressure from the news media which insisted on knowing every detail while playing watchdog on foreign policy. Carlisle had some highly restrictive rules of engagement laid on him. The biggest was a high-level confirmation of the ROE he'd originally put on Operation Squire: "This is a rescue mission; do not fire unless you are fired upon, then return fire for suppression purpose." Operation Cyclone was not to escalate into a major conflict with Iran. Although Hettrick was running the actual operation, it was Carlisle's primary job to monitor it and to make sure it didn't escalate. Hettrick wasn't to worry about the diplomatic details; she was the ROE.

The diplomatic maneuvering had taken a lot of intense work, but it was apparent that the discussions conducted with the Islamic Republic of Iran, through third parties, had been successful. Some concessions were made and some valuta were put up as guarantees against US violation of sovereign rights (which did occur and which were known to be planned), pieces of paper were exchanged between Swiss and Bahrain banking institutions, and certain fines and indemnities were "paid in advance"—although the records would never indicate this. It was all strictly legal, which is to say that the governments involved, who made, enforced, and interpreted their various laws, insured that everything which had been done was quite discreet, which

407

meant that the funds as well as the discussions couldn't possibly be traced. This might have disturbed some people who had to say in public that they believed mankind should follow certain moral codes, but these codes are often a bit hazy about who can do what to whom and for how much. And lawyers in any country find them adaptable.

As a result, the CIA reported through the DIA that the Iranian Air Defense Army of the Baluchistan and Kerman Military Districts had been ordered to stand down for a special inspection of critical aircraft power-plant components. It seemed that Teheran was concerned about some obscure engine component. These parts were ordered to be removed and inspected immediately before something could happen to the Gaspards and Super Rafaels which, although nearing the end of their useful lives, would be very expensive to replace.

The radar defense sites on the Gulf of Oman were alerted to the presence in the skies along the Pakistani border of a large number of unstealthed aircraft of a "friendly nature" that would be conducting a "humanitarian relief mission" from the Gulf to the Zahedan area and then returning within hours. Although this was a "peaceful mission," it was also quietly inferred that any military interference would be countered immediately by strong defensive retaliation.

The Pakistani government was quietly and diplomatically alerted about the humanitarian mission being conducted just inside the Iranian border to the west. As long as money changed hands, anything was possible in Islamabad, too. A small deposit was made to cover any possible damage or liability. The Pakistanis knew what was going on just as the Iranians did.

And on Kuh-e-Taftan and around Zehedan, the covert operation was proceeding as warbot brainies secretly moved into position and ensured their command and control channels.

Colonel Hettrick, Lieutenant Morgan of Carson's Companions here. Master Sergeant Kester has established contact with Captain Carson. Alexis' thought communication belied the excitement she felt. Curt was still alive! More than that, he was scheming to get out as well as funneling out intelligence data.

Please brief me, Lieutenant. I could run the tapes, but I haven't got time, the colonel told her. She was pleased about their current situation, but so much was now happening that she couldn't allow herself to become bogged down in details.

Colonel, anything Captain Carson manages to glue together on the spur of the moment is complicated. I'm not sure I can give you a "brief" report.

Lieutenant, you'll never make captain unless you can boil down a situation to its basic elements for a thirty-second command briefing.

Uh, yes, Colonel. He's saved Sergeant Sampson, Colonel Lovell, and one of the hostages named Owen Pendleton. He can get back into soft linkage through Trajan's modules. No details yet. And he'll have the four of them ready for pickup when we implement Operation Cyclone. Kester has reactivated one of the ratbots and can maintain one-way comm with the Captain.

The commander of the Washington Greys paused. That part of it was going better than anticipated. But she fired off the thought question, *Lieutenant, are you and Carson's Companions still willing to go in there on point in person?*

Yes, Colonel. With what has to be done, we just can't handle it by remote linkage. This one could be a real wild fur ball. We could easily lose situational awareness. I don't want to trust a command link under those circumstances. Not until McCarthy Proving Ground manages to run the system at a hotter speed so the data transfer rate is boosted and more multiprocs are ginning in parallel.

Colonel Belinda Hettrick reflected that she was not only getting too old to follow some of the new technological jargon, but she was also a bit long in the tooth for personal combat . . . and that's what the Army was going back to. But she was glad that kids such as Alexis Morgan and Jerry Allen were willing to go into it when they believed it to be absolutely necessary. The staff stooges were going to have their hands full with doctrinal changes after this Zahedan affair. There would be an agonizing reevaluation of the introduction of the personal combat warrior into warbot doctrine and tactics, a discussion of the conditions under which such a mix would be justified, and of the precise roles of combat warriors and warbots when fighting together. A whole new doctrine of joint operations would be needed.

Actually, she knew it had been needed for years. But military staffs and planners never made hasty changes until some incident or series of incidents forced the issue. The pendulum of combat verities had swung to its limit with the warbot generals in control. Now it would begin to swing back as the blood-and-guts personal combat generals began to regain some power.

If the Army had any smarts at all, Hettrick thought, they wouldn't let that pendulum swing all the way. Warbots were here to stay. And who was to say what the next big technical breakthrough would be? She felt certain that the Zahedan affair had jolted Dr. Armstrong and Colonel Lovell who, as unwilling participants, had been forced to see that the Army couldn't fight with warbots everywhere in the world under every potential combat situation.

But she didn't have time for much reflection. Operation Cyclone was big and could easily get out of control. Even with high-level AI keeping tabs on routine matters, people had to take a major role in running it.

Alexis Morgan knew it, too, and so did the rest of Carson's Companions. Of all the units participating, the Washington Greys had the greatest experience, and Carson's Companions had the most in the Regiment. Thus, the Companions were on point.

But Marty Kelly and his Killers had so squandered their equipment and technically disobeyed the rules of engagement during Operation Squire that both Hettrick and Carlisle had agreed they couldn't risk letting the Killers participate in Operation Cyclone. Hettrick had wanted to throw the book at Kelly; it was Carlisle who told her not to break the spirit of that company. There might be times when they would be useful, but this wasn't one of them. So Kelly's Killers were temporarily detatched to Maputo where some violent terrorist activities were going on.

But the Warriors and the Maruders were going to be

411

in the thick of it. Neither Edith Walker, Manny Garcia, or their officers and noncoms had liked the idea of pulling out of Zahedan and leaving RI people behind in spite of the general doctrine which they expressed as "Have no pride when it's time to get the hell out of Whiskey Creek!" Operation Cyclone gave them a chance to make their names shine again, to restore the honor and integrity of their outfits. Morale and unit pride were rated high in the Army, which is why the divisions and regiments had taken the names and traditions of the great regiments of the United States Army and why companies also had names, although they might be referred to by alpha-numeric designators in combat.

The strength of tradition was nowhere stronger than the empty organizational box in the Table of Organization at Fort Riley. It was labeled "D Troop, 7th Cavalry." For nearly two hundred years, that outfit was traditionally considered missing, not having reported back from the little Big Horn River. In fact, no cavalry regiment, armored or otherwise, had ever had a D Troop since.

Colonel Hettrick didn't want the same sort of tradition established for A Company, 3rd Robot Infantry Regiment, 17th Division (Robot Infantry), otherwise known as Carson's Companions.

But she fought off the urge to become a mother hen about it. She'd done her planning. Her staff done their work. Now she was counting on her oft-maligned "staff stooges" and "warbot weenies." She was depending on everyone being where they were supposed to be and behaving according to schedule and plan. Even with AI equipment and robotics, she couldn't follow every aspect of the large and complex operation.

As anticipated, Operation Cyclone wasn't running as well as had been expected. Hettrick would have been surprised and even a bit worried if it had been going too smoothly. She didn't panic, but knew that big operations never run smoothly; if they do, it probably means something's wrong.

The space-based portion was running late due to a combination of equipment malfunction on the launch pad and refusal of the Orient Space Traffic Control Center to grant clearance at the time requested. Orient Center was cooperating to the fullest extent it could by getting commercial traffic clear of the requested operational space in the upper atmosphere, but there were some flights that just couldn't be rerouted or rescheduled. Four unmanned ore carriers inbound from the asteroid belt couldn't be delayed and had to dip into the upper atmosphere for aerobraking at the precise time their precleared flight plans called for the maneuver; otherwise, four months' of deep space flight time and perhaps all four carriers would have been lost.

Thus, Operation Cyclone was running two hours behind schedule, and every additional delay might make the operation more difficult or might reveal the existence of Hettrick's forces to the Jehorkhims. The aerodynes were at their initial positions but were holding on the ground to conserve fuel. Plenty of time still existed to bring the operation off as closely as possible to the plan, but it would be far more effective if it were launched against Zahedan at night.

If Operation Cyclone were delayed until first light,

the powerful psychological elements would be compromised. And Colonel Hettrick was relying heavily on these.

She was also hoping that Carson wouldn't drop out of communication in Zahedan. If his location wasn't known when the strike began, the chances of recovering his group dropped dramatically and the chances of their being slaughtered rose.

She would have felt better, if she'd had constant two-way communication with Carson. One-way or simplex was better than nothing, but there was no way for Curt to "talk" to her except through linkage when he could manage it.

For Curt, that was enough. As long as he knew the ratbots were scurrying about on the edges of things, he also knew that the Washington Greys were aware of his location, and the pickup, when it occurred, would happen quickly and cleanly—*if* he could keep the other three with him or nearby.

Curt could estimate the possible time lines of Operation Cyclone, he was aware of the general disposition of Army forces in the Middle East, and he was familiar with the transportation capabilities of the military services. Operation Cyclone could occur as early as that night. If not, it would certainly occur within twenty-four to thirty-six hours. If the later time was chosen, he'd have to stall.

He told the three others in linkage, *Act like this wasn't a totally successful experiment. A little gold-bricking would help. Headaches, disorientation, confusion—that sort of thing. Edie, you and Owen might want to do some fiddling with the equipment. We've*

414

gotta stall for time. Okay, let's start getting back to the real world ...

Coming out of that soft linkage wasn't as difficult as returning from hard linkage in which soldiers had control of warbots. But things were a little confusing nonetheless. Curt's first act was to ask Edie Sampson, "You okay, Sergeant?"

She smiled wanly and winked so that Taisha couldn't see her do it. "Feel lousy, Captain. Something wrong with the phasing. I've gotta go back into the hardware and realign the timing and synchronization. Sound right to you, Lieutenant Pendleton?"

Owen Pendleton revealed a sense of humor for the first time. "Yeah. Something wrong. Fasarta is delinked in such a phase relationship that the thrimaline is being forced to bast. I can fix it. Couple hours, at least, if the equipment is available. Maybe a day otherwise."

Colonel Willa Lovell was shading her head and holding her temples between her palms. "Bad headache," she muttered.

Curt believed she was playing her role very well. "Need an analgesic from the medikit?"

"No. Don't want to shut down any capillary flow in the cortex. Let it run itself out. I'll be all right in an hour or so."

"It worked, didn't it?" Dr. Rhosha Taisha asked.

"The multiple linkage? Yes, but we've got some problems with it. As you can see," Curt told her.

"I do know something about this sort of thing," Taisha remarked, not totally believing Curt. "I would like to try it with you."

415

"Uh, Doctor, I take it you've had a lot of experience in robotic linkage?" Curt asked diplomatically.

"Only a few hours during elementary field lab experiments in graduate school. But I can do it. I was monitoring the datastream just now. It doesn't appear to be that much different from what I'm doing in my machine-man interface control work," she explained.

"Well, it is different, but in subtle ways," Curt told her earnestly. "I certainly can't keep you from trying it if you want, but the Army spends at least six months training warbot brainies before they even go into soft linkage with an AI. And that's using tested equipment. What we've got here is an experimental lash-up. I couldn't guarantee your safety, Doctor."

"Nonsense! I'm an experienced electroneural researcher!" Taisha insisted.

"Colonel, what do you think?" Curt turned to Willa Lovell.

Willa was doing an excellent job of goldbricking. She managed to look pale and shaking. "I'd say no way. Not until we get it adjusted better. Unless, Dr. Taisha, you are willing to risk triggering some deep-seated psychosis or, at worse, ending up catatonic. If that happens, I don't have the means here to treat you. You know how tricky and delicate it is to match a human nervous system to a computer; you've done it yourself, with another approach."

Dr. Rhosha Taisha wasn't convinced. "I think you're lying. The four of you think you know more about robotics than I do. You're wrong!"

Curt shrugged and spread his hands. "So? Probe me with your own equipment if you wish."

416

She shook her beautiful head with its black, shoulder-length hair. "You have a disciplined mind. You are familiar with linkage. I may not have the capability to break through your mental barriers."

Curt played a bluff. "As I told you, probe me."

"I may do that. But there's one way I can find out for sure, and that is by working at the level of basic beliefs using my Jehorkhim indoctrination technique of your sergeant, the woman robotic expert, and your new officer."

"But we have work to do," Curt objected.

Taisha hesitated for a moment, then added, "I do not trust you, Captain. I will begin now. And do not try to oppose me. I took the liberty of requesting a suitable guard. I asked the Imam for two specific Jehorkhims because I took a personal interest in their indoctrination. Harun! Jemal!"

The Jehorkhims Curt had seen thus far hadn't been large people. Few Baluchis stood as tall as he. But the two turbaned soldiers who stepped through the doorway were big and powerfully built. They didn't strike Curt as looking particularly intelligent, but they were brawny.

Taisha spoke to them in their language, then told Curt, "I have instructed them to stay with us constantly. If you make any sudden move toward them, they have orders to kill you instantly!"

There was a scurrying in the back of the room and Edie Sampson jumped up suddenly. Something had managed to come through the open laboratory door despite the Jehorkhim guards.

"What's the problem?" Curt asked, but thought he knew what it was.

"Place is not only full of bugs, it's infested with rats, Sampson said with mock distaste. She knew what she was seeing.

It was a ratbot that had been left in Zahedan by the recon mission.

One of the huge Jehorkhims unsheated his yataghan and moved toward the rear of the room, obviously intent on killing the rat. But Taisha stopped him. In English, she said, "If we stopped to kill all the vermin around here, I could never get any work done. It's just another harmless rat. Someday, I shall have a proper laboratory that I can keep clean."

To Curt the active ratbot meant that the Washington Greys had reestablished an RCP nearby, if not on Kuh-e-Taftan then on one of the other volcanic hills close enough to run this ratbot.

The cavalry was coming over the hill in the nick of time.

CHAPTER TWENTY-FOUR

Curt wasn't apprehensive as Dr. Rhosha Taisha began Sergeant Edwina Sampson's indoctrination. Sampson was experienced in linkage, and she was a disciplined soldier. But she was tired and stressed. She might lose her temper and become stubborn. She might even violently resist the Jehorkhim indoctrination.

But Sergeant Edwina Sampson came through it like a trooper. She even managed to act suitably dazed and amazed when she came out of it. "Wow!" she exclaimed with real excitement in her voice. "That was really something! Was that really what the Imam saw?"

It was Willa Lovell who came apart.

Whether or not this was due to poor linkage was a question Curt couldn't answer. As warbot brainies, both he and Sampson had their heads shaved for better contact with the linkage sensor pads. Willa Lovell didn't. She still sported a beautiful head of hair. Curt guessed that she'd started on the Orient Express flight coiffured in the latest fashion, but after a week in Zahedan, that was long gone. Save for a brief opportunity to wash up, she hadn't even been able to remain clean. Her long, unkempt locks could well have resulted in bad contact with Taisha's primitive, hand-made electrode pads during the indoctrination linkage.

Less than twenty seconds into the session, Willa started to twitch. Then she flailed her arms wildly and went into what appeared to be convulsions.

"She'll hurt herself! Help me!" Taisha snapped to Curt and Edie as the robotics expert screamed and thrashed about in the chair, the linkage harness still strapped to her. "Hold her down! She could rip that harness off!"

Dutifully, the Americans obeyed. They knew that severe psychological trauma might result from a sudden and violent disruption of Taisha's primitive system, and they didn't want Willa Lovell to turn into a vegetable. It was going to be difficult enough to get out of Zahedan with everyone mobile.

Resilient as Dr. Willa Lovell had been during the siege on the rooftop yesterday, she now seemed terribly vulnerable. Something about the Jehorkhim indoctrination apparently had pushed her over the edge. Perhaps some fearsome aspect of the hallucination had triggered a long-buried childhood nightmare or terror. Or one of the raw memories that most people manage to keep well under control.

It was also possible that Dr. Willa Lovell had a theoretical knowledge of robotics but little experience in remote linkage. Curt wondered if this was something totally new to her. He found that hard to believe, but he'd seen recruits come apart during their first linkage

420

experience. Many exhibited the same reactions as Willa Lovell.

Or was Willa Lovell a consummate actress really doing an outstanding job of faking these responses?

When Taisha stopped the indoctrination recording at its end, Willa slowly came out of the linkage and returned to the real world. Her eyes were glazed, her pupils dilated, her complexion flushed. She was breathing in short gasps, and Curt could feel her pulse racing. There was a terrorized look on her face, and when she recognized where she was, she buried her face in her hands and sobbed, "My God! Oh, my God!"

Dr. Taisha was standing before her; syringe and needle in hand.

Curt shook his head. "No, Dr. Taisha! I'll handle this!"

"Stand aside, Captain! I'm the one who's in charge here. This will tranquilize her."

"And drive her unleashed mental terror back down inside so it may pop back up again at any time in a flashback," Curt told her. "She's got to cope with it herself. I've handled recruits with the same syndrome."

"Stand aside," Dr. Taisha repeated. "That's an order!" She glanced up to where the two Jehorkhim guards were standing passively at the side of the room.

"Colonel Lovell is one of my officers. I'm experienced with this sort of thing. I've brought people out of it before. Let me try," Curt replied firmly. Then he offered, "If I can't snap her out of this, you can use drugs."

Without waiting for a reply from Taisha, Curt grabbed Willa Lovell by her shoulders, pulled her to her feet, and shook her like a bitch shakes an unruly puppy. "Willa! Willa! Listen to me! Hear me! No one is hurting you! Nothing is going to hurt you! You are in control of yourself! Face it! Beat it down! Conquer it! You can! You must!"

The physical ruffling that Curt gave Willa Lovell was something new to her. Except for her recent experience as a hostage in Zahedan, which had caused a deeper personal trauma than most people would have guessed, she'd lived in a world where people didn't touch one another except in personal and intimate ways, and certainly not harshly. The shock effect of his action was what Curt was counting on.

"It . . . it was awful! It was terrifying! I'm so frightened!" Lovell mumbled in a little girl's voice. Then she wept on Curt's shoulder.

"But it's all inside you, Willa," Curt told her. At that instant, he knew the child in Willa Lovell had slipped out as a result of the indoctrination. She was very vulnerable. "It's you frightening yourself! Who are you?"

She suddenly looked up at him. "Huh?"

"Who are you?" He was using his command voice.

"Uh . . . Why, I'm Colonel Willa Lovell, United States Army."

Bingo! He'd gotten through. "And where are you?"

"What?"

"Where are you?"

"I . . . Zahedan."

"And what are you doing here?"

422

"I'm being held prisoner in the dungeons . . . No! No, I remember now! I know! I let you take command even though I outrank you because you're pretending we're joining the Jehorkhims so the Imam won't kill us when the rescue mission arrives."

In her totally confused state of mind, Colonel Willa Lovell had let the cat out of the bag. There was no more time for guile. No time for a con job. No time for explanations. They must act.

Taisha suddenly moved, the syringe full of tranquilizer aimed at Curt.

But Edie Sampson was faster. And she was bigger and physically tougher than the beautiful but small Eurasian bioscientist. She caught Taisha's wrist with a hard chop. The syringe smashed to the floor, shattering into uncounted pieces, its mind-numbing liquid splattering in all directions.

Edie was an expert in hand-to-hand combat, and she wasn't afraid to use her know-how. In a single motion, she spun Taisha around, clamped one arm around her throat, and twisted the doctor's other arm up behind her back, the wrist sharply bent. Now Edie didn't have to exert much force on Taisha to create exquisite pain, and Taisha was unable to move without increasing her discomfort.

Thus held, Taisha was between the four of them and the two Jehorkhim guards.

The Jehorkhim guards drew their scimitars but, to the surprise of the warbot brainies, just stood there. They were big and powerful, but they weren't able to think very fast. They appeared to be frozen in indecision.

423

Edie clamped down on Taisha's throat as she bent her arm farther up behind her back. Taisha screamed, but the sound came out as a choking gurgle.

"Stop screaming!" Edie snapped in her meanest sergeant's voice. "I'm going to release your throat just enough for you to tell them to drop those swords! *Now!* Or I'll just keep right on squeezin' and bendin' until we see what breaks first!"

Taisha croaked an order in Baluchi, and two scimitars clattered to the floor.

"Now their yataghans," Edie added.

On Taisha's order, two short sabers also hit the floor.

Curt already had one of the scimitars in hand, and he kicked the two yataghans back toward Willa. "Pick them up, Willa! Taisha, tell the guards to turn around and face the wall!"

One of the huge Jehorkhims moved toward Curt, counting on the fact that they were in close quarters, a scimitar is a slashing weapon.

Curt wasn't trained to use a scimitar, so he wasn't saddled with the concept that it was only for slashing. He used it as a thrusting weapon, and that worked. Much to the surprise of the Jehorkhim, the blade, driven in under his rib cage, punctured his diaphragm, and tore into his heart. It made a nasty wound and it couldn't be withdrawn.

Curt let go of the hilt and scimitar, and a dead man fell to the floor.

He was immediately hit by the other Jehorkhim whose sheer bulk took him down. The guard got his hands around Curt's throat and began to squeeze and twist at the same time. This was the quickest way to choke a man, at the same time tearing the esophagus and trachea, and thereby causing permanent damage that would kill.

Curt tried to drive his fist up into the man's solar plexus, but there wasn't room enough to move his arm so he could gain enough momentum. The Jehorkhim's hands were tearing at his throat, and his lungs were aching for air.

Suddenly the huge, heavy form atop Curt jerked spasmically, and, without warning, the death grip on Curt's throat relaxed. The Jehorkhim then went limp. Curt found himself underneath a hundred kilograms of sweaty, smelly dead meat.

Colonel Willa Lovell was driving one of the yataghans again and again into the dead Jehorkhim's back.

"Stop it, Willa! He's dead!" Curt told her between gasps of lifesaving breath.

Only when she heard Curt's voice did the Colonel seem to realize what she'd done. Her jaw muscles twitched. "I did it! I did it! I've wanted to do that to one of them for days," she declared as she stood holding the bloody yataghan with both hands.

Curt rolled out from underneath the corpse. "Looks like you'll have the chance to do more of that if you want. We've got to fight our way out of here and hold them off until the rescue mission arrives." He stood up and took the short yataghan from her. He placed it in Edie Sampson's hand—the one she had pressed tightly against Taisha's throat. Edie closed her fingers around the weapon, but didn't take her attention from the doctor. Curt then retrieved the other scimitar and yata-

425

ghan. He handed the shorter blade to Willa with the remark, "Thanks for quick thinking."

"We're even now." Willa remarked. She had regained her composure.

"Who's keeping score? Nothing's even until we're safely out of Zahedan," Curt reminded her. "Are you all right now?"

Willa shook her head. "No. I'm frightened, scared."

"We all are. But do you know who you are and where you are and what we have to do now?"

She nodded, her breath coming in short and wavering gasps. "Yes. I killed one of them. That helped . . . At least, I think I killed him. Did I really kill that man?" She acted as though she couldn't believe what she'd done. Throughout her career, she had worked saving lives; now, she'd just taken one.

"Yes, you did."

"I shot people on the roof; that was different. This time, I killed a man with a knife. I've never done that before."

"Neither had I before I got to Zahedan," Curt admitted. It might have seemed a strange remark, coming from a combat soldier. "Edie, got things under control there?"

"You bet!" The sergeant had shifted her arm until the knife in her hand was against Taisha's throat. To her captive she said harshly, "One wrong move, one wrong word, sweetie, and *zzikk,* you breathe through a new hole for about ten seconds before you die."

"Owen! Lieutenant Pendleton! We're probably going to have to get the hell out of here, and damned fast. Can we get into linkage harnesses and take the electronic linkage gear along with us when we leave? Can we maintain contact with Georgie?''

Pendleton shook his head negatively. ''A lash-up. A kluge. Might work except for power. Energy cells were dead when we pulled the gear. Haven't had time to recharge them. Even if we put one person into harness for comm purposes, we haven't got enough power to run the hardware. Unless we're going where there's a convenient household outlet. I don't think any Baluchi household has . . .''

Curt looked around the room. ''Where's that ratbot? Is there a ratbot in here?''

A rustling sound came from a far corner of the laboratory, and a ratbot scrabbled out into the light.

''Okay, we fall back on Plan B. I'm going to pick up this ratbot and carry it. It's our one-way comm system and locator,'' Curt explained, as much for Willa and Edie as for Henry Kester who was operating the ratbot from some unknown location nearby. He scooped the small bot off the floor and was surprised at how heavy it was.

''Henry,'' he told the ratbot, ''you've seen what happened. We've got to get out of here. I'm counting on you for directions. Move the rabot's head for standard yes-no answers. Wiggle its front paws to indicate left-right directions.''

The ratbot's head slowly moved up and down.

Curt held the bot out to Willa. ''Here, you carry it.'' It would give her something to do, he figured.

She recoiled momentarily for the bot appeared to be a big gray rat.

427

Curt noticed and said, "Hey, Willa, it's a robot, and you're a robot expert."

"It looks so real."

"Yeah, your design people are pretty good, aren't they?" He handed the ratbot to her, then said, "Owen, help me bust up this equipment of ours so Taisha can't use it against us in the future."

Owen Pendleton looked aghast. "Bust it up? Destroy perfectly good equipment?"

Curt picked up a mobile linkage harness. "Yeah, I know, that's not what you're taught to do. But give me a hand with these linkage harnesses; they're the first critical items. Next we can bust some AI modules." Curt threw the mobil linkage harness onto the floor and began to grind the heel of his combat boot into the delicate electrode pads and wiring.

Owen Pendleton was reluctant to do the same.

"Treat it as a game," Curt told him.

In less than a minute, they'd stomped all four linkage harnesses and had started kicking the panels and modules that held the delicate, microminiaturized, artificial intelligence computers and amplifiers.

"You've gotten the critical stuff," Willa said. "Everything else is standard robotics technology that they can buy off the shelf."

"Okay." Curt faced the others. "Now we go out the door and up the street, slow march, behind me. Sheath your scimitars and yataghans, but keep them in plain view so it's obvious we're armed. Prisoners don't go about armed, so we should create enough indecision in the Jehorkhims to enable us to pull this off. Act like we know exactly what we're doing. If someone asks you a question, just shrug and point toward me, the glorious leader. Edie, follow me. Force Taisha to go ahead of you . . . and don't let go of her."

"I won't," Edie Sampson promised. "Do I get to kill her?"

"If she makes one sound, slit her throat." It saddened Curt to speak of killing such a beautiful woman, but the world was full of beautiful women and the Jehorkhims would sure as hell slaughter them if given the chance. "Willa, follow Edie and Taisha. Owen, bring up the rear and lock the door behind us if there's a lock on it. The longer it takes the Jehorkhims to realize what's going on, the better . . . and that lab is probably off limits to them when the door's closed."

"What's the plan, Captain?"

"Edie, it will be revealed in my final mission report."

"Yes, sir. I thought so. Standard procedure when things go to slime."

It was dark in the streets, and no one was around in the building. Curt realized that everyone was at late evening prayers except for the absolutely essential guards. Maybe the breaks were beginning to fall his way.

"Suppose we run into Jehorkhim troops?" Owen Pendleton asked as they walked along the street.

"We've got their Imam's girl friend," Curt pointed out. "If I run up against any Jehorkhims who speak English, I'll tell them we're moving to new quarters out by the aerodrome."

It was a bold, audacious, balls-out move. *L'audace! L'audace! Toujours l'audace!* was now Curt's motto as it had been Napoleon's and Patton's. Against Jehorkhim soldiers who'd been brought up with the fatalistic attitude that went along with submission to the will of Allah, such American rashness would be unsuspected, unanticipated, and hopefully unopposed. At least, Curt was counting on it working that way.

And it did. Henry Kester, who was in control of the ratbot carried by Willa, occasionally indicated a turn at an intersection of the narrow streets. Walking in the van, Curt was challenged once. He flipped a quick salute in the direction of the Jehorkhim sentry and replied authoritatively, "Captain Carson and contingent, moving to our newly assigned quarters at the aerodrome as ordered by the Imam! Is this the right direction?"

The sentry didn't understand a word, but he recognized the tone of authority in Curt's voice. He flashed a quick, nervous smile, saluted, and waved them down the street.

Dr. Rhosha Taisha said nothing. Sergeant Sampson had released her hold on Taisha's neck and the hammerlock on the bioscientist's arm, but she walked so closely beside Taisha that it was impossible to see the yataghan. Taisha knew it was there; however; it pricked her side beneath her ribs as a constant reminder that Edie would not hesitate to plunge it upward into her heart.

Dr. Rhosha Taisha wasn't a fanatic; she knew if she called out, she'd be killed instantly by a quick thrust of that yataghan. She wasn't interested in giving her life for Allah; she was interested in surviving to carry on

430

her research ... so she waited for an opportunity to make a break for freedom.

It didn't take long to get to the outskirts of Zahedan. Even in the moonlight, enhanced occasionally by a single electric light bulb on a building or by lamps and lanterns that threw wan beams through windows, Curt could see that they were approaching open country near the aerodrome, which was dark save for a few lights on hangars and building.

As the five people moved down a footpath toward the aerodrome—it couldn't really be called a road—shouts came to them from Zahedan.

"The Imam just found out," Curt announced. The ratbot in Willa's arms indicated a left turn into a date grove with widely spaced palms. "Okay, troops, let's gather 'round here and sit down. Edie, get a close grip on the doctor, please. She may be our bargaining chip until the cavalry gets here."

It was easy to see the mass of white-turbaned Jehorkhims running toward them from Zahedan.

Curt waited. There wasn't much else he could do. When the closest Jehorkhims spotted them and began to run toward them, Curt stood up, waved the scimitar in the air, and called out, "Halt! Who goes there?"

Chatter in Baluchi was the response. The Jehorkhims, prepared to give gleeful chase, apparently did not suspect that Curt and his group would stand their ground. Such behavior puzzled them. Amid shouted orders, the group of about fifty Jehorkhims slowly surrounded Curt and his contingent, keeping a respectful distance of about twenty meters and remaining partly hidden by the undergrowth around the circle of palm trees.

"Keep a cool stool, folks," Curt advised. "They're confused. They don't know what to do. Don't break and run."

It wasn't ten minutes before the Imam himself showed up. When the Jehorkhim leader stepped through the surrounding ring of troops, he called out, "Captain Carson! I don't believe I gave you orders to go to the aerodrome."

"You didn't," Curt replied.

"Then take your unit back into Zahedan at once!" the Imam ordered. "Dr. Taisha hasn't completed her indoctrination of your people."

"Yes, she has!"

"I won't converse with you any longer. Back to Zahedan! Or you'll all be killed right here."

Curt played his trump card. "Not while we hold Dr. Taisha! Sergeant, stand up with the doctor, please. Let them see you in the moonlight."

"Rhosha!" the Imam called when he saw her.

"I am here, Abdul," Taisha replied coolly and calmly. "I'm glad you've come. Now I can leave these renegades who threatened me!"

Without showing the slightest fear, Dr. Rhosha Taisha turned to Edie and said in her icy and logical manner, "Put away the yataghan. If you kill me, you'll all die anyway. So why have my blood on your hands?"

Curt had to admit, she was one cool customer. God, what a fantastic warbot brainy she'd make if her mind weren't twisted by a lust for absolute power. And she'd

432

play her cards just right. If he carried out his threat to kill her, the Iman's men would immediately attack.

"Captain?" It was Edie Sampson. She didn't know what to do, but she wasn't going to let Dr. Rhosha Taisha go unless ordered to do.

But Curt didn't have time to respond to his gutsy platoon sergeant.

The sky over Zahedan suddenly lit up.

Thousands upon thousands of shooting stars sparkled and sprayed and glittered above, their brightness overcoming the light of ordinary stars. They seemed to come from everywhere, brightly spraying sparks and trailing long tails of brilliant colors behind them, ejecting pieces that flamed and then faded.

These were celestial fireworks of the greatest magnitude.

In the light from individual sparkling streaks the date palms cast shadows, as did the men ringed around them. Curt could even see the hulking black form of the hypersonic transport sitting on the aerodome not half a kilometer away.

Strange sounds accompanied the light show. Like distant thunder, the low rumbles in the subsonic scare frequencies reached into the body and vibrated vital organs, creating uneasiness and panic.

Those on the ground suddenly felt prickling sensations. The hair on their heads and bodies stood up. Sparkling, scintillating electrical discharges emanated from every object—from the leaves of the date palms, the tips of the Jehorkhims' scimitars and bows, the tips of fingers, and from individual body hairs.

Hot Sierra! Curt thought. He didn't dare call out

433

aloud. He knew what was going on: a military celestial fireworks show with thousands of pyrotechnic and pyrophoric dummy entry bodies plunging from space into the Earth's atmosphere over Zahedan, their pyro charges burning and popping while their surfaces ablated and sluffed off. The sounds were coming from the hypersonic shock waves caused when bodies slammed into the atmosphere, and were attentuated by a hundred kilometers of air.

Added to this was the electrostatic effect created by low-level passes of specially equipped spaceplanes using Tesla Effect. By tapping the earth-space current flow, they concentrated a very strong charge over Zahedan, effectively electrifying the very dry desert air.

Curt knew what was coming next, and he wasn't disappointed.

More rolling thunder came from the cloudless sky. But this was louder, sharper, more local. Source: Hypersonic vehicles passing over at thirty kilometers, their rapid cleavage of the thin air creating massive pressure waves.

The rumble was suddenly punctuated by a sharp double clap of thunder, two quick explosions—followed by more. And more. And more. Source: Supersonic aircraft at Mach-2 and ten kilometers altitude.

At the same time, bolts of lighting cracked down out of the clear night sky all around Zahedan, hitting the volcanic cones and striking date palms. Source: More Tesla Effect equipment, probably mounted in aerodynes this time and getting power from microwave energy beamed from solar-powered satellites in orbit above them.

The *coup de grace* however, and something that caught Curt by surprise, was a shaft of bright, intense, coruscating red light that streamed down from the heavens, brighter than the midday sun, and lit the grove of date palms. The stream of light began to waver and flicker like flames, and things seemed to take on a shimmering glitter in its brilliance.

Curt really felt good about that little touch. The crimson light had to be coming from an orbiting laser of moderate power, defocused to throw a one-hundred-meter diameter circle of light on the Earth's surface at the date palm grove.

The RI was *really* going all out on this one!

And this time they'd called in some expertise on psychological warfare.

And it was working. The Jehorkhim soldiers panicked. Some dropped their sparking weapons and merely stared at the sky. Others were temporarily blinded by the sudden laser light. And many prostrated themselves in prayer.

The Imam Abdul Madjid Rahman stood in the brilliant crimson light, mouth agape. He was having trouble believing what he was seeing. He knew the power of modern technology, but he'd never suspected it could be applied in this manner, although he had made a compact with Dr. Rhosha Taisha to use technology for psychological effect. He suddenly knew that unless he acted fast, his power as Imam of the Jehorkhims would vanish before this overwhelming display of power that was, to his followers, completely supernatural.

But he didn't know what caused these magical effects. He was almost as ignorant of modern technology

435

as his followers, in spite of the fact the he'd lived and studied in England. The Imam hadn't been interested in power over the universe, which this technology exemplified; he'd been interested only in power over people's minds. Now he saw that those with power over nature could exercise power over minds which viewed technological feats as magic or gifts from Allah.

Freed of Sergeant Edie Sampson's strong grip when the fireworks started, Dr. Rhosha Taisha stumbled over to the Imam. She did, indeed, understand something of what was happening. She knew it was harmless, a show, a display of power. "Abdul!" she screamed at him over the yells and shouts of his men who were about to go amuck. "Abdul! Rally your men! This is just a show! These things you see are harmless!"

When the Imam stood woodenly, himself awed, she began beating on the men around him and kicking those who were folded in prostrate prayer. "It's not *jinn* doing these things, you ignorant savages! It's other people! These are tricks of modern magic! Up! Kill these infidels now and it will stop!"

A new sound rent the air: the roar and howl of wind. It came from everywhere. Wind was nothing new to those who lived in Zahedan, where the north wind blows constantly most of the year. But this wind didn't blow; there was only the sound of it.

In contrast to the brilliant crimson of the laser beam illuminating the date-palm grove, columns of brilliant green light sprang into being all around them. Each beam lit a boiling cloud of dust and sand about a kilometer away. The neighborhood of the aerodrome was surrounded by these boiling whirlwinds.

436

Only aerodynes hovering less than ten meters above the ground could make such roiling clouds of dust and sand. The blanket of air blown rapidly over an aerodyne's upper surface was bent downward. This enormous downwash—a disadvantage that aerodyne users had to live with under normal operating conditions, and one that had caused trouble during the inbound flight of the Operation Squire—howled like a hurricane when it impacted the ground all around the 'dyne.

There were dozens of aerodynes out there. The RI must have pulled every 'dyne available into the region.

Several aerodynes, hidden in their clouds of dust, were heading toward the aerodrome and the hypersonic transport. As Curt watched, two of them hovered over the black hulk, long tubes extended from their bellies like insect probes. As they refueled the transport, they looked like giant insects mating.

Then the Jehorkhim opposition began. The aerodrome guards, seeing what was happening, began to open fire. They were armed with old Soviet rifles.

But the response was quick. Other 'dynes moved i' Their rotary machine cannon, firing with the particular ripping, tearing sound of high-rate weaponry, spit out streams of tracers in a deadly fireworks display.

The Imam saw it, and he suddenly tried to rally his men. But before he could get a word out, the columns of boiling sand and dust, illumined by green laser light, started moving toward the Jehorkhims.

The green whirlwinds suddenly began to speak.

The words were in Baluchi, but Curt thought he recognized the youthful voice of Hassan!

He couldn't understand what was being said, but he

caught the words *jinn, si'lat, 'ifrit,* and *manaya.* He'd read *The Thousand and One Nights* and he remembered that these words had to do with angels and devils. These spirits weren't supposed to exist according to the true Islamic religion, but they were a part of the Mideastern folk legends, and had been incorporated into the religion of Mohammed by the local people.

Irregardless, the voice, coming out of dozens of whirlwinds, cut right to the heart of the Jehorkhim conditioning so carefully programmed by Dr. Rhosha Taisha's mind-bending equipment. The Jehorkhims who didn't panic and run lay prostrate and quaking.

Seven large aerodynes bathed in green light moved to the edge of the circle of red light illuminating the palm grove. There, they settled to the ground in a howling maelstrom of sand and dust. Ramps plopped down and assault warbots poured down them, weapons ready.

Through the settling dust, Curt saw something else coming down the ramps behind the warbots from four of the 'dynes: Carson's Companions—Alexis Morgan, Jerry Allen, Henry Kester, and Nick Gerard, all clad in body armor, all armed with personal weapons, and all ready to complete the rescue.

A few of the Jehorkhims prostrated on the ground looked up, saw what was really happening, and started to react. They raised scimitars and charged. They fired Soviet AKMs. The rules of engagement for Operation Cyclone were quite clear; the warbots shot them without hesitation.

"Curt! Edie!" Alexis Morgan's voice cut through the whine of turbines and the roar of idling aerodynes.

Curt moved. "All of you!" he yelled to the other three. "Let's move!"

When Alexis saw him, she rushed over. "Captain! Second in command reporting. The Company command is yours, sir!"

He clapped her on the shoulder and wished that he could be even more demonstrative, but this wasn't the time or the place. "I'm in no condition to resume command, Lieutenant! Keep it for now! Let's get the hell out of Whiskey Creek!"

"Where's the Imam? And that woman scientist?" Alexis asked, looking around the grove.

Neither the Imam Abdul Madjid Rahman nor Dr. Rhosha Taisha were anywhere to be seen. Together, they must have faded into the night during the aerodyne landings.

"Gone," Curt observed.

"We were supposed to bring them with us if we could."

"Why?"

"Iranian government requested it."

"They'll have to do their own pick up. Looks like we missed."

"Not really," Lieutenant Jerry Allen muttered. "We said we'd try. We didn't promise anything. Let 'em round up their own troublemakers."

"Attention, all personnel!" Colonel Belinda Hettrick's voice came through the loudspeaker systems on the aerodynes and warbots. "About to spool-up and roll! We've got a schedule to meet and a plan to follow! Shag your buns aboard!"

439

"Or don't you really want to get out of here, Captain?" Alexis asked unnecessarily.

"You twisted my arm!" Curt replied, and he sprinted up the ramp of Alexis' aerodyne.

CHAPTER TWENTY-FIVE

Diamond Point was "home" for the Washington Greys of the 17th "Iron Fist" Division (RI). Insofar as Captain Curt Carson was concerned, it was an infinitely better place to be than Zahedan. But he didn't really look forward with great joy to his return

The reason was simple: Staff stooges and intelligence officers would keep him very busy in debriefing and analysis sessions.

He felt he'd been kept busy enough in the past week. And he was tired.

One of these days, he told himself, he'd take some accumulated leave and sleep . . . and sleep . . . and sleep. But he'd probably have to wait until he got to Fiddler's Green because Heaven was once defined as the place where a soldier finally has time to do all the things he never had time to do before.

No soldier ever gets enough sleep or rest except in peacetime, and in a world that had never stopped fighting, peace was an elusive state of affairs. During one of those hurry-up-and-wait delays, Curt had calculated that of five-thousand four-hundred and eighty-six years of recorded history, only two-hundred seventy-two had seen no war.

Thus, he had determined that it was the lot of a combat soldier, especially an officer, to be always hovering on the ragged edge of exhaustion.

The ghosts of long-dead generations of warriors must have laughed as they agreed with him—the Greek hoplites, the Roman hastati, the Byzantine cataphracts, the French poilus, the British tommies, and the American doughboys, GIs, and grunts.

The warbot brainy was no different, even though the warbot was actually exposed to the hazards of war, not the human being. That had been hailed as one of the greatest breakthroughs in military technology since the invention of gunpowder. But robot warfare didn't always work out that way, as the Army had found out at Zahedan.

The problem that most warbot brainies faced coming off a big mission was letdown followed by interminable debriefings and critiques. These had to be done as soon after the operation as possible before memories faded and ideas germinated in the heat of action disappeared from the elusive circuits of human brain. As a result, these debriefings and critiques were always attended by exhausted, and hurting people. Mostly they were just plain fatigued because combat, no matter how it's conducted, is probably the most intensive human activity.

True, Curt had gotten some badly needed rest and some medical treatment for his bruised arm after the flight out of Zahedan. Biotech Sergeant Helen Devlin had practiced her usual skillful therapy, and Colonel Willa Lovell had insisted on supervising, which had made Helen a bit testy because Curt was *her* Captain and she was responsible for taking care of him. The four evacuated from Zahedan had been landed on the hospital surface ship CHS *Pierce* on which they'd gotten an immediate medical checkup, a hot meal, a hot shower, and a good sleep while heading for Karachi at 90 knots.

Curt noticed during the voyage to Karachi that everyone was already treating the Zahedan experience like a bad dream which should be forgotten as quickly as possible.

Except Brevet Second Lieutenant Owen W. Pendleton. He'd undergone an amazing change. Although he still stammered and sometimes hesitated over his words, he seemed far more outgoing now. During a quiet period while they were both sunning on deck, Pendleton asked Curt, "How long does a temporary commission last?"

Curt looked at him, and replied with another question, "How long do you want it to last?"

"Long enough to sign Form DA 71 on the dotted line. Missed the chance to get a reserve commission through ROTC."

"Sure you want to jump into this way of life?"

"It's not bad."

"Maybe. Maybe not. But why? You've already got it made on the outside as an independent consultant."

"Solving stupid problems somebody else created. Fun for a while. Now I've got some ideas that Dr. Armstrong and Colonel Lovell might find useful. We'll meet Doctor Rhosha Taisha again, and I'll be ready for her."

"How about the Imam and his Jehorkhims?"

443

"They had nothing to do with robotics. The Imam was trying to wage psychological warfare, and was beaten by it." Owen Pendleton pointed out.

"Well, Owen," Curt told him, "you're a scientist who fights as well as he thinks. I'll recommend you for a permanent commission if that's what you want."

"That's what I want," Pendleton said with finality; then he added, "And I'm not a scientist. I'm an AI mentor."

Colonel Willa Lovell spent a lot of time with the Companions during the trip, and seemed a bit miffed that she wasn't treated as one of them. Curt was much too exhausted to attempt to figure out her intent. Later, it occurred to him that Willa had made no friends among the hostages, and had attached herself mostly to him during the operation in Zahedan. This bothered him. She was older than he—far more educated, intelligent, and powerful. He hadn't totally figured her out in Zahedan, and her actions had been even more enigmatic afterward. She moved in a different world: Dr. Robert Armstrong and Major General Bernard J. Irwin, head of the Medical Service Corps, were waiting for her at Karachi to whisk her back, on the general's personal aircraft, to her familiar world of Army high-brass.

The battle-weary men and women of the Washington Greys were returned to Diamond Point for debriefing in a civilian contract airlift aerodyne. The trip took eighteen hours.

Curt got some sleep on the ship and during the flight home. But he was still fagged out and somewhat impatient at the thought of days of debriefing sessions at Division Headquarters. He knew the sessions would be

444

long ones. No RI soldier had been in physical combat for a very long time, and his information was essential to the staff stooges and medics.

He really wanted to head for the Caribbean where it was warm, wet, green, and restful, a place totally different from Zahedan. He needed to get into a friendly culture dedicated to fulfilling his every wish and desire . . . which mostly involved rest, lying in the sun, throwing away the clock, and not doing one damned thing according to schedule or plan.

He could sense the same cravings in Carson's Companions. Not all of them had been stranded in Zahedan. But those who'd gotten out had been anxious about those who'd had to stay. There was now a strange new bond between them. It was different from the relationships of warbot brainies. Any twentieth-century GI or grunt could have told them about the close relationships between people who've actually been shot at and lived through it. They last a lifetime.

But leave might be out of the question. There was the still-unresolved matter of the death of Mahmud. Would it be decided that Curt acted in the line of duty? The investigating officer hadn't reported yet. Curt could be looking forward only to a court-martial, although he believed he'd be found innocent.

Carson's Companions congregated at the Club for a little on-base R&R the night after their return. Colonel Belinda Hettrick showed up at their private alcove. She sensed that something was different. She was curious about it, but she felt it herself. "Let an old battleaxe join you?" she asked as she approached, a glass in one hand and a bottle in the other. Her casual reference to herself signaled that she wanted day-to-day military courtesy relaxed—considerably. "Especially if she brings a bottle of twelve-year-old Scotch?"

The Companions looked at Curt who simply replied, "Pull up a stump, Belinda."

"Especially when it's a bottle of good Scotch," Alexis Morgan added.

"Sure, Colonel," Edie Sampson said brightly. "Nobody here but us warbot brainies."

"I understand you took some fire when you evacked the command post on Kuh-e-Taftan when Operation Squire went to slime, Colonel," Jerry Allen observed.

"Right through a connecting cable," Hettrick said as she set the bottle down on the table. "Didn't count as being KIA, though. I was on backup in milliseconds when my AI caught the loss of signal and performed an autoswitch."

"Don't tell me it didn't shake you up," Master Sergeant Henry Kester observed. "And careful with that bottle. Don't bruise the stuff inside. Why don't you let me pour, m'am?"

"Don't spill it, Henry. KIA or not, yes, it did shake me up just a tad."

"Too bad it doesn't even rate a Purple Heart." Kester was easily familiar with the high brass, counting on his years of service and experience to leaven things. "Don't worry. If I spill a drop, you can have my stripes."

"I'm not worried. And not even General Carlisle could take your stripes, Henry—unless you defect to the Jehorkhims or something. Like Lovell though, Curt was doing, I understand. Curt, how did you figure out that whole caper?''

Curt shrugged and offered his glass to Kester to be filled. ''To quote an old field manual, 'A good field sojer if captured will continue to resist by all means available.' The only means I had at hand was to spoof the Imam. I figured he couldn't have been too smart because of some of the goddamned dumb things he did—like hijacking the Orient Express, torturing people on videotape, and even letting us know where he was. That might have worked a hundred or two hundred years ago, but not today.''

''He should have known we'd come in and curdle his buns,'' Alexis added.

''He expected it, but not the way we finally did it,'' Hettrick put in.

''No, there was something else involved,'' Henry Kester interrupted, pouring himself a bit of the Colonel's Scotch. ''People like the Imam and Taisha and even the Jehorkhims still think of us Americans as being overarmed giants afraid to use our clout. They remember Teheran and Beirut because they greased our skids there. But they forget Asmara and Tarakhan where we got 'em by the short hairs. They celebrate their victories and don't dwell on failures. On the other hand, what do we remember? Our defeats: Pearl Harbor, Bataan, Changjin Reservoir, Saigon ... places where people got the big medals for hanging tough in impossible situations.''

''Speaking of medals, Curt, you and Sergeant Sampson are in for the Distinguished Service Cross and the rest of the Companions have been cited for the Silver

Star." Hettrick raised the glass Kester had poured full of the brown, aromatic liquid. "Ladies and gentlemen, the Greys."

Around the table, eight glasses were raised amid the quiet murmur, "The Greys."

Curt turned and looked at her. She wasn't hard to look at tonight, but Curt initially dismissed his reaction as the result of combat and fatigue and being away from home base too long. He replied quietly, "If it's all the same, I'll take the Silver Star along with the rest. I don't deserve a DSC just because I was stupid enough to get left behind."

"Yeah, I'll go along with that. Stupidity shouldn't be confused with bravery," Sergeant Edwina Sampson put in.

Hettrick shrugged. She looked considerably less formidable in her off-duty attire, an attractive cocktail sheath. Unlike the Companions who were warbot brainies with shaved heads and proud of it, Belinda Hettrick was wearing a wig. "I figured you'd say that. So I didn't hear it. Besides, it's too late. Procedure has been initiated. And you know this outfit: once a procedure is set in motion, it takes an act of God to stop it. We need only the corroborative data from debrief."

"I was going to talk to you about that," Curt put in. "None of us look forward to a couple of days of intensive debrief. Can anything be done to expedite it, shorten the sessions, that sort of thing?"

"Nope. Especially not on this mission. It wasn't a typical one. We were in actual physical combat. Nobody in the Army for the last twenty-some years has done

what we did—or gone through what we went through."
Hettrick said flatly.

"Dammit, Belinda, we're wrung out!" Curt complained in an irritated tone.

"I confirm Curt's sit-rep," Alexis added. "This has been a week of hi-tense attention requiring a lot of situational awareness. I don't think any of us has had more than one good night's sleep since ... since ... Well, I don't remember when."

"Alexis," Hettrick remarked quietly, swirling her drink in the glass and savoring the aroma, "the Washington Greys held General Burgoyne at Saratoga until Gates could smash the center. We were the rear guard at Bladensburg. We hung on with Scott at Vera Cruz when the other troops decided to go home. We fought in the Wilderness under Grant. We were once on the line near the Saint-Mihiel salient in France for six months of trench warfare. We slogged our way up the Italian boot with Mark Clark's Fifteenth Army Group for a whole year after damned-near getting creamed at Anzio and Monte Cassino. We were the ones who took Sfax and held it for five months against General Mahdhi's desert legions. Pusan, Tet, Haleb, the list goes on. Those, young lady, were real honest-to-God high-tension situations that lasted for a long, long time. The whole Zahedan operation took about a week."

"Colonel ... Belinda," Master Sergeant Henry Kester put in quietly in his rough voice, "Zahedan was three operations heel-and-toe, and the only one you mentioned that involved warbots. The others were physically demanding ball busters for sure. But none of them was near as intense over a short period of time. Save

449

the pep talk for the recruits. Carson's Companions have had it."

Belinda Hettrick looked at Kester. Here was a man who knew. How could she argue, much less dress down, one of the few who'd made a successful transition from physical combat to warbot operations . . . and then back again? "Sorry, Henry. My apologies for mouthing off to an outfit that got a unit citation out of the Zahedan fracas."

"No kiddin'? Hero medals galore!" Nick Gerard remarked. "What color? Will it match the rest of the streamers on our standard?"

"Combination green and yellow ribbon this time. Green for the Muslim Jehorkhim opponents, yellow for the hostage retrieval. Nice touch, I thought," Hettrick explained.

"Who came up with that one?" Jerry Allen asked.

"The general."

"Doesn't sound like Knox," Curt said.

"Carlisle," his colonel told him.

"Oh."

"He's been around." Hettrick was quiet for a moment, then she suddenly said, "And, by the way, I know it's been orgasmic out there; I was on Kuh-e-Taftan for both Squire and Cyclone. I don't want to drag out the debrief, so I requested Carlisle to ask Armstrong and Lovell if they'd please use something brand new they've got in the way of debriefing technology. Would you like to try it?"

Curt replied noncommittally, "Depends on what kind of guinea pigs you want us to be. I've already been a guinea pig for one mad scientist this week."

"What have they come up with down at Fort Dreamland now, Colonel?" Nick Gerard asked.

"Direct memory dump in linkage prompted by Georgie."

"Is that the 'mind probe' rumor that's been flitting around since we got picked up in the date grove?" Edie Sampson asked.

"Yes. Georgie goes right in and makes you relive it."

There was silence around the table for a minute.

"Hell, no!" Edie Sampson muttered. "I don't want to relive one goddamned second of that frigging mission in that stinkin' hellhole."

Curt added, "Thanks for nothing, Belinda. I'd rather endure a couple of days of regular interrogation. In that I can lie a lot."

"Wait!" Belinda Hettrick said quickly. "I went through it today. It's fast. Direct memory dump in linkage does a lot of good things for you. Edie, although you'd just as soon not relive the Zahedan episode, the new linkage debrief provides a good outlet, like talking to the padre or a psychiatrist. Know what I mean?"

Platoon Sergeant Edie Sampson looked askance at the other woman. Hettrick outranked her and had been shot at, but Edie didn't fear her colonel. She respected her and would follow her orders, but in this social atmosphere she felt capable of letting down her hair—if her head hadn't been smooth shaven. "Once you talk about it, you feel better? That psychology crap? Bullshit."

Colonel Belinda Hettrick looked directly back at Edie.

451

"Believe me, it takes a lot of the rough edges off. Might help. Give it a try."

Sergeant Nick Gerard took a swig from his glass, thought about what he was going to say, then remarked, "I'm told it also does some other things. Tends to make a warbot brainy a bit horny."

"Well ..." Colonel Hettrick paused, then went on, "even warbot combat does that to brainies. Reliving physical combat under such realistically perceived conditions does tend to reinforce it. That's one of the little bugs they haven't worked out yet."

"Got news for you," Curt added. "We don't need reinforcing at the moment. If the Army still did such prudish and childish things as bed checks—which, thank God, it doesn't—I wouldn't make one tonight. Half the beds are going to be empty, and it's not my job to keep score."

"When Rule Ten isn't in effect, I don't give a damn who does what to who as long as they report for duty fit and ready when they're supposed to," Hettrick admitted bluntly.

"Well," Curt said with a sigh, "I'll try it. I can always duck into a cold shower afterward."

"It's probably more fun to nullify the side effects naturally," the regimental commanding officer said in a way that was neither coy nor blunt. "All I'm saying is: Try the new technique. It worked for me. And Mahmud would probably still be alive if we'd had it out there on the *McCain.*" She sipped at her Scotch and remarked to Curt, "By the way, meant to tell you, the Temporary Juridical Investigation Officer I assigned to the Mahmud death matter turned in her report today."

"Her report?" Curt stressed the first word. "Who was the TJIO?"

"Lieutenant Ellie Aarts of Manny's Marauders," Hettrick replied.

"Good officer," Henry Kester said.

"She reports it as an unintentional accident," the colonel explained, "which means that you're off the hook, Curt, subject to my endorsement of the report and review by Division staff."

"And?"

"I endorsed the lieutenant's finding based on Georgie's record of evidence. Carlisle will sign it off in a few days. It'll be forwarded to the JAG and never go in your file. Relax."

"I wish I could. I need some relaxation. So do we have Hassan to thank for that great celestial fireworks and thunder show?" Curt asked, although he thought he already knew the answer.

Hettrick nodded toward Alexis. "Thank your second in command. She pulled it out of Hassan."

"Hassan thought women inferior," Curt recalled. "How'd you do it, Alexis?"

"Used my feminine wiles." Alexis grinned self-consciously and tried to explain, "Actually, the kid just needed some mothering."

"Don't we all?" Curt asked, not expecting an answer. Alexis ignored his remark, although the look she shot in his direction answered his question. "Hassan gave Georgie a solid data base on the way the Baluchis think. With that, we knew how to effectively design and use psychological warfare tactics that, hopefully, wouldn't kill anyone."

453

"And the effectiveness was continually cross-checked with feedback data obtained by your Master Sergeant who reactivated and ran the ratbot." Hettrick went for an hors d'ouvre and then observed, "Incidentally, Curt, you were right. Hassan's smart. Damned smart. He's on his way to transition school in Tucson tonight, then on to Kemper when he can speak and read English . . . and has learned our customs."

"Orgasmic! That kid deserves a better life than searching for rocks in that godforsaken desert!" Curt observed.

"He'll have some problems at first," Jerry Allen opined. "He's different. The old cadets will haze his ass off. His plebe year will be rough."

"You sound like you speak from experience, Jerry," Hettrick observed.

"Some. Tell you all about it sometime . . . if you ever get me drunk enough."

"Henry, pour him another one. I want to hear it. By the way, while you're at it, pour me another before I dry up and get wrinkled like a prune." As the colonel held out her glass for Henry, she added offhandedly, "I gather you're in a hurry to get debriefed because you want to take some leave?"

"You read my mind."

The colonel shook her head. "Not a chance."

"What the hell, Belinda? I've got it coming. Why not?"

"Got other things in mind for you. How'd you all like a little TDY?"

"Temporary duty often has its drawbacks. Where? Doing what?"

454

"I've been ordered to pull Carson's Companions out of the line temporarily."

"Little recruiting tour?" Alexis wanted to know. "Heroes of the hour? Show us off to the world now that the general can't keep the news media off our backs any longer?"

"That, dear lady, was no easy job, believe me. General Carlisle knew better than to let the news hawks and harpies into Zahedan in the first place. He pulled a Grenada on them. But after Operation Squire, he put the best man on the job of spinning war stories to the press and keeping them happy. Turned out to be pretty good at newsmongering, too."

"Someone we know?" Curt asked.

"The hero of Tunis and Zahedan, General Victor Knox."

"Well, I'll be damned!" Curt breathed. "Finally found the right slot for him!"

"Wondered why he suddenly disappeared from view," Alexis muttered.

Edwina Sampson lifted her glass. "Here's to General Knox! Uh, Colonel, I hope someone changed his rated position code."

Colonel Hettrick said nothing, but her smile was reply enough.

"Well, where are you going to send us this time? Some place interesting, maybe . . . like Antarctica? Lunar Base? Deepest, darkest, dankest Africa?" Curt asked.

"How about the Staff College in Charlotte Amalie?"

"The Vee-Eye? Orgasmic!" Alexis chirped.

"Staff College?" Jerry Allen followed. "They going to turn us into staff stooges?"

"No. The Army wants to look into developing new doctrine. Carson's Companions have more experience than anyone at the moment," Hettrick explained.

"Well, there are worse places to be sent," Curt admitted, thinking that he was perhaps going to get his Caribbean R&R without cutting into his leave time. "But what's this doctrine stuff?"

Hettrick looked surprised. "Hell, Curt, you certainly ought to be able to figure that one out without me drawing a picture!"

"Sorry. Brain working at only fifty-percent power. Been a rough week."

"Personal combat is now seen as an important adjunct to warbot combat," the colonel remarked.

"Oh? Someone finally admitted that a warbot can't do everything that a human being can?" Master Sergeant Henry Kester remarked, reaching over to refill the colonel's glass yet again.

"About right. The availability of the warbot led to the doctrine of nonphysical combat—take the human being completely out of danger and let the warbot take it in the pan instead. Looking back, some staff stooges now see the doctrine didn't work real well in Tunis or La Paz. Adequate, but not outstanding. It took Zahedan to show them how dangerous it could be." Hettrick said sharply to Kester, "Henry! Take it easy! This stuff has more kick than a rogue bot!"

Kester just nodded and kept on pouring. "Lady, you brought it to the table. You told me to pour it. I figger if I keep it up, you'll eventually make the TDY permanent and even work out some way to cut yourself in on it."

"How'd you ever make sergeant in the first place?"

"By doing just what I was told, like I'm doing here."

"Good Soldier Schweik," Hettrick observed and went on. "The military mind works in strange ways. I don't need to tell you that. Even when there's plenty of fighting around to prove theories, staffers have a tendency to go off the deep end."

"Like the French belief in the overwhelming superiority of the attack. *Cran* or just plain guts was supposed to win the day, except it didn't work diddly against automatic firearms," Jerry Allen said.

"So that's the new doctrine? We're going back to crawling on our bellies in the mud?" Alexis asked.

Hettrick shook her head. "Not this decade. The doctrine people are looking for is a better mix between brainies and bots. Carson's Companions were selected as the outfit to work it out—on TDY with overseas pay, I might add."

"The carrot helps," Alexis remarked.

"Oh, plenty of those! Like step increases for everyone. And, Morgan, you might pick up some silver bars in the Exchange. Sorry, Allen, your brown bars stay that way until you get minimum time in grade, but you still get the step boost. Making you now would set a bad precedent."

Jerry Allen only smiled. "Well, that shouldn't bother anyone. Sure as hell wouldn't bother me. I've always set a bad precedent."

"Just watch for the next make sheet," Hettrick advised, knowing that the young officer would undoubtedly be on the next promotion list. "Same goes for Gerard and Sampson, by the way. As for you, Kester, you old banty rooster, nobody can figure out a way to put tassels on those chevrons and rockers." Henry Kester had turned down two field promotions and G-1 Personnel had quit counting how many times he'd backed away from a warrant. The man was where he wanted to be: the top of the heap, the highest ranking frog in the noncom puddle. And he'd told the brass that was the way he wanted it. Furthermore, he had the clout to make that stick.

Hettrick looked around the table. "I've got to get some food before this good Scotch goes too far. How about the rest of you. Eating ... or eaten?"

"Neither," Curt said. "Too damned tired."

"Well, then you need to chow down," the colonel remarked, and pushed the call button. "Meal's on me. I got a step increase, too."

A service robot showed up. After days of field rations and Baluchi food, Curt decided he could stand a high-energy meal after all. He ordered steak, barely dead. The other Companions also ordered high-energy food loaded with protein and carbohydrates. When the robot disappeared to retrieve their orders, Edie Sampson said, "That's one thing I didn't understand. How could those people in Zahedan, those Jehorkhims, do what they were trying to do on the miserable diet they had?"

"Oh, the food wasn't too bad, Edie," Curt told her.

"The hell it wasn't! Heavy on cereals. Some goat meat. And not much at that."

"It kept them alive. You probably didn't eat the

458

kumquat rinds. Did a world of good for me." Curt was kidding her, but she didn't get it.

"Not what I meant. Didn't give them much extra juice to fight with. How did they do it?"

"Religious fervor."

"No substitute for a full stomach."

"Oh? Well, you saw them fight, Edie."

"Yeah, but the Jehorkhims couldn't possibly have much staying power when the crunch got tight."

"Gee-two made that assessment, too," Hettrick put in. "For once in this operation, they're probably right. Fighting a modern war takes a lot of physical and mental energy, which you get through food."

"Sure as hell don't breathe it in," Gerard added. "Although that's just about what I'm going to do. Here come the feed bags."

As several service bots showed up with their dinners, Curt saw Hettrick hole the chit, and he was sure that she wasn't using her personal punch. RHIP, but Curt figured she was using one of the discretionary funds for postmission on-base R&R. He didn't argue. Captain's pay wasn't super, but it was competitive with that of nonmilitary bot supervisors. Still, a company commander doesn't turn down a free meal.

"While we're talking about this sort or thing, Curt, did the Jehorkhims seem a little slow to you? Maybe a little dense?" Hettrick wanted to know.

Curt nodded. "They weren't stupid, but we could sure think faster. I could never have gotten the group out of Zahedan otherwise."

"Oh, come on!" Jerry Allen interrupted, irritation in his voice. "They're just people like everyone else."

"Jerry, my boy . . . sir," Kester said flatly, "that's a bunch of bot flush. Sure, maybe people are just people. But when you've been around a little more, you'll find they're very different everywhere. Heard a lot of high-powered research types talk about heredity and environment, and I still don't know which makes the most difference. But some people don't get enough new blood, some don't get enough of the right things to eat, and some end up on the short end of both. How can a guy that eats nothing but fish heads and rice—less than a thousand calories a day—outfight, outthink, and outlast somebody that eats five times as much? Hey, eat up! You're on the top end of the bell curve."

"So are we rid of the Jehorkhims because they're too hungry to fight well?" Nick Gerard wanted to know.

Curt shook his head. "Hell, no! As the colonel said, sometimes religious fervor can overcome a lot of deficiencies. The Jehorkhims are still around. We're going to run into them again . . . and the Imam, too. He'll be a little more wily next time. Same goes for Dr. Rhosha Taisha. You know, that woman is so godawful beautiful she could get damned near anything she wanted from any man in the whole world if she only used what she already has plenty of."

"Yeah, but she's dangerous, Captain," Edie decided. "I can't figure her out. If I had her looks and her brains—"

"I can't either, Edie, and it bothers me. She's nuts. Crazy as a pet ferret. Beautiful but deadly. I'm worried about her," Curt admitted.

"Intelligence will be tracking her now," Hettrick promised.

"Don't bet on it, Belinda!"

As the evening wore on they became more relaxed. Curt needed that. They all did—a bit of ethanol flavored with various concoctions, good food and lots of it, soft music, some dancing, and relaxed camaraderie. Those things were few and far between in a warbot brainy's life.

The party thinned out, but no one paid any attention to who left together or alone.

A bot came up to the booth and announced, "Telephone for Captain Curt Carson."

Curt raised his hand. "That's me. Bring it here."

"Request for private communication, Captain. You may take the call in the hush booth opposite the bar."

"Damn! Excuse me," he told Belinda Hettrick.

Who could it be? he wondered. The Scotch and the meal and the relaxation had worked their magic on Curt. The edge had come off.

He found the hush booth, punched in his code, and was mightily surprised to see the image of Colonel Willa Lovell appear on the screen.

"Captain! You're looking much better! I'm glad you made it back to Diamond Point!"

He inclined his head in greeting. "Low and slow in a contract airlifter. And I might add that you're looking better than when I first saw you about a week ago. Even better than when you left Karachi yesterday. No, that was the day before ... or was it? Hell, my circadian rhythm's all screwed up. We crossed an international date line somewhere in the process, I think."

"I'm feeling better, too. I thought you might like to see something I got from Bob Armstrong, who didn't

461

get his cut off until he got out of Zahedan." She held up her left arm on which she now wore one of the hostage shackles as a polished iron bracelet. "It's just to remind me that there are other places and other kinds of people."

"That surprises me," Curt admitted. "I want to forget that place."

"Oh? Why? It changed my whole life, Curt."

"Mine, too, Colonel."

"You act as though nothing happened in Zahedan."

"Pardon?"

"My name's Willa, remember?"

"Sorry, Willa. I guess I'm slipping back into the military routine here."

"That's better! Tell you why I called, Curt. I understand that you're being temporarily assigned to Charlotte Amalie."

Apparently, Colonel Willa Lovell had had something to do with the new TDY assignment. But he answered her, "My entire company is being detached to the Staff College there."

"I know. How wonderful! I understand you'll be there next Saturday."

That was news to him. "I haven't received my orders yet, Willa."

"You will. I'll be there next week at our tropical environment test lab. Will you have dinner with me Sunday night?"

Curt Carson had often thought that being a warbot brainy was perhaps the loneliest job in the world. But he suddenly realized that the sort of high-tech linkage now possible between a human being's nervous system

462

and a computer/robot brought him close to and intimate with personalities like Georgie, Beauregard, and Trajan ... and with Carson's Companions and other people in the RI. On the other hand, Colonel Willa Lovell, at the top of the robotics R&D heap, was probably far lonelier. Career must have been everything to her before Zahedan. But even though she was now a gorgeous lady, having availed herself of the services of a beauty salon since she'd got back, Curt knew that she was vulnerable, a woman who'd built a career to protect herself from the outside world.

And he knew what she was up to. But she was older then he. On the other hand, he thought, did age make that much difference?

"I'd be delighted, Willa. Pick you up at nineteen hundred hours at your quarters?"

"No, I'll send a car around to the Staff College VOQ for you. I know a lovely little place on a hilltop where we can have dinner."

"I'd like that."

"So would I. See you Sunday."

He switched off and turned to find Colonel Belinda Hettrick quietly looking over his shoulder. She smelled good close-up.

"I don't have a lovely spot on a hilltop, but would comfortable quarters inside a mountain do just as well?" she asked.

"Belinda, it's not proper to eavesdrop, even on a subordinate."

"RHIP," she replied. "I didn't think you went for older women."

"What has age got to do with it?"

463

"I also thought you were bushed out from the Zahedan operation."

"I thought you were, too."

"When I get too tired for other people, which our rules have a tendency to subdue in the name of military dicipline, then it's time for me to turn off."

"Obviously, you're still turned on."

"Obviously." She took his arm.

"Rule Ten in abeyance?"

"You soldiers are all alike, Captain Curt Carson."

"Speak for yourself, Colonel."

GLOSSARY OF ROBOT INFANTRY TERMS AND SLANG

Aerodyne: A saucer- or frisbee-shaped flying machine that obtains its lift from the exhaust of one or more turbine fanjet engines blowing outward over the curved upper surface of the craft from an annular slot near the center of the upper surface. The annular slot is segmented and the sectorized slots can therefore be controlled to provide more flow and, hence, more lift over one part of the saucer-shaped surface than another, thus tipping the aerodyne and allowing it to move forward, backward, and sideways. The aerodyne was invented by Dr. Henri M. Coanda following World War II but was not developed until decades later because of the previous development of the rotary-winged helicopter.

Artificial Intelligence or AI: A very large, very fast computer which can duplicate or simulate certain functions of human intelligence such as bringing together or correlating many apparently disconnected pieces of information or data, making simple evaluations of importance or priority of data and responses, and making decisions concerning what to do, how to do it, when to do it, and what to report to the human being in control.

Biotech: A biological technologist, normally a non-commissioned officer in the Robot Infantry but often a specialized noncombat officer.

Bot: Generalized generic slang term for robot which takes many forms as *warbot, reconbot,* ratbot, etc.

Bot flush: Since robots have no natural excrement, this term is a reference to what comes out of a highly mechanical warbot when its lubricants are changed during routine maintenance. Used by soldiers as a slang term which refers to anything of a detestable nature.

"Check minus x": Look behind you. In terms of co-ordinates, *plus x* is ahead, *minus x* is behind, *plus y* is to the right, *minus y* is left, *plus z* is up, and *minus z* is down.

Double-lobed Lebanese systolic stroke: Warbot brainy slang for being killed in action, suddenly losing all contact with one's war robots.

Down link: The remote command link or channel from the robot to the soldier.

Fur ball: A complex and confused fight, battle, or operation.

Go physical: To lapse into idiot mode, to operate in a combat or recon environment without robots; what the regular infantry does all the time.

Golden BB: A lucky hit from a small-caliber bullet that creates large problems.

Greased: Beaten, conquered, overwhelmed, creamed.

Humper: Any device whose proper name a soldier can't recall at the moment.

Idiot mode: Operating in the combat enviroment

without robot support; especially, operating without the benefit of computers and artificial intelligence to relieve battle load.

Intelligence Amplifier or IA: A very fast computer with a very large memory which, when linked to a human nervous system, serves as a very fast extension of the human brain allowing the brain to function faster, recall more data, store more data, and thus "amplify" a human being's "intelligence."

KIA or "killed in action": A situation where all of a soldier's data and sensory input from one or more robots is suddenly cut off, leaving the human being in a state of mental limbo. A very debilitating and mentally disturbing situation.

Linkage: The remote connection or link between a human being and one or more war robots. This link or channel may be by means of wires, radio, laser or optical means, or other remote control systems. The robot/computer sends its data directly to the human soldier's nervous system through small electrodes positioned on the soldier's skin; this data is coded in such a way that the soldier perceives the signals as sight, sound, feeling, smell, or the position of a robot's parts. The robot/computer also picks up commands from the soldier's nervous system that are merely "thought" by the soldier, translates these into commands the robot can understand, and monitors the accomplishment of the commanded action.

"Orgasmic!": A slang term. It means outstanding!

Pucker factor: The detrimental effect on the human body that results from being in an extremely hazardous situation, such as being shot at.

Robot: From the Czech word *robota* meaning work, especially drudgery. A device capable of humanlike actions when directed by a computer or by a human being through a computer and a remote two-way command-sensory circuit. Early war robots appeared in World War II as radio-controlled drone aircraft. They were used as targets or to carry explosives. The first of these, the German Henschel Hs 238 glide bomb, was launched from an aircraft against surface targets and guided by means of radio control supervised by a human being in an aircraft who watched the image transmitted from a television camera in the nose of the bomb.

Robot Infantry or RI: A combat branch of the United States Army which grew out of the regular Infantry upon the introduction of the robots and linkage to warfare. Active RI divisions are the 17th (Iron Fist), the 22nd (Double Deuces), the 26th (R.U.R.), and the 50th (Big L).

Rule Ten: Slang reference to Army Regulation 601-10 which prohibits physical contact between male and female officers and soldiers other than that required for official business while on duty.

Rules of Engagement or ROE: Official restrictions on the freedom of action of a commander or soldier during confrontation with an opponent. Generally used to refer to those that increase the probability that said commander or soldier will lose the combat, all other things being equal.

Simulator or sim: A device which can simulate the sensations perceived by a human being and the results of the human's responses. A simple toy computer with an aircraft flight simulator program or a video game simulating a human-controlled activity is an example of a simulator. One of the earliest simulators was the Link Trainer of World War II. Without leaving the ground, it provided a human pilot with the sensations of instrument or "blind" flying.

Sit-guess: Slang for "estimate of the situation," an educated guess about the situation.

Sit-rep: Short for "situation report."

Spasm mode: Slang for killed in action (KIA).

Staff stooge: Derogatory term referring to a regimental or divisional staff officer.

Tiger error: What happens when an eager soldier tries too hard to press an attack.

Up link: The remote command link or channel from the soldier to the war robot.

Warbot: Abbreviation for "war robot," a mechanical device that is operated remotely by a soldier, thereby taking the human being out of the hazardous activity of actual combat.

Warbot brainy: The human soldier who operates war robots.

APPENDIX A
ORGANIZATION OF THE
ROBOT INFANTRY

(Excerpted from *The United States Army Officer's Manual,* Revision 3.1.2, by Colonel Carl H. Styer AUS (Ret.), the Armed Forces Data Base (AFDABA), Department of Defense Open Network (DODON).

Flexibility of organization is encouraged in order to more adequately meet the wide variety of tactical situations and missions in which the Robot Infantry may engage. Thus, commanding officers have the ability to internally restructure their organizations in accordance with well-defined guidelines in order to meet the challenges of modern high-technology robot warfare. However, the four basic units are the division, the regiment, the company, and the platoon.

The Robot Infantry Division is the largest force that is trained and employed as a combined arms team. It is a balanced, self-sustaining force that is capable of conducting independent operations. Although it is concentrated around four Robot Infantry combat regiments, it contains staff and support units. For administrative and operational purpose, the combat units of a division may be divided into two tactical brigades, depending upon the situation. A division is normally commanded by a major general. Two or more brigadier generals may be assigned administrative and/or operational command of the brigades. Robot Infantry Divisions are not only numbered but have nicknames such as the Iron Fist or the Double Deuces. A division normally has both color standards and a divisional insigne which is worn on uniforms as a cloth patch or a metallic emblem except in combat. Four RI Divisions are currently organized and active in the US Army: 17th Iron Fist, the Twenty-second Double Deuces, the 26th R.U.R., and the 50th Big L.

The Robot Infantry Regiment is a complete tactical and administrative unit and is the basic unit of maneuver. It is composed of three to four Robot Infantry combat companies (which may be operationally or administratively assigned to two tactical battalions, depending upon the operation or mission), a headquarters company consisting of a staff platoon and a communications platoon, and a service company consisting of a maintenance platoon, a supply platoon, and a biotechnology platoon. For operational or administrative purpose, a regimental commander may from time to time divide the tactical units into two battalions which may be under the command of the regimental commander or one of the company commanders. A regiment is normally commanded by a colonel or a lieutenant colonel. Regiments have adopted the names, traditions, colors,

471

ROBOT INFANTRY REGIMENT

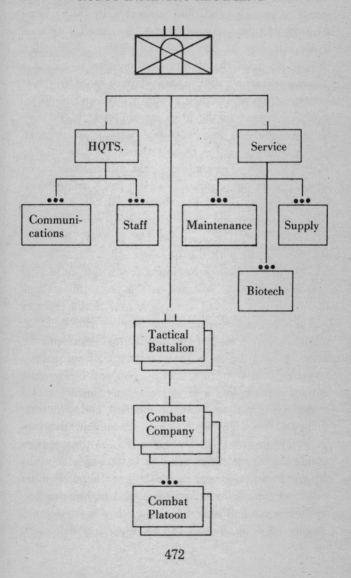

and battle streamers or old-line Army regiments. Thus, some units such as the Old Guard, 1st Regiment, 17th Iron Fist Division (Robot Infantry) or the Washington Greys, 3rd Regiment, 17th Iron Fist Division (Robot Infantry) have traditions, battle streamers, and unit honors extending back to the Revolutionary War.

The Robot Infantry Company is the smallest self-contained tactical and administrative unit capable of sustaining itself in action. It consist of two platoons—the Alpha fire base platoon and the Bravo maneuvering platoon. It is commanded by a captain or a major; however some companies have been led in combat by lieutenants. The detailed operation of a company is carried out by a first sergeant or a master sergeant assisted by two platoon sergeants. The rank of sergeant is the lowest noncommissioned officer grade in a Robot Infantry combat company; noncombat companies may have a complement of noncommissioned officers and specialists in the full range of ranks. Combat companies adopt and are known by motivational names selected by the personnel.

The use of war robots allows combat companies to be made up of three officers and three noncommissioned officers who control up to thirty-six war robots or aerodynes all-terrain transportation vehicles, armed or unarmed. The largest are headquarters and service companies or the divisional support and special operations companies or regiments. However, because of automation, artificially intelligent computers, intelligence amplifiers, and robots, the personnel of a regiment is slightly more than two-hundred while a full division consists of only about two-thousand. All personnel at the regimental level and below carry personal weapons and may have to defend themselves physically, although it is unlikely that anyone outside the combat companies has more than a remote chance of being exposed to physical risk in battle.

APPENDIX B.
ORDER OF BATTLE
OPERATIONS SQUIRE & CYCLONE
ZAHEDAN HOSTAGE RESCUE

17th "Iron Fist" Division (Robot Infantry)
Major General Jacob O. Carlisle

  First Robot Infantry Brigade (Tactical Strike)
  Brigadier General Victor Knox

   3rd Regiment "Washington Greys"
   Colonel Belinda J. Hettrick

    First Battalion (Tactical)
    Colonel Belinda J. Hettrick

     A Company, "Carson's Companions"
     Captain Curt C. Carson
      Second Lieutenant Alexis M. Morgan
      Second Lieutenant Jerry P. Allen
      Master Sergeant Henry G. Kester

Platoon Sergeant Nicholas P. Gerard
Platoon Sergeant Edwina A. Sampson

B Company, "Walker's Warriors"
Captain Edith M. Walker
First Lieutenant John G. Ward
Second Lieutenant David F. Coney

C Company, "Manny's Marauders"
Captain Manuel X. Garcia
First Lieutenant Joshua M. Rosenberg
Second Lieutenant Eleanor S. Aarts

D Company (assigned), "Kelly's Killers"
Captain Martin C. Kelly
Second Lieutenant Steven B. Calder
Second Lieutenant William B. Prentice